Beyond the Dreams of Avarice

Beyond the Dreams of Avarice

Walter Besant

MINT EDITIONS

Beyond the Dreams of Avarice was first published in 1895.

This edition published by Mint Editions 2021.

ISBN 9781513281339 | E-ISBN 9781513286358

Published by Mint Editions®

 **MINT
EDITIONS**

minteditionbooks.com

Publishing Director: Jennifer Newens
Design & Production: Rachel Lopez Metzger
Project Manager: Micaela Clark
Typesetting: Westchester Publishing Services

Contents

I

A Surprise and an Injunction

L ucian!" The sick man was propped up by pillows. His hands lay folded outside the coverings. All that could be seen of a face covered with an iron-gray beard was deathly pale. His deep-set eyes were bright. His square, strong brow, under a mass of black hair hardly touched with gray, was pale. "Lucian, I say." His voice was strong and firm, although the patient repose of his head and hands showed that movement was either difficult or impossible. "Lucian, it is no use trying to deceive me."

"I do not try to deceive you. There is always hope."

"I have none. Sit down now and let us talk quietly. It is the last chance, very likely, and I have a good deal to say. Sit down, my son—there—so that I may see you."

The son obeyed. He placed a chair by the bedside and sat down. He was a young man about seven-and-twenty years of age. He had the same square forehead as his father, and the same deep-set bright black eyes; the same straight black eyebrows. His face was beardless; the features were strong and clearly cut; it was a face of resolution: not what girls call a handsome face, but a face of intellectual power, a responsible face, a masterful face. His broad shoulders and tall, strong figure increased the sense of personal force which accompanied the presence of Lucian Calvert.

"The weakest point about human knowledge," said the sick man, philosophizing from habit, "is that we never seem to make any real advance in keeping the machinery in order, or in setting it right when it gets wrong." He was a mechanical engineer by calling, and of no mean reputation. "When the machinery goes wrong, the works stop. Then we have to throw away the engine. She can't be repaired. Why don't you learn how to tinker it up, you doctors?"

The son, who was a physician, shook his head.

"We do our best," he said. "But we are only beginning."

"Why don't you learn how to set the thing going again? Let the machine run down, and then take it to pieces and mend it. Get up steam again, and then run her for another spell. That's what you ought to do, Lucian."

"You are talking like yourself again, father."

"I suppose," he went on, "that if men had by their own wit invented this machine of the body, if they had built it up, bit by bit, as we fellows have done with our engines, they would understand the thing better. As it is, we must pay for ignorance. A man finds he has got to die at fifty-five because the doctors know nothing but symptoms. Fifty-five! In the very middle of one's work! It's disgusting. Just beginning, so to speak, and all his knowledge wasted—gone—dissipated—unless, somehow, there's the conservation of intellectual energy."

"Perhaps there is," said his son. "As you say, we understand little more than symptoms, which is the reason why there is always hope."

But he spoke without assurance.

"Never mind myself," the father replied. "About you, Lucian."

"Don't think about me; I shall do very well."

"I must think about you, my dear boy, because it is impossible to think about myself. Last night I had a dream. I was floating in dark space, with nothing to think about. And it was maddening. I don't suppose that death means that. Well, I shall learn what it means in a day or two. There's the money question. I never tried to save money. I was set dead against saving quite early in life. Had good reason to hate and loathe saving. But I believe that Tom Nicholson has got something of mine—something that rolled in—and there's your mother's money. You won't starve. And you've got your profession."

"I shall do, sir."

"I think you will. I've always thought you would. You've got it written on your face. If you keep your eyes in the right direction—in the direction of work—you'll do very well. You will either go up steadily or you will go down swiftly. It is the gutter or the topmost round for you."

He paused. The exertion of talking was too great for his strength.

"Rest, father," said the son, touching the sick man's pulse. "Rest, and talk again tomorrow."

"Who will talk with me tomorrow? Wait a moment, Lucian. Lift my head. So. That's better. I breathe again. Now—as soon as I am buried, you must communicate the news of my death—to my father."

"To whom?" Lucian started. He thought his father was off his head.

"To my father, Lucian. I have never told you that I have a father still living."

Imagine, dear reader. This young man had lived seven-and-twenty years in the world, and always in the belief that his father was an only child, and that his grandfather was dead, and that there were no cousins, or if any, then perhaps cousins not desirable. If you remember this, you may perhaps understand the amazement of this young man. He sprang to his feet and bent over the sick man. No; his eyes were steady. There was no outward sign of wandering.

"My father, Lucian," he repeated. "I am not delirious, I assure you."

"Your father? Why? Where is he? What is he? Is he—perhaps—poor?"

"He is a very old man; he is over ninety years of age. And he is not poor at all. His poverty is not the reason why you have never heard of him."

"Oh! Then, why—"

"Patience, my son. He is neither poor nor obscure. He is famous; in fact, so famous that I resolved to begin the world for myself without his reputation on my back. A parent's greatness may hamper a young man at the outset. So I left him."

"His reputation? We are, then, connected with a man of reputation." But Lucian spoke dubiously.

"You are, as you will shortly, perhaps, discover. I suppose he no longer follows his profession, being now so old."

"What profession?"

"Destruction and Ruin," replied the sick man, shortly.

"Oh!" His son asked no further questions. Perhaps he felt that to learn more would make him no happier. A strange profession, however, "Destruction and Ruin."

"I changed my name when I left the family home. So that you have no ancestors, fortunately, except myself. You are like Seth, the son of Adam."

"No ancestors? But we must have ancestors."

"If you want to learn all about them, you can. Tom Nicholson knows. Tom Nicholson, the lawyer—he knows. He has got some papers of mine, that I drew up a long time ago. It might be better for you to go on in ignorance. On the other hand—well, choose for yourself. Read the papers, if you like, and find out what manner of people your ancestors were. Nicholson will give you your grandfather's address. Tell him, without revealing yourself or the name that I have borne—or your own relation to me—tell him simply that I am dead."

"Very well, sir. I will do what you desire."

"One thing more. It is my earnest wish—I do not command, my son; no man, not even a father, has the right to command another—but it is my wish that you may never be invited or tempted to resume the name that I abandoned, or to claim kin with any of the family which I have renounced, or to take one single farthing of the fortune which your ancestors have amassed. Our money has been the curse of us for two hundred years. You may learn, if you please, from Tom Nicholson the history of the family. From father to son—from father to son. It was got by dishonor; it has been increased and multiplied by dishonor; it has been attended with dishonor. Fraud and crime, madness, selfishness, hardness of heart—pitiless hardness of heart—have gone with it. Lucian, when you have learned the history of your ancestors, you will understand why I left the house full of wretched memories and renounced them all. And if I judge you aright, you will be ready to renounce them, too."

"I shall remember your wish, sir," said his son, gravely. "But I do not understand how the question of money can arise, since your father is in ignorance of my very existence."

"Best so; best so," said the sick man. "Then you cannot be tempted."

For one so weak this long conversation was a great effort. He closed his eyes and spoke no more.

The young man sat down again and watched. But he was strangely agitated. What did his father mean? What kind of profession was that which could be described as Destruction and Ruin?

Nothing more was said upon the subject at all, for the machinery proved so much out of gear that it suddenly stopped. And as no one could possibly set it going again, there was nothing left but to put away the engine in the place where people put away all the broken engines.

When the funeral was over, the two principal mourners, Lucian Calvert and a certain Mr. Nicholson, old friend and legal adviser of his father, above referred to as Tom, drove away together. They went back to the house.

"Now," said Lucian, "tell me things. All I know is that my name is not Calvert, and that my grandfather is still living."

"That is all you know, is it? Well, Lucian, in my opinion you know too much for your own happiness already. I advised your father to keep you in ignorance. I saw that you would get on, as he had done, without the help of money or the hinderance of connections. But he thought you ought to have the opportunity of knowing everything if you choose."

"Certainly, I do choose."

"Well, then, your father was my oldest friend. We were boys together, at Westminster School. He was unhappy at home, for reasons which you may learn if you like. At the age of seventeen he ran away from home and fought his way up through the engineering shops. His name was not John Calvert, but John Calvert Burley."

"Burley? My name is Burley, then? Go on."

"Your grandfather lives in Great College Street, Westminster. Your father never had any communication with him after he left the house." Mr. Nicholson lugged out of his coat-pocket a little roll of papers. "Here is a bundle of papers which have long been in my keeping. They contain an account of the Burley family, drawn up by your father for you. There are also some letters and memorials of his mother and others, taken from her desk after she died. And that is all."

"You have told me nothing at all about the Burley people."

"No. Read the papers which your father prepared for you, and you will learn all you want to learn, and perhaps more."

He took his hat. "And, Lucian, if you choose to resume your true name and to join your own people, I will look through the papers for you and communicate with your grandfather. But I rather think, my dear boy, that you will prefer to remain Lucian Calvert. Don't change your name. Far better to be the son of John Calvert, civil engineer, than the grandson of John Calvert Burley. Toss the papers in the fire when you have read them, and think no more about the matter."

Lucian, left with the packet of papers, handled them suspiciously, looked at the fireplace in which there was no fire, began to untie, but desisted. Finally he put the roll into his pocket and sallied forth. He was engaged—not an unusual thing for a young man—and what is the good of being engaged if you cannot put a disagreeable task upon the *fiancée?*

II

A Packet of Papers

The girl, Margaret by name, sat with her hands folded in her lap, looking up at her lover as he stood over her.

It has never yet been decided whether those marriages are the happier when the couple are alike or when they are unlike in what we call essentials. For my own part, I think that the latter marriage presents the greater chance of happiness, if only for the infinite possibilities of unexpectedness; also for the reproduction of the father in the daughter and the mother in the son. These two were going to try love in unlikeness. The girl was fair in complexion, with blue eyes which could easily become dreamy and were always luminous; there was at the moment the sweet seriousness in them that so well becomes a beautiful woman; she was a tall girl, as becomes the fashion of the time, dressed as one who respects her own beauty, and would become, in her lover's eyes, as attractive as she could; a strong and healthy girl; able to hold her own yet, as one might conclude from her attitude in the presence of her lover; one who, when she promised to give herself, meant to give everything, and already had no thought but for him. As she sat under him, as he stood over her, every one could understand here was man masterful, the Lord of Creation, and here was woman obedient to the man she loved; that here was man creative, and here was woman receptive; that out of her submission would spring up her authority. What more can the world desire? What more did Nature intend?

"Now that everything is over," he said, "it is time for us to talk and think about ourselves."

"Already, Lucian?"

"Already. The dead are dead; we are the living. His memory will live awhile—longer than most men's memories, because he did good work. With us his memory will last all our lives. Now, Marjorie, I have got something wonderful to tell you. Listen with both ears."

He took a chair and sat down, and held one of her hands.

"Both ears I want. Two or three days before he died, my father told me a thing which greatly amazed me. I said nothing to you about it, but waited."

"What was it, Lucian?"

"After the funeral, this morning, I came away with Mr. Nicholson, my father's old friend and his lawyer. He drove home with me and we had a talk."

Lucian told his tale and produced the packet of papers.

"I confess," he said, "that I shrink from reading these documents. If I were superstitious, I should think that the reading of the document would bring disaster. That's absurd, of course. But it is certain that there must be something disagreeable about it—perhaps something shameful—why, else, did my father run away from home? Why did he, as he said, renounce his ancestors? Why did he speak of a fortune created by dishonor? Why did he say that my grandfather's profession was 'Destruction and Ruin'?"

"'Destruction and Ruin!' Did he say that? Destruction and Ruin? What did he mean? What kind of profession is that?"

"I don't know. Now, Madge, this is the position: I have never had any cousins at all, or any ancestors on my father's side. His people don't know of my existence, even. But there is in this packet the revelation of the family to which I belong—to which you will belong. They may be disgraceful people—probably they are."

"Since they do not know of your existence, it is evident you need not tell them who you are."

"They must be in some way disreputable. 'Destruction and Ruin!' That was my grandfather's profession. Do you think he is Napoleon the Great, not dead after all, but survivor of all his generation? 'Destruction and Ruin,'" he laughed. "It would make an attractive advertisement, a handbill for distribution on the curb outside the shop door—'DESTRUCTION AND RUIN!' There's your heading in big letters. 'By John Calvert Burley!' There's your second line. 'Destruction and Ruin'—this is where your circular begins—'Destruction and Ruin in all their branches undertaken and performed with the utmost certainty, secrecy, and despatch—and on reasonable terms. The Nobility and Gentry waited on personally. Everybody destroyed completely. Ruin effected in the most thorough manner. Destruction superintended from the office. Recovery hopeless. Ruin, moral, material, physical, and mental, guaranteed and executed as per order. Strictest confidence. Customers may depend on being satisfied with same.' They always say 'same,' you know. 'No connection with any other house. Tackle of the newest and most destructive kind to be had on the Three Years'

Hire System. Painless Self-Destruction taught in six lessons. Terms—strictly cash.'"

"Hush, hush, Lucian! Not to make a jest of it." But she laughed gently.

"We need not cry over it. But—hang it! What can it be—'Destruction and Ruin'?"

"Do you think—do you think—he made a quack medicine that will cure everything?"

"Perhaps. 'The Perfect, Pleasant, and Peremptory Pill. Children cry for it. The baby won't be happy till he gets it.' Very likely. Or he may be a Socialist."

"Ye—yes;—or—do you think he is a solicitor? Your father always hated lawyers."

"I don't know;—or the proprietor of a paper on the other side? He was a great Liberal."

"Perhaps;—or a jerry builder? He hated bad workmen of all kinds."

"Perhaps;—or a turncoat politician? Or a critic? Or a cheap sausage-maker? Or the advertiser of soap? Or—" When one is still young it is easy to turn everything into material for smiles, if not laughter. These two guessed at many things for a profession which could fitly be described by these two words. But the real thing did not occur to them.

"It was a fat profession," the young man continued, "because my father was so anxious that I should never be tempted to take part in the fortune. Since my existence is unknown, it is not likely that the temptation will arise. I wonder what it was?"

"You wish to know the contents of those papers?"

"Very much."

"You will never rest till you do know them. Well, Lucian, let me read them for you. Perhaps you need not inquire any further. Perhaps your curiosity will be satisfied with a single broad fact. It"—"It" meant the profession—"it could not have been so very disgraceful, for your father was a Westminster scholar, and has been a life-long friend of Mr. Nicholson, a most respectable person."

Lucian gave her the papers. "Take them, Madge. Read them, and tell me this evening as much as you please about them."

In the evening he called again. Margaret received him with a responsible face and a manner as of one who has a difficult duty to perform.

"Well, Madge? You have read the papers?"

"They are written by your father. Your grandfather's address is 77, Great College Street, Westminster, and his name is John Calvert Burley."

"Yes—so much I knew before. And the wonderful profession?"

"Lucian, it is really disagreeable. Can't you let the matter just rest where it is?"

"Not now. I must know as well as you. What? You are to be burdened with disagreeable discoveries and I am not to know? Call this the Equality of Love? What about that profession? What about Destruction and Ruin?"

"My dear Lucian, your father began a new family. You may be contented with him."

"So long as you carry it on with me," said her lover, with a lover-like illustration of the sentiment, "I shall be quite contented. We will renounce our ancestors and all their works and ways—their fortunes and their misfortunes. But who they were, and who they are, I must know. Tell me, then, first, what is that profession called Destruction and Ruin?"

"Well, Lucian, your grandfather had several professions, and all of them disgraceful. First of all—he must now be a very old man—he began by keeping a gambling-house—a most notorious gambling-place."

"Kind of Crockford's, I suppose?"

"Burley's in Piccadilly. It was open all night long, and the keeper was always present looking after the tables, lending money to the gamesters, and encouraging them to play. Thousands were ruined over his tables. He provided supper and wine and everything. Well, that is the first part of it."

"A noble beginning. Pray go on."

"Then he was the proprietor of a place where people, detestable people—danced and drank all night long. It appears to have been a most horrible place."

"Oh! Do we get much lower?"

"I don't know. In addition to all these things he was the most fashionable money-lender in London—and that appears to have been, of late years, the profession by which he was best known. And because he was such a byword, your father could not bear to remain at home, and ran away, changing his name. And that, Lucian, is all that you need to know about your people. There is a lot about his forefathers and his brothers. There is a great deal of wickedness and of misfortune. The story is all told in these papers." She offered them, but he refused them.

"Keep them, Margaret. I think I have heard all I want to know—at least, for the present. I will write to the old man. I should like to gaze upon him, but that is out of the question, I suppose."

"He lives in the house that has been the family house since the first Burley of whom anything is known built it."

"I'll go and see the outside of the house. Don't be afraid, my child. I will not reveal my existence. I will not try to see this gentleman of so many good and pious memories. But he is over ninety; surely he must have outlived his old fame—"

"His infamy, you mean," she corrected him, severely.

"Fame or infamy—it matters little after all these years. If you were to talk about Burley's gambling-house of sixty or seventy years ago, who would remember it? It is forty years and more since my father left him. I suppose that, forty years ago, there might have been some prejudice— but now?"

"Some prejudice? Only some, Lucian?" She spoke with reproach. She expected much more moral indignation.

"The world quickly forgets the origin of wealth. My father, had he pleased, might have defied the opinion of the world. Still, he was doubtless right. Well, Maggie, I am glad to know the truth. It might have been worse."

"What could be worse?"

"You yourself suggested quack medicines. But we need not make comparisons. Burley's Gambling-Hell; Burley's Dancing-Crib; Burley's Money-Lending Business. He must have been a man of great powers. Wickedness on an extensive scale requires genius. There are retail dealers in wickedness by the thousand; but the wholesale merchant in the wicked line—the man who lives on the vices of his fellows—all the vices he can encourage and manipulate—he is rare. Looking at John Burley from the outside, and not as a prejudiced descendant, I can see that he must have been a very strong man. Now I will tell him that his son is dead."

III

"The Child is Dead"

In his back parlor—since the building of the house in 1721 the house had always contained a front parlor, a back parlor, and a best parlor—the owner and tenant of the house sat in his arm-chair beside the fire.

It was quite a warm day in early summer, yet there was a fire; outside a leafy branch of a vine swept windows which had not been cleaned for a longer time than, to most housewives, seems desirable; the same vine—a large and generous vine—climbed over half the back of the house and the whole of a side wall in the little garden; there was also a mulberry-tree in the garden; and there were bumps, lumps, and anfractuosities of the ground covered with a weedy, seedy grass, which marked the site of former flower-beds in the little enclosure.

The man in the arm-chair sat doubled up and limp—he had once been a tall man. Pillows were placed in the chair beside and behind him, so that he was propped and comforted on every side; his feet rested on a footstool. His wrinkled hands lay folded in his lap; his head was protected by a black silk skull-cap; his face as he lay back was covered with multitudinous wrinkles—an old, old face—the face of a very ancient man. The house was very quiet. To begin with, you cannot find anywhere in London a quieter place than Great College Street, Westminster. Then there were but two occupants of this house—the old man in the chair, and an old woman, his housekeeper, in the kitchen below—and they were both asleep, for it was four o'clock in the afternoon. On the table, beside this aged man, stood a decanter containing the generous wine that kept him alive. There were also pens, paper, and account-books, one of them lying open, his spectacles on the page.

Literature to this man meant account-books—his own account-books—the record of his own investments. He read nothing else, not the newspapers, not any printed books; all his world was in the account-books. Of men and women he took no thought; he was as dead to humanity as a Cistercian monk; he was, perhaps, the only living man who had completely achieved what he desired and lived to enjoy the fruit of his labors: to sit rejoicing in his harvest.

How many of us enjoy our harvest? The rich man generally dies before he has made enough; the poet dies before his fame is established; but this man, who had all his life desired nothing but money, had made so much that he desired no more; his soul was satisfied. Perhaps in extreme old age desire itself had died away. But he was satisfied. No one knew except himself how much he had accumulated; he sat all day long in his old age reading, adding, counting, enjoying his wealth, watching it grow and spread, and bear golden fruits. For this man was Burley of the gambling-hell; Burley of the dancing-cribs; Burley the money-lender—in his extreme old age, in his last days.

The house was always quiet; no one knocked at the door except his manager, the man who was the head of the great house filled with clerks—some of them passed solicitors—where his affairs were conducted, his rents collected, and his vast income invested as it came in day by day. Otherwise the house was perfectly quiet. No letters came; no telegrams; the occupant was forgotten by the world; nobody knew that he was still living. The old money-lender sat at home, by himself, counting the money which he lent no more; most of those with whom he had formerly done business were dead—they could curse him no more; all those who had thrown away their money at his gaming-table were dead—they could curse him no more. As for the nightly orgies, the dancing-cribs, the all-night finishes, if their memory survives, that of their proprietor had long since been forgotten. And the dancers themselves—the merry, joyous, laughing, singing, but their voices were hoarse; careless, yet their eyes were restless—happy company of nymphs and swains of sixty years ago, not one was left to curse him for the madness of the pace or to weep over the memory of a ruined youth.

He had outlived, as his grandson suggested, his infamy. Nobody talked about him. In his own den he had quite forgotten—wholly forgotten—that at any time there had been any persons whom he had injured. He was serenely forgetful; he was in a haven of rest, where no curses could reach him, and where no tempests could be raised by memories of the past.

Those who study manners and customs of the nineteenth century have read of Burley's Hell. It was a kind of club to which every one who had money and wore the dress and assumed the manners of society was freely admitted. The scandalous memoirs of the time talk of Burley's *chef* and his wines, and the table at which he was always present all night long, always the same—calm, grave, unmoved; whatever the fortunes of the night, always ready to lend anybody—that is, anybody he knew—any sum of money he wanted on his note of hand. Great fortunes were lost at Burley's. Men walked out of Burley's with despair in their hearts and self-murder in their minds. Yet—old history! old history! as Lucian Calvert said. Only those who are students of life in London, when the Corinthian and his friends were enjoying it, still talk about the Finish—Burley's crib—where the noble army of the godless assembled night after night, young men and old men, and ladies remarkable for their sprightliness as well as their beauty, and danced and laughed and had supper and drank pink champagne—too sweet—in long glasses. There was generally some kind of fight or a row; there was always some kind of a gamble in some little room upstairs. But—old history! old history! Those who read it never thought of Burley at all. Who cares, after fifty years, to inquire about a man who once ran an all-night dancing-crib? Mr. Burley had outlived his infamy.

And always, till past eighty years of age, the prince of money-lenders. Everybody went to Burley. He found money for everybody. His terms were hard, and you had to keep to your agreement. But the money was there if the security was forthcoming. No tears, no entreaties, no prayers, no distress would induce him to depart from his bond. It is indeed impossible to carry on such a business successfully without an adamantine heart. But it was nearly fifteen years since he retired from practice, and the world spoke of him no more. He had outlived his infamy.

He was startled out of his sleep by the postman's knock. He sat up, looked about him, recovered his wandering wits, and drank a little port, which strengthened him so that he was able to understand that his house-keeper was bringing him a letter.

"Give it to me," he said, surprised, because letters came no more to that house. He put on his spectacles and read the address, "John Calvert Burley." "It is for me," he said. He then laid the letter on the table and looked at his house-keeper. She knew what he meant, and retired. The old man at his time of life was not going to begin doing business in the presence of a servant. When she was gone he took it up again and opened it slowly.

It was short, and written in the third person.

"The writer begs to inform Mr. Burley that his son, John Calvert Burley, died five days ago, on the 16th of May, of rheumatic fever, and was buried yesterday. At the request of the deceased this information is conveyed to Mr. Burley."

There was no date, and there was no address. But, the old man thought, there could be no reason to doubt the fact. Why should it be invented?

His memory, strong enough about the far-distant past when he was young, was weak as regards matters that occurred only forty or fifty years ago. It cost him an effort to recall—it was a subject of which he never liked to think—how his son had left him after protesting against what he called the infamy of the money-lending business. Infamy! he said. Infamy! Of a respectable and lucrative business! Infamy! when the income was splendid!

"An undutiful son!" murmured his father. "A disrespectful son!" He read the letter again. "So : he is dead." He threw the letter and the envelope on the fire. "I have left off thinking about him. Why should I begin again? I won't. I will forget him. Dead, is he? I used to think that perhaps he would come back and make submission for the sake of the money. And even then I wouldn't have left him any. I remember. That was when I made up my mind what should be done with it. Ho! ho! I thought how disappointed he would be. Dead, is he? Then he won't be disappointed. It's a pity. Now there's nobody left, nobody left at all."

This reflection seemed to please him, for he laughed a little and rubbed his hands. At the age of ninety-four, or there-abouts, it is dangerous to give way to any but the simplest and most gentle emotions. It is quite wonderful what a little thing may stop the pulse at ninety-four, and still the heart.

Even such a little thing as the announcement of the death of a son one has not seen for forty years, and the revival of an old, angry, and revengeful spirit, may do it. When the house-keeper brought in the tea at five o'clock she found that, to use the old man's last words, "There was nobody left at all."

"Look, Marjorie." Lucian showed her a newspaper. "The old man, my grandfather, is dead. Read. 'On the 15th, suddenly, at his residence, Great College Street, Westminster, John Calvert Burley, aged ninety-four years.'"

"On the 15th? Two days ago! That was when he received your letter."

"If he did receive it. Perhaps he died before it reached the house. Here is a paragraph about him. See that? He did not quite outlive his infamy."

The paragraph ran as follows:

"The death, this day announced, of Mr. John Calvert Burley, carries us back sixty years and more, to the time when gambling-hells were openly kept, and when there were all-night saloons; to the days when the pace of the young prodigal was far faster than in this degenerate generation. Mr. Burley was the firm friend of that young prodigal. He gave him a gambling-table with free drinks; he gave him dancing-cribs; he lent him money; he encouraged him to keep the ball a-rolling. Sixty years ago Mr. Burley's name was well known to all followers of Comus. For many years he has lived retired in his house at Westminster. The present generation knows nothing of him. But it will be a surprise to old men, if any survive, of the twenties or the thirties, that John Burley lived to the age of ninety-four and only died yesterday. He must have outlived all those who drank his champagne and lost their money at his tables; he must have outlived most of the young prodigals for whom he ran his dancing-saloon and to whom he lent money at 50 percent"

Margaret read it aloud. "Yes," she said, "some prejudices linger, don't they, Lucian? Better to be a Calvert without any other ancestors than an honorable father, than a Burley with this man behind you."

"Perhaps," said Lucian, thoughtfully. "But a man can no more get rid of his ancestors than he can get rid of his face and his hereditary tendencies. Well, my dear, the name may go. And as for the money—I suppose there was a good deal of money—that has been left to some one, and I hope he will enjoy it. As for us, we have nothing to do with it."

IV

An Inquest of Office

The door of the house in Great College Street stood wide open—a policeman was stationed on the door-step. Something of a public character was therefore going on: at private family functions—as a wedding, a christening, a funeral—there is no policeman. But there was no crowd or any public curiosity—in fact, you could not raise a crowd in Great College Street on any pretext whatever. Once a horse fell down in order to try. He had to get up, unnoticed. From time to time a man stepped briskly up the street, spoke to the policeman, and went in.

Presently there came along the street a young man—Mr. Lucian Calvert, in fact—who walked more slowly, and looked about him. He had come to see the outside of a certain house. He arrived at the house, read the number, and saw the open door and the policeman on the steps.

"What is going on?" he asked.

"Coroner's inquest."

"An inquest? Is not this the house of the late Mr. Burley?"

"Yes, sir. That was the party's name. He's left no will, and there's an inquest. You can go in, if you like. It's in the ground-floor back."

The young man hesitated. Then he accepted the invitation and stepped in. He had come to see the outside of his grandfather's house. Chance gave him an opportunity for seeing the inside as well. Other men walked up the street and spoke to the policeman and stepped in. Then there drove up to the door a cab with two men. One had the unmistakable look of a man in office; the other the equally unmistakable look of a middle-aged clerk. After a certain time of life we all appear to be what we are. This is as it should be: in early life we can make-up. I have known a young duke look like a carpenter, and a young compositor like a belted earl. When these two had entered, the policeman left the door and followed the others into the ground-floor back—more poetically, the back parlor.

The twelve men gathered there were the twelve good men and true who had been summoned to form a jury. They represented, after the manner of their forefathers, the wisdom of the nation. The man of office represented the ancient and honorable post of coroner. The policeman represented the authority of the Court. A reporter, together with the young gentleman who had been invited to assist, represented the publicity of the Court—no Star-Chamber business there, if you please. All above-board and open. There were one or two others—an elderly gentleman, well dressed, with the look of ability and the air of business experience—this was Mr. Burley's manager; an old woman in black, who held a handkerchief in her hand and patted her eyes with it at intervals with a perfunctory moan—these were witnesses. There was also a young man who might have been something in the City. He was in reality a shorthand clerk employed at the office where the Burley estate was managed, and he came with the manager to take down the proceedings. And standing in a corner Lucian observed, to his astonishment, Mr. Nicholson, his father's friend and solicitor.

"You here, Lucian! Who told you?"

"I am here by accident. What does it mean?"

"It means that they can't find any will. Good Lord! What a windfall it will be for somebody!" He remembered that Lucian was the grandson. "That is, for anybody who would proclaim his relationship to such a man."

Lucian looked about the room. It was wainscoted and the panels were painted drab—a good, useful color, which can absorb a good deal of dirt without showing it, and lasts a long time. It was formerly a favorite color for this if for no other reason, all through the last century. In the panels were hanging colored prints, their frames once gilt, now almost black. The low window looked out upon a small garden, in which stood a mulberry-tree, while on the wall grew an immense vine. Curtains which had long lost their virginal color hung from a mahogany curtain-pole. On the mantel-shelf was a tobacco-jar with two broken pipes, and two wax candles in silver candlesticks. The floor was covered with a worn carpet, faded like the curtains; in front of the fire it had gone into holes—there was no hearth-rug. As for the furniture, it consisted of a ponderous mahogany table, black with age, a mahogany sideboard of ancient fashion, with a large punch-bowl upon it and a copper coal-scuttle below it; a tall bookcase filled with books, all in the leather and sheepskin binding of the last century; three or four chairs of the straight-backed kind and a modern wooden arm-chair stood against the wall. The fireplace was of the eighteenth-century pattern, with an open chimney and a hob: on the hob was a copper kettle. The brass fender was one of the old-fashioned high things, to match the grate and to keep as much heat as possible out of the room. Two benches had been placed in the room for the accommodation of the jury.

The coroner bustled into the room, and took his seat at the head of the table in the arm-chair. His clerk placed papers before him and stood in readiness, the New Testament in his hand. The reporter and the short-hand clerk took chairs at the lower end of the table—the policeman closed the door and stood beside it on guard—the jury took their seats on the wooden benches, the old lady renewed her sobs, the manager took a chair behind the reporter, and the public, represented by Mr. Nicholson and Lucian, shrank deeper into the corner.

"Gentlemen," said the coroner, rising and looking slowly round the room with importance, "I am about to open the Court—this Court," he repeated, "for this inquest."

The jury murmured and cleared their throats.

"Gentlemen," said the coroner, "you will first be sworn."

This was done by the coroner's clerk, who handed round the New Testament with the customary form of words.

"And now, gentlemen," the coroner began, absently, "we will proceed to view the cor—I mean, of course, we will proceed to the business before us. This, gentlemen, as you have heard, is not an ordinary inquest; it is not, for once, an inquiry into the cause of death of any person for which I invite your intelligent assistance this morning. It is a more formal duty that lies before us. Equally important—even, in this case perhaps, more important. It is what lawyers call an 'Inquest of Office.'" He repeated these words with greater solemnity, and every man of the jury sat upright and cleared his throat again. "An Inquest of Office!" Not an ordinary inquest, you see. This was an Inquest of Office.

"Gentlemen," the coroner continued, after a pause, to allow these words time to settle in the collective mind, "the facts are these: The owner and tenant of this house, who died and was buried a fortnight ago, was one John Calvert Burley."

"Known to all of us," one of the jury interrupted.

"John Calvert Burley," the magistrate repeated, with a judicial frown, "upon whose estate—not his body—we now hold this inquiry. He has died, so far as has been discovered, intestate. An announcement of his death has appeared in the papers; paragraphs concerning him have also gone the round of the papers—for the deceased was, as most of us know, a person formerly of considerable—of unenviable—notoriety. But so far, oddly enough, no heirs have appeared. This is the more extraordinary as it is reported that the deceased possessed very great wealth. In fact"—the magistrate assumed a confidential manner—"the estate is reported to be enormous—enormous!"—he spread out his hands in order to assist the jury to give play to their imaginations—he sat upright in his chair in order to lift up the grovelling—"we must rise to loftier levels. However," he sank back again, "the magnitude of the estate does not concern us. This Court has to do with an estate, large or small. And now, gentlemen, I shall offer you such evidence as we have to show that there is no will, and that there has been, so far, no claimant. I call Rachel Drage."

The old lady in black answered to her name, wiped her eyes, and stood up to give evidence.

She said that she had been house-keeper to Mr. John Calvert Burley for forty years. Asked if he was a married man, she said that she had always understood that he was a widower; but he had never spoken to her about his family. She could not say what caused her to believe that he was a widower. Asked if there were any children, supposing there had been a marriage, she said that there was a nursery which had a child's crib and a chest of drawers with children's clothing in it, but she knew nothing more. Her master never spoke of his family affairs. Asked if there were any relations, said that she had never heard of any. If there were any, and if they ever called on the deceased gentleman, it must have been at the office, not the house; not a single visitor had ever called at the house or been admitted to this room—Mr. Burley's living-room—during the forty years of her residence. He had no friends; he never went out in the evenings; he never went to church or chapel; he lived quite alone.

"Gentlemen," said the president of the Court, "the important part of this evidence is the fact that for forty years no one ever called upon the deceased—neither son, nor grandson, nor cousin, nor nephew. Yet his wealth was notorious. Rich men, as most of you, I hope, know very well, are generally surrounded by their relations."

One of the jury asked a question which led to others. They bore upon the deceased's way of living, and had nothing to do with the business before the Court. But since we are all curious as to the manners and customs of that interesting people—the rich—the coroner allowed these questions. When the jury had learned all about the conduct of an extremely parsimonious household, and when the old lady had explained that her master, though near as to his expenditure, was a good man, who was surely in Abraham's bosom if ever anyone was, she was permitted to retire, though unwilling, into the obscurity of a back seat.

The manager gave his evidence. He had been employed by the deceased for thirty years. He was now the chief manager of his estates. Everything connected with the estates was managed at the house, where solicitors, architects, and other professional people were employed on salaries. He was familiar with the details of the estate; there were enormous masses of papers. He knew nothing of any will. Had a will passed through his hands he should certainly have remembered it. Naturally, he was anxious to know what would be done with so great a property. He supposed that Mr. Burley had employed a solicitor outside his own office for the purpose of drawing up a will. He had never spoken to Mr. Burley on the subject; he knew nothing of Mr. Burley's family or connections; he understood that Mr. Burley had once been married; he believed, but he did not know for certain, that there had been a child or children. He had himself sent the announcement of the death to the papers; he had seen one or two paragraphs concerning the early life of the deceased, but could not say, from his own knowledge, whether they were true or false.

He was asked by one of the jury whether the deceased was as rich as was reported. He replied that he could not tell until the report reached him. Other questions as to the extent and value of the estate he fenced with. There was, he said, a great deal of property, but he declined absolutely to commit himself to any estimate at all. So that the curiosity of the jury was baffled. They had learned, however, that the estate was so large and important that it had to be managed at a house specially used for the purpose, by a manager and a large staff of accountants and clerks. This was something—such an estate must be worth untold thousands.

"Gentlemen," said the coroner, "you have now heard all the evidence that we have to offer. Here is an estate. Where is the late owner's will? There is none. Where are the heirs? They do not appear. For forty years no member of the deceased's family has visited him. He might have had sons, grandsons, great-grandsons. None have turned up. But there must be, one would think, nephews—grand-nephews—cousins. If he had brothers, they must have had descendants; if he had uncles, they must have had descendants. Now, in the lower classes nothing is more common than for a man to change his place of residence so that his children grow up in ignorance absolute of their ancestry and cousins.

But this man, whatever his origin, was at one time before the world, notorious or famous, whatever you please; he was a public character; he was owner of theatres, dancing-places, gambling-hells; he was a well-known money-lender. All the world knew the usurer John Calvert Burley. He stood on a kind of pinnacle—unenviable, perhaps, but still on a pinnacle of publicity. His relations must have followed his course with interest—who would not watch with interest the course of a childless cousin? Yes, he is dead; and where are the cousins and the nephews? It is a very remarkable case. A poor man may have no one to claim kinship at his death. But for a rich man, and a notorious man—It is, indeed, wonderful! Gentlemen, you have only to declare the estate, in default of heirs, escheated and vested in the Crown. You all understand, however, that her Majesty the Queen will not be enriched by this windfall. The Treasury and not the Sovereign receives all those estates for which an heir is wanting."

The jury thereupon returned their verdict—"That until, or unless, the lawful heirs, or heir, shall substantiate a claim to the estate of the late John Calvert Burley, the said estate shall be, and is, escheated and become vested in the Crown."

"Then, gentlemen," said the coroner, "nothing more remains except for you to affix your signatures to this verdict, and for me to thank you, one and all, for the intelligence and care which you have brought to bear upon this important case."

In this manner and with such formalities the estate of the deceased was transferred to the Treasury, to be by it held and administered in the name of the Crown unless the rightful claimant should be able to establish his right.

"That's done," said Mr. Nicholson. "Now, let us look over the house. I haven't been here for forty years and more. Come and see where your father was born, Lucian."

V

The Fortune and the House

M argaret!" She had never seen her lover so flushed and excited. Mostly he preserved, whatever happened, the philosophic calm that befits the scientific mind. "Margaret, I have had the most wonderful morning! I have made discoveries! I have heard revelations!"

"What is it, Lucian?"

"It is about my grandfather. I told you I should go to see the house. Well, I had no time to go there till today. I have been there—I walked over there this morning. And I have been rewarded. A most remarkable coincidence! The very moment when I arrived there was opened an inquest in the house itself. Not an ordinary inquest, you know—the poor old man has been buried a month—but what they call an Inquest of Office. For since his death they have been searching for his will, and they haven't found it. And it really seems, my dear Margaret, as if the one thing most unlikely of all to happen has happened: that this rich man has actually died intestate, in which case I, even I myself, am the sole heir to everything!"

"Oh, Lucian! Is it possible?"

"It is almost certain. They have searched everywhere. There are piles of papers: they have all been examined. No will has been found. Now, if he had made a will, it is certain that I could not have come into it, unless through my father, and it is not probable that he would have had anything. But there is, apparently, no will, and the estates are handed over to the Treasury until—unless—they find the rightful heir—me—whom they cannot find."

"Oh, Lucian! It is wonderful! But, of course, you are not going to claim this terrible money—the profits of gambling-saloons and wicked places and money-lending?"

"No, my dear, I am not. Yet"—he laughed—"my dear child, it is a thousand pities, for the pile is enormous. You sit there as quiet as a nun: you don't understand what it means. Why, my dear Margaret, simple as you look, you should be, when you marry me, if you had your rights, the richest woman in the country—the richest woman, perhaps, in the world!"

"Don't take away my breath! Even to a nun such an announcement would be interesting."

"The richest woman in the world! That is all—wealth beyond the dreams of avarice—only that. And we give it up! Now, I'll tell you—I can't sit down, I must walk about, because the thought of this most wonderful thing won't let me keep still. Very well, then. Now listen. Mr. Nicholson, my father's old friend, you know, was there. He had heard of the inquest from the manager. All the Burley estates are managed at a house in Westminster—it is a great house filled with clerks, accountants, solicitors, architects, builders, rent-collectors—everything, all under a manager, who is a friend of Mr. Nicholson. Nobody knows what the estate is worth, but when this old man's father died he left the son an income of £20,000 a year, which at 5 percent is £400,000. That was what he began with at five-and-twenty. There was no need for him to do any work at all. But he did all those things that we know."

"Yes?"—for Lucian paused.

"He lived quite simply. The whole of that income must have accumulated at compound interest. Do you know what that means?"

"No. But these figures are beginning to frighten me. What does it matter to us how much there is?"

"Why, my dear, I am the heir—only in name, I know; still—well, Marjorie, money at 5 percent doubles itself every thirteen years or so. That is to say, the sum of £100 in seventy years would become, at 5 percent, £3200, and the sum of £400,000 would become in the same period over twelve millions. I don't suppose the old man always got his 5 percent, but it is certain that the original principal has grown and developed enormously—enormously! Without counting the money-lending business and the other enterprises, there must be millions. Nicholson says there is no doubt that the estate is worth many millions. My father knew of this enormous wealth, but he kept silence."

"Your father would not touch that dreadful and ill-gotten money, Lucian. Tell me no more—I cannot think in millions; I think in hundreds. So many hundreds—you have two or three, I believe—will keep our modest household. Do not let us talk or think about other people's millions."

"They are mine, Margaret, mine, if I choose to put out my hand. I only wish you to understand, dear, what it is—this trifle we are throwing away in obedience to my father's wish."

"Do not let us think about this horrid money, Lucian. We should end by regretting that you did not claim it. Your father renounced his name and his inheritance."

"Yes"—but he looked doubtful. "If that binds me—"

"Of course it binds us. It must bind us, Lucian. Besides, there is a curse—remember your father's words—a curse upon the money. Got with dishonor—"

"My dear child! A curse! Do not, pray, let us talk mediæval superstitions. The money may be given to anybody, for all I care. At the same time, to throw away such a chance makes one a little—eh?—agitated. You must allow, pretty Puritan, for some natural weakness."

"Yes, Lucian. But you are a man of science, not a money-grubber. What would money do for you?"

"Let me tell you about the house."

"I do not want to hear about the house, or the occupants, or the money, or anything. I want to forget all about it. I am sorry we read those papers, since they have disturbed your mind."

"Listen a moment only, and I will have done. The housekeeper took us up to the first floor—Nicholson and myself. It is a wonderful place. The furniture is at least a hundred years old. Neither the old man nor his father—who was a miser: quite a famous miser: they talk of him still—would ever buy anything new or send away anything old."

"I should like to see that part of it."

"Of course you would. On the walls are portraits—my ancestors; although my grandfather ran dancing-cribs, they have been a respectable stock for ever so long."

"They have been disreputable since the time of Queen Anne," said Margaret. "I do not know what they were before that time."

"Very well. There they are, in Queen Anne wigs and George II wigs, and hair tied behind. And, I say, Margaret, you know, whatever they were, it *is* pleasant to feel that one has forefathers, like other men. Perhaps they were not altogether stalwart Christians—but, yet—"

"One would like, at least, honorable ancestors."

"We must take what is helped. We can't choose our ancestors for ourselves. This is their family house, in which they have lived all these years. It is a lovely old house. Three stories, and garrets in the red-tiled roof; steps up to the door like a Dutch stoop; the whole front covered with a thick hanging creeper—a green curtain; the front window looking out upon the old gray wall of the Abbey garden; at the back a little garden with a huge vine—"

"Your father must have played in it," said Margaret, attracted against her will by the description.

"Then he played under a mulberry and beside a splendid vine. The stairs are broad and low; the whole house is wain-scoted. Marjorie mine!" He sat down, stopping suddenly, and took her hand.

"What is it, Lucian?"

Now these two young people were not only engaged to each other, but they were fully resolved to gather the roses while they might, and not to wait for the sere and yellow leaf. They would marry, as so many brave young people do now marry, in these days of tightness, on a small income, hopeful for the future. What that income was, you may guess from the first chapter of this history.

"I have an idea. It is this: The house will suit us exactly. Let us take it and set up our tent there. Don't jump up, my dear. I renounce my ancestors as much as you like—their trades and callings—their little iniquities—their works and their ways. Their enormous fortune I renounce. I go about with a name that does not belong to me, and I won't take my own true name. All the same, they are my ancestors. They are; we cannot get clear of that fact."

"But why go and live in their house and be always reminded of the fact?"

"Can one ever forget the fact of one's own ancestry? They are an accident of the house; they won't affect us. We shall go in as strangers. As for that curse of the money—which is an idle superstition—that cannot fall upon us, because we shall have nothing to do with the money; and it is so quiet; the street itself is like—well, it reminds one of those old-fashioned river-side docks—quiet old places which the noise of the river seems never to reach. Great College Street is a peaceful little dock running up out of the broad high river of the street for the repose of humans. And it is close to the Abbey, which you would like. And at the back is a Place—not a street—a Place which is more secluded than any Cathedral Close anywhere. You would think you were in a nunnery, and you would walk there, in the sunshine of a winter morning, and meditate after your own heart. It is as quiet as a nunnery and as peaceful. Now, child, let me say right out what is in my mind. I want a place—don't I?—where I can put up my plate and make a bid for a practice—Lucian Calvert, M.D. Well, I looked about. The position is central;

the street is quiet; there are lots of great people about. The members of Parliament would only have to step across Palace Yard; the Speaker can run over and speak to me about his symptoms, noble lords can drop in to consult me; the Dean and Canons of Westminster have only to open the garden gate in order to find me."

"Oh, Lucian! I am so sorry that you have seen the house. Oh! I am so sorry that you ever heard anything about this great fortune."

"Of course I mean that we should take the house with all that it contains."

"All your ancestors' portraits?" she laughed, scornfully. "Why, if you knew who and what they were—"

"I do not expect virtue. Their private characters have nothing to do with us. We have cut ourselves off. Only, it will be pleasant to feel that they are there always with us. My dear, after all these years, say that it *is* pleasant to find that one has ancestors."

"And you want to go and live with them! You have changed your name and refused your inheritance. Why, Lucian, if you live among them, it will be like a return to the family traditions—and—and—I don't know—misfortune and disaster—you have not read the history of the family."

"A family curse!" he repeated, with impatience. "Nonsense! The place is most suitable; the house is most convenient—and—besides—the house should be mine; my own people have always lived in it; I belong to the house. The portraits are mine; I ought to be with them. One would say that they call me."

VI

The Nursery

L ucian turned away and said no more that day. But the next day—and the next—and every day he returned to the subject. Sometimes openly, sometimes indirectly; always by something that he said, showing that his mind was dwelling on his newly recovered ancestors and on their house at Westminster. She knew that he walked across the park every day to look at it. She perceived that his proposal to take the house, so far from being abandoned or forgotten, was growing in his mind, and had taken root there. Her heart sank with forebodings—those forebodings which have no foundation, yet are warnings and prophecies.

"You are thinking still," she said, "of those portraits."

"There is reproach in your voice, my Marjorie," he replied. "Yes, I think of them still, I have seen them again—several times. They are the portraits of my own people. A man cannot cut himself off from his own people any more than he can cut himself off from his own posterity."

"If you will only read the history of your ancestors as your father set it down, you will no longer desire to belong to them."

"Wrong, Marjorie, wrong. It is not a question of what I should wish; it is the stubborn fact that I belong to them. Their history may be tragic, or criminal, or sordid, or anything you please; but it is part of my history as well."

"Then read those papers."

"No, I will not read them. You shall tell me, if you please, some time or other. Now, I have talked it over with Nicholson. He quite thinks the house would suit us."

"Does Mr. Nicholson, your father's old friend, approve?"

"I have not asked for his approval."

Lucian did not explain that Mr. Nicholson had expressed a strong opinion on the other side, nor did he inform her of Mr. Nicholson's last words, which were: "If you take this house, Lucian, you will end by claiming the estates. I have no right to say anything; but—it is ill-gotten money."

"I say," Lucian repeated, "that I act on my own approval. Well, Nicholson has found at the office—my grandfather's office—that I can take the house on reasonable terms, and that I can have the furniture and everything at a valuation."

"Oh! Those portraits drag you to the house, Lucian."

"They do. I am not a superstitious man, my dear; I laugh at the alleged curse on the money; yet I accede to my father's wish, and I will not claim that great fortune—we don't want to be rich; nor will I resume my proper name, which would cause awkwardness. But I want to feel myself a link in the chain."

"Alas," she sighed, "what a chain!"

"And I want to return to my own people. They may keep their fortune. But since they have transmitted to me their qualities—such as they are—I would live among them, Marjorie!" He held out his hands. "You know my wish."

She took them. She fell into his arms. "Oh! my dear," she cried, laughing and crying, "who can resist you? Since you must, you must. Being so very wilful, you must. We will go—those faces on the walls are stronger than I—we will go there—since nothing else will please you. But, oh! my Lucian, what will happen to us when we get there?"

This step once resolved upon, it was agreed that she should first see the house. But she made one condition.

"If," she said, "we take that house and buy those pictures, I must tell you who and what were the people whose portraits they are. At least, Lucian, you should not be tempted to pay them any reverence."

"As you please, Margaret," he replied, carelessly. "Of course, I don't expect chronicles of virtue; they would be monotonous. I am sure that the forefathers of the deceased must, like him, have had a rooted dislike to the monotony of virtue."

And then occurred a very curious thing. The girl's mind had been filled with terror, gloomy forebodings, presentiments. She had read those papers, she knew the family history, she was weighed down by the sins of all these ancestors. But when it was resolved to take the house, when the possible became the actual, she found to her astonishment that the ghosts vanished—as Lucian had said, the past was old history— old history—what did it matter to them?

It was, she found, a lovely old house. Steps, side steps, with a good old iron railing, led to the stoop and to the front door. There were three stories, each with three windows; there was a steep red-tiled roof with dormer-windows. Over the whole front hung a thick green curtain of Virginia-creeper. The shutters, indeed, were closed, which partly concealed the uncleaned condition of the windows. On the other side of the street was the old gray wall of the Cathedral precincts—did Edward the Confessor build that wall, or was it an earlier work still?—the work of Dunstan, what time his Majesty King Edgar endowed the Abbey?

"Is it a lovely old place outside?" asked Lucian, eagerly. "Is it a quiet, peaceful spot?"

"It is all that you say, Lucian."

"Now, my dear, you shall see the inside of it. Remember that it has not been cleaned for ever so long. Don't judge of it, quite, by its present aspect."

With his borrowed latch-key Lucian opened the door, and they stepped in. The place was quite empty; the old woman was gone; the shutters were closed; the furniture, it is true, was left; but furniture without life makes a house feel more deserted than even when the rooms are empty. Another well-known point about an empty house is that, as soon as people go out, it is instantly seized upon by echoes; if it remains long empty it receives a large collection of echoes. When Lucian shut the street door, the reverberation echoed up the walls of the stairs from side to side; then it came down again more slowly, and then more slowly still climbed up the walls again, dying away with obvious reluctance. Lucian said something, a word of welcome; his voice rolled about the stairs, and was repeated from wall to wall; he walked across the hall, his footsteps followed his voice, as his voice had followed the shutting of the door.

"The house is all echoes," said Margaret. Her voice was not strong enough to be rolled up the stairs, but her sibilants were caught, and Echo returned a prolonged hiss.

"Only because it is empty. Echoes are odd things. They never stay in an inhabited house. They like solitary places, I suppose." Lucian opened the door of the back parlor, which, with the shutters closed, looked like a black cave in which anything might be found. "This is the room"— he lowered his voice—"in which the old man lived and died. Quite a happy old man, he is said to have been. Serenely happy in the memory of his little iniquities. He was no more troubled with remorse in his age than he was with scruples in his manhood. Curious! Most very wicked people are happy, I believe. Seems a kind of compensation—doesn't it?" He pulled back the shutters and let in the sunlight.

"There! Now, Margaret, my dear, you behold the consulting-room of Lucian Calvert, M.D. Here he will sit and receive his patients. They will flock to him by crowds—the lords; the members of Parliament; the Canons of West-minster; the engineers from George Street; the people from the Treasury, the Colonial Office, the India Office, the Board of Works, the Board of Trade, the Educational Department— they will all flock to me for consultation. They will wait in the front room. Not a physician in Harley Street will be better housed than I. We will breakfast and dine in the waiting-room. Upstairs you shall have your own rooms—drawing-room, boudoir, everything. This is to be the patients' waiting-room."

He opened the door of communication with the front room, and strode across in the darkness to open the shutters. The room was furnished with a dining-table, but no one had dined in it for a hundred years. In the miser's time there was no dinner at all; in his successor's time the room at the back was used as a living-room. The place was inconceivably dirty and neglected.

"Oh! what dust and dirt!" cried the girl. "Shall we ever get it clean and presentable? Look at the windows! When were they cleaned last? And the ceilings! They are black!"

"Dirt is only matter in the wrong place. Bring along a mop and a bucket and transfer it to the right place. We will transform these rooms. A little new paint—pearl-gray, do you think? With a touch of color for the panels and the dado, a new carpet, new curtains, white ceiling, clean windows—"

"What a lot of money it will take!"

"We will make the money. Patients will flock in; I shall finish my book. Courage, dear girl. And now, if you please, we will go right up to the top floor first. How the old house echoes!" He lifted his voice and sang a few bars as they stepped back into the hall. Instantly there was awakened a choir of voices—a hundred voices at least, all singing, ringing, repeating the notes backward and forward and up and down.

"I believe the house is full of ghosts," said Margaret. "Without you, Lucian, I should be afraid to go up the stairs."

"I wish it was full of ghosts," Lucian replied. And up and down the stairs the echoes repeated: "I wish—I wish—I wish—it was—was— was—"

Margaret laughed.

"When I am the wife of a scientific person," she said, "I must leave off believing in ghosts. Just at present and in this empty house I seem to feel the ghosts of your ancestors. They are coming upstairs with us."

They were broad and ample stairs, such as builders loved when these were constructed.

"But they were made for hoops," said Margaret.

The old carpet, worn into holes and shreds, its outlines gone, still stuck by force of habit in its place.

"There were two misers in succession," said Margaret; "therefore this carpet must be a hundred years old at least. I wonder it has lasted so long."

"My grandfather stepped carefully upon the holes," said Lucian, "in order to preserve the rest. I think I see him going up and down very carefully."

"If we were to meet one of the ancestors stepping down the stairs in a satin coat and a wig and laced ruffles, should you be surprised, Lucian?"

"Not a bit. First floor. Let us go on. It is a noble staircase, and when we've got through with the whitewasher and the painter, and have the stair-window cleaned, it will look very fine. Second floor—one more flight."

They stood on the landing at the top of the stairs; two or three dust-covered boxes lay scattered about carelessly, as if no one had been up there for a very long time. Two closed doors faced them. In one was a key; Lucian unlocked it and threw the door open.

"It's the nursery!" cried Margaret. "Why, it is the old, old nursery!" She stepped in and threw open the windows—they were the two picturesque dormers that had caught her eyes in the street. "There! A little fresh air—and now—" She turned and looked again at the evidence of ancient history. "Why!" she said, sitting on the bed. "Here grew up the innocent children who afterwards—they were innocent then, I suppose—afterwards became—what they were. Here they played with their innocent mothers. Oh! Lucian, my history says so little about the wives and mothers. They had some brief time of happiness, I hope, in this room while the babes grew into little children, and the children grew tall—and my history says nothing about the girls. There must have been girls. Did they run away? Did they disgrace their name and themselves? Do you think they were girls as much ashamed of their people as we can be, Lucian?—because thy people are my people, you know, and where thou goest, I go too. And in this house I shall become a successor to these wives, whose sons were your grandfathers." The tears stood in her eyes.

"Nay, my Margaret, but not an unhappy successor. What does it matter if these women were unhappy? Old histories—old histories! Let us trust, my dear, in ourselves, and fear no bogies."

"Yes, we will trust in ourselves, Lucian." She got up and examined the room more closely.

Against the wall there stood a cradle; not one of the little dainty baskets of modern custom, but a stout, solid, wooden cradle, with strong wooden rollers, carved sides, and a carved wooden head; a thing that may have been hundreds of years old. The little blankets were lying folded up ready for use on the little feather-bed, but both blankets and bed were moth-eaten and covered with dust—for the room had not been opened for fifty years. Beside the cradle was a low washing arrangement, for children's use, a thing used before the invention of the modern bath; in one corner was a small wooden bed, a four-poster, without head or hangings, but with a feather-bed also eaten in holes and gaps; in another corner the children's bed, a low truckle-bed of the time when children were put two and three together in one bed; on the mantel-shelf were basins and spoons, and a tinder-box, and an old-fashioned night-light in its pierced iron frame. There were two or three chairs, a chest of drawers, a small table, a high brass fender, and a cupboard.

"The nursery," Margaret repeated, with a kind of awe. The discovery moved her strangely. The dust lay thick upon the beds and the cradle and everything. When the last children died, and the mother died, and the last son left the house, the door of the nursery was shut, and for fifty years remained shut. She pulled open the top drawer of the chest. There were lying in it, carefully folded and put away, the complete trousseau of a baby. Such beautiful clothes they were, with such cunning and craft of embroidery and needle-work as belonged to the time when things were made and not bought. In those ancient days things, because they were made, and excellently made with skill and patience and pride, were much prized, and were handed down from mother to daughter-in-law, insomuch that this dainty frock in long clothes might have served for generation after generation of babies in this family of Burley. Margaret turned over the things with the artistic curiosity of one who recognizes good work more than with the sympathetic interest of a possible matron, who considers the use for which it was designed.

The other drawers contained things belonging to children a little older—frocks, socks, shoes, sashes, ribbons, petticoats, and whatever is wanted to adorn and protect a child of three or four.

"See," she said, holding up a long baby frock, "the beauty of the work. Ah! In such a house as this it relieves the mind only to see such evidences of loving work. Love means happiness, Lucian, for a woman at least. While the patient fingers were embroidering this frock, the woman's heart must have been at rest and in happiness. Yet they were going to be so miserable from mother to daughter-in-law, all of them. Oh! I am so glad we have seen this room. It is like a gleam and glimpse of sunshine. Five generations of women lived here—all of them, one after the other, doomed in the end to misery. Five generations! And we, Lucian—we begin afresh. If I thought otherwise—but these poor women had unrighteous lords—and I—"

He stooped and kissed her hand. "We begin anew," he said. "Courage! we begin anew."

She threw open the cupboard. There were hanging up within two or three dresses of ancient fashion.

"Strange," said Margaret, "that these things should be left. See, they belong to the time of George IV. The sleeves are returning to that fashion. I suppose the last two tenants would suffer nothing to be destroyed. Look—here are their toys—even the children's toys kept! Here they are: broken dolls, battledoors, Noah's arks, cup and ball, wooden soldiers, puzzles, picture-books. I must come up here again," she added; "I must come up alone and turn out this cupboard at my leisure. Lucian, in such a place as this—in the old nursery one feels the reality of the family. There are women and children, mothers, wives, daughters, in the family. You can't understand it simply by reading about the wickedness of the men. It is like a history which concerns itself only with the campaigns of generals and the oppression of kings. Here one feels the presence of the mothers and the children." She sighed again. "Poor unfortunate mothers!" she said. "Lucian, I charge you, when you send in your workmen, leave the nursery untouched. This shall be mine."

"Yes, dear, it shall be yours—your own."

"The room is full of ghosts, Lucian. I am not afraid of them; but I feel them. If I were to stay here long, I should see them. Let us go into the next room."

VII

The Prodigal Son

The other room, the back attic, was locked, and there was no key in the door. Lucian turned the handle and pressed with his shoulder. The lock broke off inside, and the door flew open.

"Ouf!" cried Lucian. "What a dust! What an atmosphere!" The sun was struggling through the window, which was covered inside with cobweb, and outside with the unwashed layers of many years' coal smoke. He tried to throw up the sash, but the cords were broken; he lifted it up and propped it with a book which he took from a shelf hanging beside the window. "So!" he said. "Why, what in the world have we here?"

The room was furnished with a four-post bed. The hangings, which had never been removed, were in colorless tatters; everything was devoured by moth; but the bed was still made—sheets, blankets, and coverlet—and so had remained for a hundred and fifty years. There was a single chair in the room—a wooden chair; there was a mahogany table, small, but of good workmanship; on the table were the brushes and palette of a painter; a violin-case lay half under the bed; the inkstand with the quill pens, the paper, and the pouncet-box still lay on the table as they had been left; the books on the shelf—Lucian looked at them— were chiefly volumes of poetry.

"See, Lucian! The walls are covered with paintings!"

So they were; the sloping walls of the attic, which had been plastered white, were covered all over with paintings in oil. They represented nymphs and satyrs, flowers and fountains, woods and lakes, terraces and walks, gardens and alleys of the Dutch kind, streets with signs hanging before the houses, and ladies with hoops. The paintings were not exactly executed by the hand of a master; the drawing was weak and the color faded. Each picture was signed in the left-hand corner "J. C. B.," with dates varying from 1725 to 1735.

"What is the history of these things?"

"I think I know," Margaret said, softly. "There is a picture. Oh!" she shuddered, "I am sure the date corresponds. How shall I tell you, Lucian?"

The picture hung over the mantel-shelf, turned face to the wall. Lucian turned it round. It represented a young man about twenty-five years of age. He was richly dressed in the fashion of the time—about 1735; he wore a purple coat with a flowered silk waistcoat and lace ruffles. His hat was trimmed with gold lace; his fingers, covered with rings, resting lightly on the gold hilt of his sword.

"The man was a gentleman, at least!" cried his descendant.

His handsome face was filled with gallantry and pride. One could see that he was a young man with a good deal of eighteenth-century side and swagger; one recognized his kind—always ready for love or for fighting; one could picture him standing up in the pit of the theatre, sitting among the rufflers and bullies of the tavern, the terror of the street, a gallant in the Park.

Margaret said something to this effect, but not much, because, in truth, her knowledge of the eighteenth century was limited. "He is handsome," she said, "but not in the best way. It is a sensual face, though it is so young. See—Lucian! There are his initials, J. C. B., with the date 1735. It is the painter of these pictures. I will tell you about him, Lucian. This is clearly his own room, the place where he practised art when he was a boy—where he lived until he left his father's house. His name was the same that they all bore, you know, John Calvert Burley, and he was the son of Calvert Burley—of whom I will tell you presently—the man who began the fortunes of the family. When this man was young he was full of promise; he was an artist—these must be his paintings; he was a musician. See—" She pointed to the violin-case. "He was a poet, or at least a writer of songs." The book-shelf was filled with books of verse. "He was a dramatist who wrote a comedy which was played at Drury Lane; and there were other things in which he was skilled that I do not remember. All these facts are noted in your father's papers."

Lucian nodded to his ancestors. "I am glad," he said, "that I have a forefather of so much distinction. Permit me to say so much, sir, although I have renounced you."

"Wait, Lucian. This room has been locked up since his death. That was in 1750. Your father mentions the room that was always locked up. It was this man's room. Upon him, your father writes, the vengeance first fell for his father's sins."

"Oh!" Lucian interrupted, impatiently, "please do not talk to me about vengeance for another man's sins. How can such a thing be? Besides, had this man none of his own?"

"Unfortunately—yes. That was part of the vengeance. He was all wickedness. Clever as he was, bright and clever, and good-looking when he was young, he became a profligate and—and—everything that you can imagine in the way of wickedness, after he grew up. People must have spoiled him when he was a boy. There is a great deal about him in your father's papers. His name should have been Absalom. I have been thinking lately about this unhappy man. People should not spoil clever boys. He was good-looking—well, look at the portrait. Handsome Jack Burley they used to call him. He quarrelled with his father—I do not know why—and then he lived by his wits—lived on the town. How did young men live on the town, Lucian, a hundred years ago?"

"I don't very well know. Much as they do now, I suppose. They played cards and won; and games of chance, and won; they borrowed money of their friends and did not pay it back; they took presents from rich ladies—whose hearts they afterwards broke; they ran away with heiresses; finally, they got into the Fleet Prison and starved, or they took to the road and were hanged. Then my ancestor here was quite a model profligate, I take it. Perhaps Tom Jones had this man's career before him as a model."

"You have stated his case exactly. He married an heiress and he squandered her fortune. Then she left him and came here with her child. He was brought up in the nursery we have just left; I suppose that we have seen his baby-clothes."

"Well, and what became of that prodigal? Did he repent and come home again? Or was he presently brought to the Fleet Prison?"

"No, Lucian," she replied, gravely. "This bright and gallant gentleman"—she pointed to the picture—"who looks as if there were no laws of God to be feared, chose one of the two lines you have indicated. But it was the road, and not the Debtor's Prison. And it led to—the other kind of prison."

"Oh!" But Lucian's face flushed a little. "You mean, Margaret, that this gay and gallant gentleman was—in point of fact—"

"Yes. A fitting end for him, but it was disgraceful to his people. This ancestor was hanged at Tyburn for a highway robbery. His father turned the portrait to the wall and locked the door. That was in the year 1750. And the room has never been opened since."

"Humph!" Lucian stroked his chin gravely. "Have you any more such stories to tell me?"

"Two or three more."

"After all—old history—old history! Who would care now if one's descent from a man who was hanged in the year 1750 was published from the house-top? No one. Old history, Mag. And as to vengeance for his father's sins, why, you've made it clear that he had enough of his own to justify the final suspension. Shall we ever use this room, Maggie?"

She shuddered. "Who could sleep here?" she said. "We will turn it, perhaps, into a storehouse of all the old things—the children's dresses and the dolls, perhaps, out of the nursery; and the toys and the cradle and everything else that belongs to the innocent life. If the ghost of this wicked man still haunts the room, he may profitably be reminded of the days of innocence. Perhaps he has repented, long since, of the days of prodigality. I don't think we could make a bedroom here."

"Call you that renouncing of my ancestors, Marjorie? Why, you are bringing all the mischief you can upon your own head by acknowledging that you know the stories. The wisest thing to do would be to clear out the room—both rooms—burn the rubbish, put the portrait somewhere else, and give the old-fashioned things to a museum of domestic manners and customs. Let us go downstairs."

VIII

The Portraits

They closed the door and went down to the next floor. Here there were three bedrooms, all furnished alike and with solidity. Each had a great mahogany four-poster, a mahogany chest of drawers, a mahogany dressing-table, and two mahogany chairs; there was a carpet in each; and the hangings were still round the beds, but in dusty, moth-eaten tatters and rags. There were also shelves and a cupboard in each room. On the shelves were books—school-books of the early part of this century. Latin grammars in Latin, Greek grammars in Latin, Ovid and Cicero and Cornelius Nepos, Gordon's Geography, the Greek Testament, and so forth. There seemed no reason to linger in the room. But Margaret opened the drawers. Strange! they were all filled with things. She looked into the cupboards; they also were filled with things—clothes, personal effects. "Why," she cried, "they did not even take away their clothes! Oh! I know now. They left them here when they ran away, and here they have remained ever since. I will tell you directly all about them, Lucian. Look! These silk gloves must have belonged to Lucinda—your great-aunt. She ran away. And in the other room there are things with the initials H. C. B.—your great-uncle Henry; and others with the initials of C. C. B. and of J. C. B.—your great-uncles Charles and James. They, too, ran away. I will tell you why presently."

On the first floor there were two rooms only, at the front and the back. They opened the door of the room at the back.

It was furnished exactly like the rooms overhead, only that the four-poster was larger. The carpet and the hangings and the curtains were quite as moth-eaten and ragged as those upstairs.

"This is the room of the master," said Margaret—"your grandfather's room. For fifty years he was alone. His wife died about the year 1850; and when his son, your father, left him he was quite alone, and the house has been in silence ever since. Fancy a house, a thing that ought never to be without young people, condemned to silence for fifty years! It isn't used to noise. The echoes take up your voice on the stairs; the walls whisper it, as if they were afraid to speak out loud. All these years of silence! And all the time downstairs he sat and reckoned up his money."

She turned away and closed the door.

"Lucian!"—she laid her hand upon his arm—"before we go to see the portraits, think. In your father's papers is an account of them all. Better have nothing to do with them—better know nothing about them."

"Oh, nonsense! If I do not hear now I shall be wanting to read the confounded papers myself. You need not soften the facts, Margaret. I am not afraid. Besides, old histories! old histories!"

He opened the door of the drawing-room, which in the old days when it was furnished was called the best parlor. This was the state-room of the house, never used at all except for weddings, christenings, and funerals.

The furniture was stiff and rather quaint. The chairs and sofa had been upholstered with stuff once green; there had also been gilt about the legs and backs; there was a round table in the middle; there was a card-table between the windows; there was a cabinet containing a few curiosities; there was a faded carpet, partly moth-eaten; the fireplace and fender were of the old fashion; and there was nothing else in the room.

"I wonder," said Margaret, "if there has ever been any festivity at all in this room? Certainly there can have been none for two hundred years. Is there anywhere else in this city a house with a drawing-room which for two hundred years has never been used?"

But the walls! Round the wainscoted walls there were hung on every panel the portraits of the family; the men were all there; the wives and the daughters were all there. Two or three of the upper shutters of the windows were half open, and the faces were just visible in the dim light. Lucian threw open all the shutters.

It was the custom all through the last century in every family of the least pretensions or importance to have all their portraits taken. In the time of great Queen Anne the limner went about the country from house to house. He charged, I believe, a guinea for a portrait. You may see specimens of his skill preserved in country-houses to this day. Portraits, in time, began to rise in price; it became an outward sign of prosperity to have your portrait taken. During this present century many most respectable families have gone without portraits altogether. Photographs, of course, do not count. In the Burley family the custom prevailed during the whole of last century and well into this. All the sons and daughters of this House were figured and hung in frames, which sadly wanted regilding, upon the walls.

"My ancestors." Lucian bowed with a comprehensive sweep of his arm. "Ancestors! I present to you your granddaughter-in-law that will be. We have renounced your works and ways, but we recognize the fact of the relationship. Maggie, you have something rather uncommon to tell me about our ancestors, I believe? With your permission, ancestors!" Again he bowed gravely.

"Yes, but what is it? Very odd! Oh! I see. Most of them are following me with their eyes wherever I go. What an uncanny thing! How came the painters to make all their eyes like that? It looks as if they were curious to see the living representative."

"Let them follow," said Lucian. "Now, historiographer of the ancient House of Burley, I listen—I sit at your feet—I wait to learn."

Margaret was walking round the room looking at the names and dates on the frames. "Yes," she said, "these are your ancestors; all are here, except that unhappy man for whose sake the room upstairs has been closed all these years. Now Lucian, if you are prepared—mind, I could tell you a great deal about every one—but I will confine myself to the principal facts. You will find them bad enough."

"You ought to have a white wand." Lucian sat down. "Now—it *is* odd how the eyes are staring at me—I am ready to hear the worst."

Over the mantel-shelf hung the effigy of a gentleman in a large wig—a wig of the year 1720, or thereabouts. A certain fatness of cheek with a satisfied smugness of expression characterizes most portraits of this period. Both were wanting in this face. It was hard; the eyes were hard; the mouth was hard; the face was determined; the forehead showed power, the mouth and chin determination. Time, who is often an excellent finisher of portraits, and occasionally brings out the real character of the subject much more effectively than the original limner (but he takes a good many years over the job), had covered this face with a cloud of gloom and sadness.

"We begin with this man," said Margaret. "He is Calvert Burley. He began, however, as a clerk, or servant of some kind, to a City merchant. He must have been a young man of ability, because he rapidly rose, and became factor or confidential clerk. What he did was this: He persuaded his master, who entirely trusted him, to invest a great sum in South Sea stock. With a part of the money he bought shares in his own name, falsifying the figures to prevent being found out. The shares, as he expected, went higher and higher, till they reached—I don't know what—and then he sold his own shares to his own master at the highest price. Then the crash came. He really looks, Lucian, as if he heard every word we are saying."

"Let him answer the charge, then."

"Well, the unfortunate merchant was ruined; his clerk who had made an immense profit upon every share he held—I know not how many there were—stepped into his place. This was the origin of the fortunes of the House."

"And the confiding merchant?"

"He died in the Fleet. His former clerk would not send him so much as a guinea when he was starving. Well, Calvert from a servant became a master; from a factor he became a merchant. I suppose that no one found out what he had done."

"How was it found out, then?"

"I do not know. I read it in your father's papers."

"Humph! I should like to hear Mr. Calvert Burley's own account of the transaction."

"That was what your father meant when he said that the fortunes of the House were founded on dishonor."

"Yes." Lucian looked at the portrait, who fixed upon him from under black eyebrows a pair of keen, searching eyes. He got up and looked more closely. "Yes," he repeated, "I should like to hear your own account of the transaction, my ancestor. Because you look as if you could put it differently."

"Lucian, stand there a moment beside the portrait, so the light upon your face is the same. Oh! you are so like him. You have the same strong face, the same eyes, and the same mouth. Lucian, your strength was his, but he turned his strength to evil purposes."

Lucian laughed. "At all events, my Marjorie, I shall not invest my master's money in my own name."

"You are exactly like him. But, of course, what does it matter? Well, you heard upstairs how vengeance fell upon this man through his son."

"Not at all. I heard upstairs how the son was rightly punished for his own crimes—not for his father's crimes at all. I am quite sure that the judge who sentenced him made no allusion to his father."

"Well, he had no happiness with his money; for his eldest child ended as you have heard, and his only daughter died of small-pox at the age of twenty-two. I expect this must be her portrait." It was one of a very pretty girl; dark-eyed, animated, evidently a vivacious and pleasing girl. "Poor child! to die so young; and his youngest, a boy of sixteen, disappeared. They thought he was kidnapped. It is all in your father's papers."

"How did he know?" asked Lucian.

"I think I can tell you. Beside the men of a family, there are the women. The men work—for good or evil. The women watch; they watch, they observe, and they remember. Do you think that the wife of Calvert Burley—the unhappy wife of this man—did not know what her husband had done? When her sons and her daughter were taken from her, do you think she hid in her heart the things she knew—the money got by fraud, the starving prisoner in the Fleet? Oh no! She told her daughter-in-law, who in time told hers, and so the story was handed down as far as your mother, who told her son."

"It is possible. I did not think of that."

"Men never think of the women who watch. If they did, how long would the wickedness of the world endure?"

"You are bitter, my Margaret."

"It is because my mind is full of the women of your own House. Am I not going to become one? See—the next panel is empty. That is because the portrait is upstairs in the room that you burst open. This one is his wife. Poor wretch! She is young now, with all her troubles before her—and an heiress. See how beautifully she is dressed! My dear Lucian, when her husband had spent all her money and deserted her; when she came here with her infant; when the news arrived of her husband's shameful end—do you think that the bereaved wife and the bereaved mother did not sit and whisper to each other words of the Lord's vengeance?"

"It is possible," Lucian replied, gravely. "Old superstitions!"

Margaret went on to the next portrait. It had upon it the date of 1760. The big wig had given place to a more modest gear. The face was that of a young man. "He is the son of the man upstairs," said Margaret.

There was little of his father's swagger visible in this young man's face. He was like all the men of the family, endowed with black eyes and black hair; there was no force of character in his face: his mouth was weak; his eyes looked upward—there was a strange, expectant light in them—while his forehead was marked with a straight vertical line. The expression of this man's face seemed out of harmony with those around him.

"The only son of his mother," said Margaret. "He married and had children, but I know not how many, nor what became of any except the eldest. I believe that they all died young except that one. And this poor man—what he did I know not—whether he advanced the fortunes of the family I cannot tell you—but—he went mad—"

"Mad! He doesn't seem mad." Yet as Lucian looked closer, he saw the possibilities of madness in those eyes.

"It was a time, you know, when people thought a great deal about the safety of their souls. Many became mad from religious terrors. It was in this way that he went mad. For twelve years he was chained to the floor in one of the rooms upstairs. I said there was nothing to keep us there—I was afraid of finding the marks of the bolt in the floor. After twelve years he died. This was his wife."

"The history becomes more cheerful as we go along. Really," said Lucian, "there never was such an unlucky House. And all because of that little fraudulent transaction in stocks. Pray go on."

"There is not much more in the way of horrors. The next picture, this with the hair tied behind, is the son of the madman. You see it is dated 1790. He lived to the year 1820, when he died, at the age of fifty. What should you say, from the look of the man's face, was his character?"

"Well, it is a dark and rather a gloomy face; it has a look of the original Calvert, but without his power. This man was small; he looks small and narrow; there is some determination in his face; and, somehow, the painter has left out the intellect. Perhaps he had none. What did he do? To look at him he might have been a small retail trader, counting up his little profits every day."

"Lucian, you are cleverer at character-reading than I thought. He *was* a little retail trader—that is to say, he became a miser—quite a celebrated miser—one of the misers you read of in books. He used to wander about the streets picking up crusts and bones; he would have no fire in the coldest weather; he would have no servant in the house—had he not a wife and a daughter? He went in rags himself; his sons should learn to do the same. It is said that at night he would beg in the streets, or hold a horse or call a hackney-coach. But he left off going into the streets because the boys followed and hooted him. He weighed out the food, which was of the commonest and cheapest kind. He bought scraps of the butchers and stale loaves of the bakers. Nothing was too bad for him."

"Oh! This was my great-grandfather. Very pleasant, indeed—a charming ancestor!"

"I suppose he had some family feeling, because he had actually spent money on having his children painted. Perhaps he got it done for nothing. But here they are—first his wife; I suppose they are the family jewels which she wears. You must have an immense number of cousins, Lucian; but I do not know who they are because the papers contain no information about their wives. She is a handsome woman, is she not, your great-grandmother? That is her daughter Lucinda. Whenever there is a daughter, the name is always Lucinda. You see, she wears the same jewels as her mother; she borrowed them, no doubt."

"Did she distinguish herself?" asked Lucian.

"She rebelled against the miserly rule at home and ran away. It is also stated that she married, but her married name is not recorded, and I know nothing more about her. These are the four sons—there were five children altogether. They are a good-looking lot of boys, are they not? Do they look like the sons of a miser?"

Their portraits had all been taken in the same year—probably at so much the job—by a painter very much down in his luck. They were not ill-painted. The young men were from seventeen to two or three and twenty; their hair was curled for the occasion, because a sitting for a portrait was like going to a party. They wore high stocks, and every one had a watch-chain hanging from the fob.

"It is the same watch and chain," said Margaret, "lent to one after the other."

"These are my grandfather and my great-uncles."

"Yes. That is your grandfather. He is like Calvert, is he not? Curious how the face reappears—first in him and then in you. It is a much larger face than his predecessor's: there is more intellect in it. As for the others, tell me what you think of this one—the second."

"He is exactly like the gallant highwayman. Did he also take to the road? Was he, too, conducted in triumph to the fatal tree?"

"No. Like the highwayman, he had all kinds of clevernesses: he could make music on anything, and he could sing and make verses. He ran away as soon as he was eighteen years of age—he ran away and became an actor."

"Very sensible thing, too—much better than taking to the road."

"Much better. He succeeded, too. He was a good actor, and became, at one time, lessee and manager of the York Theatre."

"His grandchildren will put in a claim to the estate, I suppose!"

"You will not mind if they do," Margaret replied quickly.

"Very well. Let us go on to the next. Who is this fellow? Why, he looks like the man who went mad—his grandfather. Has he a history, too?"

"That was Charles. I said that there were other tragedies. This unlucky young man ran away from home, and I think there is something said about an aunt who befriended him. He was put into a place in the City, and—I hardly know what he did; I think it was a forgery" (Lucian groaned); "and he was tried and sentenced to be hanged, but the sentence was commuted to transportation for life. So he went to Australia."

"Australia is not so far off as it was. The convict's grandchildren are doubtless on their way home to get the estate."

"Very likely." Margaret went on to another: "This was the youngest son, James."

"There is a touch of the highwayman about him, too," said Lucian. "How did he distinguish himself?"

"Well, he ran away, of course; and he became a solicitor—I don't know how; and then he—he took away his employer's young wife, and went to America."

Lucian sat down. "Why!" he cried. "It is a great—it is a glorious family! They vie with each other in greatness."

"That is all, Lucian."

"Thank you, dear cicerone. You have spun out a very pretty history—one that could be told of very few families—very few indeed. I think I ought to be proud of such an ancestry."

He lapsed into silence. As he sat there looking up at the portrait of Calvert Burley the resemblance became stronger. His face assumed a gloomy look, which still more increased the resemblance.

"After all, Margaret," he said, presently, "why should we not take over this great inheritance? We only know, in general terms, how it was amassed. Old histories! Old histories! What does the world care about the long string of obscure money-grubbers and criminals?"

"Is it the question what the world knows, Lucian?"

He sprang to his feet and shook himself. "I believe, with that old fellow looking down upon me, I could persuade myself into anything. Come, my dear, let us have done with them. We have renounced their works and their ways."

"Take down the portraits and burn them, Lucian. Put an end to the memories of this house."

"No; I like feeling that I can sit among my forefathers, though their record is disgraceful. But, Marjorie mine, you have seen the house. Do you think that you can make your home here, in spite of all these memories?"

"I think, Lucian," she replied, slowly and with hesitation, "that when we have had the place cleaned and painted and whitewashed, and these pictures regilt, and carpets laid down, and modern things put in, and some of the old hangings carted away, that it will be different. And there is the nursery. And if the men who have sinned are here upon the walls, so are the women, who have suffered and wept and prayed. It seems as if they will protect us from sorrows like their own."

"Child of superstition! You to become the wife of a scientific man? From sorrows, my dear? I will protect you from sorrows."

He laid his arms—his strong arms—about her neck and kissed her forehead.

"Now," he said, "claimants will turn up from the children of all these grand-uncles. Of one thing I am quite resolved, my dear. If I am not to take this inheritance, I'm hanged if anybody else shall. My ancestors"—he waved his hand comprehensively—"you approve, I hope, of this resolution?"

It was as if the portraits all with accord bowed their heads in affirmation. I say "as if," because neither would have asserted, positively, that the portraits actually showed this interest in things mundane; but Margaret afterwards declared that she had a feeling—a creepy, supernatural feeling—as if something of the sort had happened. The whole science of spiritualism is built upon foundations no stronger.

"Oh, dear Lucian!" she said, "it is only by giving up what they valued so much that we can escape the consequences of belonging to this House. Do not scoff. In some way or other the children must suffer from the father's sins. You are the grandchild of the man who ruined thousands by his money-lending; of the miser who ruined his whole family for the sake of his hoards; of the poor madman, chained to the floor upstairs because he thought his soul was lost; of the highwayman who was hanged; of the man who grew rich by ruining the master who trusted him. What a record! Oh, my Lucian! if I thought that you would resemble any of these men, I would pray—since I learned their history I *have* prayed—that you might die suddenly and at once—that we might die together. But you cannot resemble them!"

"Margaret, dear"—his eyes and his voice softened—"do not be troubled. I make you a promise that I will never act against my father's wish unless with your approval. Are you satisfied?"

IX

The Press Upon Windfalls

It was about this time—viz., a month or six weeks after the death of the old man—that the newspapers began.

First there appeared in all the journals a paragraph reporting the Inquest of Office; but, as the news editor was not posted up in the difference between an ordinary coroner's inquest and a coroner's Inquest of Office, and he had no time to ask questions and to hunt up nice points of law, the report appeared among those of the ordinary inquests. In most of the papers it was jammed in between an inquiry into the death of a man found drowned and that of a child run over by a cab. Therefore, the thing attracted, at first, little attention. Moreover, the reporter, a young man of small imaginative power, was not in the least carried away by the coroner's flights of fancy and poetical dream of half-millions. He went by the evidence. Nothing in the evidence proved the extent of the estate—in fact, as you have seen, little was said in the evidence on this point. Therefore, with a moderation and self-restraint unusual in his profession, he only said that the coroner appeared to think that the estate might prove to be of considerable value.

Nothing could be more guarded, or less likely to excite any interest. "Considerable value!" One would use this adjective, for instance, in speaking of an estate worth a thousand pounds. "Considerable" means anything. Nobody could possibly divine the truth, or anything like a fraction of the truth. Such a colossal truth as this cannot be divined or imagined, or even realized. We realize great riches by one simple rule or formula. Man says to man—with mouth wide open and awe-struck eyes: "Sir, he might give me a thousand pounds and never feel it!" That is the only way in which we can arrive at anything like an understanding of the rich man's mind and the rich man's fortune.

As the present order continues, fortunes increase, so that he who was a very rich man indeed a hundred years ago is now reckoned to be no more than easy in his circumstances. Our ancestors thought very highly of their success if they found themselves worth a hundred thousand pounds, poetically called a "plum!" But what is a plum now? The word itself remains of course, a comfortable, soft, self-satisfied word—a

WALTER BESANT

plum; but what is it? A bare hundred thousand pounds—no more than three thousand pounds a year. Call that great wealth? Why, a man with a modern fortune of ten millions or thereabouts—which is, one admits, a large fortune, even in America—gets three plums and a half every year at a little over 3 percent; he gets more than a thousand pounds a day, not counting Sundays. That is something like a fortune, and since there are but one or two men in our country who possess anything like this income, the possibility of so much belonging to anyone man is by the general run of us quite unsuspected.

No one, then, outside Mr. Burley's office, where the estate was administered, had the least suspicion of the truth, nor was the whole truth known to anyone, not even excepting the chief manager, so mixed up and spread about was the property. At the office, however, they knew a good deal, and from that centre, which the journalists speedily found out, the talk began. At first it was nothing but the plain fact that another person had died intestate, and apparently without heirs. The Crown had, therefore, got something. Everybody supposed that the Crown meant the Queen; one or two papers waxed indignant over this prerogative of the Crown; people asked each other how much fell into her Majesty's lap every year by these windfalls; the intelligent outsiders who wrote letters to the papers asked scathing questions about the Royal conscience. But their letters did not appear.

Then those journalists who were barristers saw their opportunity in the novelty of the court—an Inquest of Court. Nobody knew anything about such a court; they began to hunt it up, they wrote paragraphs, short leaders, long leaders, letters, communicating their information; they contradicted each other, they carried on a wordy war, they wrote sarcastic things concerning each other.

Next, for the subject proved of unexpected interest, they wrote about the history, the duties, and the attributes of the ancient office of coroner.

This opened up a very lively discussion. For some maintained, and very learnedly argued, that the office, as shown by the illustrious Verstegan, Leland, Ducarel, and Dryasdust, was established by King Alfred himself, and that the first court was held on the body of a Dane found just outside the Royal wagon, with his brains beaten out at the back of his head. The verdict was *Felo-de-se*, which the King, with an arch smile, received as a very proper verdict, and what he expected of such a judge and such a jury, and that the office should, therefore, be permanently established. Others—with the late learned Dr. Freeman—

rejected the legend of the Dane, and would have it that the office was established in the thirteenth century by King Henry III.

The next step was a discussion on the whole subject of unclaimed property. Then followed a boom of letters on this subject. Indeed, it interests the whole world. For what could be more delightful than to learn suddenly that one had inherited a noble fortune? Everybody read these letters; the circulation of the paper advanced by leaps and bounds. In train and in tram and in omnibus everybody became pensive, dreaming that he had become heir to a vast fortune, which lifted him far—very far—above the heads of his fellows, and won him the respect and the affection of the whole world. This was last year. No one, since the appearance of these letters, has, so far as I have heard, unexpectedly stepped into a vast estate, but the dream of "coming in" for an immense fortune still continues. It has its uses; it shows the young man and the young girl what a very noble person he or she would become if he or she were suddenly to "come in" for money. For in these dreams about it they always picture themselves as gods making crooked things straight and compelling all to virtue.

Lucian read all the letters and laughed over them. "They haven't found out," he said. "Presently they will—then from Greenland's icy mountains and India's coral strands, from Australia's dingy deserts and Wisconsin's prairie-lands, the claimants will begin to flock in. If they only knew! Because, my dear Maggie, as I said before, if I can't tackle this pile, no one else shall!"

"Don't think about them, Lucian," she replied. "Let who will fight over the fortune: let who will enjoy it."

The thing made him restless. He thought of it night and day; he talked of it continually. When he did not talk of it, he was thinking about it; he had long moods of silence.

"I *must* think about it, Maggie," he said. "Why, I don't believe there ever was a man in such a strange case. I have been without a family and without ancestors for six-and-twenty years. Then I find out my people—only to be told that I must renounce them, because they are too disgraceful for any decent descendant to acknowledge. And the next moment I find myself the sole undisputed heir to wealth colossal—and that I must not, on account of scruples as to the way it was gotten, put in my claim. Isn't that worth thinking about?"

"It is worth forgetting, Lucian. What was your grandfather's profession?"

"Destruction and Ruin. The Profession of the Tornado. Let me talk about it a little with you, dear girl. Let me have my little grumble, and then we will settle down contentedly to poverty and pinch."

She shook her head and sighed. He had never before grumbled at his poverty, which, after all, was an independence, and he had never before felt any pinch. Had he not four hundred pounds a year? It is a competence.

"I must think about it, Madge. I dare say I shall get accustomed to the thought of it. Presently it will become—what? A tender regret? A thing to be ashamed of?"

Then the papers found out the truth—something like the whole truth; an approach to the colossal reality. The manager told some one something about it; the clerks talked; representatives went to the office and interviewed the manager; some of the people at the Treasury got to know the facts. Then—we know how to present things dramatically—there was an announcement. Not a little paragraph in a corner—but an announcement in large type, after the leading articles, which informed a gasping, gaping, wondering, admiring, envying world that the estate of the late John Calvert Burley, which was in the hands of the Treasury by reason of intestacy and the failure of heirs, was ascertained to be worth—if the property was to be realized—in lands, houses, and investments of every kind—that is, of every safe kind—over eleven millions certainly; perhaps over twelve millions—possibly more. And you could hear the national gasp all over the islands of Great Britain and Ireland.

Of course there was an article upon the subject. What follows is a part of this remarkable commentary:

"The Treasury seems to have received a windfall in the estate of the late John Calvert Burley which surpasses all previous experience. It beats the record of windfalls. One or two there have been in which the estates have been valued at the hundred thousand. The estate which has lately been escheated to the Crown in failure of heirs—who may, however, turn up—is now, it is said, proved to be worth nothing less than the enormous sum of eleven or twelve millions sterling.

"So great a fortune, representing an annual income of at least £400,000, places its possessor among the very few really rich men of his time. How many men, in fact, are there in the world whose rent-roll, with all deductions made, actually touches these figures? How many men are there whose investments, scattered about in every kind of security, actually produce the income of £400,000 sterling? Are there five-and-twenty in the whole world? Probably not so many.

"Great—very great—has been the increase of incomes and the magnitude of fortunes during the last fifty years, especially in America; but there have been few cases on record of so large a fortune being amassed as that which has now fallen in 'to the Crown.' It is so splendid a windfall that the Chancellor of the Exchequer—unless, which is not improbable, an heir presents himself—will have to reckon with it as an asset of no inconsiderable importance. It would pay the income-tax for a whole year; it would give us twenty new war-ships; it would pay the whole expenses, forever, at British rate of pay and maintenance, of an army of 4000 men; it would pay for education, science, art, law, and justice for a whole year; it would be easy to enumerate the way in which such a windfall of eleven millions might be spent. Probably the importance of the amount may be realized when we consider that, suppose others of corresponding wealth were to give, or to lose, their fortunes to the country, it is easy to perceive how the national burdens might be lightened.

"The questions which everybody will ask are, how this immense sum was accumulated? and who was the fortunate man its last possessor? John Calvert Burley was once as well known a man in London as Crockford. Like him, he ran a gambling-house, which was open to all comers; like him, he advanced money in large sums to young spendthrifts. If any player had lost his money, he had but to ask, and there was more—for John Burley knew the private history and resources of every one who frequented his place. The gamester was supplied with the means of continuing his play so long as any means were left. He then had to go away. In addition to his gaming-house, John Burley practised the trade of money-lending, which he carried on with the relentless, pitiless hardness of heart by which alone this trade can be made successful. There was no necessity for him to carry on any trade, for he began life with such a fortune as should have satisfied him. But to make money—more money—always more money, was with him an instinct. As a usurer he enjoyed a much better reputation than many of his brother practitioners, for though he took great interest, and exacted his bond to the letter, he advanced his money in full without making his victim take half in bad champagne or villanous cigars. For this reason he enjoyed the reputation, such as it was, of being the prince of money-lenders. He acquired at one time, so little did he care how his money was made, some interest, if not the whole, in an infamous all-night dancing-den.

"Theatrical speculations, newspaper speculations—even racing speculations—were undertaken by him, with, it is reported, an unvarying success. Fortune followed him. Until a few years before his death, when he retired, he continued to carry on the trade of money-lender. Of late he led a perfectly retired life, quite alone, friendless and childless, but not, it is said, unhappy, because he could contemplate the great pyramid of gold which he had erected. He died at the great age of ninety-four, illustrating by his long life the lesson that he who would live must avoid emotions, and know neither love, nor hatred, nor jealousy, nor envy, nor any other passion whatever.

"It is certain that there have been many usurers, but none have been so abundantly successful as this man; and that to amass eleven millions of money even in a life of nearly a hundred years is a task which might well be deemed impossible save by some exceptionally lucky accident, some discovery of diamonds or emeralds, some purchase for next to nothing of a silver mine when silver was worth digging up.

"Some explanation of the mystery is found in the history of the family. This man's father was one of those mentally diseased unfortunate persons who become misers. He was an historical miser—in any of the books which treat of eccentric characters and uncommon traits, the misers are always portrayed—among these, next to John Elwes comes John Burley. He was born to a good fortune—perhaps not an enormous, but a respectable fortune. He lived for fifty years; for thirty he was in possession of this fortune. He developed the disease in its most pronounced form. He would spend nothing; he pursued his morbid parsimony to the utmost limits; he would have no fire in cold weather, no light after dark, no new clothes, the coarsest and simplest food. He prowled the streets at night in search of crusts and remnants; he bought the odds and ends of the butchers.

"This man was a perfectly well-known character in Westminster; the memory of him still lingers, it is said, though there are not, probably, any living men who remember the ragged old miser who used to prowl about the streets in the twilight; he died about the year 1825, of his self-inflicted privations. He left his son the whole of the property thus increased and multiplied. According to his biographers, the fortune amounted to £400,000. His son proved to be as eager to make money as his father, yet not contented with the slow process of saving it. He appears also to have inherited much of his father's parsimony without the extreme developments of the miserly character. His eagerness to make more money caused him to embark in business of the kind which requires the greatest astuteness and the coldest temperament. His desire to save caused him to live in so simple a fashion that he may fairly be said to have saved the whole of his income every year.

"In other words, besides the money which he made by his profession and his investments, he saw for seventy years his original capital multiplying at compound interest. Now the sum of £400,000 at compound interest and at 5 percent becomes £800,000 in thirteen years, and in seventy years it has become more than twelve millions. Since, therefore, Mr. Burley's estate is said to be no more than about eleven millions, it would seem as if the unfortunate gentleman must have had losses. Or perhaps he did not of late years manage to make so much as 5 percent. Smaller men than he have had to be contented with three.

"Who—what—where are the heirs? They must be somewhere. Anyone who casts an eye on the line of descent as set forth in a certain well-known law-book must understand that it is almost impossible for a man to die without heirs. For the property either descends or mounts up the main line. First, the man Burley: had he children? Presumably not. Then, had he brothers and sisters? Perhaps not. If he had, it is not credible that they, or their children, would ignore their connection with this incredibly rich man. A very wealthy man is the head of the family; he is like the man who enjoys the family title, and has inherited the family estates; he is the great man of the family. For this man, we must remember, did not hide himself away until he grew very old; he lived, so to speak, openly. He personally conducted his gaming-house; his money-lending was openly conducted in a public office with clerks and servants. It was always in evidence.

"Again, he was not a self-made man; he began life so rich that he needed not to work at all. He did work because he had an active intellect, and he chose what is thought to be disgraceful work because he saw that he could make money by it, and because he was indifferent to the opinion of men. Again, his father, the miser, inherited, and did not make his fortune. How was it made? That is not known; but we have certainly three generations of easy circumstances. If the miser had one child only, had he any brothers and sisters? Was he an only child? This is very improbable. Then where are the descendants of these brothers and sisters? Or had the miser's father any brother and sisters? If so, where are they? It is perfectly certain that somewhere or other the main stock must be struck by some branch which will thus become the heirs to this vast property.

"Here we find a remarkable illustration of the strange apathy displayed by the middle-class Englishman concerning his own ancestry. He neither knows nor cares to inquire into his origin and connections. Considering this family, it seems almost impossible that its members should be so split up as actually to lose in two generations the knowledge of their own relationship to so rich a man. Yet it is not impossible. Mr. Galton has somewhere pointed out that it is unusual for a middle-class family to know their own great-grandfather. They do not investigate the question; partly they do not care; partly they fear to find their ancestors in the gutter, or at least upon the curb. It is foolish fear, because when one says middle-class one says everything; the middle-class is perpetually going up or going down. It should be most interesting for a family to know its own history, whether that has been passed in obscurity or otherwise.

"Our people do not care for ancestry, unless they can claim descent from a distinguished House; in that case they care very much for the connection; so that we see, side by side with the greatest neglect of ancestry, the greatest respect for ancestors. This very neglect it is which cuts off so many branches which have fallen into poverty and deprives them of their forefathers. Probably that branch of the Burleys who at this moment are the true and lawful heirs of all this fortune are down in the gutter, or on the curb; behind a counter, or carrying a rifle; absolutely unable, for want of knowledge or want of papers, to connect themselves with the money-lender, the prince of money-lenders—or his father the miser of Westminster, or his unknown father who, perhaps, first made the money by careful attention to business among the nobility and gentry of Tothill Street and Petty France."

"There's a leading article for you!" Lucian read it right through to Margaret.

"It makes one burn with shame," she replied, "only to think of putting in a claim. The miser—the money-lender—the money-lender—the miser—the contempt of it all!"

"But they have found out—they have found out at last. I knew they would, and now for the claimants. They will come forward in shoals."

First, however, everybody read this leading article, or some of the others on the same subject, which, as you have seen, was of a kind which goes straight to everybody's heart. An immense fortune, with nobody to claim it! Heard one ever the like? Why, it might be—as the coroner wisely said—you, or me, or both of us—Quick! Where is the family genealogy? Who knows what our grandfather was?—mother's father? Perhaps he was a Burley! Does nobody know? Cousin Maria knows; she knows everything, good old girl—capital thing to have a Cousin Maria. Who was he, then? Not a Burley at all; he was a Smithers, and a journeyman shoe—Oh! Cousin Maria knows nothing, stupid old thing! Has she no pride of family, then? And what about the family coat of arms?

There was a great searching into family records and origins, and such secret humblings of family pride as the world has never seen. But, then, the world did not see these things because they were kept in the family; the girls hid away the papers or destroyed them, and went to church next Sunday with their chins stuck out more than ever, and the family arms displayed upon the covers of their prayer-books.

Other papers, of course, took up the subject from other points of view; they hunted up stories of great fortunes, unlooked-for inheritances, men suddenly raised from the deepest poverty to great wealth; a *Book of Successions* was drawn up in twenty-four hours by an eminent hand for an enterprising publisher, who did well with it; people reminded each other also, by letters to the papers, that there were other estates unclaimed. Everybody bought the *Gazette*, which contains the official list. It was not the Burleys only that were in demand, but all kinds of names. Surely in such a long list it would not be hard to make out one's right to something. Alas! the lists are long, but after all they only amount to a few hundreds, whereas the number of families in Great Britain, Ireland, and the Colonies amounts to—I know not how many; but as there are five millions of families, of whom a great many come from the same stock, perhaps we may reckon as separate families those families so far and so long separated that they have forgotten their relationship and changed the spelling of the name. Very possibly there are a million of separate families. The list is therefore a lottery—an immoral, speculative, gambling, unsettling, corrupting State lottery, in which there are a million of tickets (one for every family) and about two hundred prizes.

The *Spectator* had an article which very nearly guessed the truth. The writer assumed for his purposes that family pride was the leading characteristic and the strongest passion of the modern Englishman.

"Here," the article said, "we see one of the greatest estates ever known; an estate comparable with that of the famous widow of the Peloponnese, or with that of the landlord of New York, or with that of any American railway king, and it fairly goes a-begging. The heirs will not come forward. Why? Most probably because they are ashamed— they dare not face the shame of proclaiming themselves. The heirs of the money-lender and the miser—they will not touch money so made. At first one respects this dignity, this self-respect. Then one asks whether a truer courage would not be shown in accepting the whole—the awful— responsibility of so much wealth as a trust, to be devoted to some form of good works which shall not pauperize or demoralize. It is easy to think of many ways in which such a trust would be usefully employed, and no doubt a whole life might be nobly devoted to the administration of such a trust. But perhaps the courage is wanting—the courage of taking the first step—that of advancing to the front before all the world and saying aloud: 'The heir of the money-lender and the miser? Behold him! He stands before you!'"

"There!" cried Lucian, reading this article aloud. "You see, Madge, the *Spectator* has got the truth—not quite by the right way; but still— the pride of family will not, however, be strong enough to deter more than one possible claimant from stepping forward. How devoutly does all the world wish that they could so step forward and declare themselves! Claimants? There will be claimants by the thousand!"

X

Are We Cousins?

Five fair daughters, running up, like Pandean pipes, from fourteen to twenty, named respectively, though their names matter little to us, Lucy, Cathie, Polly, Nelly, and Dot—or, in full, Lucinda, Catherine, Marian, Eleanor, and Dorothy—composed the greater part of Sir John Burleigh's family. Lady Burleigh was, however, in herself a considerable part, and the Reverend Herbert Burleigh, B.A., formerly of Radley and Trinity, and now curate, or assistant priest, of St. Lazarus, Bethnal Green, completed the family.

Sir John, ex-Premier of New Zealand, and K.C.M.G., arrived in this country in the month of June. It was fifty years since he had exchanged, being then of tender years, and therefore not consulted in the matter, Great Britain for New Zealand. His wife and daughters had never before visited the mother-country. Everything was new to them: it was their first journey; it was their first evening in England; they were all excited and happy; and they had their brother with them, the first time for ten long years.

On the hearth-rug stood the father of this family, a gentleman of fifty-six or so, bearing his years cheerfully, his arch of black hair tinged with gray, his figure somewhat portly, but erect and strong, his face capable, his smile kindly, his appearance prosperous; his whole manner contented. He surveyed the group before him with the satisfaction of one who is proud of his daughters, able to leave them something substantial, and willing to postpone that legacy as long as possible. Oh! the unspeakable cheerfulness of the man who has "got on," in ways esteemed honorable, beyond his own expectations, and keeps his teeth and his taste for claret, and "enjoys" nothing nasty in the way of rheumatics or other blessings, and has daughters pretty and loving and sweet-tempered! Beside him, in an armchair, sat his wife, comfortable and satisfied, well dressed and happy.

Nothing could be prettier than the group before him. There were the five girls, all animated, rosy, graceful, formed in a hollow square or linked in a loving circle round their brother. They took his hands and held them tight; they laid their own hands on his shoulders;

they kissed him in turns; they purred over him; they discussed him openly.

"Oh!" cried one, "I like him so much better in his clerical dress. It is much more becoming than the football blazer."

"So much more intellectual," said another; "but is it *quite* so becoming as the undergraduate cap and gown? Perhaps, however—" she laid her head on one side. "The collar is sweet."

The Reverend Herbert was a youth of striking appearance, tall and strongly built. His smooth-shaven face, with the high and narrow forehead under an arch of black hair, like his father's, was already, though he was still a deacon, distinctly ecclesiastical. Even in ordinary tweeds, even in hunting scarlet, he would be recognized as a cleric. He was very properly attired, as becomes an ecclesiastic who respects himself. Whether in the slums or at court, the modern abbé is always dressed for the part. In the Church there is no Piccadilly. What struck one most in Herbert Burleigh were his keen, piercing black eyes set deep under square eyebrows. They were not only bright eyes, but they were restless; they made one think of the zealot; they were the eyes of the Dominican eager for the true doctrine; they were the eyes of the Dominican eager for the true doctrine; they were the eyes of the martyr.

He suffered his sisters' caresses with a patience which one could see would be but short-lived. They had not seen him for ten years; his youngest sister, Dot, could hardly recollect him.

"He looks pale," said another; it was quite true—the young man had the pallor of an ascetic. Perhaps he wore a hair shirt; perhaps he lived on lentils. "It is that nasty parish work."

"Nelly," he interrupted, "it is the work of the Church."

"Yes, I know." The girls had the colonial freedom from respect to authority. "We shall have to take him away with us when we go home. New Zealand sunshine is what he wants. At present all he gets is New Zealand mutton, poor dear!"

The young clergyman smiled faintly. "As for my dress," he said, "we must remind ourselves daily and hourly of our sacred profession. And in this outward and visible manner we must remind the world. A clergyman going about the world should be a standing and silent sermon, or catechism at least. What is he? Why is he? What power has he? How shall we use him?"

"You make us afraid, Herbert," said one. "Suppose you change your coat for one of father's jackets. Then we could all sit down and laugh and tell stories just as we used to do." The clergyman smiled sadly. "You remember, when we used to make up and pretend? Do you never laugh now?"

"We have our idle moments. They are rare. But—perhaps—sometimes—" he sighed.

"Well," said the sister who preferred the undergraduate, "you can't be always taking services or tramping around the slums. Then you will come to us and sit in your shirt-sleeves, if you like."

"My work," said the young man, solemnly, "lies among the slums, at present. But all the world is a slum—rightly considered."

"If that is the case," the same girl answered, "we are all in the same boat, and we should try to make the best of the slum."

"Oh!" cried the eldest. "And we haven't asked him about the most important thing of all. Herbert, what about the long-lost family?"

"Yes, yes; what about the family?" they all cried in concert.

At this question—which was by no means new—Sir John winced and changed color slightly. No one noticed the emotion. He quickly recovered, and, glancing at his wife, laughed aloud.

"What about the family, Herbert?" he repeated. "You were going to restore us to our family, remember."

"I remember, but—"

"It was resolved unanimously, Herbert," said Lucy, the eldest, "that you should undertake the search."

"Yes. But I have no clew. Without something to connect us—"

"You have all the facts," said his father. "Fifty-two years ago, when I was four years of age, we landed in New Zealand, my father, my mother, and I. Where we came from, who our people were, I have never learned. And there is not a scrap of paper, not a letter, or a book, not even a baptism or a marriage certificate, in my possession that will tell you anything more. Nothing to show you the maiden name of my mother, or the place where she was married."

"Quite so," said the son. "And I have long since given up thinking about it."

"Grandfather must have been a gentleman, to begin with," said the eldest girl.

"Of course!"—from all the other girls.

"A gentleman," said Sir John, "to end with, at any rate."

"And he never spoke of his own people. The inference is that he had quarrelled with them."

"That might be so," said Sir John.

"It must be so," said the girl. "Oh! we've talked it over and over, till we seem to know exactly what happened."

"I have not forgotten," Herbert explained. "But I have not been able to do anything. You see, it is pleasant when fellows talk about their own people to remember that one's father is a public man of position and respect. Nobody in such a case as ours ever asks what the great-grandfather was. And when you talk about New Zealand, nobody considers that all the people there have gone out from the country within the last sixty years. Still, one would like to have cousins at home. There must be cousins somewhere. Why, there must be two branches of cousins."

"We thought you were looking for them all the time."

"Not all the time. You see, a man cannot give out to the whole world that he is in search of cousins."

"That you were, in fact," said another sister, "the Reverend Japhet in search of a grand-uncle."

"A grand-uncle." The eldest girl again took up the theme, standing upright, and emphasizing her points with her forefinger. "In search of a grand-uncle. He can't be the Lord Burleigh, or the Earl of Burleigh, for their people are Cecils. Could he, however, have been the Lord John Cecil, son of the Marquis of Exeter, who changed his name to Burleigh when he married the poor, but illustriously descended, family governess? There's a chance, Herbert! We must prosecute the inquiry, now we are come home, seriously and all together. The search for the long-lost family. When you are not at work, Herbert, you shall help us. I mean to begin at the beginning—with the dukes and marquises. We will next go on to the bishops. My great-grandfather the Archbishop of York would sound nicely. My grandfather left home—the archiepiscopal palace—in consequence of his father's anger at hearing that he had been to a theatre. If not the bishops, then the earls and the viscounts and the barons, the baronets and the City knights. After them the professionals. We shall say, perhaps, with mock humility: 'We have always been middle-class people. My great-grandfather, Sir John Burleigh, was Attorney-General in the time of George II.'"

"Very good," said Sir John. "But suppose you have to go lower down?"

"In that case, it will be in order to satisfy our own, not the public, curiosity, and we shall keep the melancholy secret to ourselves and be quite satisfied"—the girl laid her hand upon her father's shoulder—"with the dear old dad that we are so proud of."

"Of course," said one of her sisters, "if we find the cousin, grandson of the grand-uncle, on the curb, so to speak, arranging his cheeses and his bacon in the shop-window, we shall not reveal the relationship, nor shall we fall into his arms and marry his assistant in the white apron. And if he happens to be in the gutter—which may be the case, for families in this country, they say, do climb up and fall down in the most surprising manner—we shall pass him by like a family of Levites, and we shall say nothing at all about blood being thicker than water—no, not even if they are cottage folk in smocks and scrupulously clean and doggedly virtuous."

"You are a most unprincipled set," said their father, laughing, "and I sincerely hope that you never will find your people."

"A change of name. That is what seems to me," said the eldest girl, "the most likely. But how to find the real name? Given the facts. Somewhere about the year 1841 there arrived in New Zealand an immigrant with a wife and one child. His name was So-and-so. He is believed to have changed his name. What family in England had a son who, in 1841 or thereabouts, had a row with his own people and took another name and went out to New Zealand? Did he do this openly or secretly? Did his wife's people know what he was doing and where he was going? Did he break altogether with his own people? Then, can we find out a family whose son disappeared about that time, taking with him a young wife—somebody's daughter—and an infant son?"

"My dear," said her father, "it is a wild-goose chase. For there is nothing to connect him with anybody. And as for disappearing sons, why—you've all known them for yourselves—among my shepherds—men who never communicated to their own people anything at all about themselves. Better enjoy London, children, and leave unknown cousins alone."

"What I think," said another daughter, who had imagination, and will, perhaps, become a novelist, "is that our grandfather was another Adam, created especially for New Zealand, and miraculously provided with an Eve, also specially created. That explains everything."

And so they all laughed and changed the subject, going back to the worship of the brother, which shows what an uncivilized, colonial, half-finished, unadvanced set of sisters they were. For the girl who worships the brother will presently worship the lover, and even, such is the depth of this girl's degradation, the husband.

Later in the evening the young man returned again to the subject. "You know," he said, "that my work takes all my time. I cannot go about with you as I should wish. But I will do what I can. Meantime, is there not another solution possible about these cousins of ours? Perhaps our grandfather preserved silence about his people because they were quite humble. Our cousins may be low down—very low down. I could wish it were so. I wish I could find them in my own parish. It might help me in my work if I could say to them: 'I am a son of the gutter, like you. I am your cousin—one of yourselves—my great-grandfather, a laboring man, perhaps even a criminal.'"

"Oh!" cried Sir John, "you'd like that, would you?" He did not laugh, but spoke fiercely.

"Dear Herbert!" cried his sisters. "Let us, above all things, believe, until the contrary is proved, that we come from an honorable stock at least."

"I was thinking of my work," said the assistant priest. "For the sake of my work, I would willingly be the grandson of—"

"Thank you, Herbert," his father interrupted. "And now we will have no more said about it. Our first evening in England must not be disturbed by foolish speculation into remote possibilities which would only humiliate us."

But the harmony of the evening was broken. A discordant note had been struck. Presently the son went away, promising to return for breakfast at half-past nine, after early service. Then the mother and the girls talked about him, and about the nobility of his character and his deep sense of religion, and thought humbly of themselves as walking—and actually feeling quite comfortable—on levels so far below his. But Sir John took no part in this discussion. He did not even listen. Something had put him out.

The next morning was that on which a certain leading article, which you have seen, came out in a certain morning paper.

Sir John appeared, clad in his usual cheerfulness—his face serene, his brow unclouded. He sat down to breakfast with a colonial appetite; he worked his way through the vivers with his accustomed energy. When he had laid the foundation for a day of activity, he took a fresh cup of tea, and half turning his chair, so as to get the light, he opened the morning paper and began to read.

He read on with the ordinary show of interest until he lighted on the leading article, which was the third. Then he started; he changed color; he laid down the paper and looked about him, seeing nothing. At this point the girls became aware that something had happened, and left off chattering. He then began to read the article again, and read it right through a second time.

"What is it, dear?" asked his wife, who perceived those signs of interest.

"An article in the paper," he said, "concerning a certain person of my name—our name—one Burley, name spelled differently—who has died enormously rich without any heirs. So rich that it seems incredible. They say that his estate is worth about twelve millions sterling—twelve millions! Without heirs, so that the estate will be seized by the Crown. Twelve millions! Is it possible? And we call that man rich who can save a poor hundred thousand or so."

"And of our name?" said his son. "Was he a gentleman? What was his profession?"

"Among other things"—Sir John hesitated—"he was—he was—a money-lender."

"Then," said his son, with decision, "I suppose he is no relation of ours?"

"Yet, yesterday, Herbert, you expressed yourself anxious to be connected with the criminal classes," said his father.

"Well, I said so for the sake of my work. But to be the nephew of a rich money-lender would not help me at all, unless I could pour the whole of his misgotten gains into the lap of the Church. Then, indeed, I would confess and acknowledge the relationship."

"Twelve millions," said one of the girls. "It seems almost enough to gild any trade. Why should not a man lend money?"

"It is the most ignoble of all callings. What was his name, father—Burley? Is it spelled our way?"

Sir John handed his son the paper and buried his nose in his teacup. Because, you see, his son's full name was Herbert John Calvert Burleigh, which contained the name of the deceased Dives.

The young clergyman observed this fact, and read the article with flushed cheeks.

"Do you know, sir—" he began.

"My dear boy," said the ex-Premier, gravely, "we had a little playful talk, which very nearly became a serious talk, over this matter last night. I confess to grave misgivings about any attempt at investigating the family history. That my father told me nothing concerning the social position of his family is a conclusive proof, it seems to me, that he had reasons for wishing a complete severance with his own people. For this reason I have never attempted any inquiry into the matter; nor do I intend to attempt any. If you, however, choose to undertake such an inquiry, you are, of course, free to do so. Here, then, is a man who appears, according to his Christian names, which are the same as yours and mine, to be some kind of connection. His name is ours, with a little difference in the spelling."

"Give me the paper, Bertie"—from the five daughters, simultaneously.

"I think that, most likely, we are cousins of a sort to this man. That fact, however, if we could prove it, would not necessarily make us his heirs. Very well, then. He was not, apparently, a man whose kinship could raise us in the eyes of the world. Are we prepared, before we embark upon a serious inquiry, to be labelled as the cousins of a man infamous for the way in which he made his fortune, or are we prepared to be advertised as the cousins, and perhaps unsuccessful claimants, of such a man? My father's name was Charles Calvert Burleigh—perhaps he altered the surname from Burley—l-e-y. I do not know. My own name is John Calvert Burleigh. Your name is Herbert John Calvert Burleigh. The Christian names of the deceased were John Calvert."

"Such names cannot be mere coincidence," said his son.

"Perhaps not. I think certainly not. We *must* be of the same family. Are we prepared to dig up old scandals—old quarrels—and to publish them for all the world to laugh at them?"

"No, my dear," said Lady Burleigh, decidedly, "unless the money is clearly yours. In that case, perhaps—an old scandal is not generally a very important thing."

"Why should there be scandals?" asked the son. "I confess the connection with a money-lender and a keeper of dancing-saloons is not an ideal; but if we could pour this money into the coffers of the Church—"

"You forget, my son, that it would first have to be poured into my coffers."

"Well; but suppose the widest publicity. There cannot possibly be anything in our branch that we should be ashamed to parade before all the world."

"Nothing? Humph! Well, I have known a good many families, and I do not remember one in which there were not some black sheep—some scandals best forgotten. I remember sitting one night over the fire with an old fellow who gave me the history of his family. It was a good family, old, with honorable men in it, and fools in it, and criminals in it. My dear Herbert, the whole of the Decalogue had been broken by various members of that family. Very well, then. If by opening up the old stories you could establish a claim upon this vast property—I do not say—though I doubt—it is more than doubt—I am sure—" Here Sir John grew obscure and hesitated. "I mean, Herbert, that I think we had better let things alone."

Herbert made no answer. The girls were reading the article.

"My dear," said Lady Burleigh, "if it is a question of obscure origin only, I think that would not matter."

"No; not much. We are too strongly placed to dread any discovery about obscure grandfathers. But there may be scandals. Why did my father keep silence on the subject of his own people?"

"Father," said the girls, "it is such an enormous fortune. Fancy! If we were really the heirs to all that! If you were the heir—the only heir. Why, they would have to make you a duke. It is enough to develop the whole possibilities of the colony."

"Here is another thing, however," said the father, persistent. "Suppose you found that a certain Charles Calvert Burley and his descendants were the heirs, how would you connect this man with your grandfather? Without documentary proof it would be impossible. To begin with, how to prove the change of name?"

"There are no proofs, as yet," said the son. "But proofs may be found. The man was married. There must be the register somewhere. There must be relations—cousins—somewhere in the world; there must be some one living who can remember that young married pair. For my own part, I care very little about old scandals. Let us take steps, at least, to prove the relationship if we can. I hope I am not greedy; if I had all those millions in my own hands I should not wish to live differently. But the Church—the Church wants so much."

"The colony wants it a great deal more than the Church," said one of the New Zealand wardens.

"It is a very big estate," said Sir John—"a bigger property than ever yet started a noble family. Take the other side—at present we do very well; we are rich after our humble way. You, Bertie, are the son of a man who has, to a certain extent, distinguished himself; you are the grandson of a man who—" here he stopped for a moment—"who, however he began, ended in a good position. If we go into court with our claim we may,

I repeat, have to publish for the whole world all kinds of things best forgotten—family scandals, perhaps—even—even—disgraces—who knows? Children, it is for you to decide. Shall we go on as we are, or will you rake up the past in the hope of succeeding to all this money?"

The girls all looked at their brother.

"I think," said Herbert, "that we should prove the connection, if possible, for our own satisfaction, and then decide what to do next."

"You are not afraid of—these family scandals, then?"

"One may discover them. One need not disclose them to the world."

His father regarded him gravely. "As you will," he said. "I advise you rather to let sleeping things remain undisturbed. But, as you will."

"I have no fear," replied the son. "Let us, at least, have the choice, if it prove to be our lawful choice."

"Japhet!" cried the girls, with one consent. "Japhet is, at last, in search of a grand-uncle with millions and millions and millions. Oh, Japhet!"

Later on, the father and son were alone.

"You meant something, sir, when you hinted at family scandals and disgraces. Can you tell me anything definite?"

"No, Herbert. If there are scandals—I don't say so—you may find them out for yourself. My father, I repeat, never spoke about his people, nor did I ever ask him. His name you know—Charles Calvert Burleigh. He died twenty years ago, when you were a child of five or six—you remember him, I dare say. He was then seventy-three years of age. He was born in the year 1800, and he went to New Zealand in the year 1841. There are no books, no papers; nothing whatever to help you but these facts, and such other facts as you may discover for yourself. If they are disagreeable facts, you need not, of course, tell your mother or the girls."

XI

Youth in a Garret

Youth, who formerly lived in a garret with lean-to walls and a low ceiling, where the only furniture was a truckle-bed and a crazy table, a three-legged chair, and a toasting-fork for the toothsome bloater, now takes on lease an æsthetically decorated flat at the top where the garret used to be. Youth now furnishes his flat according to the latest lights. Youth, who formerly wasted his treasure of the golden years in vain regrets, in miserable poverty, and in beating the air with angry hands, an operation which never produced anything but a harvest of wind, now occupies himself profitably, and rakes in an income by a thousand different ways; and he spends that income on those objects which are naturally dear to his time of life. Youth has a very, very much better time than ever he had before, and all because there are now so many different ways, to him who is clever, of making money. Formerly, Bohemia meant the dingy tavern and the cheap chop-house; now, Bohemia means the flat, the club, the stalls, the studio, the greenroom, the editor's room—with frequent champagne. The chop and the pewter and the sanded floor have disappeared with the short pipe of clay and the shabby great-coat. The young man of the New Bohemia closely resembles the Gilded Youth. He dresses so like him that you cannot tell them apart; he dines at the same places and as expensively; he enjoys the same pleasures; he is seen at the same haunts; he has the same friends. The only difference is that the latter is living on his inheritance, and that the former lives on his wits. If he spends every penny that his wits bring him in, that is his affair, not ours.

Mr. Clarence Burghley, a young gentleman very well known in certain circles, occupied a set of upper chambers with his friend Mr. James Pinker, in a mansion between Piccadilly and Oxford Street—one of those great barracks in red brick which are transforming the West End. The situation is in the exact centre or hub of the universe. Therefore, it suited Clarence Burghley. For the profession of this young man demanded a central position. His profession was the Making of Amusement. He was not an amusing young man; he was an Amuser.

Other people go about and throng together seeking to be amused; he went about promising to amuse. He could play the piano with a light and dexterous touch—and sing to it with a light and flexible tenor. The songs he sang were light and bright—little songs of society—songs about smart people—songs about flirtation—songs of the ball-room, the race-course, the yacht—songs of the surface; they were so light and so actual that they seemed to be improvised. You could not buy these songs, and nobody else had them to sing. Then he could play the violin and make it do tricks like a trained dog, and he could touch the banjo with a master's hand. He gave, at private houses, little entertainments, consisting of songs and burlesques, parodies and talk. He also had a collection of original comediettas, little dramas, and proverbs, unprinted, unpublished, and not to be procured anywhere, with which he furnished the private theatricals, he himself being stage-manager and actor. Clarence was the son of an actor and the grandson of an actor, and therefore to the manner born. All that he did was dexterously done; all that he sang or acted or played was light and frothy, without reality, without emotion, without passion. He lived by these performances, but he was not accepted as a professional. If he went to a great house, either on a visit or for the evening, he went as a guest; he was treated as a guest, but he was paid as a professional—a professional Amuser. It is a most difficult profession—one that demands many and varied qualities, and therefore one that should command the highest respect.

In appearance Clarence Burghley was slight and even delicate; nothing of the athlete in him; his limbs were not those of a football-player; his face was smooth, except for a slight mustache; it was fine in features and in expression; his black eyes were keen, bright, and swift, under straight and strongly marked eyebrows; his black hair, parted at the side, rose in a natural arch which helped to give him a look of distinction. In such a profession a look of distinction is invaluable.

For a youth in this profession it was natural that he should wear, in his own rooms, a brown velvet coat, no waistcoat, a crimson sash, and a white silk tie. It was also natural that the rooms should be decorated and adorned up to the latest note of æsthetics. In a word, this young man looked exactly what he was—a young man of Piccadilly; the flower, or fruit, whatever you please, of the London pavement; a young man born in the town, brought up in the town, and unable to live out of the town.

His friend, Mr. James Pinker, who shared the chambers with him, shared also, though the fact was not proclaimed abroad, the profits and proceeds of the business. The division of work was simple. James, not Clarence, was the poet and dramatist. He it was who wrote the songs and comediettas and the musical entertainments. Clarence sang and acted them. James arranged the engagements and accepted the invitations, modestly signing himself "Private Secretary." A very promising partnership it was, and one that became more lucrative every day. At ten guineas a night, if you can arrange for five nights a week and nine months in the year, the returns mount up to £2000 a year. And there are no expenses at all, except cabs. Nothing was said in public about the partner. Not that Clarence went about pretending to be the author of the songs and things. Not at all. Nobody ever asked him who was the author. People think that an entertainment grows spontaneously out of the brain of the singer; they regard the author no more than they regard the service which provides the dinner.

Mr. Pinker was not brought up to the profession of entertainment poet; quite the opposite. He was destined by his parents, who did not belong to the upper circles, to advance the family one step by becoming a solicitor. He was duly admitted. But he then found, what no one expected, that there was no room for him anywhere. Not even as a clerk could he obtain a living. It was the stimulus of necessity which caused him to become a poet. In fact, he had always written verses for his own amusement. His old school-fellow Clarence used to sing them, also for amusement. At a certain crisis in their fortunes, both being stone-broke, and with no prospect of any further supplies from any quarter, Jemmy Pinker hit upon the private-party plan, and the evening entertainment of funny society songs. For himself, he had never gone into society. He knew nothing at all about smart people; he had no occasion for a dress-coat; he preferred—not that he ever got the choice—a steak and a pint of Bass in a tavern to the company of countesses; he was quite satisfied with what his partner told him about society and the simple wants of after-dinner people.

In appearance the poet was "homely"—a good old word fast dying out; his features, that is, were undistinguished; his hair was of a warm hue, approaching to red; his figure was short; his very fingers were short and broad. He sat with his short legs curled under his chair; his gray eyes were sharp and bright; his face was habitually serious, as becomes one who is always meditating responsible and money-getting work; he seldom smiled; he never laughed.

The profession of entertainment poet—writer of topical songs—is not quite the highest branch of the poet's art. It is not, however, within everybody's reach. There must be the genius or natural aptitude for the work. It must be studied and practised. After a time, in the case of one to the manner born, it becomes easy—the easiest thing in the world; that is, after the time when the poet has not only cultivated his own powers, but has gauged and grasped exactly the requirements of his audience. The jokes and quips and turns, for instance, need not be too original; people, especially after dinner, like their old and expected friends; new work—unexpected work—makes them uncomfortable; they expect the usual situations, the usual ending, the usual jokes; novelty interferes with digestion. This limitation Mr. Pinker thoroughly appreciated. And it made his work easy; in fact, no young man in London, working for his daily bread, had a more easy life. He had no misgivings about the dignity or value of his work; he liked it. He made rhymes upon everything, and noted them in a pocket-book; he thought in rhyme, and he talked in rhyme sometimes, just to keep his hand always in. It was a perfectly grave and serious business—that of providing metrical means for mirth.

"Courage, Clary," said the poet, finishing his breakfast. "The season is almost over."

"Thank goodness!—yes."

"Only two more engagements. Tonight at the Baroness Potosi's. Tomorrow at Lady Newbegin's. The Baroness expected you to go up the back stairs, but I explained."

Clary was a little jumpy this morning. He cursed the Baroness. At the end of a fatiguing season, with champagne every day, one is apt to be jumpy.

"What is it, old man? Come, things couldn't look rosier. We've had an excellent season, and you are booked for half September and the whole of October and November—good houses—pleasant houses—all of them."

"It's the fag of the work, I suppose. And sometimes I begin to worry about what we shall do when they get tired of me."

"Look here, Clary"—his partner got up and slowly filled his pipe— "they never do get tired of anybody so long as he can make 'em laugh. When he can't make 'em laugh any longer, he may go and hide himself. You go on singing and I'll go on making 'em laugh for you. Next year we'll make a clear thousand apiece out of it—see if we don't." He lit his pipe and sat down again, tucking his feet under the chair. "Make 'em laugh. Something in that idea, isn't there?" He pulled out a pocket-book.

"Mouth gaping, cheeks aglow, Laughlit eyes—is 'laughlit' right?—in mirthful row, When fun and farce begin. He that pleases—not you, Clary—he may try Tears and groans to make 'em cry. Let me sing—you, that is, Clary, if you please—to—" He bit the point of his pencil. "Let me sing," he repeated gravely, "to make 'em grin." He made a note of these beautiful and suggestive words, and looked at them critically.

"As for you," grumbled the other, "it's always the same. You are always satisfied."

"Generally. I have reason to be. I have a partner, by whose help my verses are a small gold-mine. Quite satisfied. Give me my pipe and my beer, and my Chloe—my Chloe—there's no good rhyme to Chloe—and I ask no more."

"As for me," said Clarence, whose temper was short this morning, "I've got to do the work. I belong to the service. I ought to wear woollen epaulettes and white-thread gloves."

"Rubbish! People don't know, or if they do, it doesn't matter. They think your father left you money."

Clarence laughed. "If they think that," he said, "they will think anything. My father leave me any money? My dear James, you don't understand my father's ocean-like capacity for absorbing all the money there is. He left me nothing but his debts, which, of course, I did not pay. Why should I? On account of his good name? The dear man had none."

"Ah! No name! The Nameless One!—the Nameless One—" But he shook his head.

"They carried on, he and the granddad, as if there was no such thing as money at all, or as if they had millions. Wonderful men both, but especially the granddad. He got whatever he wanted; he wanted everything; he paid for nothing. How? I don't know."

"Unspeakable are the gifts of the gods."

"Of course they led the Joyous Life all the time. Never anything but Joyousness in the house as long as I can remember. Joyousness, with troops of topers, girls, and merrymakers, and men in possession looking on with a grin."

"I would I had known your sainted ancestors, Clary. We want, in fact, more Joyousness—a great deal more Joyousness. Let us start a Joyous Club. I am sure it would succeed with troops, as you say, of topers, girls, and merrymakers. Couldn't we have a Lament over past Joyousness?" He took out his pocket-book, and improvised:

> *"Where are they gone—the merry, merry men?*
> *Where are they gone—the merry, merry days?*
> *Why did they leave us, who were so merry then?*
> *Why did they take with them their merry, merry ways?*

I'm afraid that's pitched just one note too high for our people, Clary. They don't like real sentiment. Yet it looks as if it might be worked up, too. 'Merry, merry days'—even the smart people ain't always young."

"Why, I dream of millions, just from habit, because they were such excellent actors that I really thought they did have millions. Wouldn't it be glorious to have a million or two? If you were offered your choice of things, wouldn't you choose a million down in hard cash?"

"Perhaps I would."

> *"Some Johnnies march in glory's ranks—*
> *Some toy with Chloe's locks;"*

that's how Chloe's got to come in—

> *"I'd find my joy in City banks,*
> *And, if I could, in stocks."*

Again the note-book. "The millionaire, you see, could buy up all the locks of all the Chloes and a fair slice of glory too. Some Johnnies—it isn't very bad—march in glory's ranks, some toy with Chloe's locks."

Clarence laughed. He sat down, took the morning paper, unfolded it, then he went on talking.

"I wish you had known the granddad," he went on. "Good old man! He only died ten years ago, having being born about the beginning of the century. He acted and told stories and made love to the very end. I think he always believed that he was only thirty." He threw himself back in his chair and opened the paper. Then he jumped up and screamed aloud: "O Lord! O Lord! Here's a wonderful thing!"

"What is it?"

"What were we saying? Millions we talked about. Good Lord!" He stared at his friend as one too much amazed for speech.

"Well, but what is it?"

"There's an estate said to be worth twelve millions and more waiting for an heir to turn up."

"Does it concern either of us?"

"I don't know. We were talking about millions," Clarence said, breathlessly. "About millions! You shall hear. Here is the article. Read it!"

The poet read it through, taking five minutes. "Well, it doesn't matter to us, does it?"

"To you? No—to me? I don't know. Look here, Jemmy. This is a most wonderful coincidence, if it is a coincidence. The dead man's name was John Calvert Burley. My grandfather's name was Henry Calvert Burghley, spelled with a 'gh'; my father's name was Elliston John Calvert Burghley; and my name is Clarence John Calvert Burghley. Is that coincidence?"

"But, Clary, my boy, your surname is different."

"My grandfather may very well have altered his name—put in the 'gh' for pretty. It's quite the theatrical way, and what one would expect. The proper spelling, I expect, was Burley, without the 'gh'; the way this Dives—this master of millions—spelled it. Well, now—if I am right, what relation was Dives to my grandfather, to whose generation he belonged?"

"What do you know about your own people outside your grandfather?"

"You see before you, my friend, a man who has no people except the limited number of progenitors I have already mentioned."

"But you must know something. Have you no cousins?"

"I've got nobody. I don't even know who my mother was. She died when I was quite young. I never once asked my father about her, nor did he ever tell me anything about her. I suppose she must have had relations, but they never came near me. And my grandfather must have had cousins, but I never heard of them. I know nothing about anybody but these two. Nothing separates relations more than the habit of borrowing. If you carry on the Joyous Life, you must borrow. Now, if you had known my father, James, you would understand that he was not the kind of man to talk about the domestic affections. The affections that are not domestic might—and did—engage his serious attention and his continual conversation, but not—no—not those of the home kind."

"Well, there was your grandmother."

"I don't know anything about her. She is prehistoric. The old man resembled his son in that respect that the home affections were insipid to him. They lacked flavor; he liked his food spiced and seasoned and curried—deviled, in fact. We never talked about such things as wives in that pagan tabernacle which we called home. The old man, I say, led the Joyous Life. He was never serious; I believe he dreamed jokes and made love-songs in his sleep. 'Life to the end enjoyed, here Roscius lies,' is written on his tombstone. Not original, but it served. His life was one long, continual banquet, for which somebody—I know not who—footed the bill. Well, the fact is—I don't know anything."

"After all," said his partner, reflectively, "a man cannot be without any relations at all in the world. And here we have a clew to the family. Clary, let us have a shy at those twelve millions. If we get them, you can go out and make 'em cry, if you like."

"What are we to do? We can't ask a dead man anything."

"No. But there are registers and wills and letters and documents of all kinds. Have you got your grandfather's will?—your father's will?"

Clarence laughed. "You might as well ask me if I have his landed estates. Even your poetic brain, my partner, cannot realize the existence of a butterfly. Make a will? That is providing for the future from the past! These two had no past and had no future. They had nothing but the present. And in the present they spent all they could get or borrow. There was no will, bless you."

"Have you got no papers at all?"

Clarence sprang to his feet. "There's a desk. It was the old man's. Since he never opened it, there is probably something in it that other people might call useful. I once opened it to see if there was any money in it. There wasn't. Only papers. I will go and get it."

He brought back not only a small rosewood desk, but also a bundle of papers tied up with string. "Here's the desk," he said, "and here are some papers that I found after my father's death, all piled in a drawer. I tied them up, but I have never looked at them."

"Now, then"—the poet-solicitor looked immensely important—"what we've got to do is this. I know. I have not served five years in a solicitor's chambers for nothing. We must first prove that you are the lawful son of Ellliston John Calvert Burghley; then, that he was the lawful son of Henry Calvert Burghley; then, that he was something pretty close to the late John Calvert Burley, After that. . . I say, Clary, if this *should* come off! What a thing it will be for both of us!"

"Don't, Jemmy, don't. I can't bear it. My throat swells. I can't speak. Twelve millions!" He did not apparently resent the assumption of partnership in the inheritance as well as the business.

"Go away now, Clary. It's lucky you have got a man of business for your partner. Go and walk somewhere; get out among fields and daisies and skylarks and the little cockyolly birds; sit by the babble of the brook; catch the fragrance of the brier-rose; Nature calls; go listen to the voice of Nature."

"I hate the voice of Nature," said the young man of the town. "The daisies and the skylarks would just now drive me mad. I feel as if I shall go mad with the mere thought of the thing. I don't want silence; I want noise and action. I will go and play billiards with the windows open, so as to get all the noise there is. That will steady the nerves, if anything can. And, I say, Jemmy, how long, do you think, before—"

"Come back to lunch at half-past one. Now go away."

He went away. He put on his boots and his hat. On his way out he put his head in at the door. "Found anything yet? I say, twelve millions! Oh, if the old man could have had that almighty pile! Get it for me, and I'll show you how to spend it!"

He came back about one o'clock.

His partner looked up from his papers. His face was serious. "Clary," he said, "this is no laughing matter. Sit down. Now, then, are we to continue partners? If so, you shall have all my business energies as a solicitor. Mind, it's an *awful* big thing. If I pull it off for you I shall be content with ten—a simple ten percent. A million and a quarter! It isn't much, but with thrift I could make it do. Yes—oh yes—with thrift and care and scraping I would make it do."

"I agree. Only get it for me."

They shook hands upon the bargain.

"I will put our agreement in black and white presently; meantime, I have discovered one secret. Your grandfather, Clary, was certainly a brother of the deceased Dives. I am quite sure he was. So that you are a grandnephew, and therefore one of the heirs. Of course we don't know how many other heirs there may be."

Clarence turned perfectly pale; he staggered. He sat down, and for a moment he heard his partner talking, but could not understand what he was saying. He revived and listened.

". . . will take jolly good care not to part with it until we have established the case beyond any doubt. They will want a case complete at every point. Don't wriggle about in your chair like that, Clary. Sit quiet, man!"

"I can't. Things are too real. Go on—get on quicker, man. One would think it was a ten-pound note—not twelve millions—millions—

millions! Oh!" He threw himself back into his chair, and leaned his head upon his hand and groaned. "Oh! I feel like a woman. I could cry. Millions! Millions! Oh! Do you think—do you think—we may—"

"Pull yourself together, old man. Now listen. This is our case, so far. Your father and grandfather had some sense. Their marriage certificates are among the papers. I confess, Clary, when you talked about the butterfly and the domestic affections, I began to fear—but that's all right. These certificates are the first essentials, at any rate. Well, most of the papers are notes quite unconnected with the home affections. There are verses of a jocund and amatory kind—even I, the modern Anacreon, couldn't write better lines—there are play-bills, there are papers connected with this and that event. Your grandfather was lessee of the Theatre Royal, York, for many years. His son was born there; he came to London and played here; his son grew up and went on the boards; his son married a lady of the company in which he played. All these things are plain to make out. But who was Henry Calvert Burghley, to begin with? Now here is a letter which gives us a clew."

The solicitor-poet handed over a letter written on the old-fashioned letter-paper, folded with a wafer on it. "Dear Harry," it began: "We are all glad to hear that you have made a start. You can't be more pinched for money than when you were in Westminster, which may console you. Father said nothing when you did not come home, except that there was one mouth less. I shall run away too, as soon as I can. Jack says that if you want money he will buy out your chance of getting anything out of father's will for a pound or two if you like. But Jack says that father is only forty-five, and if he was eighty-five he wouldn't leave you anything because you ran away. So I remain your affectionate brother, Charles."

"You see, this is not conclusive proof, but it puts us on the track. Your grandfather came out of Westminster; his father was a miser. The intestate Burley's father was a miser living in Westminster. We must prove that there was a brother Henry and another brother Charles— Jack seems the eldest brother, probably John Calvert Burley, and Charles is clearly younger than Henry. I must say that the case looks promising. We should have to prove the change of name, and—and—and there may be other things to prove before we establish the connection."

Clarence gazed stupidly on the letter. He gasped.

"Mind," said the poet, "I am quite sure, perfectly sure, in my own mind, that you are the deceased's grandnephew. But we shall have to make the lawyers sure. And, Clary, my boy, this material is not quite enough so far."

"Oh!" Clarence murmured. "Oh! It would be too much, this wonderful stroke of luck! too much! too much! If I were to get it I would—I would turn respectable. And as for going out to sing—old man!" He turned away. His heart was full. The Joyous Life, the only life he cared for, seemed within his grasp—not like his grandfather's, impecunious, loaded with debts, troubled with duns; but free, with a capital of twelve millions fully paid up. The poet looked at him curiously. And he murmured, making a note of it on the spot:

> *"Rich and respectable. Oh, what a change it is!*
> *Once a poor vagabond singing his verse!*
> *Solemn and smug he is: look at him! Strange it is:*
> *Rich and respectable: guineas in purse."*

But he was wrong. Clary's ideas of respectability went no further than the respect which attaches to one who pays his way—neither begs, nor borrows, nor earns his way, but pays it—along the Primrose Path.

XII

"Aunt Lucinda"

A unt Lu-cin-da!"

The girl laid down the paper she was reading and squalled—it is a rough and rude word, but it is the only word which expresses the excitement and amazement shown in this cry.

"Aunt Lu-cin-da!" she repeated.

The elderly lady, who was engaged in some needle-work, looked up quietly.

"Well, my dear! Another dreadful murder?"

"Not nearer than Buffalo, and that only an Italian family. But, Auntie, listen to this." She took up her paper. "No"—she put it down again—"tell me first what was the full name of grandfather—your father?"

"Why do you wish me to tell you? Surely you know already. He was named James Calvert Burley."

"Yes; I wanted to make quite sure. And father's full name was John Calvert Burley. John C. Burley he wrote it. Yes—yes. Oh! it's the same name." She jumped up and clapped her hands. "Auntie, where'd they come from—our people—your people?"

"Well, my dear, you seem very much excited about something. They came from a place in London called Westminster. I believe the Queen lives there. Your grandfather often told me about the family house. It stood in a street called College Street, looking over the gardens of Westminster Abbey."

"Oh! It's the same—it's the same." She clapped her hands again. "Oh, go on, Auntie! What were they—by trade and calling, I mean?"

"I don't know that they were anything. Father always allowed that there was considerable money in the family. He got none, because he ran away and never went back to ask for his share, nor learned anything at all about them."

"Oh! He ran away. What did he do that for?"

"They all ran away. He had four or five brothers, and they all ran away because, you see, my dear, their father was a miser, and made the home too miserable to be borne."

"Oh! There were brothers. But they couldn't have had children, or there would be heirs."

"What are you talking about, dear? What heirs? Your great-grandfather was a most dreadful miser," Aunt Lucinda continued. "Father used to tell how he would go out with a basket and bring it home filled with bones and crusts and broken vegetables—everything he could pick up. The boys were half-starved and went in rags—so they ran away. Your father was helped by his mother's people, who made him a lawyer, and then—then—he—came over"—she hesitated a moment and changed color—"and settled here, you know."

The girl nodded, and clapped her hands again. "Why," she cried, "there can't be any doubt! The miser only died the other day—at least, I suppose it was the miser—and—Aunt Lucy—Aunt Lucy"—she fell upon her aunt's neck, and laughed and cried—"oh! our fortune is made. Oh! we are the luckiest people in the whole wide, wide world. Oh! you poor thing! Never was anyone so lucky. It isn't too late to enjoy yourself, though father was so unlucky with the money. We must begin to consider at once what is best to do. There is no time to lose. Perhaps we can get a lawyer in London to do the thing; but English lawyers are dreadful, I believe. Perhaps we shall even have to go over ourselves."

"My dear, I do not understand one single word that you are saying."

"We could borrow some money, we shouldn't want much; I suppose they'll give up at once when they see the proofs. Oh! Auntie—you shall be the richest woman in the whole world; you shall have new frocks by the dozen—"

"Dear child! What is it?" she repeated, with some trouble gathering in her eyes.

"Listen, Auntie! Only listen! Oh! listen. It takes my breath away only to think of it. Listen! listen! listen! Oh! it's the most wonderful thing that ever happened to anybody. All the good things—the lucky things—are coming to America. This is the real land for fairy stories. All the fairies are coming here. I am Cinderella—I am Cap o' Rushes—I am Belle Belle—Oyez! oyez! oyez!"

"Dear Ella"—the elder lady began to grow alarmed—"are you in your senses?"

"No, Auntie. I am out of them. But listen!" She had been jumping about and waving the paper in her hand. At last she stood still and read:

"Heirs Wanted!
AN IMMENSE FORTUNE!
TWELVE MILLIONS STERLING!
SIXTY MILLION DOLLARS!
ALL DROPPING INTO QUEEN VICTORIA'S LAP!
HEIRS WANTED NAME OF BURLEY!"

"These are only the head-lines, Auntie, just to wake you up. There, sit up now. Open your mouth and shut your eyes and see what I will send you. I am Titania, Queen of the Fairies. I am the Lady Best of Good Luck. Listen! listen! listen!"

"'People named Burley are invited to read the following with attention. People whose mother's name was Burley may also find it to their advantage to read it with attention. People whose grandfathers and grandmothers were named Burley may read it with singular advantage and profit. Till one fatal day four or five weeks ago there lived in a little street called Great College Street, Westminster, an old man, by name John Calvert Burley'—John Calvert Burley, Auntie. Think of that!— father's name!—John Calvert Burley," she repeated. "'He was so old that he had apparently outlived all his friends. At all events for forty years, as his house-keeper bore witness, no one had called at the house except his business manager. He was ninety-four years of age. Those few people who knew of his existence knew also that he was very wealthy. He was so very wealthy that his affairs were managed for him at an office, where he had formerly transacted business as a money-lender, by a large staff of employés—lawyers, architects, builders, accountants, and clerks. The old man, who died suddenly, has, it appears, left no will. The estate, therefore, in default of heirs, falls to the Crown, and it is the biggest windfall of the kind that has ever happened. For the property left by this obscure old man is now estimated to be worth more than sixty millions of dollars. As yet no claimants have appeared, though it is extremely improbable that so great a fortune will not give birth to endless claimants. It is most certain, moreover, that the British Treasury will require the most rigid proof before admitting any claim. Meantime we advise everybody named Burley to investigate their line of descent. If the deceased left brothers (which is not likely) or nephews and nieces, these will be the heirs to the whole estate. If there are neither nephews nor nieces the inheritance passes upward to the children, or their descendants, of the deceased grandfather. This opens up a wide vista of possible claims. For suppose the deceased's grandfather was born, say, in 1740, and had six children—of whom five are concerned in this inheritance. These five children, born, say, between 1765 and 1775, may have had five children each; these in their turn five each, and so on—until we arrive at a grand total in the present year of grace of 3125, all with claims to this estate. This gives to each the sum of £3520 or $17,600, a painful illustration of the reducing power of common division.'"

"There, Auntie, what do you say to that?"

This conversation took place in a small house—a wooden house, painted a light, yellowish brown, with a green porch and green jalousies, and at the side a small orchard. The house stood in the main street of a little New England town which had a special industry in chair-legs. It was quite a small house, containing only one sitting-room, a veranda, a kitchen, and two or three bedrooms. Of the two ladies who lived in this house one, the elder, was a lady of a certain age, who had a little—a very little money. The other, her niece, a girl of twenty-one or two, was engaged as cashier in the most considerable factory of chair-legs in the place. The appearance of the elder lady, formal in her manner, precise in her dress, indicated the great respectability of the family. Nobody, in fact, could be more respectable.

Tewksbury, Mass., is a town in which the feminine element largely predominates. The girls take all the places, berths, and appointments, and do all the work at half the pay that should be given to the men for the same work. Therefore the men—the few men who are born in this town—go away West, and the women, thus achieving their independence, are happy. The future of Tewksbury, Mass., is uncertain, but as the greater part of a chair-leg can be made by women just as well as by men, it is calculated that another fifty years will see the end of the town. This will be a pity, because it is a very pretty place, and in the summer most umbrageous with shade-trees. Yet who would not rather be a cashier in a chair-leg factory than a mere wife and a meek mother, slaving for a husband and for children? Tewksbury stands for many other places—we ourselves, if we live long enough, may witness the destruction of our own towns, when women have fully resolved on their independence and have driven the men out of the country.

In the town of Tewksbury, not only do women predominate, but women rule. Theirs is the literary society; theirs is the circulating library; they form the committee for the lecture programme; they get up the school and church feasts and treats and social teas and summer picnics. It is a Ladies' Paradise, with as little as possible of the other sex, and, in fact, there are very few husbands and no marriageable bachelors, and the boys have to sit on the same benches as the girls, and are not only taught to behave pretty, but to acknowledge the superiority of women's intellect, being admonished thereon by the result of every examination.

The Tewksbury Paradise is an Eden of culture with the disturbing element left out. Also, needless to say, that it has its commonplaces or maxims generally admitted—of which the one about the insufficiency of money to satisfy the soul naturally commends itself to a community of women living on a very few dollars a week. Yet, you see how Philosophy may break down. What power had this maxim over the soul of Ella Burley when she read this intelligence and was tempted by the prospect of these millions? Alas! Poor Philosophy! Whither wilt thou fly?

"Auntie!" cried the girl again. "Don't look like that! Say something! Get up! Get up!"

Miss Lucinda Burley took off her spectacles and gazed into space.

"Sure enough," she said, slowly. "Father came out of that street—and I suppose the man just dead must have been his brother. Sure enough! One brother, I know—the eldest brother—remained at home—ninety-four. Yes, he must have been my uncle—ninety-four! It's like a dream."

"Sure enough, then, that great fortune is ours—isn't it? Unless the other brothers—but that isn't likely, or they would have come forward. It is ours, Auntie—ours."

To the girl's amazement her aunt at this juncture turned perfectly white, and began to tremble and to shake.

"Oh, my dear!" she cried, "put it out of your head—we mustn't claim it. We mustn't think of it. Oh! it cannot be ours. Don't so much as think of it."

"Not claim it? Not think of it? But, Auntie, it is ours by right. What is the matter, dear?" For now Aunt Lucinda appeared to be nigh unto fainting. "It is the sudden shock that is too much for you. Dear Auntie, lie down—so. Oh! and I thought you were sitting so calm and quiet over it—and I was so excited. Lie down—so—and let me talk. What was I saying? Oh! Yes, you are the niece and I am the grandniece of the rich man's brother. There were other brothers, but their descendants have not put in a claim. Now all that is wanted will be to establish the relationship. Well! here we are. Grandfather settled here. He was a lawyer here. He lived here and died here. People remember him well;

everybody remembers James C. Burley. I remember him; an old man who walked with a stiff knee and a stick. He died fifteen years ago; he was about seventy-five when he died. Then everybody remembers father—John C. Burley—who was only forty-five when he died. We shall have nothing to do but just to connect grandfather with the house in Westminster."

"Is that all, Ella?" The elder lady sat up. She was still pale and agitated. "Is that really all that we shall have to do? Shall we not have to go into court and swear all sorts of things?"

"Why—of course—what more can there be? If we can prove that James C. Burley was the dead man's brother, and that we are his descendants, what more can they want? Did you think you would have to stand up to be bullied by a brutal British lawyer? Or were you afraid there would be heavy law expenses, Auntie? Was that what frightened you?"

"Yes, dear, yes. Oh! that was what I meant. I was afraid. It occurred to me—but since that is all—"

"Why, dear, what nonsense! Of course that is all. It will all be as plain as possible. We shall simply have to show that grandfather was this dead man's brother."

Aunt Lucinda sat up and took the paper. But her eyes swam—she could not read it; she lay down again, murmuring: "After all these years—all these years—no—no!"

"After all these years, Auntie—yes—yes; after all these years! Oh! To think that we shall be so rich—so rich—oh! so rich. Let us sit down and make out what we will do when we are so rich."

The girl was a slight and slender creature, bright eyed, rather sharp of feature; her hair nearly black, her black eyes deep set; she spoke and moved with animation. She was thoroughly alert and alive; she was a well-educated American girl who knew her mind and had her opinions. On one table lay the library books she was reading; in the bookcase were her own books; on the writing-table lay the sheets of an unfinished paper on the "Parleyings of Browning," which she was writing for the literary society. This was a flourishing literary society, including all the ladies in the town—two hundred and fifty-five; most of them wrote critical papers for the society; the rest wrote poems; one or two had written for New York magazines. Fiction was, very properly, excluded from the work of the society. It was, you see, a profoundly critical town. Many of the ladies, including Ella Burley, believed that the verdict of their society on the merits of an author made or marred that author.

Ella sat down beside the sofa on which her aunt lay, still agitated, and began to talk. She enjoyed the pleasures of imagination for half an hour. Then she remembered that supper had to be prepared, and she ran out into the kitchen which adjoined in order to make it ready. And at intervals she ran back again to add another detail.

But the elder lady sitting upon the sofa looked about the room with troubled eyes. "She can find out nothing," she murmured, "Oh! I burned all the letters and papers. Oh! nobody knows except me—nobody else in the whole wide world. If it were discovered now—after I've hidden it away all these years! After all these years!"

"Auntie!" The girl ran in again. "I'm real sorry for Queen Victoria. She little thinks that over here in the Land of Freedom there lives the heiress who is going to make her disgorge those millions. Of course, she reckons they are hers already. Fancy! At Buckingham Palace—I see them quite plainly—they are all sitting in a circle round the table, the Queen in the middle and the Prince of Wales on her right hand, contriving how to divide and to spend the money—and now they won't have any of it. Oh! what an awful blow for them it will be."

She disappeared again.

When they sat down to supper neither could eat anything for excitement.

"I have made up my mind, Auntie," she said, as if the elder lady's mind was of no account whatever. "I mean to carry this business through with a rush. I will give up my post in the factory tomorrow. We must get some money—an advance—a loan—a mortgage on this house will do—it won't cost much—we will go second-class to Liverpool; then I suppose a week or two will be all we want to get the business settled. Why, it's as plain as can be—we must get certificates or something that we are the persons we claim to be, and you must get whatever proofs you have to connect grandfather with the—What is it, dear?" For Aunt Lucinda was beginning to tremble again.

"Oh! Are you quite sure—quite sure, dear—that there will be nothing more wanted? Only these certificates? I've got old letters upstairs— letters from his mother to my father—"

"Why, of course. What should be wanted more than what we have? Get out every scrap of paper you can find, and, Auntie, dear, don't look as if we were going to be hanged. You shall be crowned, not hanged, my dear, with a coronet—a countess's coronet. Oh! I feel so happy—so happy!"

THREE WEEKS LATER THEY WERE sitting in a London lodging—it was in Westminster, so as to be on the spot, close to Great College Street; in fact, it was in Smith Square, where stands the huge mass of stone called the Church of St. John the Evangelist. And it was a cheap lodging of two rooms that they took.

"Now, Auntie"—it was the day of their arrival; their boxes were unpacked; they had taken tea; they had tried the chairs and the sofa; and they were preparing to settle down—"let us bring out our papers. Oh, how I used to wake up at night on board the horrid ship, dreaming that we were in London and that we had lost the things. Here they are." She opened a brown leather hand-bag and took out a bundle of papers. "Here are the certificates of baptism; yours, father's, and mine. They're all right. John Calvert Burley, son of James Calvert Burley, lawyer, and Alice, his wife. Yours, too, Lucinda Calvert Burley; and mine, Ella Calvert Burley. They're all right. Next, here is the certificate to show that the late James Calvert Burley, an Englishman by birth, lived in Tewksbury, Massachusetts, and practised as a solicitor until his death in 1875. Here is the certificate of his death, with his age. That, of course, will correspond with his birth certificate at Westminster—in this great ugly church, I dare say. Here is my poor father's death certificate. Also the certificate about his residence and practice. Then, here are the letters which you have kept—the letters of his mother (my great-grandmother)— only five of them, but two are enough. 'My dear James,'"—she took up one of the letters; it was folded in the old fashion, without an envelope, and fastened with a wafer—"'I am rejoyced to hear that you are Well and Safe and that your Uncle Jackman has been able to find you Employment. Your Father remains Obstinately Sett against Forgiveness, and you must expect nothing from him but Resentment, unless you quickly return, which I fear you will not do. Write to me often. You can bring or send the Letters to save Postage. Push them under the Door. Be Good, my son, and you will be Happy. Your Loving Mother—Frances Burley.' The letter is dated," the girl went on, "December 20th, 1825."

"That was about five years before he crossed to America," said Aunt Lucinda. "The other letter is very much like it—written a year later."

"My grandmother died about the year 1878, I believe. Auntie, the evidence is crushing."

"Are you quite sure—quite—that they can ask no other questions?" Aunt Lucinda asked, anxiously.

"Why, of course not. What other questions can they ask? There may be other nieces and nephews. But the property could be divided, I suppose. Come, Auntie, the way lies plain and easy before us. We have nothing to do but to send in our claims. We will find out the way somehow. We will not have any lawyers to send in bills. A lawyer's daughter ought to know better. We will just draw up our statement, make copies of the letters and papers, and send them in—the copies, of course. Why, Auntie, I wouldn't trust even Queen Victoria's lawyers with the originals. There, we will put them all back for tonight, and tomorrow—ah!"—she drew a long breath—"we will spend in drawing up our case. I suppose it will be examined at once, and as there can be no doubt about it, we shall have the property at the end of the week. Poor Queen! She's a good woman; everybody says so. I'm sorry she will suffer through us. But, of course, we can't help it. Perhaps a little present—a silver teapot, say—would partly console her. We'll find out how such a trifle, as a mark of respect from an American girl, would be received. I don't mind the disappointment of the princes a bit. And now, my dear, you are tired with the day's journey, though it's nothing—really—to get across this little bit of an island. You ought to go to bed and rest. Otherwise there will be a headache in the morning and—mind—lie down with a joyful heart. There's no more doubt, mind—no more doubt than there is about the Stars and Stripes."

Aunt Lucinda obeyed. But she did not immediately go to bed. She sat on the bed and trembled. Then she locked the door, and, falling on her knees, she prayed with all the fervor of a faithful Christian, while the tears ran down her cheeks. "O God!" she murmured, "grant that it may never be found out or suspected. After all these years! And no one knows except myself. After all these years! And he a deacon! And our folks respected in the town! Oh! keep the sin a secret. Let it burn in my heart and shame me and torture me. Kill me with it, and I will never murmur. Let mine be the suffering and the secret shame. But keep it— oh! keep it from the innocent girl. O Lord, if the fortune cannot come to us by reason of that sin, let me alone know that it is the sin which stands in the way."

In the other room the heiress sat at the open window watching the lights of the house and listening to the clocks. She was not ignorant of the long, long history which the Palace Yard and the buildings around it illustrate and commemorate, but her thoughts were not with English history. She was thinking of the house close by, where her great-grandfather, the miser, had lived, from which her grandfather fled. She must contrive to see that house somehow, as soon as the case was drawn up and handed in, but not before. She would present herself as the heiress—it would be her own house—as soon as the property was handed over to her; that is to say, in a week or so at the outside.

XIII

The Vision of the Mothers

I t was in the evening, in the first glow of an early autumn sunset, that Lucian brought his bride to her new home in Great College Street.

He had accomplished, you see, that strange desire to live in the house of his forefathers. He had obtained a lease from the administrators of the property; he had bought the whole of the furniture and fittings, books, pictures—everything as it stood, and he had cleaned, painted, decorated, and whitewashed the house. It was his for seven years on the customary conditions.

The street was peaceful as the cab rolled into it; the house, clothed with its Virginia-creeper, just putting on its September splendors, looked truly and wonderfully beautiful; the door, opened by Margaret's two maids with smiling faces, showed a light and cheerful hall. The stairs were carpeted, the walls newly painted; the echoes were gone. Margaret ran in with a light heart.

"Oh! how changed!" she cried. She opened the dining-room door. The table, laid for dinner and decorated with flowers, was in itself a welcome; the dingy old walls had disappeared, and in their place were dainty panels of gray and green. "The house looks young again! Lucian, the past is gone and forgotten. It is your house; the old house, but transformed. Lucian, I am glad we came here."

"It is your home, my Margaret." He kissed her. "May it prove a happy and a fortunate home."

Then they talked of their plans. The brass plate was on the door, "Lucian Calvert, M.D.," as an invitation to enter and be healed. The book which this young physician was preparing was nearly ready; his reputation would be made by that book. Formerly a young man could not take his degree till he had maintained, before all comers, a thesis; in these days he takes his degree first and advances his thesis afterwards. Oh! he would get on; he had confidence in himself. And not a word was said about the ancestors upstairs, or the millions waiting for him at the Treasury.

Next day, breakfast over, her husband gone to the hospital, which took his mornings, Margaret began a new exploration of the house. First, she went into Lucian's study—the consulting-room of the future—the back parlor where the old man spent the last fourteen years of his long life. No sign of him was left; that is, no outward and visible sign in this room or in any other room. Since his profession had been, as his son called it, "Destruction and Ruin," I dare say there were evidences of his industry to be found outside the house—in poverty-stricken ladies, sons gone shepherding, and broad lands that had changed owners. However, here the signs and marks of him were all swept and carried away; the windows were bright and clean; the sun shone upon the panes through a frame or fringe of vine leaves; the old bookcase now contained her husband's scientific books—the old books, which were chiefly theological dialogues, essays, and sermons, were gone—packed off to the twopenny boxes of the second-hand booksellers; the old table was covered with her husband's papers and writings; the colored engravings still hung in the panels, but their frames were newly gilt; as for the walls themselves, they were newly painted a pearl gray, with a little warmer color for the dado and the cornice. Window-curtains were put up; there were new photographs, new knick-knacks on the mantel-shelf, and the portrait of Lucian's father was placed in this room, apart from the ancestors whom he had renounced. Could this be the dingy room of only six weeks ago? That represented age, squalid, low-minded, without dignity; this meant youth and manhood, with noble aims and lofty studies.

The young wife had nothing to do in her husband's room. She looked in simply because it was his room; it made her feel closer to him only to stand in his room. She was perfectly happy in that foolish satisfaction with the present which newly married people ought to feel. There are periods and seasons when time ought to move so very, very slowly. During the first three months of marriage, for instance, so as to prolong the happiness of it; during the last three years of an old man's life, so as to prolong the time of reminiscence—or, perhaps, repentance; when one is engaged upon a work of art, so as to prolong the delight and the joy of the work. That time will not move any slower to accommodate anybody is part of the curious lack of sympathy between Nature and the individual.

Margaret, for her part, living in the present, had forgotten those forebodings. How should forebodings linger in the mind of a happy bride of twenty-one? Besides, the house, so lovely within and without, so quiet and peaceful—what had it to do with the dingy, dirty, memory-stricken place that she had seen six weeks ago?

Yet she was to be reminded that very morning of these forebodings.

She sighed—for very happiness. She smoothed the papers and arranged the pens—just in order to touch something of her husband's. Then she looked out of the window into the little garden with the mulberry-tree and the vine, and then, as if reluctantly, she left the room and softly shut the door.

Heavens! What a change that magician, the house-painter, had effected! Nothing could look brighter than the stairs, broad, covered with a soft carpet, running up between walls newly painted and hung with framed engravings, lit by a spacious window, glorified by a broad mahogany balustrade. When she lifted her fresh young voice and began to sing as she climbed the stairs there was no echo. All the echoes had gone. Why? Because, as Lucian suggested, they love the empty places of the earth? It is one of the many scientific questions which cannot be answered. All the echoes had gone. Margaret opened the door of the drawing-room. Similar changes had transformed this room. The old furniture was there, but it was supplemented by modern things, imported by Margaret herself. New tables, new chairs, new blinds and curtains, new carpets. The walls were painted in a soft, delicate shade. The frames of the portraits were regilt. There were new books, and a bookcase full of them; and there were fresh flowers on the table.

Margaret looked at the ancestors. She began to examine the pictures again. Once more she felt those curious eyes—deep set, searching, under straight black eyebrows, like Lucian's, which followed her about the room—and once more she remembered their history, as related by Lucian's father in those pages which she had read. Since she saw them last they had somehow—but that was nonsense—changed their expression. How can pictures change? Perhaps it was the new gliding of the frames; perhaps it was the general brightening of the room. Whatever the reason, the ancestors did certainly look more cheerful. The original Calvert no longer brooded over past misdeeds and impending punishment—he now meditated deeply some great, if not noble, enterprise. The highwayman, his son, whose picture had been brought down from the garret and restored to its panel, had put aside the swagger which formerly distinguished his portrait, and now appeared with something of the modesty of a gallant soldier to whom death is no evil compared with dishonor. Even the miser looked as if he were satisfied with the result of his last counting, and could reward himself for his success with a few extra privations.

The ladies, for their part, appeared to smile upon her. A strange fancy; yet Margaret could not shake it off. They were smiling. No doubt these changes were entirely due to the cleaning of the pictures and the brightening of their frames. But still, it was surprising. These ladies smiled upon her. Why? Because she was now one of the House? You may live under a false name, you may renounce your ancestors, but you do belong to them; there is only one set of ancestors possible for a man; one set of ancestors, one cast, or mould, or type of face, with two or three hereditary tendencies for choice. Therefore, when Margaret appeared in the drawing-room as the new mistress of the house, and the wife of the heir, these ladies naturally smiled a welcome.

A little of the former terror fell upon Margaret. Not much; but some. She remembered their evil lives, their misdeeds, and their misfortunes. A family specially marked out for misfortune; pursued by crime, dishonor, and sorrow. Lucian, like his father, had renounced his forefathers. No harm would happen to him, therefore. Yet Margaret trembled, only to think of the long inheritance of sorrow. Her piano stood in one corner of the room. She sat down and began to play—idly at first. Then the feeling came over her that the ancestors were all listening. She lifted her head and looked round—all were looking at her; the women, she now thought, with compassion rather than welcome—the men, with curiosity. She changed the music—it became a grave and serious meditation; it became sacred music; she played pieces of a mass she knew; finally, she played a hymn—one of the solemn hymns which we never sing now—an eighteenth-century hymn—with a beautiful melody—a hymn in which the soul feels her helplessness, and cries out for help to the place whence only help can come. All her soul went heavenward with the music. As she bent her head over the keys she became dreamily conscious that the men were listening unmoved, but curious, and that the women were weeping in their frames. And the house was so silent—so silent—and she was alone in it with her ghostly company. But she was not afraid. Only she felt excited and restless.

She arose—pale, with set face and eyes dilated; her limpid eyes, which could so easily become dreamy. Then, as in a dream, not knowing what she was doing, or why, she left the room, closing the door after her, and climbed the stair, up—up—up, until she reached the highest floor, and then she walked into the nursery and sat upon the bed.

Why was she there? She knew not, save that her head was filled with the thoughts of the mothers and the children. Here, in this nursery, generation after generation, the wives and mothers had their brief time of happiness while the children were yet little. This room was theirs; it was sacred to them; she was one of them now; she was the wife of the heir; it was right that she should make this room her own.

In all "communications," appearances, conversations, and correspondence with the other world, it has been remarked, over and over again, that we never learn anything which we did not know before. Human knowledge has never been advanced a single step. If any revelation is made as to the kind of existence led in the other world, it is exactly the kind of life led at the present moment by ourselves in this generation. This makes certain scoffers ask the use of interrogating the spirits, or of expecting any help from them. In what followed, for instance, Margaret heard and saw nothing but what she had already imagined. The vision that came to her was already in her own brain. In what had gone before, the threatening faces of the portraits, she saw what was in her own brain. Nothing supernatural in it at all? Nothing at all. Quite a natural phenomenon.

She sat on the old moth-eaten bed. Presently she closed her eyes and fell back upon the mattress. How long did she lie there unconscious? I know not. As for what follows, it is exactly what she told her husband that evening. One can only write down what one is told. History is often mystery. We see what is not there to be seen; we hear voices where there is silence; our ghosts are all created in the brain; which, again, is the real reason why ghosts never tell anything that we did not know before.

Margaret opened her eyes. It did not surprise her that she was lying on the bed in the nursery. Nor was she in the least surprised to see, standing round the bed, all the women of the house; the wives, the mothers, the daughters. She knew them by their portraits. In fact, they stepped straight out of the frames and came upstairs, dressed in the things they wore in the pictures, in order to greet the newly arrived wife of the heir. But their faces were all alike, pale and sad. Their hands were clasped. And when they smiled their sadness only seemed the stronger.

And another thing. Behind the mothers were all the children, all the little children that ever played in this nursery—twenty little children, every one three years of age, all running about and tumbling down, and, without making the least noise, going through the forms of laughing and crying; some played together and some played apart; children of the last century and children of this. And they were so lovely, all these children; the gift of beauty was theirs from generation to generation.

But Margaret turned from the children to their mothers, for they spoke to her. At first they spoke all together, with the same faint smile, and with the same sad, soft voice.

"Welcome," they cried, "welcome, daughter of the House! Now art thou one of us; one with us."

"One of us, and one with us," they repeated, all with the same sad smile; "to suffer and to weep with us—with all who marry into this House."

Then they spoke in turns, each telling the new-comer her story of sadness.

"I," said the first, who had on her head the Queen Anne commode—"I married the man who committed the crime for which you have all since suffered in your turn. Would to God I had died first! How should I know that he had ruined his master, and starved him to death in prison, and made his children beggars? I knew nothing till, in the agony of bereavement, he confessed it all. My daughter, my lovely girl, died in her very spring. My lovely boy was kidnapped and carried away, I know not whither or to what hard fate; my eldest, as brave and as beautiful as David's own son Absalom, was carried to Tyburn Tree and hanged upon the shameful gallows. Oh! my son—my son! Oh! my daughter! Oh! wretched mother! Thus began the expiation. Listen, thou newly made one of us!"

"As for me," spoke the second, "I lived to so great an age that I thought I should never die; and I had sorrow and shame for my companions night and day. I had to look on helpless while my husband squandered my fortune among wantons—till love was turned to hate, and hate was changed to shame when he was taken out to die. Thus have we women wept for the wickedness of men."

"And I," said the third, "married one who lost his reason, and raved for twelve long years. And so my life was ruined, save that my children were left to me."

"Whose lot was worse than mine?" said a fourth. "For my husband became a miser. He was mad for saving money. I had to pray and threaten before I could get money even for my children; as for clothes, I had to make them myself. When the boys grew up they ran away and left the miser's home; all but one, who found means of his own to live and clothe himself until his father died. My only daughter left me.

No one would stay in the House. Oh, wretched House! Oh, loveless House! Oh, House of evil fortune!" She wept and wrung her hands.

"And I," said the last, "married the miser's son. Like his great-great-grandfather, he cared nothing how he made money, so that he could make it. Like his father, he could not bear to spend it. I had children, six, but five of them died, and when I lay a-dying, my son whispered that he could not endure to live in the house without me, and that he could no longer endure being called the money-lender's son, and so, I think, he, too, ran away."

"One of us," said the first—"one of us! With all these memories to fill thy mind and these our sorrows to share—O fair, new daughter of the House!"

"The money was gained with dishonor," said the last, "and has grown with dishonor. How should this couple who inherit the money escape the curse? They cannot take one without the other."

"Shame and dishonor! Shame and dishonor! These things go with the fortune that Calvert Burley founded and the miser and the money-lender increased."

You will observe in the report of this vision, first of all, that Margaret was alone in the house, save for the two maids in the kitchen below; next, that she knew the history attaching to every portrait; then, that the vision told her nothing new; and, lastly, that she had been from the first strangely moved by the nursery and its associations. One would not willingly explain away, or suppress, anything supernatural—things really and undoubtedly supernatural are, despite the researches of the Psychical Society, only too rare. At the same time, we must remark the predisposition of this young wife to such a vision. It was a warm autumnal morning; her imagination was excited by the sight of the portraits; she sat on the bed; she either fainted or she fell asleep; and she dreamed this vision of the mothers. It ceased; the unhappy mothers vanished. Margaret sat up, looking around her, listening to the voices which died away slowly in the chambers of her brain.

She was married to a scientific husband; she was accustomed to hear derision poured upon all spiritual pretensions and manifestations and revelations. "It was a dream," she said—"a dream caused by what I had been thinking about." Yet she arose with a sense of consolation. "Shame and dishonor," said one of the women, "go with Calvert Burley's money." Therefore no harm would fall upon those who refused part or share in that money. It was the belief of Lucian's father. No harm would come to her or hers so long as they continued that great refusal. "It is a dream," she said, wondering why she came to the nursery, and remembering no more after she had played that sacred music which prepared her soul for the dream of the mothers. "A dream," she repeated. Yet—strange that one should, in open daylight, walk in sleep.

She descended the stairs, feeling a little dizzy and still confused about this dream. When she reached the first floor she stopped, hesitated a moment, then turned the handle and went into the drawing-room. Why, there was nothing at all in the pictures out of the common; poor paintings, for the most part; stiff in drawing, and conventional; very probably good likenesses. But as for that feeling of being watched by them, or of any intelligence in them, or of listening by them, or anything in the least unusual—it was absurd. "I have been dreaming," said Margaret.

She took a chair in one of the windows and sat down, taking a book of verse to read. The poetry did not appeal to her this morning; she laid the book aside; she closed her eyes and dropped off to sleep.

At one o'clock she awoke; she sat up with a start; she looked round, expecting the mothers to be surrounding her chair. There was nothing; the mothers were on the wall, but they were evidently thinking of themselves. "It was a dream," she said. "But how clear and vivid! And, now, I know them every one. 'One of us—one with us—to share our sorrows!' Oh, hapless House! There may be sorrows for me, and there will be; but not the shame and dishonor that go with all this money."

"LUCIAN," SHE SAID IN THE evening, "I must tell you what a strange thing happened to me this morning."

"You have something on your mind, dear. Tell me, if it will relieve you."

"I will not tell you quite all. I must keep something back, because even to you, dear, I feel as if I could not tell everything—just yet."

"Tell me just what you please."

She was ashamed to tell him of the strange terror which seized her in the drawing-room; she was ashamed to tell him of the hymn she played for strength against these airy terrors; she was ashamed to tell him that she could not remember how she got upstairs to the nursery.

"I went there," she said, "and I sat upon the bed, and began to think of the children and the poor mothers. And—I don't know—perhaps it was rather a close morning, and the window was shut. I am afraid I fainted, for I fell back, and when I was recovered I was lying on the bed."

"Fainted? My dear child!"

"And I had a most curious dream. Well, the dream was in my head before I went off. I dreamed that round the bed stood all the mothers of the House—those unhappy women whose portraits are upstairs, and they welcomed me as one of themselves, and lamented their unhappy fate, and they said that shame and dishonor go with the money that Calvert Burley began to save."

"A strange dream, my dear," said her husband. "Truly a strange dream."

"Oh, it was only a dream, Lucian," she concluded. "Oh, I do not need to be told that. But it has brought home to me so vividly the sorrows of these poor women. Oh! how they suffered, one after the other! If men only knew the sufferings their vices bring upon women, I think half the wickedness of the world would cease. One after the other—yes—I know what you would say—their husbands sinned and caused their sorrows. Yet your father thought so—as I think. Dishonor and shame go with Calvert Burley's money."

Lucian laughed, but with grave eyes. "My dear," he said, "it is strange for you to have visions. But you are too much alone. We must get your sister to come here for a spell when she returns home. It is a very quiet house, and you are not accustomed to be so much alone. One easily gets nervous in such a house. If I were you, dear, I would not spend too much time in that nursery. Let me clear it all out and make it a lumber-room."

"No, no. It is my room, Lucian. I will not have it touched. Besides, I haven't half explored the cupboard yet."

All that evening Lucian watched her furtively. She sat with him in his study. And when she said it was time to go upstairs, he did not remain for a pipe by himself, but rose and went up with her. For it was not Margaret's custom to grow faint and to see visions.

XIV

A Visit to the Treasury

I suppose we are not forwarded any, Ella dear?" Aunt Lucinda looked up with a forced smile as her niece came in.

"Not a bit." Ella threw her hat upon the table and pulled off her jacket. The girl was changed already. The face, which was so bright and eager when first she resolved on bringing over her claim in person, was now pale and set as with endurance and resolution. It was a fighting face. You may often see this face among the women of the good old stock, which is said to be fast dying out in New England; it means the iron resolution which they inherit from the Puritan Pilgrims. I should be rather afraid to confront such a face if I had a weak cause or a wrong cause. This face meant perseverance to the end. It also meant anxiety.

"We are not advanced a bit," she repeated.

"Were they civil?"

"Oh, they are civil enough, now. Quite polite, in fact. I don't think they will ask me any more to sit on the doorstep and wait. But it's no use being polite, as I told them, if we don't get on. It's always will I wait? Will I have patience? Will I consider that this is a very important business? The lawyers have all the claims sent in as yet. All must be considered. Well, these may be considered; but how many are from nephews and nieces? Then they say that there may be other nephews and nieces—why don't they come forward, then? Then they say that there was a son. They must get proof that the son is dead, and further proof that he left no children, or that these children are dead. How long do they expect to keep me waiting? They don't know. It is impossible to say. A great deal depends upon the proof about the son. It may be a long time."

"Oh, Ella, what do they call long? Is it weeks or months?"

"I don't know, Auntie; I don't know"—she sat down wearily.

"My dear, the suspense is killing me."

"Auntie, you look frightened always. Why does the claim frighten you? Is it that the fortune is so huge?"

"Don't ask me, dear. I try not to think about the money; but I must. The gracious Lord knows, Ella, that I do not desire it. I desire only that the thing may be settled one way or the other. I wish we were back in Tewksbury again, and all was as it used to be—and I was arranging for the reading of the Literary Society's papers."

"Things can't ever go back, Auntie. We've got, somehow, to see this through."

"And how are we to live, dear, until things are settled?"

"I don't know, Auntie. I'm thinking all day and all night. I don't know what we are to do." She sat down and folded her hands. "Let us see— we say the same thing every day. . . Let us see again." She took her purse from her pocket and poured out the contents. "We've spent all the money we brought for our expenses here; and we've spent most of the money for our passage home. Auntie, we've got exactly three pounds ten shillings and sixpence—about seventeen dollars. Our rent is ten shillings a week; say that we have four weeks' rent in hand, that leaves us one pound two shillings and six-pence—about five dollars and a half—for washing and for food. Can we make it last for three weeks? Three weeks more—and then? My dear Auntie, I don't believe that they mean to settle this case in three weeks, or in three months—or, perhaps, in three years."

"And after three weeks, dear?"

"We must wait in patience if it's thirty years. For whatever happens, we shall not withdraw our claim. They may try to drive us back to our own country; but no—we will wait."

"But how to live, dear?"

"I don't know yet. They *must* give in sooner or later, Auntie; it is a certainty."

"Suppose we were to go home again, dear, and wait there," said Aunt Lucinda, timidly. "I should like to see the old street again."

"We can't, my dear. We've got no money to take us back, not even if we went as steerage passengers. We must stay here somehow. Besides, if we went back, how should we ever pay back the money you borrowed? We should have to sell the old house, and how long should I have to wait before I got another situation? There are twenty girls in Tewksbury wanting places to every place there is for them."

"But, my child, how are we to live?"

"I don't know yet. We've got three weeks to find out. Well"—she jumped up—"I must find out something. Don't be afraid, Auntie. There's the American Minister here; I will go and ask him to get me some work. Perhaps they want a girl clerk at his place. Or, there's the American

Consul. I will go there and ask for advice. We don't want to borrow money; we want a little work that will keep us going, in ever so poor a way. They say it is so hard for a woman to get work in this city. But we shall see. I will write to the Queen herself and tell her our case. Perhaps she wants a short-hand girl clerk; or a cashier; or a type-writer—who knows? I suppose she wouldn't bear malice because we want to take this money? They say at the Treasury that she won't have it, in any case. I don't know why they say so. The papers all declared that the estate would go to the Crown. You shall see, Auntie; I *will* get something somehow."

"Well, my dear," said Aunt Lucinda, feebly, "you are very brave, but you can't make people find you work or lend you money. Oh! my dear, you are young and clever, but I know more than you. Money it is that makes people hard, and cruel, and unjust. They will be hard and unjust to you here just as much as at home. This dreadful money! We were happier when we wanted none. At Tewksbury we taught ourselves to despise money. Remember that we put up a petition and a thanksgiving every morning against the prevalent and sinful greed of money."

"Yes, dear, we did. But you must remember that we have not sought this fortune nor asked for it. The gift came to us. You are this dead man's niece; I am his grandniece; it is our bounden duty to take what is given, and to show the world how such a gift may be used aright. That is what it is meant for. If we'd prayed for it night and day we should not have got it. A millionaire is put upon a pillar, like a king, for the world to watch. Everything that he does is watched and recorded. In a few weeks or months, you and I, simple as we are, will be the two women in the world the most talked about—and it is laid upon us to show the world how so great a gift should be administered."

"Well, dear, it will be a most awful responsibility—I dare not think of it. The mere thought of millions makes my head dizzy."

"As for that, you must not let yourself think of the figures. They are bewildering; and you will gradually, without hurting yourself at all, come to understand that whatever you want to have, you can have. Don't be afraid, Auntie—you will want and do nothing but what is good."

"I will try, my dear. Meantime—after the next three weeks—how shall we live?"

"I don't know—I am thinking and thinking—and, so far, nothing has come of it. I'm not afraid, but I am a little anxious. We are so much alone; we know nobody; if we go to a lawyer we shall have to pay him. If we could go and consult a minister! There is the great stony church out there in the square; I have thought of going to see the pastor, but then he's Episcopal, and we are Methodists. I wrote to Mr. Gladstone—I didn't tell you, Auntie, because you might think it was mixing ourselves up in politics, and an American girl over here oughtn't to take a side. He answered very kindly—says he can't help. Well—he's too busy, I suppose. As for his not being able to help, I wonder if there's any single thing in the world that old man can't make the people here believe and do."

"I don't know, dear; I am beginning to feel—"

"No, don't say that, Auntie dear," the girl interrupted, quickly, "anything but that. It's only waiting for a little while—a week or two—a year or two. Only patience for a bit. These solicitors! I asked for their names, meaning to go and sit upon their door-steps until they attend to me, as I threatened to do at the Treasury."

"But, Ella, we must remember the other claimants. There may be some with quite as good case, until they come to ours. We must take our turn, after all."

"I'm so restless about it; I can't sleep for thinking of it; I can't sit still. Yesterday, in church, I was obliged to get up and go out, because my thoughts wouldn't let me sit still. I can't sit here in this room; it is too small. I am choked. Auntie, put on your bonnet, and, for goodness' sake, let us go out and walk up and down."

Aunt Lucinda obeyed; she always obeyed. She belonged to that class of women who are born to obey. She meekly rose, and went to her room for her bonnet.

The girl's face lost all courage when she was alone. She waved her arms in a kind of agony. "Oh!" she cried. "Hundreds of claimants! Hundreds! and more coming in every day! They will not decide until they have received and considered all. And it may be years, they told me—long years of expectation. Oh! What shall we do? What shall we do?"

Then her aunt returned with red eyes. The two hypocrites smiled at each other and went down the stairs, and so into the square, called after an unknown Smith—perhaps allegorically as connecting the church, which covers three-fourths of the space, with the work of men's hands. The whole of the square was formerly the burial-ground of the church, so that these ladies were unconsciously walking over the dust of their forefathers—parishioners since the parish was first begun.

They walked nearly round the square, their thoughts far away. Then Ella turned into a street, for no reason, her aunt following her; and in two or three minutes they found themselves in an unexpected Place—a continental Place—which brought their thoughts back to Westminster. So long as you walk along streets and houses that you expect, and see the sights and hear the sounds to which you are accustomed, you can think as well and let your thoughts go roaming as far as if you were alone in the fields. When you see and hear the unexpected you must leave off thinking. Ella looked round her, awakened by the unexpected. For she stood suddenly in the most quiet and peaceful spot of all London. Houses of the early eighteenth century, with porches, and pillars, and flat façades, stand round this place, houses built for the comfort that our forefathers placed so far above artistic show and æsthetic display. Many generations of peace and home lent to this place the very atmosphere of seclusion. No one was walking in it; the houses and the street lay in sunshine—each home a hermitage. Perhaps in the month of September the people are away, but even in merry May there can never be the noise of the street.

"There's a street in Albany," said Aunt Lucinda, "which looks like this. Ah! if only we were once more safe—"

"Don't, Auntie. Oh, we shall pull through, somehow. I've got my watch still, and you've got your ring. We will go to a money-lender and borrow. Auntie," struck with a sudden thought, "your uncle, the rich man who died, he was a money-lender; he lived somewhere here—I suppose the business is still carried on. Let us go there. His successor might lend us some money on the security of our claim—we will give him any interest he wants. It is a chance—an inspiration, perhaps." It was; but not in the sense she meant.

"Where was the house?"

"It was a place called Great College Street, Westminster. The number was 77, I think."

They asked a postman. The street was close by—first turn to the right and straight on. They followed the direction, and speedily stood in the street beside the old gray wall and before the door numbered 77.

"It can't be the house," said Aunt Lucinda. "A miser and a money-lender couldn't live in such a lovely house; and see,—'Lucian Calvert, M.D.' on the plate. It is a doctor's house; Ella, you mustn't."

"I must. I am desperate. I suppose the house has been done up fresh, painted and everything, since the old man died. It doesn't look like a miser's house. But I don't care, I will ask." She rang the bell. The question she wanted to put was delicate. Was Dr. Calvert the successor of the late Mr. Burley, in the money-lending business? When the door was opened by the neat and well-dressed house-maid, the girl found herself unable to put that question. She had expected the physician himself. She hesitated, therefore, and stammered, and finally asked if "Dr. Calvert was within."

He was not. If the ladies wished to consult him he would be at home in the afternoon.

"We do not wish to consult him professionally," said the claimant. "That is—"

"Mrs. Calvert is at home," the maid suggested.

"That will be very much better. Would Mrs. Calvert see us? No; she does not know our names."

Mrs. Calvert would see them. They were shown into the dining-room, where they found a lady quite young, apparently newly married.

"You do not know us at all," said Ella, stepping to the front. "My aunt's name is Lucinda Burley, and I am Ella Burley, and we are Americans, and claimants for the Burley estate."

"And you wish to see the house where Mr. Burley lived and died?"

"N—no—that is, we should like to see the house, but we came on other business."

"You had better tell this lady the whole truth, my dear," said Aunt Lucinda, with the sagacity of age.

"Then it is this way. My great-uncle—"

"You are the granddaughter of James Calvert Burley?"

"You know about the family, then? Your name is Calvert? You are a cousin?"

"We are not claimants," said Margaret. "I know that James Burley went to America. That is all."

"We thought that our claim would be acknowledged in a day or two. We have spent most of our money, and it occurred to me that the money-lending business might be still carried on somewhere—perhaps here—but I see I was mistaken; and that, if we could learn where the office is, we might try to borrow money on the security of our claim."

"The money-lending was discontinued long before Mr. Burley died. My husband is a physician."

"Oh! then that idea has fallen through. Well, Mrs. Calvert, we are sorry to disturb you, and very much obliged to you. I hope you won't be offended because we asked."

She got up to go.

"I am not offended at all; I am interested in your case. Would you like to see the house where your grandfather was born?"

"If it will not trouble you too much," said Aunt Lucinda. "My father often spoke to me about this house and the old days. His father was a dreadful miser."

"I perceive that you know something of the family history. I suppose you have brought over proofs of your descent, and—and—everything that will be required."

"Plenty of proof," said Ella, stoutly, "all the proofs that can be asked for."

Margaret looked doubtful. For a moment she hesitated. Then she rose, and without further question led the way.

"Come with me," she said, "and I will show you the house. My husband is connected with the family. We are cousins, in fact—distant cousins. We took it over with all the furniture, only we have painted and decorated the place. James, through whom you claim, was the youngest son. He was born in 1804."

"We do not know much about our relations—not even how many brothers he had."

"Two brothers came between John, the man who died the other day, and your grandfather. So far as I know, neither of these two brothers, through heirs, has yet put in a claim. You are the first claimants who have called here. Come upstairs, and you shall see the family portraits."

She led them into the drawing-room, where the heads of this remarkable family adorned the walls.

"Father came over to America in the year 1830, with mother," Aunt Lucinda explained, her pale cheeks turning rosy red, no doubt with excitement. "My brother was born in 1831, and I was born in 1832. I am sixty-one years of age. This child was born in 1873, and my brother died in 1886. Father and son were lawyers. We've got the certificates of baptism and everything, and they've gone into the Treasury."

"They will try to cheat us out of our rights, if they can," said Ella, with determination. "But they've got an American girl to deal with."

She looked round the room. "That's like father," she said, pointing to the original Calvert. "He could look just as determined as that—you remember, Auntie?"

"Yes, my brother had that look sometimes, though he was unlucky in money."

"And you are like this lady; who was this, Mrs. Calvert?"

"That is Lucinda—wife of John Burley, the celebrated miser. She is your grandmother, Miss Burley. There is a strong likeness, but I hope you will be more happy than this poor creature."

They looked about them with curiosity. "Oh!" cried Ella. "To think that we are gazing upon our own people! Don't tell us, Mrs. Calvert, which is grandfather; Auntie, find him on the wall. What lovely pictures! what wigs and what head dresses! I always thought that we belonged to a grand family."

"I will tell you directly something about the family grandeur. Miss Burley, do you think you can find your father's portrait among them?"

The historian is naturally gratified at being able to state that Aunt Lucinda behaved exactly like Joan of Arc in a somewhat similar historical situation. She looked once round the room, and placed her hand upon a picture. "This is my father," she said, "though I remember him only as a middle-aged and elderly man."

"You are quite right. That is James Calvert Burley. His granddaughter is like him—and like all the Burleys. Theirs is a strong type, which repeats itself every generation; and now, if you will sit down, I will tell you something about your family history."

They spent an hour and more in that portrait-gallery, listening breathlessly to the story of the family grandeur. Margaret, with intention, emphasized the misfortunes that followed them all, from father to son. She said nothing about the curse which her husband's father believed to cling to the possession of the fortune. She left them to make out for themselves, if they chose, a theory on the subject. They did not choose; in fact, they did not connect the misfortunes with the money, but with the extraordinary wickedness of the men. They were like Lucian in this respect. A family curse, you see, is not a thing that can be tolerated under a democratic form of government.

They were impressed. For the first time they realized the meaning of a family. It is a dreadful loss, which we of the English-speaking race inflict upon ourselves, that we do not preserve the family history. Through the gutter, in the mire, among criminals, in degradations even, the family history ought to be followed and preserved. We should guard the records of the past; we should preserve the traditions. Ella, the American, who had never thought of the past in connection with herself, listened with rapt eyes while Margaret unfolded the history of the eighteenth century in its relations to herself.

"Oh," she cried, at last, "it is terrible! Yet—Auntie—don't you feel taller for belonging to such a family?"

"The extreme wickedness of man," sighed Aunt Lucinda, "in the effete European states is awful to contemplate. In Tewksbury there couldn't ever be such a record. The ladies wouldn't allow it."

"Come upstairs," said Margaret. "I have still something else to show you. This is the portrait-gallery of them all; and here you have heard the history of the men. Upstairs you shall see the rooms of the women—the unfortunate women—your great-grandmothers, who had to endure the consequences of the men's wickedness." She showed them the nursery, which had been left just as she found it: the wooden cradle, the bed, the cupboard, the infants' clothes, the dolls and toys. She gave them each a doll from the family treasures. "Do these things," she asked, "make you feel that you really do belong to the House? Here are the very dolls that the little girls of the family played with. It must have been before the miser's time, because he would certainly never allow such a waste of money as the purchasing of dolls."

They went downstairs again.

"Oh," cried Ella, in the hall, "how can we thank you enough?"

She held out her hand; Margaret took it and held it.

"You have no friends in England," she said; "make me, if you will, your friend. Let me call upon you. I have plenty of time on my hands, and I may, perhaps, be able to advise and help." The American girl hesitated. She was proud, and she was going to become destitute. "I believe that I know all about you," said Margaret. "You have betrayed yourself. You seem to me to want advice."

"We certainly do."

"Then—if you think you can trust me—make me your friend."

"But you must know more about us," cried Ella, persuaded into confidence. "We are desperately poor; we live in quite cheap lodgings close by; we have spent nearly all our money; we want all the advice we can get."

"I will call upon you," said Margaret, with her grave smile.

"Oh! you are so kind—and you have got such a *good* face! But you mustn't think we are grand people." Ella was very anxious on this point. "At home, Auntie has got the house we live in for her own; and I've got—that is, I had—a situation as cashier in a store, at five dollars a week. And so we got along somehow, and we were quite contented, until the papers began to ring with this fortune wanting an heir—and we've given up everything, of course, for this claim—and—and—now we begin to want advice very badly."

"I understand," said Margaret, gravely; "only, for Heaven's sake, do not build upon your claim. Do not count upon it—oh! I implore you, do not! Try to go on as if you had no claim. There will be long delays; there may be dreadful disappointments; there may be terrible surprises."

Aunt Lucinda began to tremble and to shake. It was her strange way, from time to time. "Terrible surprises?" she repeated. "Oh! what kind of surprises? Who can tell what the future may bring forth?"

"It must be ours," said Ella, lightly; "but it is kind of you to warn us. We will not think about it more than we can help. And, oh! I am so thankful and happy! For we have made a friend in this horrible, heartless place. Come some—come today—or tomorrow—come to tea with us. Auntie, dear, leave off looking so frightened, or you'll drop your grandmother's doll. I feel as if everything was fixed up now. Good-bye, Mrs. Calvert." She hesitated a little, and then threw her arms round her new friend and kissed her. "We are cousins, are we not? And you are not a claimant, and we can be friends."

"Ought I to have told them, Lucian? They do not know the truth. They have no claim, and they don't know, clearly, the horrid truth, and they look as if they would sink into the earth with shame if they did know."

"Don't tell them, dear. Do what you can for them, but don't tell them; there is no reason whatever for telling them. And they never will know. Because, you see, before the Treasury decide between the claimants, I must step forward and forbid the banns of marriage between this estate of mine which I am not to touch and any of my cousins."

XV

Hundreds of Claimants

H undreds of claimants," said the people at the Treasury.
There were hundreds. New claims were sent in every day.
The name of Burley is not one of the most common, but a good many
people rejoice in it. Everybody who answered to that name, or had a
Burley among his ancestors, made haste to send in his claim. One man
wrote that his grandmother's name was Burley, and invited the Treasury
to send him the estates; another wrote that from information received
privately he knew that, early in the century, his great-grandfather had
married a Burley—the Treasury could easily prove the fact; a lady wrote
to say that she had married a Burley, now dead, and he had always
assured her that he was of good family—the fortune could be sent to her
lodgings; another lady sent up a certificate of good character from the
vicar of the parish, and explained that her father's name was Burley—
she would call for the money on the following Monday, and would be
glad of an advance for her railway fare; solicitors by the hundred wrote
that they were instructed by their clients to forward their names as
claimants—the case would follow as soon as completed; another wrote
from his establishment in the City Road, to say that his name, which
was Burley, proved his right to the estates, and "speedy settlement of
same" would oblige; another, who had an imagination, sent up a carefully
prepared work of fiction, containing the history of his connection with
the Westminster branch, hoping that his allegations would be accepted;
another Burley, who understood more about the necessities of the case,
sent up an historical essay on the family with a genealogy, which looked
very pretty. He hoped that the weak point—the connection—would
not be too closely investigated.

And from every country of Europe, America, from India, from China,
from Australia, from every part of the known and habitable world, letters,
demands, claims, threats, entreaties, questions, began to pour in. For
we never know—nor can we know, until we die intestate, leaving large
possessions—how many cousins we have in the world. Cousins of every
remove, but mostly removed a good way, poured in. Next—for the law
of descent is but imperfectly understood, owing to the prejudice which

prevails, and the favoritism shown in the making of wills—the families and descendants of the families which intermarried with Burleys began also to send in their names and their descents.

The Burley millions became the stock subject for the paragraphist; when all other material failed, he would always invent something about them. "Sixty-five more claimants sent in their papers last Saturday; the total number is now said to be nine hundred and eighty-nine." Or, again, "It is reported on good authority that a granddaughter of the deceased gentleman has been discovered in a laundry not a hundred miles from Latimer Road Station." Or: "A surprise awaits the literary world. A well-known novelist is said to have discovered that he himself is the sole heir to the Burley estates." Or (a paragraph which was repeated in several papers): "The son of a well-known actor and grandson of another is completing the papers which are to establish his claim to the Burley estates." In certain circles men showed this to each other, and asked if it was really possible that Clary Burghley was the lucky beggar pointed at in these lines.

And then, somehow, it became known to all the papers at once that the family of Burley belonged, and had always belonged, since the creation of the parish in the year 1716, to the Church of St. John the Evangelist, in Smith Square, Westminster.

If you come to think of it, all the really interesting and remarkable things that happen in the world are sure to become known at the same moment over the whole world. By the remarkable things I mean, of course, the personal things. The superiority of the American press, for instance, is proved by its recognition of this fact and by the prominence it gives to the personal items. How comes this simultaneous knowledge of all the interesting things? No one knows. There are unseen electric wires which connect everything and all the world; it is a mark of civilization to be connected with this electric machinery. The lower forms of man are outside it. The negro, for instance, knows and cares nothing about the personal items; like the poet in the hymn, one step is enough for him—that, namely, to the nearest melon-patch.

When all the world understood that the registers of the Burley family were preserved in the vestry of St. John the Evangelist, they wrote for copies, they called for copies, they went to that remarkable church—which they then saw for the first time—and demanded copies. One of the evening papers, with more enterprise than its brethren, actually procured copies, and made a splendid coup by forming a genealogical table out of the registers of the Burley family, from one Calvert Burley, who was the first person of that name on the books.

This document, which is not without interest to the reader of this narrative, is reproduced on the following page. He will understand that a parish register cannot fill up the history of a family, though it may give with accuracy the three leading dates of birth, marriage, and departure. This genealogy, therefore, does not contain the histories of those members who were born in the parish but married and died outside it.

The papers pointed out that the John Calvert Burley born in 1836 was the first and sole heir; and, in the event of his death, his sons and daughters. But where was he? Where were they? The whole world was ringing with his name, "John Calvert Burley, born in 1836." Where was he? Nobody knew. Now, if you come to think of it, it is a very remarkable circumstance for any man to disappear so completely. Did he die young? Not, at least, in the parish. Therefore he grew up, presumably. Where were his mother's relations? Did they know? One of them wrote to the papers: he said that he was the younger brother of Emilia Weldon, who was married in 1835 to the recently deceased John Calvert Burley; that his sister had five or six children, all of whom, except the eldest, died in infancy; that she died in the year 1850; that there never had been any cordial relations between his family and his sister's husband; that after her death no pretence of friendship, or even acquaintance, was kept up; and that he could not tell what had become of the surviving son, whom he had last seen at his mother's funeral in the said year 1851, the boy being then about fifteen years of age. It was wonderful that a young man should disappear so completely. Had he no friends? His father was a miserly and morose recluse—that was evident. The boy, perhaps, had gone away. But whither—and why? Had he any school-fellows who remembered him? Two men wrote to say that they had been at school with him in the years 1844 to 1851, or thereabouts; that he was known to be the son of the notorious money-lender; that he was an ingenious boy, who made and contrived things and rejoiced in mathematics; that he left school suddenly somewhere about the latter year; and that they had never since met him or heard what became of him. Lastly, another old school-fellow wrote to say that he had met John Calvert Burley, looking prosperous, in the year 1870, in Cheapside; that he addressed him by name, shook hands with him, and made an appointment to meet him again, which the latter never kept. All this was very curious and interesting, and fired the imagination a great deal more than the Irish

Question. It was one of those subjects which invite the whole world to write about it. The whole world rose to the occasion. The letters sent to the papers were legion. For the moment there was but one topic of discussion: Where was John Calvert Burley, the younger, born in 1836, left school in 1852, and last seen in 1870?

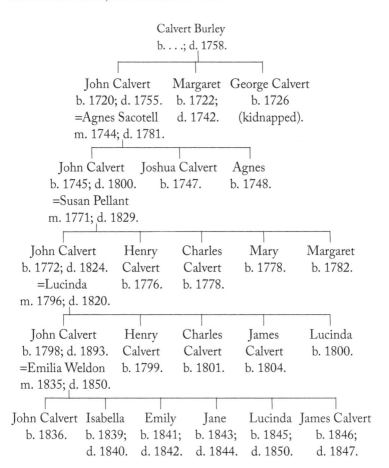

"We have only to keep silence, Lucian," said Margaret.

"Until such time as they think sufficient to prove the death of the heir has elapsed. Then, before they give the estates to any claimant, I shall step in—"

"And then?" asked his wife, anxiously.

"Then we shall see. Perhaps the occasion may not arise for years."

It is an age of great imagination. Almost as many guesses were made as there were writers. Emigration, said one. Emigration, an up-country station beyond the reach of papers; but there are no such stations left. Death in some obscure place; but, with all this racket and inquiry, some one would recollect that death. It must have been within the last twenty-three years. A lunatic asylum, under some adopted name; there was a man in Melbourne some time ago who actually forgot his own name and history. Might not John Burley be suffering somewhere from this strange disease? A prison; was he a criminal, undergoing a sentence? Or was he a criminal who had accomplished his term and was afraid to return? Or, perhaps, he might be in a monastery. But then, oh! how joyfully would the brethren seize upon the estates! Was he in one of the few places where the papers do not arrive—in Patagonia, perhaps?—or in Stanley's mighty forest, among the Pygmies?

Then began the stories of miraculous disappearance. Everybody remembered the disappearance of the Englishman in Germany about the year 1812 as he stepped from one carriage to another. And there was the disappearance of Grimaldi's brother between the last scene but one and the last scene of the pantomine.

Next: how long would the Treasury wait before they considered this last heir to be dead? And upon this point a journal of common-sense spoke words of wisdom. "We offer this advice," said the paper, "to all those who have sent in claims and have come up to London in order to look after them on the spot. It is that they leave their papers in the hands of the Treasury, and go home again and betake themselves to their ordinary pursuits, without thinking about their claims more than they can help. The chances will probably prove a disturbing element as long as they live, for only to be able to think that one has a chance of so great a property is a thing calculated to disturb the most philosophic soul. Let them, however, go home, and take up their daily task again with what calm and patience they may find."

And from Pole to Pole, unto the uttermost ends of the earth, was raised that cry, "Where is John Burley, the younger, born in the year 1836, last seen in the year 1870?" And to all their calling, no answer. Silence—as deep as the silence of the heavens; as deep as the silence of the grave! Wonderful! Was there no one—not one single living person who would remember anything at all about a man prosperous and flourishing, to outward seeming, only twenty years ago? Silence—as deep as the silence of the heavens; as deep as the silence of the grave!

XVI

The Missing Link

"Have you seen this?" Clarence held up a paper—that which published the pedigree as taken from the parish registers. "Have you seen this?"

It was about five in the afternoon when his partner, who had been out all day, returned.

"I saw it before you got up this morning. I've been all day engaged in verifying the thing."

"Well?"

"It's all right; and now it's clear that your grandfather, Clary, was the second son, Henry Calvert Burley. There he is." The poet's broad forefinger covered the name. "Second son. You couldn't be closer, unless you were actually a grandson."

"Yes—yes—the second son. Why—there!—there! Man alive! What more do you want?"

"Softly, Clarence. Let us sit down quietly and talk this thing over. We have to prove our claim. You and I know very well that there is no doubt possible. Everybody who reads our case must feel that there is no doubt possible. Yet, you see, it isn't proved."

"What on earth do you want more?"

"We want to prove, not to assert, things. I'm a lawyer, now, Clary, not a poet. Sit down, man—don't jump about so."

His eyes had that look of expectancy which belongs to an inventor or to a claimant. The look speaks of a thought which never leaves one, day or night—of hope deferred; of doubt; of rage because of the stupidity or the malignity of people.

"For God's sake, finish this job soon," said Clarence. "I don't think I can bear it much longer."

"Why, man, we've only just begun—I am afraid that it will prove a waiting job, unless you can establish the death of the son and his heirs. You can't expect the Treasury to hand over this enormous property to the first claimant, can you?"

"All I know is that the thing haunts me day and night."

"It does, my boy. Your eyes are black-edged and your forehead is wrinkled."

"Lucky it has been summer. But work will begin again soon, and—I say—the thought of work makes me shudder—I am heir to all that property, and I have to go out and be paid for singing comic songs."

"Humph! You are paid pretty well. Come, now—but about the inheritance—where's that son?"

"He must be dead. After all the fuss made about him, he would hear it at the South Pole. Oh! he must be dead."

"Very likely—most likely."

"Dead—and without heirs, or they would have turned up long since."

"Very likely—most likely; only somebody must prove it, or you will have to wait. When did he die? Where did he die? Has he left any heirs? These are the questions, you see. So we may just go back to our old work, and make new engagements, and write new songs. It's a horrid nuisance, Clary, for you are certainly the grandson of the next brother. But, so far, we haven't got evidence enough to prove the connection. And we may have to wait for years. If the son and his heirs were out of the way I should begin"—he became a poet again—

> *"Begin to hear the rustling of the notes—*
> *Oh! crisp and soft and sweet upon the ear!*
> *No softer, sweeter music rolls and floats—*
> *And none, my brother, rarer and more dear.*

And I should begin to hear the footsteps," he added, going back to prose—"the footsteps of those who humbly bring pieces of silver—I don't think there is any rhyme to silver. Meantime, old man, it is going to be a long job. Therefore," he laid a friendly hand upon Clarence's shoulder, "don't think too much about it. Go back to your old thoughts. Let us get to real business. My new songs are nearly ready, and I've got a capital little entertainment for you—"

"I can't—" The young man turned away impatiently. "I am sick and ashamed of it."

"Nonsense. If it's all you've got to live upon—"

"I can't. It's all so small. What's a thousand a year, or two thousand? It's such a trifle compared with this immense mountain of money. It's the comparison. See, I work as hard as I can—five engagements a week, say, for half the year. What is it compared with the income of that fortune—four hundred thousand a year, a thousand pounds a day? Think of it that way."

"Well, Clary, I can't think of it that way. The figures are too big—my limitations as regards money are narrow. They allow me with difficulty to include a thousand a year. But, Clary, you were not wont to do sums in long division to please yourself. Doing sums isn't in your blood, I should say."

"No, it isn't," Clarence replied, slowly. "Show-folk don't, as a rule, care for money. You see, it's easily made and easily spent. They live from week to week. But, now—do you know what it is to think and crave and yearn for drink?"

"Rumor, report—has reached me concerning a thirst insatiable. What says the old song?—'We cannot drink an hour too soon—nor drink a cup too much.'"

"Well, with that same craving I yearn for this money. It is my great-grandfather, the Westminster miser, coming out again in me. I dream of it; I feel as if I shall have no rest or peace until I have got it."

"No heroics, Clary. You mean it?"

"I mean it all; I am like that drunkard with the craving in his throat. I want this inheritance; all of it. Oh! it is so close to me, and yet I cannot lay my hand upon it."

"After all, what could you do with it, if you had it? The thing is far too big for anyone man to handle."

"Too big?" Clarence turned upon him fiercely. "What could I do with it? Your limitations are indeed narrow. Well, you haven't thought of it so much as I have. What could I *not* do with it? First of all, I would have my own theatre for my friends. There we should act our own pieces with a free hand as to subjects. We shouldn't have it open all the year, but one may sink a good deal in a theatre properly conducted. Then I should want my own newspaper. I know exactly what I should want: no politics; no money markets; no beastly reviews; nothing but Art and Literature and Music, and things artistic and æsthetic, and, again, a free hand as to subjects. Then there must be a yacht. If one must go out of town some time in the year, a cruise in a yacht is the best way. Of course, there would be a town house, and open house; no beastly charity or philanthropy or stuff; no pretending to care about anybody else; pure selfishness; that's what I want, my friend. All the people about me shall be hired to make our lives—my life—run smoothly. I shall be an Eastern king, with art and culture added. You shall see; I will show you, as soon as the business is settled, how a rich man ought to live!"

"You'd get rather fat in the cheeks after a bit, wouldn't you? and a little puffy in the neck. Philanthropy is humbug, and man's brotherhood is rot"—he dropped, as usual, into verse—"and my only pal, my only friend, is Me. Rather a good tag, the last line. Don't you think—" He stopped and made a note.

"Well, Jemmy, there's my plan of life in the rough. I am only afraid that it may prove too costly, even for my large fortune."

"Meantime, Clary, it will be better for you if you descend to facts and consider how we stand."

"There is nothing new, is there?"

"This: We are now in August. Work begins in September, and you are not fit for work—and you've got to make yourself fit, Clary—you've got to mend." The poet spoke like the master rather than the partner. But there are some occasions when mastery in speech is useful.

"Well?"

"As for the case, I tell you that it will be years, perhaps, before it is decided; and if it were decided now, your case could not be proved. Come out of your dreams, man. Shake yourself; face the facts."

Clarence shook himself, but he did not face the facts.

"Consider," his partner went on, "the attitude of the Treasury. They say there is a man named Henry Calvert Burghley, an actor. Where is the proof that this Henry Calvert Burghley was originally Henry Calvert, the second son of Burley the miser? Where is it? That's what they say."

Clarence made no answer.

"We want proof that the boy who ran away became an actor. We want to know when he changed his name; in fact, we want to recover the early history of an obscure country actor—and we have as much hope of finding it as we have of any name taken at random from a London cemetery."

"We have a letter."

"Yes; that is something. It is signed 'Your affectionate brother, Charles.' And it comes from Westminster. Well, there was a younger brother, Charles, as well as a second brother, Henry. But there is nothing to prove that the letter was written by this younger brother to the elder brother. If we had other letters to prove the handwriting— but we haven't. No, Clary, our best chance is delay. Time may give us something. Let us see," he went on, after a pause. "He ran away; he had very little money; he joined a strolling company; he began at the very bottom of the ladder, and worked his way up. Men very seldom talk of the first start. The lessee of the York Theatre, the favorite London actor, wouldn't talk much about the early days. It must be eighty years ago. How on earth are we to trace the beginnings of a lad who ran away from home eighty years ago? And he never talked about his people, and you never inquired. I suppose you were satisfied with having a grandfather. To be third in a succession of frockcoats and top-hats is enough to make anybody a gentleman. And, besides, when your grandfather had arrived at his pinnacle, he wouldn't be proud of the Burley brother—Burley the Money-Lender; Burley the owner of the Dancing-Crib; Burley of the Gambling-Hell; not a character likely to attract the light comedian—the squanderer—the Père Prodigue. We can understand the situation, but it's unfortunate. What are we to do?"

Clarence shook his shoulders.

"Perhaps the Treasury have got papers that prove the connection. Hang it! A single letter would do."

Clarence got up and leaned on the mantel-shelf, gazing into the empty fireplace.

"I remember," he said, speaking slowly, "a little play that my grandfather cribbed from the French. It was a comedy, in which he played the principal part. That was easy, because it was himself. In it he did everything, without the least reference to morality, that would help him to what he wanted. He sold secrets, he forged signatures, he opened private letters; and all with such a delightful simplicity that nobody blamed him. I have often wondered, if the chance came, whether one could rise to that level?"

"Speaking as a lawyer, Clary, I should say that it was dangerous. As a poet, I think the situation capable of treatment. Have you got any portraits of your grandfather?"

"In character?"

"In character. That might be something. If we could get hold of an early portrait and could find some old friend—but that is impossible, I fear—or if we could find any other descendants, or if we could advertise for anyone who might remember him as a young man—Wanted: a Methusaleh!" He stopped. "Well, Clary, dear boy, that's where we are. It is not encouraging, but one need not despair. Meanwhile, it may be years before the claimants are even considered. We've got to work and live. Get the Joyous Life out of your head. Don't dream any more—for the present, at least—about the golden possibilities. Forget them—and set to work again. You must."

"I can't forget them," groaned the Heir Expectant.

"Well, unless I am to starve—which afflicts me much more than the certainty of seeing you starve as well—you will just sit down, get rid of that hangdog face of yours, which would damn the funniest song ever made, and get something like sunshine in your face—and try this new song of mine:

> *"Wanted, a Methusaleh! To tell us how they kept it up—*
> *Our fathers in the by-gones when they made the guineas spin;*
> *How they wasted time and drank it up,*
> *and anything but slept it up—*
> *And always ere the old love died a new love would begin."*

XVII

The Beginning of the Cloud

Does anyone ever remember the first beginning of an evil thing? Does anyone remember the first observation of the dark spot which grows darker, broader, deeper, till it covers over and hides the summer sky and darkens the summer sun?

The young married pair of Great College Street were much alone; they had few friends in London; they led the most quiet and regular life possible. In the morning the husband went to the hospital; in the afternoon he worked in his study, ready for the patient who did not come. In the morning the young wife looked after her home, walked in the park or about the quiet courts of the Abbey; in the evening, after dinner, she sat in the study while her husband carried on his work till half-past ten or so, when he turned his chair round, filled his pipe, and they talked till midnight.

There was nothing to disturb the happiness of this honeymoon prolonged, unless it was that strange dream of the mourning mothers, which came back to Margaret continually—in the night, in the daytime—a vision unbidden, that would suddenly float before her eyes—the company of sad-eyed, pale-faced, sorrow-stricken women, who held out hands and cried, "She is one with us—she is one of us!" It was a persistent dream—perhaps the very strangeness of it caused Margaret to return to it again and again. How could she belong to these hapless ladies when they were separated by Lucian's change of name and his refusal to claim the great inheritance? The dream troubled her, but not much, though it persistently remained with her.

How long was it?—a week?—a month?—after they went into their house that the anxiety began? When was it that the young wife, reading her husband's thoughts, saw in his mind doubt and disturbance; heard a temptation continually whispered; saw an ear ever readier to listen? The discovery of the temptation—the knowledge that he was listening—filled her soul with dismay. In the afternoon, when he should have been at work, she heard him pacing the narrow limits of his study. Like most young scientific men, he wrote for medical papers and scientific magazines; he reviewed scientific books; he wrote papers on such of his subjects as could be made popular in the weekly reviews; and he had a book of his own on the stocks, a work by which he hoped to gain a place as a specialist; an advanced book with all the recent medical lights; a work psychological, biological, and everything else that was new and true and uncomfortable. He read a great deal in the medical journals of Germany, France, and Italy; in short, he was without any practice except that in his hospital. Lucian Calvert led a very busy life, and, like most men who are fully occupied, he was a perfectly cheerful creature. The maiden expectant of a lover should pray, above all things, that he may turn out to be a man with an active brain, and belonging to an intellectual profession, for of such is the kingdom of cheerfulness. Margaret loved to see him absorbed in thought; she sat perfectly still so long as he was working, contented to wait till he should turn his chair, take his pipe, and say, "Now, Madge!"

But when Lucian was walking up and down the floor of his study he was not working. He was disturbed in his mind; his thoughts were diverted. By what? At dinner, at breakfast, when they took their walks abroad, he would become distrait, silent, thoughtful—he who had been able to convert even a stalled ox into a feast of contentment and cheerfulness. Why?

In his study, after dinner, his wife saw that he sat with his eyes gazing into space and his pen lying idle. What was he thinking of?

Alas! She knew. Women who love are all thought-readers. She saw, I say, that before his eyes there was floating continually the temptation that she feared. Her heart grew sick within her—more sick and sorry day by day—as she saw that the strength of the temptation was daily growing. And the light died out in his eyes and the ready smile left his lips, and Lucian, while he listened to the voice of the Tempter, was transformed and became as black-avised and as dour and as resolute of aspect as his ancestor, the first great Calvert Burley.

One night when he turned his chair and mechanically took his pipe, she spoke. "Where have your thoughts been all this evening, Lucian? You have done no work, unless, perhaps, you were devising some. Your gaze has been fixed."

"I have been upstairs," he replied, with a little laugh. "I have been among the grandfathers and the grandmothers."

"Is it good to live among them, Lucian? Does it make you taller or stronger to live among these poor people? They crept and crawled through life, did they not? But you—oh! Lucian—you walk erect."

"I go among them sometimes—" he began.

"Sometimes? You were among them this afternoon, and at dinner, and all the evening. And yesterday the same. I begin to think, Lucian, that we made a dreadful mistake when we came to this house."

"It is not exactly a house which preaches contentment to the disinherited, is it?"

"If we cannot get contentment, dear Lucian, for Heaven's sake let us go elsewhere and leave these memories behind. My dear, what will our life become if we are not contented?"

"Do not fear, Marjorie"—he roused himself with an effort and laughed—"I only pay occasional visits to the portraits. The family, as you say, did mostly creep and crawl. They have had their divagations; they have trodden the Primrose Way; still, they are our ancestors—and perhaps a little show of respect occasionally—from time to time—not often, you know—may be considered due to them. They are all the ancestors I am likely to get, you know."

Margaret shrank back, chilled. She was afraid of saying more.

Again—it was Sunday afternoon. They took their early dinner in cheerfulness—the disinheritance for the time forgotten—and they repaired—young husbands, even scientific husbands, frequently accede to their wives' wishes in small matters—to the Abbey for afternoon service. During the sermon, which was not perfectly audible in every part of the Cathedral, Lucian occupied himself in turning over the pages of his wife's Bible. The world, perhaps in prejudice, does not generally look upon young physicians as zealous students of the Bible, and Margaret observed Lucian's curiosity with some wonder. For her own part, though she did not hear one word of the sermon, it was quite enough to sit in the old Cathedral, to look up into the lofty roof, to gaze upon the marvellous window of the transept, and to breathe the air of the venerable place, which is always full of consolation to those who can open out their souls and receive its influence.

After service they walked in the park close by: in the south part of it, which is the less frequented. They walked in silence for a while. Lucian was a man of long silences at all times. It was by his face that he showed whither his thoughts led him.

"About that hereditary theory," he began. "There is heredity in disease; there is heredity in health. Drunkenness is sometimes inherited; it is, perhaps, a nervous disease, like asthma and the rest of the tribe. Any man can vitiate his blood, and can transmit that vitiation to following generations. In this sense there is constantly with all of us hereditary disease, because none of us are perfectly strong and healthy."

"Go on, Lucian."

"Yes. But you say, Margaret, that a mental twist, such as makes a man a miser or a money-lender, is the child of one mental twist or the father of another."

"I think that the sins of the fathers are visited upon the children for the third and fourth generation. And in your people, Lucian, the sins of the fathers have been followed by the sins of the sons, so that every generation has suffered for its predecessor and brought more suffering upon its successor."

"That is your view. Yes, my father—very oddly, because he was not a superstitious man—thought much the same thing."

"Why should not a man's sins be punished in his children as well as his diseases?"

"I don't know why they should not. The other question is, why they should?"

"Oh, Lucian! Because—but you do not think as I do."

"Perhaps not. I will refer you, however, to an authority which you respect. While you were pretending to listen—pretty hypocrite!—to what you could not hear, I occupied myself profitably in looking up a rather important statement of the case from another point of view. I had seen it quoted, and I knew where to look. It is a passage in the works of the Prophet Ezekiel. Says the Prophet—or words to this effect—'There is a common proverb that the fathers have eaten sour grapes and the teeth of the children are in consequence set on edge. It is a foolish proverb, because every man has got to live out his own honor or his own dishonor.' Read the passage, my child. It is put so plainly that it is impossible to misunderstand it. Nay, he is so much in earnest about it—Joshua Ben Jochanan, the great money-lender, having recently died, and his children being taunted with the proverb—that he returns to the subject again and repeats his arguments. I am very glad I went to church with you this afternoon. Will you read this Prophet and discard these superstitions?"

"He meant something else, I suppose. But, Lucian, how can you say that the children do not suffer for their father's sins?"

"Physically they often do."

"But if a man disgraces himself and loses caste or falls into poverty, his children sink into a lower place; they cannot get up again out of their poverty or their shame; they are kept down for life; their children have got to begin all over again. Oh! It is so clear that it cannot be doubted or denied."

"In social matters, and in the middle class, I dare say. Most middle-class people hang on to their social position, such as it may be, with their own hands and with no help from cousins. When they fall their fall is complete. In the case of people well connected, with some generations of affluence behind them, and with cousins all over the country, when a man comes to grief it may be grievous for his children, but it does not necessarily mean a lower level. Why, the simple annals of the aristocracy are full of the most tremendous croppers taken by the fathers, and the sons are never a whit the worse."

Margaret shook her head.

"In the case of my people, now, their misfortunes were always due to their own folly or their crimes."

"Lucian, dear, do not talk any more about it. Those who inherited that dreadful estate endured things that went with it. I have studied the faces of the mothers, and I read upon them all the martyrdom they suffered."

"You are a superstitious woman, Madge," said her husband.

He returned to the subject the next evening.

"About your view, dear—about the forefathers—you know?"

"Oh! don't think about them so much."

"There is something to be said in favor of it, so far as the mental twist can be gathered. Take the first of them—Grandfather Calvert the First, the original Burley—what do we know about him? A tradition mentioned in my father's memorandum that he acquired money by dishonest practices. Perhaps he did. At the same time, remember that we know nothing certain about him. There is no proof. For all we know, he may have been the most upright man in the world. Then there is that unlucky Shepherd who was suspended; he paid for his own diversions; when he had paid, nothing more was owing. His son went mad. So did a good many other poor wretches. Religious mad, he went. So did Cowper, the poet. But Cowper, so far as I know, never laid the blame on his grandfather. A tendency to some unsoundness of mind—some inability to recognize the true proportions of things—may be observed, perhaps, in all of them. There was, for example, the miser. It isn't absolutely disgraceful to be a miser—most people who save money have to be miserly—but it denotes their inability to understand the relative proportions of things. I can discern no signs of your famous curse in the cheese-paring life of Great-Grandfather Miser, but I do discern an unbalanced mind. Then comes his son, the money-lender and money-grubber. He did not grub for money in quite a noble way—so much must be confessed. But he was not a criminal, nor was he disgraced—"

"Not disgraced? Oh, Lucian!"

"Not disgraced by the world. And he lived to a great age, amassing money all the time. It is an unbalanced mind which puts money in the front. As for other things, we might parade them all, except one, as quite a respectable set of ancestors, and manifestly blessed by Providence, which made them rich on account of their many virtues."

"Those were singular blessings indeed, which fell upon your grandfather's brothers."

"Who, remember, had none of the inheritance, my dear."

Thus he talked, returning to the subject perpetually, as a moth flies round a candle until it falls at last into the flame.

This was the cloud that Margaret watched as it spread around the horizon, and grew day by day deeper and broader and blacker, till it covered all the summer sky and blotted out the summer sun.

XVIII

THE BOX OF ACCOUNT-BOOKS

One morning Margaret sat again in the nursery at the top of the house. The visitation of the mothers was not repeated. She sat on the bed and remembered the faintness, and then, when she opened her eyes, the company of sorrowful women gathered round her bed. She recalled this company often. The recollection of their faces came to her at odd times, by day and by night; but in this room they came no more. She had received, night; but in this room they came no more. She had received, as in a vision, their welcome and their pity once for all.

Sometimes she saw, in fancy, the same look of welcome and pity in the sorrowful eyes of the portraits. Was there really any look at all of sorrow in those faces? Had the limner caught the characteristic look, the habitual expression, which the daily life casts upon a face? Had he been inspired to foretell, by the expression of the eyes, the sadness of the future? I know not. They were stiff and conventional paintings, of little merit; a mechanical likeness was all that the artist desired to produce—he wanted people to say—they still say it at every Royal Academy—"How like! How exactly like it is!" Whether, therefore, the unknown painters who executed these works of art, between the years 1720 and 1830 or thereabouts, had put into the faces all that Margaret saw, I know not.

The morning was fine; the sun streamed through the windows, now clean, upon the floor, now swept. No other change had been made in the room; the cradle and the chest of drawers, the chairs and the bedstead, were all as they had been handed over. When the burden of her anxiety became almost more than she could bear, Margaret came up here in the morning, to find consolation in the room of the little children. "While they played here," she thought, "there was a time of hope and happiness. When they left the nursery and went forth into the world, then began again the punishment of the father's sin." For, you see, despite that chapter in the book of the Prophet Ezekiel, this superstitious person could never shake off the conviction that, from father to son, he who possessed the wealth first gotten by Calvert Burley received with it something that poisoned his whole life. And now she saw her husband daily assailed with the temptation that bade him take his own, and enjoy whatsoever his soul desired.

A morbid habit—to sit here among the rags and tatters of the past. Better, perhaps, had she put on her hat and sallied forth into the streets and the crossways. In Westminster, however, there are no streets to walk in. There are squalid old streets and ugly new streets. The absence of streets for walking is more than made up by the solitudes and places for meditation which abound in this old city. For instance, there are Dean's Yard, the Cloisters, the Abbey itself; there is the quiet and secluded Close, or *Place,* or Retreat, called Cowley Street; there is the south side of St. James's Park; there are, however, no streets. There is no Bond Street, no Regent Street, no Cheapside, no Thames Street. Abingdon Street, formerly Dirty Lane, presents few attractions; nor does Victoria Street. Better, perhaps, to meditate in the Cloisters than to sit on the old bed among the baby-clothes and broken toys.

Again, some young wives make work for themselves; they love housewifery; they enjoy directing and arranging and managing; they embroider and sew, and make things lovely for the house; they pay many calls; they read and study diligently; they write novels; they go out and look at the shops; they practise music; they lie down and bask by the fire. Margaret, in ordinary times, did all these things; she was possessed of many accomplishments. Now, so great was the fear that possessed her, she could do nothing; she was fain to climb up to this old dismantled nursery, with the remnants and remains and relics of the past about her, and to think of the mothers and the children.

We cannot get rid of our forefathers; she understood so much. We cannot shake them off even if we would; it is impossible to sever the past; the chain cannot be cut. The forefathers still live; they still try to make us act as they themselves would have acted; they work upon us by the temper and the disposition, the inclinations and the limitations, the quick or the sluggish brain, the courage or the cowardice, the quick sight or the short sight, which we have inherited from them. These are the forces of the past acting in the present. Thus are all the ages one long, unbroken chain. Whither would Lucian's ancestors lead him?

She opened the drawers where lay the children's clothes. She took them out and unfolded them. Heavens! How beautiful they were, with their delicate embroideries and the patient, skilful, fine work! For whom were they made? For the baby destined for Tyburn tree? For the baby destined for madness? For the baby who was to be the Westminster miser? For the baby who was to become the money-lender? Sweet children—innocent children once—all of them. And now these baby-clothes belonged to her—to her—and this nursery was hers. She laid back the things with a deep sigh. Her eyes fell upon the half-opened door of the cupboard, and she remembered that she had never examined the contents of the cupboard completely. In front there stood a box with half a lid, filled with the broken dolls and toys which she had seen on her first visit. In other houses this rubbish would have been swept away long ago. In this house nothing was ever destroyed or given away or swept away. To a miser even a child's doll with a broken leg means the equivalent of something in money.

She opened the door and looked in. The cupboard was a big place formed by the sloping roof and a party-wall; such a place as, in many houses, is set apart for a box-room. Behind the door were hanging three or four women's dresses of cheap material, but moth-eaten. Margaret took them down. There was no use in keeping them. Behind the box of dolls there was a heavy box, which she dragged out with some difficulty; it was not locked, and it contained boys' school-books. There was another box of school-books; there was a box containing clothes of some kinds; there was a bundle of clothes tied up. There were other bundles and boxes; lastly, when Margaret thought she had turned out the whole contents of the cupboard as a railway porter clears out a luggage-van, she saw by the dim light at the lower end of the cupboard a smaller box covered with a lid. It was quite light to lift; she took it out, placed it on the bed, and lifted the lid, which was not locked. Within the box was a heap of old papers, with a few parchment-covered books, which were household account-books. All the papers in the house had been collected and taken over by the Solicitor of the Treasury, but this cupboard had either been overlooked or had been imperfectly searched. Probably it had been overlooked altogether, because the dust lay thick on everything. Moreover, as the school-books showed, and these account-books presently proved, the cupboard had not been touched for more than seventy years. The miser, who could not bring himself to destroy anything, put away these things when his children had run away from home and when his wife was dead. Then he left the garret and the cupboard and shut the door—and so it had remained shut for seventy years and more, until Lucian opened the door and Margaret entered.

She sat down on the bed and began to examine the contents of the box with a languid curiosity.

She first took up a household account-book, dated 1817. It contained a kind of occasional diary—not day to day, but as things happened—together with the current expenditure. These details are dry reading, except to one who tries to revive the bygone life; to him there is not an entry of any kind which is not full of suggestion and meaning. This young house-keeper was at first struck with the extraordinary cheapness of living when the expenditure is ruled by a miser. In the marginal notes, recording events of the day, the boys gave trouble. They spoke rebelliously of their father. John, the eldest, was employed in keeping his father's books. Apparently he was in his father's confidence, for he was asked to plead for the others. Henry, especially, was a cause of anxiety. He spoke mutinous words as regards the food; he called it fit for pigs; he wanted money to spend as other young men could do; he wanted new and better clothes, such as other young men are allowed to wear; he wanted to be put into some profession; he wanted to enter the army; he was always wanting something that would cost money; his father always refused; the mother interceded, and was repulsed; John was asked to do what he could, and said he could do nothing, because what Henry wanted would cost money. Then came the significant words: "Henry ran away from home in the night. God help the boy! His father only said there was one mouth the less." The house went on meanwhile; whether she was bereft of her children or not, the wife must keep the house going, and the expenses grew daily less and less, or the miser grew more miserly. There were notes about the other boys. "James must have new school-books. He cannot get the money from his father; nor can I; nor can John. He says he shall do as Henry did." "Lucinda crying over her old frock." "Charles refused, today, even the outward forms of respect to his father—a sad scene!" "Letter from Harry. He has become an actor. I cannot approve it; but his father drove him away."

The entries showed a household managed by farthings. They revealed the unhappiness of the family; the hard father, growing narrower and harder; the brothers kept without pocket-money, dressed shabbily, debarred even the common and innocent pleasures of their age; the daughter grown out of her shabby frock; the mother striving to mitigate the unhappy lot of her children; and the eldest brother keeping his father's books, learning how rich he was, resolving to become the owner and disposer of so much wealth, and learning from his father those lessons of pitiless hardness which he was afterwards to practise with such eminent success on his own account. As Margaret read in the book, she realized it all; the past returned. In the quiet house she could hear the crying of the girl over her frock, and the voice of the mother trying to soothe and to console, and the growling of the miser over his pence like the growling of a tiger over her bone.

She shut up the book with a sigh. She belonged to these people; they were her people; whither her husband should go she must go; where he should lodge she must lodge; his people must be her people. And, as Lucian continually repeated, a man may call himself whatever he pleases, but his ancestors remain to him; he cannot shake them off; he belongs to them, and they to him. Wherefore we do well to envy those of honorable descent; and for this reason we should go cautiously lest we pollute the fountain of Heaven, and make the water which our children must drink a spring of shame. All these things, and more, crowded into Margaret's mind. And because it was the nursery, the room of the dead mothers, if she suffered her mind to wander, she heard whispers in the air—murmuring, singing, admonishing: "You belong to us, you and yours; you cannot separate yourself, or your children that may come, from us. Your children will be ours. You pretend not to belong to us; yet you think about us day and night; you are one of us and one with us."

XIX

CALVERY BURLEY'S ACCOUNT OF THE MATTER

Margaret carried her box of household books downstairs, and resumed her study of a household carried on under the eye of a miser a hundred years ago; but Lucian refused to be interested. He said that the figures had a hungry and starveling look, and that he was not desirous of learning more details about his great-grandfather. Margaret, however, read and pondered over these books until she realized not only the pinched and starved existence of the mother bereft of her children, one after the other, but also the daily life of the eighteenth century, which stretched without change into a third part of the nineteenth, until railways and steamboats altered the whole of the habitable globe. Can we understand a time so close to us, yet so far away? Consider. Everything was done at home; everything was made at home. There is an enormous difference, to begin with. The bread, the beer, the jam, the wine, the biscuits, the cakes, the preserving, the strong waters—all were made at home; the washing, the mending, and repairing were done at home. A housewife, then, was mistress of a learned profession; she followed one of the fine arts.

What is the chief difference, however, between our daily life and that of our grandfathers? There are small differences in manners, deportment, social forms, dress, eating, and drinking. There is a difference in the standard of living, which is now greatly raised. There is a difference in our knowledge of the world, there are differences due to our habit of reading. We have grown so much richer, and the things that make for comfort have become so much cheaper, that this is natural. We are now all growing poorer, but the higher standard of comfort as yet remains. There are differences in our religion; there are differences in our morals; there are differences in our ideas on things of state. But these things do not constitute the principal difference. That, I think, lies in the altered value of all possessions.

This was Margaret's discovery from the account-books and the marginal notes. We of this degenerate age make nothing; therefore we value nothing. We have no possessions; the things that we want we buy;

they are machine-made things, mostly. Who cares for a machine-made watch? When we had to make what we wanted to have, or to buy it, with money laboriously accumulated, of the man who made it with his own hands—a watch, a chain, a table, a fender—then we valued it and treated it tenderly, and handed it down to our successors, and called it a possession. I once read in a novel—I was compelled to read it because I had to write it—of a girl named Francesca, who had a magic knob given her by a fairy godmother. This she pressed whenever she wanted anything—and, lo! a miracle!—what she wanted was instantly brought.

All of us possess a magic knob of sorts; but its powers vary to an incredible extent. A pauper lady, for instance, may press her knob as hard as she likes; it commands nothing but the daily allowance and the annual shawl. Others, on the other hand, are amazingly powerful. And I hope that every young lady who reads these lines owns a magic knob, the pressure of which will bring her a new evening dress, new gloves, new shoes, or anything that she wants. The magic knob applied to the whole of the middle class, to which most of us belong, the class beloved and admired by Matthew Arnold—can command a glass of beer, a pot of jam, a loaf of bread, and many other useful articles. These things come to us ready-made, turned out to order by unseen work-people. We take them, pay for them, and give no heed to them. When they wear out we buy more. Now, in the eighteenth century all these things were made at home; there was a certain uncertainty as to the result. Would the beer be good? Last brew was sour, if you remember. Would the jam last through the winter? Last year's developed mildew, if you remember. Would the socks, the shirt, the collar, fit? If the result was satisfactory, there was pride. In any case, the thing which cost time, exercised judgment, showed skill, was valuable and valued. This dignified housewifery. The modern matron need know nothing, need keep nothing, need lay down nothing; she wants neither wine-cellar, nor beer-cellar, nor larder, nor stillroom, nor stores. She buys as she wants, and replaces as she uses. It saves trouble, which is a gain; but there are losses.

Her predecessor, Margaret learned, provided beforehand. If anything was omitted, the household had to go without. The amount of knowledge expected of the ancient housewife was colossal. One can only compare it with the knowledge at present expected of the oilman and his assistant. She was expected to know how to make cakes, puddings, biscuits, and to understand carving; not the miserable hacking of the present day, but scientific carving, which had its language. She must know pickling and conserving, in an age when they pickled everything, even nasturtium leaves. She must know how to distil scents and strong waters. She could make wine and brew beer. She could make washes for the complexion. She must know all the secrets of the laundry, the larder, the poultry-yard, the dairy, the kitchen-garden, the orchard, the hot-houses; the making and repairing of dresses—childish and feminine; she had to understand music, dancing, embroidery, genealogies, education, alms-giving, medicine, domestic surgery, and nursing. Finally, the housewife of the past was expected to take, or to pretend, an intelligent interest in her husband's occupations. Truly, the housewife of a hundred years ago was a most wonderful product of the age.

Margaret laid down the books with a profound respect and pity for the writer who knew so much, worked so hard, and was so wretchedly mated. The diurnal broke off abruptly on a certain day. It was then carried on by another hand, a younger hand, for a short time. Then that too broke off. The reason of the change, Margaret guessed, was the illness and death of the mother. The second hand must be that of the daughter, Lucinda. And she, like her brothers, had run away. What had become of Lucinda? Lucian's father knew nothing about her. What, again, was the end of that brother who became an actor? What had become of Charles, the third son of this remarkable family, who incurred the displeasure of the law? Of James she had, we know, been recently reminded. But of the other three no word had yet been received. Had all three perished without leaving children or a single trace of their memory?

There were other papers in the box. You would expect, perhaps, in such a house, a bag of guineas, or the directions where to find a secret hoard. You remember how the miser of old hid away his gold in odd corners. But the Westminster miser was a modern miser. Hoarded gold, to him, meant investments. The old miser gloated over his chests full of red gold, chests of wood with iron clamps; he used to lift the lid and run his fingers lovingly through the coins. The modern miser pulls out the book in which are recorded his investments; and he gloats over the columns. Margaret found no secret hoard of gold, nor any allusion to hidden gold. What she did find, however, was sufficiently interesting, as you shall learn.

There were, to begin with, certain letters, written to the miser's wife; some from her own mother, stiff and formal, exhorting her what to do in time of trouble; some from a friend who wrote to her from the country on religious topics—it was a time when religious conversation was an art greatly practised and carefully studied. This friend gave her advice of a most beautiful kind as regards patience under trial; some of the letters were from her brother; these letters also turned upon the necessity of resignation in trial and trouble. All proved that the poor woman lived in constant trial and trouble. All were the work of people to whom letter-writing was not a thing of daily use; they were written on paper of the same size, filled up carefully, so as to show a genuine desire of communicating as much news as the limits of the paper allowed, and of spending as long a time as possible over the composition of the letter. The correspondence was not, in fact, remarkable, except as an evidence of the style and fashion of the letter-writer at that period—the style stilted and formal; the fashion ceremonious. There was one letter, however, which interested her. It was from the second son, Henry, the one who began the running away.

DEAR AND HON'D MOTHER (it ran),

I write to inform you that I have been receiv'd in a Company of Strolling Players. We play in a Barn tonight—my Part, Mercutio, and some others. The Work is Hard and the Pay is Uncertain. I hope, however, to Advance both in one and the other. No Efforts of mine shall be wanting for Success, which, as has been written, if I cannot Achieve, I will at Least Deserve. On the play-bill I am described as Mr. Henry Burghley. I have not presum'd to drag my Father's Name—and My Own—upon the Stage with a Strolling Company. I do not Regret the Step I have taken, except that I would not give my Mother Pain. The miserly Habits of my Father made it Impossible for a lad of Spirit to remain in the House any Longer. I hope that your tedious Cough is better, and that you can now mount the Stairs without Distress, and that you will continue in good Health and Spirits, and that when I see you next I may receive your Approbation of my Conduct.

I remain, dear and Hon'd Mother,
Your most dutiful and affectionate Son,
HENRY

This was the only communication from any of her children.

The rest of the papers seemed to be recipes of all kinds, chiefly for puddings and highly seasoned sauces which this housewife would never be allowed to use, as being expensive. There were also written charms against warts, against quinsy, against fits—pity that most of the old charms have perished hopelessly. Against how many mischiefs could not a housewife formerly protect her house, her children, and herself? And there were notes on the treatment of children's disorders, and especially as to chilblains, colds, earaches, feverish chills, and the like.

At the bottom of the box, however, she found a small packet of papers folded up and tied with a silk ribbon. Outside was a note written in a handwriting difficult at first to read; for not only was it small, but the letters were pointed instead of being round, and the "e's" were like "o's" with a loop at the top. It ran thus:

> "The enclosed was writ by my grandfather, Calvert Burley, in the year of grace 1756, being twelve months after the melancholy event which deprived him of a son and me of a father, in the most lamentable manner possible. I found it among his papers on the 9th day of March, in the present year of our Lord, 1768. The wrath of the Lord is as a consuming fire, from which nothing can escape; it wastes not, nor is it spent until its work of woe is completed to the last letter. On account of the transgressions of my grandfather follow all these woes. Therefore my father suffered a shameful death: for this cause my father's sister was cut off in the flower of her beauty, and my father's brother was kidnapped or destroyed. What is reserved for me? I am in the Lord's hands. Let the Lord deal with me for that transgression as He will upon this earth. The things that happen to us here soon pass away and are forgotten; but let me save my soul alive, according to the promise made unto the Prophet Ezekiel.
>
> J. C. B.
>
> Nota Bene
> My grandfather died impenitent. He said that he had sinned, as all flesh must sin, but not more than other men.

WALTER BESANT

He also, with his latest breath, solemnly thanked the Lord
for the gifts which had made him rich—God is not mocked.

J. C. B.

Having made out this cheerful preface, Margaret, with some curiosity, opened the packet and read. The handwriting was large and bold, and as assured as the words which followed. Handwriting is supposed, by some, to be a test of character; this, in some unexplained way, it seems to be—perhaps because the way in which a man speaks, stands, walks, writes, looks, or does anything at all, betrays his character to those who can read the language of gesture and look. If the theory is true, then Calvert Burley was a man with a huge, an enormous, belief in himself. Such a man—he is more common than one would think—can do nothing wrong. If his actions appear to others always dictated by self-interest, to him they are never without the excuse of the highest and holiest of motives. The meanest thing that a man can do is described by him as the holy act of a Christian. The greatest crime he explains by the noblest and most conscientious scruples.

The document was written on coarse white paper, and the ink was brown. It ran thus:

"I have been assured by some Meddlers and Busybodies that God's Wrath has been Poured out upon me on account of certain former Passages in my Life. I have endured Reproach on this Account, by men pretending to be Godly, and also from my Deceased Wife, whose tender Spirit was unable to endure the Disasters which have affected us. In them she saw Manifest the Revenge taken by the Almighty on account of my past Life. I say not that these repeated shocks were not Ordered by a Wise Providence for Purposes which I cannot Understand, but as my Life has always been beyond Reproach, I cannot regard them as Expressions of God's Wrath. Therefore my Design is to lay bare, for the Instruction of all who may come after Me, the Facts of the Case on which my Departed Wife and others have ignorantly pronounced a Judgement. But let me Rehearse these so-called Judgements; and, next, let me also set against them the Manifest Mercies and Blessings which have been Poured upon my unworthy Head. And first as for the Judgements.

It is true that I who had once three Fair Children, have now none. First my younger Boy, a child of Twelve, went out to School—the said School lying no more than two Streets distance—and never reached that School, and was never seen again by us. He was therefore tempted away and either Kidnapped or Murdered. This was, I own, a Dreadful Blow. But it was shown, I am quite certain, that this affliction was not a Special Judgement, nor did it indicate the Special Displeasure of the Lord, over and above that which falls upon the general sinner, because at the same time I bought of the widow Plumer that land in Mary-lebone (for a song) which is now covered with houses.

"Next, there was my Daughter, a blooming Girl of Seventeen, whose Charms were designed (I thought) for the happiness of some young man of Quality (as I ventured to hope), who would be tempted not only by the beauty of her Person, but also by the Portion which I was ready to bestow upon her. Thus I hoped to raise my family, which was of humble Origin. Alas! She caught Small-Pox and died in a fortnight. With her these Hopes were Buried. At the same time (which forbids the suspicion or Fear of a Judgement) by a lucky Stroke I acquired (a Special Blessing) the first of those Navy Contracts by which my Fortune has been more than doubled.

"Lastly, my Elder Son, who had from Childhood given Trouble, for he would never apply his Mind to Study, nor would he learn under me how to get the better of Weak or Credulous Persons so as to transfer their Money to his own Pockets, but would continually Sing, make idle Music, Feast, Paint, and Spend. After a course of profligacy in which I did my best to Warn and Dissuade him, he madly went out to rob a noble Lord, and being Captured and Laid by the Heels, was presently Hanged—a Disgraceful Event, and one that Dashed all our rising Cheerfulness. At the same time a Signal Favor was bestowed upon me by the Lord in the fact that a violent tempest blowing over the Channel, on the very day when that unhappy Boy suffered, wrecked a large number of Ships belonging to the Port of London, while two of my richest Bottoms found Shelter in the Scilly Roads. Thus was

I singled out for marks of Approbation at the time of my greatest Affliction.

"Of these three events, the first and second were accidents which clearly belong to the changes and chances of this mortal life—In the midst of life we are in death. We know not, even for the youngest and strongest, what may happen. As for the third Event, the parents of this unhappy Young Man may reproach themselves with a too lenient and easy Up-Bringing. So far I Bow the Head and acknowledge my fault. But the whole course of that young Man seemed like a Resolve in mad Haste to reach the Gallows. And I have shown that each so-called Judgement was accompanied by a blessing much more manifest—and, I make Bold to Declare, much more Deserved.

"Why should the hand of the Lord be heavier upon me than upon any other sinner?

"I have said, above, that it was whispered, nay, spoken aloud, on 'Change that this or that Misfortune has happened to me as a Punishment for my Treatment or Conduct towards my late Master, Mr. Scudamore.

"I was a poor lad, son of a mere Fellowship Porter, my mother's brothers being Watermen, and my own fate, apparently, to be of no better station in the world than they. But, being noticed by Mr. Scudamore, then a gentleman of reputation, and having a good Business in the City and supposed to be worth Thirty Thousand Pounds at least, I was by him taken into his office, where I was first a boy at his call, to run Arrants and to carry messages. I then became a clerk in his counting-house. By the time I had reached five-and-twenty I was entirely in his confidence, and managed all his business of every kind, and he, being an easy man, and pleased to be saved trouble, and growing fonder of the coffee-house than 'Change, suffered me to go on unquestioned, and to do what I pleased and what I thought best in his interests. This was so well known that Merchants treated me with the same Openness as if I was my Master—a lucky circumstance for me, inasmuch as it taught me much concerning trade, and made acquaintances for me who afterwards became useful.

"I can boast truthfully that during the time that I thus managed my Master's business it prospered and increased.

Naturally I became discontented—who would not?—seeing that I did all the work and my Master reaped the whole Harvest. Many factors and clerks and servants do not consider this hardship, and continue to work zealously to the end of their lives, being pinched and living hardly, so that their Masters may increase and grow fat. I was not so disposed. As soon as I had gained one step I desired to take another. I would still be rising—I desired ardently to become a Master.

"The opportunity came in the Way I shall relate. At this time there broke out the Madness known as the South-Sea Bubble. Now I have ever possessed to a Singular Degree the Power of Discerning the Future as regards the Rise and Fall of Stocks and Shares. And at the outset of this Affair I clearly perceived that there would surely follow a Vast Increase in the Price of this and other Stocks; and I longed to be Trading in them—at first I thought in a small way in order to better my humble fortune. But in order to begin one must have either Money or Credit. Of these had I Neither. Therefore, I perceived that in order to attain my Object I must Secretly make Use of some of the Money belonging to my Master, as it passed through my Hands. This was difficult, because he had a Running Credit with a Goldsmith of Lombard Street. However, I devised a Plan which was Ingenious and Honest. I would but borrow the sum of £400 to begin with. Therefore I persuaded (very Easily) my Master to consent to purchase South-Sea Stock. He agreed to buy at 130 about £12,000 worth of Stock—*i.e.*, about £9230 in shares. As at this moment it was advancing rapidly, I bought £10,000 one day, of which £400 worth, or £390 of stock, I bought in my own name. By this means I was enabled to obtain a small sum for myself, and to secure for him the stock which he desired to buy. In the end, as you shall see, I faithfully repaid that advance of £400.

"How, then, did we stand? I had three Shares at £130 each—my Master held 92 shares. On my Advice he sold them out at 200. He therefore made a Profit of £70 a Share, or £6440 in all. Ought not this man to have been Satisfied with me, his faithful Steward? At the same time I sold mine at the same profit, and replaced the loan, and was £210 in pocket. Then, as I Pointed out, which was quite true, the Stock was still going up—he agreed to Buy in again. This time he would Buy about £18,000 worth, the Stock then standing at 250. I did the same thing as before. That is, I bought six Shares for myself and 66 for him. A week later, the Shares having gone up to 500, I Sold all out, and he made a Profit of cent. percent. As for me, I did very well. For I Replaced my Second Loan of £1500, and found myself the Possessor of £1710—far more than ever I Thought to own. This was all in the Early Spring. But as the year advanced, the Stock went Leaping up. I Played the same Game always, Borrowing and always Repaying, and Growing, for one of such Small Origin, every week Richer and Richer.

"Then came the Time when I perceived very clearly that the Price must Fall, and that Suddenly and Deeply; now by this my Master was Maddened, like many others, with the business, and looked for Nothing Less than to see the Shares rise to Thousands. Their highest Price was 990. My Master was eager to buy more. Next day they Fell. He was persuaded—not by me—to Hold on. They Fell lower and lower. They Fell from 990 to 150. And my Master, who had Bought in from 600 (or thereabouts) to 990, Lost his All. I, for my part, who had been Buying in and Selling out (so as to replace the various loans), and always making my profit on each Transaction, Finally Sold out at 990. The last shares my Master Bought were mine, but he knew it not till afterwards. And the end (to me) was a Modest Fortune or competence, a Capital Stock for embarkation in Trade of about £22,500. This is the history of the whole business. My Master went mad, like the rest of the Natives. I kept my Wits about me. He continued in his madness. I sold out. Remember that each Loan as I made it was paid back the next day, or a few days after, by the Differences which I had the Power (under Providence) to foretell. Who can Blame me? Was not the good success—the wonderful success—of my Venture a mark of Special Blessing? But this my dear Wife could never understand.

"Having Lost his All, my Master was ruined. It has been Objected that I should have Come to his Assistance.

But in the City of London Gratitude is never suffered to interfere with Business. I Plainly Told him that I must look after Myself. When, shortly after this, he went into the Fleet, his wife and children asked my Help. I gave it. On many occasions I have given them sums of money—a half-crown here and another there. I am not to Blame if the Woman went mad and the Man died of rage at his Ill Fortune (Foolishly Cursing Me, as if I was the Cause of his Sufferings), nor can I be Blamed if his Children (through their Father's Folly) Became I know not What—Thieves and the Companions of Thieves.

"This is the Plain History of the Events which, according to my Detractors, have Brought upon me the Judgements of the Lord.

"On the other Hand, have not His Blessings been abundantly Showered upon me? Have I not Risen from a plain Poor Boy to be a great City Merchant, an Adventurer in Foreign Ports, one whose Word is powerful on 'Change, the Owner at this moment, when I am past Sixty Years of Age, of a Hundred Thousand Pounds and More? Are not these things Plain Mercies? Would they have been bestowed upon One who, as has been Falsely alleged, rose by robbing his Master and drove him to Bankruptcy, and Suffered him to Die in the Fleet?

CALVERT BURLEY

XX

Lucian on the Document

Margaret made haste to place this document in Lucian's hands. He read it with great interest; he read it twice. He then folded it and returned it to his wife.

"Well, Lucian, what do you say?"

He made answer slowly:

"Calvert Burley's *Commentary on Himself* possesses several points of interest. It is the revelation of an eighteenth-century soul. First we have the poor boy—clever, sharp, and resolved to get on if he could—to climb out of the servitude and obsecurity of his people. I fancy there was very little climbing in those days. Where the child was born, there he grew up, and there he remained. Well, this boy had the good-luck to get into favor with a master who was clearly a man of weak nature; for he gave this sharp lad, gradually, the management of all his affairs. The lad looked about him, watching the markets and the stocks. I suppose that he grew extremely keen to foresee the probable rise and fall. Some men have a kind of prophetic instinct in such things. At last came the opportunity. In order to seize it, he had to be a villain—about this I don't imagine there was much difficulty. The finer shades of honor were not likely to be regarded by such a young man as this. The rest followed naturally. He ruined his master, and enriched himself—he tells us how. Nothing is to be gained by helping the fallen, and he, therefore, allowed his master to die in jail. A very complete villain!"

"A horrible villain!"

"Wait a little. Having become rich, he must become respectable. He marries a wife from the ranks of the City madams; in order to become respectable, he goes to church. No—that is wrong—he had always been to church; it used to be part of the City discipline—honest lads or villains, all went to church. Formerly, however, he sat in the least eligible seats. Now he occupies a pew under the pulpit, and his boy carries his prayer-book after him up the aisle. His wife talks the language of religion, such as it was—the religion of the Queen Anne time."

"Was it unlike our own?"

"I think so. Calvert shows us himself that it was a time when blessings and the approval of the Lord meant success in trade, and when afflictions were regarded as indicating the displeasure of the Lord. Very good. He prospered exceedingly. Being already rich, he could afford to be honest. Yet, we see, there were murmurs about the beginnings. Presently the troubles fell upon him, one after the other. Then the murmurs became whispers, and the whispers voices of accusation, which he heard. And in the end, to set his conscience at rest by a kind of balance-sheet familiar to the commercial soul, he wrote this narrative. Of course, it stands to reason, if Heaven's displeasure is shown in some calamity, Heaven's approval is marked by long-continued success. Thus, his eldest son becomes a profligate; marries an heiress; spends her money; goes on the road; is hanged. Very sad, indeed. But, on the other hand, during that young man's career how many cargoes safely landed! How many glorious successes on 'Change! Then his daughter dies of small-pox. What for? Why ask, since on that same day his ship alone, of all the fleet, rode out the storm? His younger boy is kidnapped. Horrible! In punishment for what crime? What, indeed, when another large slice was added on that same day to his great fortune? Therefore, as the years ran on, he grows more satisfied with himself. For some unknown sins, perhaps of his wife, perhaps of the last generation of Fellowship porters, these things have been allotted to him. But for himself it is one unbroken career of Heaven's approval and manifest blessing. There, Margaret, is my reading of this history."

He sat down. "There are people, I believe, even now, who think in the same way. A dangerous way—to look for guidance from without instead of within. Well, I said that I should like to hear Calvert Burley's account of himself, and I have had my desire. My dear, it used to be considered unlucky to speak ill of ancestors. But this Calvert Barley really was a detestable person."

"And the misfortunes fell—if not on him, for he could not feel them—on his children and on his grandchildren."

"They did. Very great misfortunes, too. Tyburn Tree and madness—a miser and a money-lender. Everybody got what he deserved—sometimes what he desired."

Margaret shook her head.

"Once more. Remember what the Prophet Ezekiel says: '*The son shall not bear the iniquity of the father.*' You will listen to that authority, I believe, my child."

"Well, Lucian, if the son, or the grandson, takes over and enjoys the harvest of iniquity, he becomes a sharer in the guilt."

"The harvest, the stored-up granaries, the result of iniquities—you see, Madge, that you beg the whole question. Take this Burley estate. How much of it is the harvest of iniquity?"

"All of it."

"Nay. The Westminster miser saved; he did not commit any iniquities. He saved, and he left nearly half a million. That alone at compound interest would mount up to many millions. How much of the rest is due to the dancing-cribs, to the gambling-hell, to the money-lending? Perhaps the old man lost money on all three. If the grandson, my dear, were to take over that estate, he would take it free from any liability on account of old injuries."

Margaret looked up. She would have answered; but on Lucian's face there lay that look of masterful resolution which made the portrait of Calvert Burley so remarkable. Lucian, at times, was strangely like the builder and founder of the House—the son of the Fellowship porter.

XXI

LUCINDA AVERY

An old woman?" Margaret looked up from her work. "What old woman? And what does she want?"

"She won't say her business," replied the maid. "Says she wants to see the lady of the house. She's an old woman out of a workhouse."

Margaret went out. She found an old woman in workhouse costume standing on the door mat. She was a thin, frail-looking old woman; she had been tall, but now walked with stooping shoulders. Her face was pinched and pale; not a face made coarse with drink and vice; a face made for pride, but spoiled by humility. She courtesied humbly when the lady of the house appeared. And she stood with her arms folded under her shawl, as one who waits to be ordered. She looked meek, even beyond the assumed meekness of the most accomplished pretender in a whole workhouse, and yet she was picturesque, with a great mass of iron-gray hair that had once been black, and eyes that were still black.

"What can I do for you?" Margaret asked her.

"I've read something in a paper," said the old woman. "A lady in the House had it and lent it to me." She unfolded her arms and produced from somewhere a newspaper. "I read it a week ago, and thought—if I was to call—"

"Let me read the paragraph," said Margaret.

It was one of the thousand paragraphs on the Burley estate, and it ran as follows:

"The house where the great Burley property was amassed is situated in Great College Street. It is now No. 77. It is reported to have been built by the same Calvert Burley who heads the genealogy compiled and published by us the other day. It is now occupied by a physician whose surname, by a curious coincidence, is the same as the Christian name of its builder. Dr. Lucian Calvert took the house with the furniture as it stood. Among the things preserved are the portraits of nearly all those persons who are mentioned in the genealogy. It was a common practice in the last century to adorn the house with the portraits of all the members of the family—a custom which photography has been largely instrumental in abolishing. Thus, even the children of the celebrated miser were painted as soon as they arrived at man's estate. The total disappearance, or extinction, of so large a family with so many branches is one of the most remarkable facts in family history ever known. Up to the present moment, we learn that only two among the many hundreds of claimants profess to belong to the miser. One is an American lady who calls herself the granddaughter of the miser's youngest son, and the other is an English claimant who announces himself as the grandson of the second son. These claims have either not been so far established or are as yet only just sent in. Surely, one would think, there should be little difficulty in establishing and proving one's own grandfather. Even if a nephew or grandnephew should ultimately turn up, the fact that so vast an estate should remain so long without an undoubted heir will remain as a most remarkable fact."

"Well?" Margaret gave back the paper. "You did not come here, I am sure, just to show me that paper."

"No, ma'am, I did not. I came here hoping that perhaps you wouldn't mind showing me those pictures." She spoke with the greatest humility, but her manner of speech was better than one generally associates with a workhouse dress.

"Yes; but will you tell me why you want to see them?"

"It's because some of them may be mother's brothers." Margaret showed some natural surprise. "It's quite true, lady. My name is Avery—Lucinda Avery—and my mother's name before she married was Lucinda Burley. And she was born in this house. It's quite true, lady," she repeated. "Mother was born in this very house. I know she was."

"You say that you are the daughter of Lucinda Burley. Can you prove what you say?"

"Oh yes, lady, I've got proofs."

"This is very strange. But come in." Margaret shut the street door. "Now sit down and tell me more about it."

The old woman sat down on one of the hall chairs. "What am I to tell you?" she asked, simply. "Mother's name was Lucinda Burley."

"Yes; there was a Lucinda Burley. Can you tell me something more?"

"Mother ran away from her home—this was the house. She's often and often talked to me about the house—this was the house. She ran away from home because she was unhappy. Her father was a dreadful miser, and wanted them to be as miserly as himself. They could hardly get enough to eat. She had brothers, and they ran away, too, one by one, all but the eldest—this was the house. So, when her mother died, she ran away too, and married father."

"Yes. What was your father?"

"Father was a gentleman." The old woman held up her head with the least possible approach to the gesture called bridling. Not every resident, if you please, in her college could boast of a gentleman for a father. "He was a gentleman," she repeated.

"Yes. A good many men are gentlemen, nowadays. What was his business?"

"He hadn't got any. He was called Captain Avery. And he was once in the army. Mother always called him the Captain. He was a very handsome man. Mother loved him, though he threw away his money—and he wasn't a good man."

"He was Captain Avery," Margaret repeated. "And he threw away his money. And then?"

"When he had no more left, they took him to prison. It was the Fleet Prison—I remember it very well, and father in it. He died in the prison."

"Oh! And this was the way that you became poor?"

"Yes. Mother was poor. Don't you believe me, lady?" She looked up with some anxiety. "Indeed, it is the truth, and nothing else."

"Why should it not be the truth? I am not disbelieving you."

"I've got the proofs, lady." The old woman produced from unseen recesses a little parcel wrapped in a pocket-handkerchief. "This is a picture of mother, made when she first married; when she was young—poor mother!"—her voice faltered. "I never remember her like this—not so young and beautiful."

Margaret took the drawing, which showed just the face and head. "Yes," she said, "I know the face. They all have it; you have the face."

It was a charming little picture, representing a beautiful girl, with something of a Spanish air, dark-eyed, dark-haired. And the poor faded daughter bore still some resemblance to the beautiful young mother.

"You all have the same face," Margaret repeated.

"I never saw her so." The old woman wrapped it up again in her handkerchief and put it back. "But I like to look at it sometimes; just to think of her as I never saw her. She looks happy in her picture—I never saw her happy. The picture was done by a friend of father's. He died in the Fleet, too. I remember him very well, because he had a bottle-nose—mother said it was rum. But a lovely painter, mother said, and good company, and sang a good song."

"It is certainly the portrait of Lucinda Burley," said Margaret. "I will show you the pictures, if you please to come upstairs with me."

The old woman's breath was bad; she mounted the stairs with difficulty; when she reached the drawing-room she was fain to sit down and gasp. Margaret sat her down before the fire, and waited. She looked timid and humble; with the timidity and the humility that come of life-long obedience to the man with the bag; of never exercising any power or authority at all. For example, a woman who had been a mother could not have that air. But she was not common or rough, there was even a certain refinement in her face; she looked like a gentlewoman out of practice. Her black eyes were fine still, but they were sad. Her face, her manner, her carriage, her voice—all together spoke or shadow, sadness, and privation.

Margaret took off her bonnet and shawl—was she not a cousin? "You shall have some tea," she said, "before you say another word." She went downstairs and brought up the tea with her own hands.

"Now," she went on, "if you are recovered, we will talk again. You shall look round the room presently. First, think that part of your mother's girlhood must have been spent in this room. Some of the things are new, the rest were here in her time. I know all the family history, and I can tell you about all the portraits. That over the mantel-shelf is the original Burley, the founder of the family. Your mother was born about the year 1802. When did she die?"

"She died ten years ago. The parish gave her out-door relief. She was bedridden for three years."

"The parish! the parish! Good heavens! And her brother ten times a millionaire! What a man! Had your father no friends to feel any sense of shame?"

"I think he had cousins. But they wouldn't help, and mother wouldn't ask them any more. Mother was too proud. She would rather work her fingers to the bone than go begging. She said she was a Burley." The old woman looked up to the lion-hearted founder of the family for approval.

"She was proud of being a Burley," Margaret repeated, not scornfully, but with a kind of wonder.

"When father died she wrote to her brother, and he wouldn't help her. But she kept his letter."

She produced again the parcel, wrapped in a handkerchief, and extracted a paper, which Margaret took. It was as follows:

Sister,

I am in receipt of your communication. I will not see you if you call. I will give you nothing. You have made your bed, and you may lie upon it. You deserted your own family and disgraced yourself when you ran away with your lover. ("But I've got her marriage lines," interrupted the daughter.) You had better apply to your brothers who also ran away. Your father is dead, and has left me his property—such as it is. ("Such as it is!" Margaret repeated. "What a man!") Go your own way and let me go mine.

Your brother,
John

"A cruel letter! A hard and cruel letter!" Margaret gave it back. "The letter of a hard and cruel man. But his profession was Destruction and Ruin."

"Mother tried to see him, but he wouldn't let her come in. Mother kept the letter. She said that she looked to see him cut off suddenly for his hardness. But he wasn't."

"No," said Margaret; "a worse thing happened to him. To be cut off suddenly would have meant reward, not punishment. He lived. He grew harder every day, till he did not know what mercy meant. A worse thing than death is to grow harder and more merciless and more insensible every day—and to live for ninety years. Go on, you poor thing."

It must not be supposed that the old woman went on quite in the connected form which follows. She was weak in the construction of sentences. What she said was extracted by questions and suggestions; if we were to put them all in, the length of this chapter would extend to a volume. She answered timidly, and only warmed, so to speak, when she began to speak of the house and what she knew about it.

"So mother took in needle-work." The whole tragedy of a lifetime in those words—she took in needle-work.

"When I was old enough I began to help her. We sat and sewed all day long."

"Where were her brothers?" Margaret knew very well, but she put the question.

"One of them did something and was transported for life. But he came back, secret, and saw mother. Then he went out to New Zealand."

"Oh! And the others?"

"One went to America, and one was an actor. Mother was so poor when she found out the actor brother that she was ashamed to go and see him. Mother was proud of her family, but there were dreadful misfortunes in it. Even when we were at our worst mother used to say she was glad she ran away from the misfortunes."

"There were misfortunes enough for her, I think," said Margaret. "But it is strange, however. Always the same feeling—ths same dread of misfortune."

"Yes, she was proud to be a Burley; but they were all unfortunate."

"And you, did you ever marry?"

"Marry?" The old woman laughed a poor little shadow of a laugh. "Marry? Do men look for wives in a two-pair back? Young men don't keep company with a girl too poor to buy a brush for her hair or a skirt to hide her rags. Ah! no, lady; I had no time to think about keeping company and marriage. What I had to think about all my life long was how to get rid of the hunger. Always that—and nothing more—unless it was to keep a bit of fire in the grate."

"Poor creatures!"

"It's over now, and thank *God* for it!" The poor old woman put on a little show of dignity and self-respect as if already in the presence of her best friend—Death. "I'm in the House for the rest of my time—till the Lord calls me. Yes, yes, it's been a long time coming, but the end has come. Sometimes I wake at night and fancy the hunger is on me again, and me so tired and my arm so heavy and the stuff so thick. It's a blessed thing when we do get old and past our work."

"A blessed thing, truly—I never thought of it before. And you were once a pretty girl."

"Pretty?" The old woman really blushed—a pale and pink suffusion it was. "No one ever called me pretty that I remember; we had no time for such talk. Why," she said, "we old women talk—we must talk, you know, now we've got no work to do. The others talk about the old days when men came courting, and they went out together in the evenings and were married. It's all strange to me. I had nothing but work—all the time."

"Yes." Margaret was looking at her thoughtfully. Had one ever before heard of a woman who never had any pleasure at all for the whole of a long life? "And so at last you gave up work and went into the House?"

"Yes. Some of them grumble all the time—I don't. It was the happiest day of my life when my forefinger got cramped and bent—look at it—and I found that I couldn't sew any longer. Then they took me in, and I've had a good dinner and a good tea every day since I went in."

"You didn't work on Sundays; what did you do then?"

"On Sunday morning we went to church. Mother never would give up going to church. She said she always had gone and always would go. After church we lay down and went to sleep. In the evenings we sat in the dark, and mother talked about her family and this house. Oh! I know all the rooms in it." She looked round the room. "This is the drawingroom. Downstairs there's the front parlor and the back parlor. They used to live in the back parlor. There is a garden at the back, with a grape-vine and a mulberry tree. Upstairs, over this room, was mother's bedroom. At the top of the house was the nursery, where the children used to play. And there was another room which was kept locked, and the children believed there was a ghost in it, and if the door was opened the ghost would come out and walk about the house."

"Yes, it is quite clear that you know the house. Now get up and look at the pictures on the wall, and find your mother's portrait if you can."

It was not difficult. "Here's mother." The old woman stood before the portrait of a girl in her early bloom, beautiful—dressed in silk—dark, black-eyed, proud, who looked down upon her pauper daughter with a kind of condescension. There was more pride in the old portrait than in the miniature.

"It's my mother—young—oh! how lovely! Oh! I never saw her like this. Oh! with a gold chain and a silk dress—and she gave it all up to run away to marry, and work on starvation wages for the rest of her life—oh, my poor mother!—and said she was happier so."

She burst into tears. The old weep so seldom that it touches one to see them. Age dries up the fountain or sacred source of tears. Or perhaps it is that the old have known so many sorrows and survived them all that they think little of another and a new sorrow. As the negro said of his imprisonments, they did not count in the record of his life. The old know that there are not really many things to weep about; they have learned one of life's many lessons—that things do not matter much if one has patience. Death? It will happen to themselves very soon. It is the cessation of pain. One would welcome death if we were only certain that the rest and the cessation of pain would be consciously enjoyed. Bereavement? Soon or late, we are bereaved of all we love unless they are first bereaved of us. Poverty? It is the average lot. Injustice? Wrong? It is the universal lot of mankind to suffer injustice or wrong. The world is full of wrong. Dependence? Most of us are slaves, and must jump when the man with the bag cracks his whip. But this old woman wept as if she were young again. She wept, you see, for her mother's sake.

"Oh!" she cried. "And I never knew what she meant when she told me about the old house, and her mother, and her brothers, and all. She was thin and starved all the time I knew her and worked beside her. I didn't understand. And now I know. She was once like this. She lived here, in this beautiful house; she was dressed like that. Oh! the dreadful life to her—the dreadful place to live in—I never knew it till now!"

"Poor creature!" said Margaret, her own eyes charged with tears.

"She used to lament of a Sunday night that she could do nothing for me. We had no books to read. You see, she used to teach me a little—oh! nothing to speak of. All I craved for, ever in my life, was new boots and a new frock, and something more to eat. I never saw anything like this before. Mother lived here—mother was like this!" she kept on repeating.

"A sad story—a miserable story," said Margaret. "We must see now what can be done. You ought not to remain where you are. Have you heard anything about the—the estate?"

"There's an old gentleman in the House who was a lawyer once—I believe he got into trouble. He says there's a lot of money waiting for somebody. He says I ought to send in my claim. But I don't know."

"Shall I advise you?"

"The man told me not to show the papers to anybody. He said that if anybody saw them he would go and pretend to be me—I don't know what he said."

"Hardly that. Well, I will tell you how the case stands. Try to follow and to understand." She explained the situation. The old woman listened, but with little understanding. Then Margaret explained it again. It was no use speaking to the old woman of millions, or of hundreds; she thought of money as shillings; she could no more realize a hundred pounds than she could realize the distance of the earth from the nearest fixed star. "Well, there is this money," she concluded, "which will be given to the proper persons when they appear. If the dead man's grandson does not appear, it will be given to the nearest in succession, and you are certainly one of them."

"When will it be given?"

"I cannot tell you. The people who order such things may think it necessary to wait for a certain number of years. If you send in your claim, you must find a lawyer to draw it up for you and to take the business in hand. That will cost you a great deal of money."

"I have got no money."

"No? Some one must do it for you. Perhaps my husband would help you. And then you must sit down and wait—for ten years, perhaps."

"I am over sixty-five now. I don't think it will be any good to wait."

"Not much, I am sure. Still, who knows what may happen? You may be the nearest to the succession—after that grandson. At any rate, you may make your existence known. You are a cousin when the other cousins turn up. And perhaps your cousins will take off this dress of yours and give you one of a—another color. It is not seemly, you know, to have cousins in the workhouse."

The old woman shook her head.

"No," she said, "I think I will stay where I am. I have never been so comfortable before. I don't want the money. I am contented and thankful. I don't mind being a pauper. Why should I? I live better than ever I did in my life before; I am warmer, and I sleep softer. And there's no more needle-work to do. It isn't a shame to me; and if it is a shame to my cousins, I can't help it."

"It is certainly no shame to you."

"You see, lady," said this model of a contented old pauper—poor and not ashamed—"if I were to ask for the money, they might turn me out of the House!" She shuddered. "They might say that if I am going to get money of my own, I had better go away and make room for those that had none." She pursed her lips and shook her head. "That would be the worst misfortune of all. Besides, if I got the money I might spend it like father spent his, in riotous living and bad companions." Margaret smiled. "And then I should get into prison for debt like they sent him. I'd rather be a pauper than a prisoner. And now, lady, thanking you for being so kind—"

She took up her shawl. But Margaret laid it over her shoulders with her own hands. And then, before she tied on the bonnet—poor old Lucinda had never experienced such attentions before—this astonishing young lady actually kissed her on the forehead; kissed a

WALTER BESANT

pauper! kissed a broken-down old needle-woman! Such a thing was unknown to her experience. In the House, to be sure, the chaplain always shakes hands with the old ladies, but he does not kiss them; the matron wouldn't allow it; the guardians would not approve of it. Therefore the old lady gasped again and fell into a shake, which brought on a cough, and made her sit down to recover. She had not been kissed for more years than she could remember. And no one but her mother had ever kissed her before. Her virginal brow knew nothing but the kiss maternal.

"We are cousins," whispered Margaret, with the kiss. But Lucinda did not understand. The chaplain certainly said that the inmates of the House were his sisters. Cousins or sisters—it meant, probably, the same thing.

This long life of privation, the undeserved misfortunes of this woman's mother—were they because her name was Burley, and because her ancestor was Calvert Burley, the man of many sins? Sorrow and disaster fell upon every generation. Yet Lucian would have it that—

"Come again," said Margaret—"come and talk to me again about your mother and yourself."

Margaret told her husband of this unexpected visitor.

"Ought we to let her stay in that place, Lucian? Remember, she is our cousin."

"And the money-lender is my grandfather. We must acknowledge all or none. If we take this woman out of the work house, it must be because she is my cousin."

Margaret made no reply. His words and his looks showed what was in his mind.

"All—all—pursued by the same ill-fortune," she said, presently.

"Ill-fortune caused by their own follies. The woman married a spendthrift and fell into poverty. What had Calvert Burley to do with that? And now, Madge, my Marjorie"—he stooped and kissed her forehead—"remember, if I cannot take this inheritance, nobody else shall. That, at any rate, is certain."

"I care nothing who has it, Lucian, so long as we do not have it; so long as I am never asked to take a crust of bread bought with the vile money of that—that—worm"—she could think of no worse name at the moment, though she felt it to be inadequate—"who condemned his own sister to a life of starvation."

XXII

The Australians

"Pater!" The five girls—they were gathered together about the teacups, their heads together, their tongues talking with animation extraordinary—all jumped up and clapped their hands, and cried out simultaneously, or with one consent, when Sir John opened the door and quietly came in to take his afternoon tea. "Pater! Come and listen! We have had an adventure! We have made a discovery! We have found the long-lost family! We are heiresses! You are an heir! Herbert is an heir! We are going to get the most enormous inheritance ever known! We are going to have the Burley estates!"

Sir John stopped short and shivered as one who has received a sudden and unexpected shock. "What have you found out? Don't all cry out at once," he said, with roughness unknown to this flock of fair daughters. "Well, what is the wonderful thing you have found out? Let one speak for the rest."

"You speak, Lucy." They chose the eldest. "Tell him everything, just as it happened."

He began drumming the arm of his chair with his fingers. He was evidently ill at ease. He looked frightened.

"Don't be anxious, dear pater," said this eldest. "Nothing very dreadful has happened. What could happen to make you look like that? Only—but you shall hear, and then we shall see what you will say."

"Go on." His face was averted and his voice was husky. "Tell me what you have discovered, and where and how you found it."

"First, then, we saw in the paper that the house where this rich man—this Mr. Burley—used to live still contained some of the portraits of the family."

"Well? How did that concern us?" he asked, roughly. What could be the matter with the pater?

"You shall hear. If we knew for certain that our grandfather came from some other family, the Burley portraits would not concern us. But as we don't know—do we?"

"We don't know—we certainly do not know, and we shall never know," he said, dogmatically. "It is now impossible to find out."

"You shall hear. Meantime, as it is naturally an interesting question with us—"

"The name is spelled quite differently," Sir John objected, *in initio*.

"But pronounced the same. And the Christian name is your own, pater dear, and Herbert's as well, which certainly means something. As for the spelling, there may have been some reason for changing it. There may, perhaps, have been a return to an older way—just as the Seymours became again St. Maurs—and our Burleigh is certainly a prettier name than his Burley."

"Go on, then. Let us hear your fine discovery." Sir John stretched out his feet and leaned back in his chair. But his lips twitched; for some reason or other he was ill at ease.

"Well, we thought we would go to the house and ask permission to see the portraits. We thought it would be at least interesting, if the people in the house would let us in. We could but try. They could but say no. So we went—all five of us—we went together."

"Well—well. You went together. You asked permission to see the portraits."

"First we had to find out the house. It is close to Westminster Abbey. To think that while we were visiting the Abbey we were close to grandfather's old house!"

"Don't jump at conclusions."

"Oh! There can be no doubt—not the least doubt."

"Not the least doubt," echoed all the girls together, in chorus.

"Only wait a little; and it is close to the Houses of Parliament. It is a most lovely old house in a quiet street. Oh! so old—so old—and quiet and homelike, one would like to live in such a street all one's life. The houses are only on one side; on the other is a gray stone wall—the garden wall of the Abbey; a wall as old as the Abbey itself. Edward the Confessor built it, I expect. The front of the house is covered all over with a magnificent creeper, the leaves crimson and purple and golden—it is like a glorified house. There is a red-tiled roof, there is a raised door and steps and old-fashioned iron railings—that's the house where he was born—the dear old granddad. But, of course, you'll go to look at it yourself, and at once?"

"We shall see."

"The street is called Great College Street. There is a brass plate on the door, with the name of the doctor who lives and practises there."

"Shall we get on a little faster?" Sir John asked, impatiently. What was the matter with him?

"Oh! my dear pater, it is all so interesting. Have patience for a few moments."

"Such a beautiful story!" cried the other sisters, in chorus. "Oh! do have patience. Let us hear the story told properly."

Sir John spread his hands. It is a gesture which means anything. Gestures are like interjections.

"Well," the eldest daughter continued, "I must tell you the whole story—it's a most wonderful adventure. We rang the bell—it was rather formidable calling at a strange house, and we were a large party—but in such a cause we dared greatly. Five female Japhets in search of a grandfather. We mounted the steps and we rang the bell."

"You rang the bell," Sir John repeated, with an effort at patience.

"And we sent in mamma's card with our names—the Misses Burleigh—in the corner."

"And they let you in?"

"Yes—we were received in the dining-room by the lady of the house. Her name is Calvert—"

"Calvert? Calvert?"

"Yes. I suppose her husband is connected somehow with the people who used to live here—our people—but she did not say so. The name on the brass plate is Lucian Calvert, M.D. One can hardly ask a strange person on the first day of meeting about her husband's family; but I suppose—oh yes, you will see—they must be connected in some way with the Burleys."

"I am listening, my dear," said her father. "We shall get to the point, I suppose, presently."

"Well, Mrs. Calvert received us. She is quite young, only a girl still—not married many months, I should say. Such a pretty girl, too—tall and fair-haired and blue-eyed. But her eyes wandered while she talked. She looks melancholy. Perhaps they are poor, but everything in the house was very nice."

"Oh, very nice!" cried the chorus of damsels.

"I was speaker. So I showed her the extract from the paper, and said that we ventured—and so forth. And she smiled gravely, and was gracious, and asked me if we were claimants. I told her that we were New Zealanders, and certainly not claimants so far, because we were doubtful whether we really belonged to any branch of the Burley family, which must have changed its name in the hands of our ancestors. So she smiled again, and said that she would be very pleased to show us the family portraits. So she took us upstairs. Pater! We can't make such a house in New Zealand if we tried ever so much. It's all wainscoted from roof to cellar. You never saw such a lovely house—the room is not big, you know, but big enough. 'I suppose,' said Mrs. Calvert, when she saw us looking about curiously, 'that people in the Colonies may easily drop out of recollection of their people at home. I will treat you as if you were cousins of the late Mr. Burley, and you shall see the house and whatever there is of interest in it.'"

"That was pleasant. And you saw the portraits?"

"Yes, we saw the portraits. And here comes the really interesting part of the story, as you shall learn. She took us upstairs, I said, and so into the drawing-room where these portraits are hanging. It is such a pretty old room, newly painted—low, with three windows, and the light falling through the creeper-curtain outside. There is an old-fashioned fireplace—with a fender to correspond."

"And you saw the portraits?" asked Sir John, a second time.

"Dear pater, you are too impatient. Yes, we saw the portraits. There are about twenty of them; they begin with the full wig of Queen Anne's time, and go right down to the curled short locks of—well—George's IV's time, I suppose; or perhaps—Dot, you're the youngest—you are the latest from school—who reigned about the year 1818?"

"George II.," said Dot.

"Well, it doesn't matter; there they are, and the women in every kind of head-dress from the high commodes to the curls of—you ignorant Dot, it wasn't George II. The pictures take us back nearly two hundred years. Many a noble lord cannot boast of respectability for two hundred years."

"To end in money-lending and dancing-cribs."

"There are the sons and daughters and the wives of the House. Well, all the men are dark, though some of the mothers are fair. All with dark hair and dark eyes."

"And the eyes follow you all round the room," said Polly, or perhaps Nelly.

"Yes; they all follow you wherever you go. It's ghostly."

"Go on with the facts, Lucy," said her father. "We'll deal with the ghosts afterwards."

"On every frame is written the name of the portrait, with the date of his birth and death."

"What did the names tell you?"

"Pater dear, do you remember grandfather before his head became white? Would you recognize him if you saw a portrait of him at the age of sixteen or so, a lad only?"

"I think it is unlikely. He was born, I know, in 1801; I was born in 1837. When I begin to remember him well, so as to recall his features, he was already a good way on towards fifty. Between the man of fifty and the lad of sixteen there must be a great difference. I remember him altogether and always as a gray-headed man, which he was, I believe, for more than thirty years."

"Well, there he is on the walls. I am certain—we are all certain—that he is there. You can go and see for yourself. There is the grandfather."

"We are all certain," cried the chorus. "We are all quite sure; there can't be a doubt about it."

"By what marks do you recognize your grandfather? How can you tell that the portrait of a boy of sixteen is that of your grandfather?"

"Because Herbert is exactly like him. That was what called our attention first to the picture."

"Exactly—exactly—exactly like him," echoed the chorus.

"Dot first saw it. She jumped up and clapped her hands and cried 'Herbert!' And we all ran and looked. It is Herbert. When you come to look into the face you see there are differences in expression. As grandfather—I must call him grandfather—was not in Holy Orders, there is wanting the spiritual look in Herbert's face. One cannot expect that; but, for the rest, the same forehead, the same nose, the same mouth, the same shape of head—everything."

"Everything like Herbert's," echoed the chorus.

"Let us examine the argument. Here is the portrait of a young man or a boy who closely resembled your brother Herbert. Therefore he is your grandfather."

"Wait a minute; we haven't half done," said Lucy.

"Not half done, not half done," from the chorus.

"Courts of law, or heralds and genealogists, want stronger evidence than a mere resemblance, my dear children. But I own that the story is interesting. Is there more?"

"A great deal more. On the frames are written the names, as I told you. The name on this frame is—Charles—Calvert—Burley—spelt their way—born in the year—1801! What do you say to that?"

"Oh! You found that name on the wall!" Sir John sat up quickly, and he became like unto himself—a Premier in the House, meeting new facts and facing unexpected arguments. "That name, too—and that date. It is curious—very curious. As yet, however, we have not got beyond the region of coincidence. For, my children, the papers have been publishing an imperfect genealogy of the family, and I find, first, that they are all called Calvert; and secondly, that there was a Charles Calvert Burley, whose birth was of the same date as my father's. I would not show you the thing, because we have already had our thoughts disturbed enough. And the name proved nothing."

"But the likeness—oh! pater, you must go yourself and see it. The likeness is most wonderful!"

"I will go, certainly. I must go, after all you have told me."

"Well, and there is another portrait also, which is exactly like Herbert, though in a different way. It is of a man who was born in 1745"—she was speaking, though she knew not the history, of the man who went mad. "The features are not so strikingly the same as in the other portrait, but there is Herbert's look—his straight, upright wrinkle—his very eyes—bright and impatient, with that queer expression which he has when he wants to be a martyr, or when he gets excited over somebody's opinions. My dearest pater, you will never, never, never get me to believe that these resemblances are within what you call the region of coincidence."

"Never!" cried the chorus. "Never—never—never!"

"Do you want more likenesses? "Well, then," Lucy went on, "I told you of one of the ladies, my great-grandmother, I believe, which they say is like me."

"Not so much like Lucy as that other portrait is like Herbert."

"And if you want still more, pater, there is the fact that your eyes are their eyes—the eyes of all the men—the same eyes. Look in the glass." He got up and obeyed. "The same eyes, as you will see when you go and look at them."

Sir John sat down, with a sigh. There was nothing to say.

"This lady—this Mrs. Calvert—acknowledged that these resemblances—what you call coincidence—were most wonderful."

"I suppose she knows nothing about—how does she come to have the portraits?"

"They bought all the furniture of the house when they took it. But she does know about the family—she seemed to know a good deal."

"What did she tell you?" he asked, sharply.

"Oh! That this one was the man who had just died, and that this other was his father, a celebrated miser—only I never heard of him—

and this and that. I asked if she knew why Charles went to New Zealand."

"Well?" Sir John interrupted, sharply.

"She said, 'No; he went—' And then she stopped short." Sir John groaned. He actually groaned as one in deep distress. "Oh!" he said. "She knows—she knows—she knows the family history. Did she—did she—tell you anything else?"

"She took us upstairs to a room at the top of the house—in the roof. She said, 'You are all girls, and so I will show you the nursery where the mothers played with their children for generation after generation.' There it was, just as it has always been. Mrs. Calvert will not have anything touched; the old-fashioned cradle with carved sides and a carved wooden head to it; the babies' things in the drawers—the things worn by grandfather, I dare say, and the dolls and toys that the children played with, all a hundred years old. Then, while we looked at them and wondered, she sat on the bed and folded her hands, and she said, talking like a woman in a dream: 'In this room I always feel the presence of the dead wives and mothers. They seem to be telling me things. You belong to the House, somehow. Of that there can be no doubt whatever. I could wish you a better fortune, for it is an unhappy House. Disaster follows those who belong to it.' So we asked her what kind of misfortunes. But she shook her head. 'There will be no disaster for you,' she said, 'so long as you do not seek to inherit the fortune. Best to forget it. Be content with knowing that you are Burleys—somehow.' She said no more, and we came downstairs rather saddened. What kind of misfortune? None ever fell upon grandfather; or upon you, dear pater."

"I have been singularly successful so far," Sir John replied. "There is still time, however, for trouble."

"I wonder who she is, and how she knows about the family. Some kind of cousin, I suppose?"

Sir John made no reply for a while. He sat with his head upon his hand, gazing into the empty fireplace. "Full of disaster—and of—what did she say?—of crime? Children, do we want to be connected with a family whose history is filled with disaster and with crime?"

"No; certainly not. But it *is* interesting; and, pater dear, won't you take steps?"

"What steps? What to do?"

"To prove that we belong to this family—perhaps, if you are not afraid of disaster, to take this estate."

Sir John rose and walked about the room. "Steps!" he repeated. "Steps! What steps? What for? To give you an inheritance of shame? Crime and shame go together—go together—unless crime remains undiscovered. That is the only chance for crime. What steps? We might easily, perhaps, find out what became of this Charles. Perhaps he went abroad—went to America or somewhere. That, however, is not the same thing as to find out about our Charles—your grandfather. In the year 1842 he sailed for New Zealand from the Port of London. There our line begins. Your know nothing at all before that date. Connect your grandfather, if you can, with this or some other family over here. Not a scrap of paper remains; not a shred of tradition or anything. Coincidences, likenesses, mean nothing. Suppose you find all about this Charles, say, up to that very date—up to the year 1842; suppose the history of him stops short there; suppose that the history of our Charles begins at the point where the other history ends—what is the use of all your investigations if you cannot, after all, connect the two? Likenesses won't do."

The girls were silent. "Oh! but," said the youngest, "he is exactly like Herbert," as if that settled the matter.

"And—we are sure and certain—sure and certain," cried the chorus.

"Very good," Sir John continued. "You have also to account for the fact that the name is changed. Why should our Charles change his name? Was he ashamed—out in New Zealand, where there were as yet not a hundred settlers, and no public opinion to consider at all about such things—of his name and his parentage? Why, his father, supposing that he belonged—of which we have no proof—to this family, was at least a gentleman, even if he was a miser. Gentlemen don't want to change their names. They are proud of them."

"Yes—but—all the same—there is the likeness. Go and see the portraits, pater dear. You can't get over the likeness. Oh! it is too striking—it is too remarkable."

"Another thing. This genealogy, of which I have spoken, this imperfect genealogy, gives the names of a dozen and more younger sons of whom nothing is stated. I suppose some of them married and had children. I suppose that hereditary resemblance may go through the younger sons as well as the elder. It is not the exclusive privilege of the elder son to be like his grandfather. Considering all that you have told me—the Christian name—these resemblances—I am strongly of opinion that we do belong to this family; but, considering other reasons,

I am of opinion that we may search—yes, we had better search among some of the earlier, younger sons. If we establish such a connection, you will have what you have been wanting so long, an English family without too close a connection with the money-lender and the miser, and the disaster and the crime."

The words, as we read them, have a show of authority. The speaker, who was a tall and, as we have said before, a portly person, stood up while he spoke, which should have lent more authority to his words. But there was something lacking. What was it? A little hesitation; a doubtful ring, as if he were making excuses. When he had finished, he turned abruptly and walked out of the room, but not in his customary manner. It was like a retreat.

The girls looked after him with astonishment.

"What ails the pater?" asked one.

"I feel," said another, softly, "as if he had been boxing my ears—all our ears—all round. Did one ever see him like that before?"

"It seems," said a third, "as if he was by no means anxious to establish the connection. Well, we don't actually want money. But it *would* be nice to have millions, wouldn't it? And I don't believe the world would much care how they were made, after all. Money-lending—"

"And gambling-places—"

"And dancing-places. Everything disreputable; though why a man should not own a place where people dance I do not know. It is not wicked to dance, I believe. If it is, we are the chief of sinners."

"I believe," said the eldest, "that it was formerly considered wicked for the working people and lower orders to dance. Well, you see the pater is a K.C.M.G., and perhaps he would rather have no uncle at all than an uncle who made his money disreputably. Perhaps it isn't nice, when a man has arrived at honors like these, to have to own an uncle who was—well—what they say this man was."

"All the same," said the youngest, "the two men in the two pictures are exactly like Herbert."

XXIII

The First Patient

Sir John fled from the house. He could not remain in it. He fled because of the terror and the shame and the sickness that filled his soul. He was like one who hears from a physician the news that he has an incurable disease which will fill his future with a perpetual pain, and will lay upon him a burden impossible to be shaken off. Such a one must needs get up and walk about; he must be alone. For he had no doubt—none whatever—that the girls had really discovered their English relations; and he had no doubt—none whatever—he divined the fact—he felt it—that this woman, this Mrs. Calvert, knew the whole of the family history, including a certain lamentable and terrible episode in the life of his father, Charles Calvert Burley. The name, the date, the resemblance—all these things together proved too strong a chain of evidence.

As for himself, he knew no more than his daughters to what family his father belonged. It was a question he had never put. But he knew certain things, and he remembered certain things; and he had learned little by little to understand that concerning these things there must be silence. He remembered, for instance, a midnight embarkation in some far country; he remembered a long voyage on board a small sailing-vessel, in which his father, mother, and himself were the only passengers; he remembered crowded streets, and then another vessel, and another voyage. And he knew—how? He could not answer that question. He knew—he had gathered—there had been hints from his mother about silence—that the place of the midnight embarkation was Sydney; that his father, if not his mother as well—a dreadful possibility which he never dared to put into words—was a convict escaping from transportation; that they were landed in London; and that after as brief a delay as possible they re-embarked for New Zealand, a colony then so thinly populated that no one would look for the escaped convict, even if any search at all was made, or any notice taken of his escape, in a place so far from British law. He knew also why his father kept on the fringe or edge of the English settlement and avoided the haunts of men. Even after years have turned the black hair white, one may be recognized.

But no one ever recognized in the peaceful, successful, and retiring settler, Mr. Burleigh, the ex-convict, Charles Burley, transported for life, in commutation of the capital offence, to the penal settlement of New South Wales.

This shameful story, then, was a secret known, first, to his mother and to himself; when his mother died, to himself alone. No one suspected it. The old man died in silence, believing that his son knew nothing, and the son had this secret all to himself.

A secret, he said to himself whenever he thought of it—in these later days seldom—which would never be discovered; it could not; there was not a possibility of discovery. The crew of the brig which brought them home knew nothing; they were all long since dispersed or dead. No one could by any possibility connect the prosperous settler with the forger. The crime itself might be remembered. You may read it in the "Annual Register" for 1825; but the criminal—he disappeared forever when he went on board that brig. The settler's purpose, in which he succeeded, was to escape, to begin again, unsuspected, and without the stigma of his crime. He had one son only to inherit that stigma, and he succeeded so far that no one except that son knew or suspected the truth.

As for the boy, the possession of the secret made him reserved, like his father. But it was his own secret to himself. He married without the smallest dread of discovery; as his children grew up around him, he began to forget his secret; when they speculated about their English origin he listened and laughed. There was not the slightest fear of discovery. It was impossible; and now, after all these years, the thing he had quite ceased to fear was upon him. In his own heart, despite his words of doubt, there was no doubt. The girls had found their grandfather; one step more and they would learn that their grandfather was a forger who had been sentenced to be hanged, and a convict who had been transported for life. What had the woman said—"Disaster—misfortune—crime?" What could she mean but the crime of Charles Calvert Burley, born in the year 1801, whose face was like his grandson's? And he had brought his wife and daughters all the way to England in order that they might hear this shameful story.

There was no man in the whole world more miserable than Sir John Burleigh when he fled from his house, and walked quickly away with hanging head and rounded shoulders. Sir John Burleigh, K.C.M.G., who usually faced the world with a frank smile and confident carriage,

WALTER BESANT

as behooves one who has done nothing to be ashamed of, walked along with the outward signs of one who had been kicked into the street.

No connection could be proved; no—that was certain—no, but the suspicion would remain; a suspicion amounting to a certainty.

Of course his footsteps took him straight to Westminster; in the midst of these very painful meditations he was dragged by the silent spirit within him, which makes us do such wonderful things, to Great College Street itself. He was startled out of his terrors by finding himself actually opposite the very door of the house. He knew it by the great curtain of gorgeous leaves and the name on the brass plate—"Lucian Calvert, M.D."

He hesitated a moment. Then he mounted the steps and rang the bell.

He asked for Dr. Calvert. He was shown into the consulting-room. The time was a little after six, when the September sun is close upon setting, and the light in a small back room, looking south through a frame of vine leaves, drops into twilight, and in the twilight men see ghosts. Therefore, Sir John reeled and gasped and became faint, and would have fallen but for the doctor, who caught him. "Why," cried Lucian, gently, "what is this?"

The ghost that Sir John had seen was the ghost of his own father. This ghost rose from his chair when he entered the room, and looked at him inquiringly. All the men of the Burley family had this strong common resemblance, and in this young man the common resemblance was stronger than in any other son of the House. But Sir John knew not that Dr. Calvert was his cousin.

The doctor put his patient in an arm-chair and stood over him. Sir John began to recover. His nerves had already received a great shock by the discovery of the day, and the aspect of this young man with the black hair, the regular features, the square chin, the black eyes deeply set, recalled to him in this unexpected manner his own father in the very house where he was born. Picture to yourself, dear reader, a visit from your own father as he was at five-and-twenty! Think how it might be to meet once more yourself as you were at five-and-twenty! What becomes of a man's old self? Last year's leaves are dust and garden mould, but where is last year's man? What had the girls told him? That the men of the family were all alike; and here was one, presumably some kind of cousin, who was what his father had been before his hair turned gray.

"Will you take a glass of water?" asked the doctor, "or a glass of wine?"

"A sudden giddiness," Sir John replied; "I am better already."

"Was it on account of the giddiness that you called?" He looked at the card. "You are Sir John Burleigh, of New Zealand? We have heard of you, Sir John."

"I heard—somebody told me—that a physician was living—in this house—and I thought—I thought—I would call and state my symptoms."

Lucian inclined his head gravely. What was the matter with this gentleman that he should faint on entering the room, that he should hesitate in his talk, and look so anxious and troubled?

He went on to describe his symptoms. There are a great many diseases in the bag, but hitherto this fortunate colonial had enjoyed none of them. He had no experiences, therefore; and as he was a very poor actor, he mixed up imaginary symptoms in a way which carried no conviction at all with them. It is rare, indeed, to find a man who suffers from insomnia, nervous apprehensions, neuralgia, giddiness, want of appetite, asthma, indigestion, headache, heaviness in the limbs, and other incidental maladies all at the same time. Lucian listened, wondering whether the man was deranged for the moment.

At last he stopped. "I think I have told you all, doctor."

"In fact," said the physician, "you have fallen into a hypochondriac condition. You hardly look it. I should say that your normal condition was one of great mental and physical strength. You look as if you were suffering under some shock. Your parents, now, were they hypochondriac? No? Well, I will write you a prescription, and you will call again in a day or so."

Sir John received the prescription with a little verbal admonition, meekly. He also deposited two guineas with the meekness of the unaccustomed patient.

"I hear, Dr. Calvert," he said, timidly, "that you have in this house certain portraits of the Burley family, the people about whom there is now so much fuss and talk. I believe that I belong to—ahem!—a very distant branch of the family. We spell our name differently. Certainly we are not claimants; my daughters have already been privileged to see them. May I venture to ask your permission—"

Lucian laughed. He understood the sham symptoms; but why did the man faint? And why was he so nervous and agitated?

"My dear sir," he said, "why didn't you say at the outset that you wanted to see the portraits? I will show them to you with the greatest pleasure. I think, however, that my wife is in the drawing-room. You will find her a better showman than I—"

In fact, it irritated him to talk about his ancestors. Margaret could relate their histories if she chose. But he could not. They were his ancestors, you see.

There was just enough light left for seeing the pictures. The faces showed in shadow, which suited their expression better than a stronger light.

Sir John looked round him. The Burley face stared at him from every panel.

A young lady rose and greeted him. "Sir John Burleigh?" she said. "I am not surprised to see you. Your daughters have told you, probably, that they called here this morning. I suppose you have learned that they discovered a very striking resemblance to their brother and to you?"

"Yes, they told me—they told me—" he began to look about the room curiously. "Frankly, I know nothing at all about my own people— of what rank or station they were. For some reason or other my father never told me, and I never inquired. I have been an active man, building up my own fortune, and endeavoring the best for my country, and I never felt any curiosity on the subject. One need not be ashamed, Mrs. Calvert, of being the architect of one's own fortunes."

"Certainly not."

"With my children it is different. They begin with the work done for them. Naturally they would like, if they could, to be connected with some good English stock."

"The portrait," said Margaret, quietly, "which most attracted your daughters was this—Charles Calvert Burley, born 1801."

"Good *God!* It is my father!"

The words escaped him. He gave away his secret at once in this foolish fashion, and then, the blackness of despair falling upon him, he sat down in a chair and gazed helplessly at Margaret.

"Is it your father? Did you not know, then, that you belonged to this family?"

"No. I did not know. It is my father's portrait."

"Sir John, do you know the history of your father?" Sir John made no reply. "Your daughters do not. They have no suspicion. But you—do you know the story?"

In such a case silence is confession. Never did a man look more guilty than this man.

"You do know it, then," said Margaret.

He groaned.

"In that case I need not recall it."

"There is no other person in the world—not my wife, not my girls, not my son—who knows or suspects this thing, except myself—and you—and anybody else whom you may tell."

"I tell these things to no one. Why should I? My husband, I believe, may know. That is, he may have heard it; but he does not talk about the misfortunes of this family."

"Your husband, he is one of them; he is exactly like myself as I was thirty years ago. He is exactly like my father. Who is he?"

Margaret evaded the question.

"The men are all alike, Sir John. Well, I shall not tell your daughters, nor shall I tell anyone. My knowledge of Charles Burley does not extend beyond his—his—exile. He went out to Australia, and there he disappeared."

"It is everything to me—my position in the world; my children's pride and self-respect; my wife's faith in me—everything—everything."

"If they persist in hunting up the past," Margaret went on, "they may, perhaps, somehow—one does not know—come across this story. Because, to begin with, it is all printed in the 'Annual Register,' where I read it."

"They are so certain about it; they are so excited about it; they are so sure to come again. Promise that—you will not tell them—I implore you. If I could buy your silence—if you are poor—I will give you £10,000 on the day when I put my girls on board again in happy ignorance." His offer of a bribe did not offend Margaret, because his terrible distress filled her with pity.

"Indeed you must not buy my silence—I give it to you. Only remember, this is an open secret. They will discover it if they examine or cause other people to examine the case. After all, there is no absolute certainty in a resemblance or a date. I suppose that without your help they could not connect your father with this portrait?"

"I cannot deny the family. I suppose that we are Burleys—we are exactly like those people; I do not think I could possibly repudiate the family."

"Find another ancestor, then."

"Eh?" Sir John looked up quickly.

"Find another ancestor. Here they are—all the younger sons; a family likeness may descend through younger as well as elder sons. If I were you, Sir John, I would choose another ancestor for them out of this collection."

A counsel of deception—and offered to the man of the greatest integrity in the whole of New Zealand; the man whose whole career had been absolutely honest, truthful, and above-board, and he adopted it instantly and without hesitation.

"Yes, yes," he replied, hastily. "It is the only thing open to me. Thank you, thank you, Mrs. Calvert. Will you kindly suggest—or recommend me—some one?"

Margaret smiled. "How would this young man do? He is Joshua Calvert Burley, born in 1747. His father was hanged for highway robbery."

"I don't care whether they find out that or not. Hanging, a hundred and fifty years ago, doesn't matter. Besides, one would say it was for killing a nobleman in a duel, or for traitorous correspondence with the Pretender. Joshua, born in 1747. What did he do?"

"I believe he died quite young, in childhood. But I am not certain, and no one will ever take the trouble to hunt up the matter."

"I shall remember. Joshua Calvert Burley, born in 1747. He changed his name to Burleigh, I suppose, and became"—Sir John looked guiltily cunning—"what do you think, now, that he would become?"

"An eminent—sugar-baker?" Margaret suggested, gravely. The two conspirators were too serious to think of smiling over their deceptions.

"Why not? Sugar-baker—made his fortune—baked sugar at—Bristol, perhaps. My father, Charles, was born—a younger son—in 1801; lost his money when he was forty years of age, and went out to New Zealand. How shall I prove all these lies?"

"That, Sir John, I leave to your advisers. I have always understood that genealogists will prove anything."

"It must be done; there is no other way out of it. Heavens! I am going to embark on a whole sea of falsehoods; but all I ask of you is silence. You have never seen me before, but your husband is my cousin—I don't know how—and you look as if you could be true as steel—true, if you give a promise even to a stranger—and a cousin whom you have never seen before."

"I have promised. It is all I can do."

"Promise again," he repeated. "Promise to forget what I said at first sight of this picture, and tell no one the story of Charles Burley's crime."

"Would it not be better, even now, to tell them? You are not to blame. And—and—I had forgotten that—you stand very near to the succession—there is this enormous fortune waiting. If you send in your claim—"

"What! Sir John Burleigh, K.C.M.G., to claim a fortune by confessing that he is the son of a convicted criminal, and that he knew it all his life? Not all the wealth of all the Indies would induce me to send in that claim!"

"But your children—they will force your hand."

"Not if I give them another grandfather. My dear young lady, hitherto, believe me, I have been an honest man. At the present crisis there is not a trick, or a falsehood, or an invention, which I would not practise in order to keep my girls from this discovery." He pulled out his handkerchief and wiped his brow.

It was true. Not a trick or a falsehood from which he would shrink in order to save his girls from this shame.

"I am very sorry for you, Sir John. I am very sorry indeed. I will keep your secret, believe me. That such a thing should be rediscovered after all these years in such a strange manner is most wonderful. But if the knowledge of it is limited by you and me, no harm can be done."

He groaned again.

"I think that the plan I have suggested will be the best. Go to some genealogist and have your family tree made out with this Joshua Calvert Burley."

"I will—I will."

"Sir John, you belong to a very unhappy family. Come here again, and I will show you how disaster and unhappiness have pursued them from father to son. They prosper only when they separate themselves from the parent stock. You have prospered—you are a great man—you are a rich man, I believe; but the moment you return to your own people you are struck with misfortune, in the shape of this threatened discovery. Good-night, Sir John. Come to see me when you have got your genealogy complete; and don't be anxious about things, because, you see, unless you own this Charles for your father, no one can possibly charge you with being his son."

Sir John went home a little lightened. If only this young lady would keep her promise! He would get out of London as soon as possible; he would take his girls home again to New Zealand six months earlier than he had intended; and he would nail that other ancestor to his pedigree.

"My dears," he said at dinner, "I have been to see those pictures."

"Well?"

"The resemblance is, as you say, very striking. But I observed that the resemblance was through all the men's faces, though the expression varies. For instance, there is an earlier one still more like Herbert, and Mrs. Calvert declares that I am myself like every one of them. Well, as you say, the resemblance is too strong to be mere coincidence."

"There!" They all clapped their hands. "He has given in."

"I have certainly given in. We belong, I am convinced, to that family. But as regards that portrait of Charles Calvert Burley, whose name is the same, and whose age would now be the same as my father's—there I do not give in, although the resemblance of Herbert to that portrait is so striking."

"Well, but who else—"

"That we shall see. Perhaps I have a clew—" he ended, mysteriously. "Perhaps the clew may be followed up. Perhaps in a little while there may be something definite discovered. Only, my dear girls, give up thinking of the great inheritance. For if my clew proves correct, you will have between yourselves and the estate all the sons and daughters of the miser and all their sons and daughters—and you will inherit no more of the Burley estates than the Queen herself!"

XXIV

Herbert and the Portraits

The girls came again—the very next day—to see the portraits. This time they brought with them their brother, the Reverend Herbert, and begged permission to show him—in one of the old pictures hanging on the wall—himself.

"I knew you would come again soon," said Margaret, welcoming them with her sweet, serious smile.

"Oh! but only think! If you had been brought up in ignorance of your own people! And then if you suddenly found out who they were, you would naturally feel curious and interested. And this is the only place where we can hear anything about them."

"I shall always be pleased to show you the portraits."

"Here, Herbert"—they led him to the portrait of Charles Burley, born 1801—"this is the picture we pounced upon for grandfather's, because it is so exactly like you. Is it not, Mrs. Calvert? Look at him—Charles Calvert—the same Christian name, and born the same year. It must be he."

"It is like him, certainly," said Margaret. "But perhaps this earlier one resembles him still more."

She pointed to the portrait of the madman. Herbert resembled him still more closely than the other. For in his eyes this morning there lay a strange light of expectancy. They looked upwards, as if waiting for a fuller faith. It is the light of religious exaltation; only one who can believe greatly has such eyes. A man with that look becomes a prophet, the founder of a new creed, a maniac, or a martyr. A monastery should be full of such eyes; I believe it is not, as a rule. But I am told there are nuns in plenty who have these eyes. You may also find them, here and there, in the Salvation Army.

Herbert looked at both pictures, one after the other. "What was this man?" he asked, pointing to the later portrait.

"His name was Charles Calvert Burley"—Margaret evaded the real question.

"What was he? and what became of the man?" Herbert affected the brusque and direct manner of the young clerics who go so far in self-mortification as to pretend not to like the society and the talk of young ladies. Perhaps this manner is designed to show that maceration still continues; perhaps it is a measure of self-protection; perhaps it is designed to assert the authority of the director.

Margaret colored and looked a little annoyed. These blue-eyed, fair girls, who seem so meek to outward view, can show annoyance, and can answer back at times.

"I do not know," she replied, shortly. If the question referred to the completion of that exile's life, she did not know—she could only guess. If it referred to the earlier part of his life, it was—Give her the benefit of the doubt. Schoolmen would allow the answer, considering the question.

"We seem to resemble all the men's faces," said Herbert, looking about him.

"See, Herbert; there is the pater, too—and there—and there—and there—you are both in all the portraits."

"It is impossible not to be convinced that this must be our family," he stated, dogmatically.

The girls clapped their hands. "He gives in, too. And the pater has given in. We are sure—we are quite sure. It must—it must—it must be our family."

"Things are strangely and wonderfully ordered," said the clergyman. "We come to England on a visit—that is, you do. We have no clew to our own people. We arrive just at the moment when publicity throws a strong and sudden light upon an obscure family; we hear of these portraits; we come here to see them, and we recover our ancestors. Perhaps, in addition, we shall step into a colossal fortune. If that is ordered, as well as this discovery of the family, it will be a great thing; a great thing to pour all these treasures—ill-gotten as they were—into the lap of the Church."

"You forget, Herbert," said the sisters, "that they will be poured into the pater's lap, and when it comes to pouring out again, the colony will certainly come before the Church."

"And," said Margaret, "allow me to point out that a resemblance does not constitute proof. You would have to establish your connection with this Charles, and it may prove difficult."

"Since I cannot give the estates to the Church," said Herbert, coldly, "anyone may have them that likes."

"Well, Mr. Burleigh, are you satisfied with these newly found ancestors?"

"No," he replied, with candor, "I am not. I should have liked either the higher or the lower class—even the lowest. These people are of the middle class—the snug, respectable, grovelling middle class; incapable of aims or desires save to be rich and comfortable; incapable of sacrifice, or generosity, or things spiritual—the outcome, the prop, and the pride of Protestantism. Except that man"—he pointed to the madman—"they all grovel."

"My dear Herbert," cried his sisters, "what do you know about them? All this from a portrait?"

"What I hoped to find, if not a noble family, was one steeped in crime—black with crime; my grandfather a criminal—all of us under the curse of the forefathers—ourselves awaiting the doom, yet rising spiritually above it, making our very punishments steps unto higher things!" His voice rose shrill and high; his eyes flashed; it was a curious outburst of fanaticism.

"Herbert!" cried the girls all together.

"So that I could go about among our poor sinners, who commit a new sin every time they speak or act, and say to them: 'Brothers, I am one with you. We have the same forefathers—criminals, drunkards, profligates. We are all alike, up to the neck in sin and the consequences of sin.'"

"How would that knowledge help your sinful brothers?" asked Margaret.

"It would make them feel me near them—one with them. They would understand me. With sympathy much may be done. With sympathy and confession, all may be done."

"It would be better for them, I should think, that they should feel that you were far above them."

He shook his head. "The Franciscans were the most successful of any preachers or teachers among the people. They lived among them—on their fare—in their cottages."

"Did they desire that their fathers should be criminals?" asked Margaret, whom the manner of this young clergyman offended. "Had they no respect, pray, for the Fifth Commandment?"

The Rev. Herbert turned his bright eyes upon her, but answered not. Young as he was, he would not allow a woman to enter into argument with him—a deacon. Then he waved his hand contemptuously at the pictures. "Middle-class respectability," he replied; "I would rather have no ancestors at all than such snug middle-class respectability."

"If you want wickedness," said Margaret, "perhaps I can find you enough among your people here—if they are your people—to satisfy even you. There is this man, for instance"—she pointed to the deceased money-lender—"to be sure, he is not your grandfather. He lived for ninety and odd years. He ruined multitudes by his gaming-tables. He ruined other multitudes by keeping houses for profligate and abandoned persons. And he ruined other multitudes again by usury and exorbitant interest. He is, apparently, a cousin of yours. What more do you want? Go among the people of your parish, sir, and tell them that you can now sit down with them proudly because you are closely related to a man whose profession, like their own, was Destruction and Ruin."

Margaret had never before spoken with such plainness. The young man winced—plain speech disconcerted him. But he recovered.

"What my people understand is not the unpunished wickedness of a rich man, but the fall and the conviction and the punishment of one of themselves. Give me a convict for my grandfather!"

Margaret turned away. Strange! What maddened the father only to think of, the son ardently desired.

"I don't think Herbert quite means what he says," the eldest sister explained, while the others behind her murmured.

"On the contrary, I mean all that I say. I should like, for the sake of the Church, to be sprung from the meanest and lowest and basest—"

"At all events, Herbert, you would not like your sisters also to belong to the meanest and the lowest and the basest? Oh no, you cannot!"

"You cannot, Herbert!" murmured the chorus. "Oh, you cannot!"

"Perhaps," Margaret added, "when you learn more of the history of these portraits, you may be satisfied."

"You know their history?"

"I know some of it. Since it is not likely that you will get exactly what you want, why do you not commit a crime of your own and go to prison for it? Then you will be really on the same level as those poor creatures, and you will spare the memory of your ancestors, and inflict on your sisters only the shame of their brother."

"You do not understand," said Herbert, coldly.

"Well, Herbert," said his sister, "look around you; choose your ancestor among them all."

"He is here." The young clergyman pointed to the madman. "This is the ancestor that I want. His eyes have a look of expectancy and of faith. I should say that he had been spiritually blessed, according to the light of his time—which was not our time, but the darkest age of black Protestantism. I have nothing more to say. Madam"—he bowed with more politeness than one might have expected—"I thank you for showing me these pictures, which I verily believe are those of our people. As for what you said—you do not understand me at all. For the sake of the Church we must resign all—even the honor of our name, even our pride in being the children of good men." He went away without taking leave of his sisters.

"He is not often like that," said Lucy. "But sometimes he is in the skies and sometimes in the depths. He has got a craze that he ought to be like the wretched creatures among whom he works—if not a criminal himself, at least connected with criminals. It is not the first time that he has flamed up in this way."

Then they sat and talked about these dead and gone people whose history was so sad. Margaret told them something, but not all—the things that saddened hut did not shame. She told about the miser, and how his children ran away from home one after the other; and about the money-lender, his successor, who suffered his sister to live in the most abject poverty. She hid from them the story of the forger who was sent to Australia, and that of the man who went mad from religious terrors, and that of the man who was hanged. She told them enough. The possession of an English family, they discovered, would not necessarily make them more joyful.

"Yet we have a family!" cried Lucy. "Even to have a family like this, laden with troubles, is surely better than none."

When they went downstairs they found, standing at the door just opened for her, a tall, thin old woman, dressed in a blue frock and a check shawl.

"Stop a moment," said Margaret. "You want to know your own people? Let me introduce you to your cousin, Lucinda Avery, daughter of Lucinda Burley, who was the sister of the rich man recently deceased. Lucinda Avery is now in Marylebone workhouse—a pauper. We are going to take her out soon—in a few days. Meantime she is, I believe, your cousin. My dear"—she addressed the old woman—"these young ladies are the daughters of Sir John Burleigh, from New Zealand, and they believe themselves to be the granddaughters of one Charles Burley—"

"Son of Charles? He was my mother's brother—her brother. Oh! now I remember—" But she hesitated, looking in wonder at these girls so beautiful and so richly dressed.

"We are not certain that he was our grandfather," said one of the girls.

The old woman shook her head. "There was never any other Charles in the family," she said. "Oh! I know—I know my own. Mother told me all she could. I don't forget—no—no; about mother's family I can talk."

Lucy took her hand. "You poor thing!" she said. "My name is Lucinda, too. I don't think a cousin of ours ought to be in the workhouse. I will speak to my father about you."

The old woman looked at her wonderingly. "Sir John!" she repeated. "Sir John! Oh! It's wonderful."

"Mrs. Calvert will tell us how we can help you," Lucy continued. "You will let us help you?"

"Sir John! Sir John!" the old woman repeated, staring.

The girls nodded and ran down the steps. The old woman looked after them.

"And their grandfather—my uncle—he was a common convict," she murmured. "From New Zealand! And their father is Sir John— Sir John. Mother said she couldn't never get over the disgrace of her brother being a common convict. And look at them now! And their grandfather was a common convict!"

She pursed her thin lips and shook her head, and went indoors to talk with Margaret.

XXV

WHO AM I?

C ome," said Margaret, taking the old woman's hand. "I think my husband is in his study. Let me take you to have a little talk with him."

But Lucinda Avery continued gazing after the girls as they walked down College Street.

"They're the daughters of Sir John," she repeated. "Sir—John—Oh! and their grandfather was Charles, who was a common convict, and came back and went out to New Zealand. I saw him before he went."

"Hush! Do not speak of that. They know nothing about it. And remember—those who know most speak least, Lucinda."

"Mother told me all about it long afterwards. Oh! and I am the cousin of those young ladies—and them dressed so lovely! And such lovely manners! They want to call at the House to see me. They'd be taken to the matron. Such sweet young ladies! and their grandfather was a—"

"Lucinda," said Margaret, sharply, "keep silence about what you know. It is quite enough to think that you and I know."

The possession of this knowledge made the old lady smile and bend her head sideways, and even amble a little—but one may be mistaken. The pride of sharing such a possession with the "lady of the house" fell upon her and gave her great comfort. How elevating and sustaining a thing is personal pride—the pride of some personal distinction, if it is only a glass eye! Never before had this old woman had any possession of her own at all, except the sticks and duds of her miserable room.

Margaret looked into the study. "If we do not disturb you, Lucian, here is our cousin Lucinda Avery, of whom I spoke. Come, Lucinda."

Lucian rose and welcomed the pauper cousin, who received his hand with a courtesy humiliating for a cousin to witness.

"Our cousin remains in the union, dear, only until I have concluded the arrangements for getting her comfortably cared for outside. You are not going back to your old quarters, Lucinda; you shall have your own room, and pleasant people to cocker you up and keep you warm."

The prospect did not seem very attractive to the old lady. She pulled her shawl more tightly round her, and said, with meaning, that the union was kept nice and warm, and she'd never had such good meals.

"But not so warm as the nest we shall find for you. Lucian, our cousin has not been in a position to acquire much book-learning; but she knows the whole history of this House, down to the miser and his five children."

"Mother told me," she repeated. "On Sunday nights she used to talk to me about them, sitting by the light of the street-lamp. Other nights we worked, and mother talked to herself with her lips all the time. I know a great deal. You are a Burley, too," she added, staring at Lucian. "They are all alike, the Burleys. A reg'lar Burley, you are, just exactly like the pictures upstairs."

"Didn't you read the name on the door-plate?" asked Margaret. "Lucian Calvert."

"I read print—almost any kinds of print," Lucinda replied. "But not door-plates. Lucian Calvert Burley, then. They are all Calvert Burleys. Every one."

"Oh!" said Lucian. "Then, pray, who am I?"

She turned her head sideways. Every gesture that this poor woman used seemed not to fit her; tall, thin, dark, with strongly marked and clear-cut features, she should have been full of dignity and authority—a Queen of Tragedy. Instead of which there was no part in the humblest comedy that she could fill. She was timid; she had never before met such people as these, who neither bullied her nor wanted to sweat her; but she had a secret shared with "the lady of the house." And she knew all about the Burleys. The mixture of pride and timidity produced remarkable phenomena in her carriage. She turned her head on one side; she smiled; she advanced one foot, and withdrew it; she took her hands from under her apron and folded them openly in front, which meant self-assertion.

"I've seen all the pictures upstairs," she said—"every one of them. And my mother's among them—with a gold chain. And the men are all alike. That's what mother used to say. 'See one,' she said, 'and you've seen all.'"

And now the old lady, who had been answering in monosyllables, began to be as garrulous as an old crow, proud to show her knowledge.

"Well?"

"You can't be the grandson of Charles, who was—I humbly beg pardon" (to Margaret); "those who know most speak least. He went abroad, and his young ladies are at home, and I've seen them. Nor you can't be the grandson of James, who ran away with his master's wife to America and never came back again. P'r'aps you're the son of Henery" (she said "Henery"); "he was an actor, and so was his son. Once, a long time ago, mother and me went to see a play in a theatre where they both acted. We sat in the front row of the gallery, and saw beautiful. Oh, it was lovely! Mother's own brother and her nephew acting—dressed up fine—on the stage. It was grand! She inquired about them—oh! she knew about all her relations. There was only one child, and he was a boy named Clarence. Mother liked to find out everything. Then there was Uncle John—him that died the other day. He married, and he had six children. Five of them died young. Served him right, said mother, for his hard heart. Then there was one son left. When his mother died, the boy ran away. Mother found out so much. Oh! she used to come round here—it wasn't very far—and ask the postman, and the pot-boys, and the bakers' boys. She never wrote to her brother any more, nor wanted to see him, but she wanted to find out everything that happened in the family."

"And what became of that son?"

"I don't know—mother didn't know. But as for you—why, you are his son, for sure."

"Oh! you think—"

"You are his son, for sure and certain. You are a Burley, and you're exactly like the picture of Uncle John, upstairs. Yes; you are his son. You can't be anybody else."

Margaret said nothing. Lucian gazed at the old woman with surprise.

"She has said it," he replied. "This convinces me, if I wanted any convincing, that all old women, and especially all illiterate old women" (he murmured these words), "are witches. They read thoughts; they know the past; they forestall the future. Go, witch! My wife will give you tea. And don't think that there are no places outside the union where you can find a warm corner."

"You are his grandson," she repeated. Then she produced from under her shawl a long, lean, and bony forefinger, attached to her poor old hand. It was the forefinger which had been cramped and bent from overwork, and to shake it in its cramped shape in a man's face was something like shaking the nightmare of a door key. But she did shake it, and she became on the spot a witch, a sorceress, and a prophetess. "Take care, you! Take care! From father to son, from man to man—

mother always said so—nothing but sin and misery, sin and misery—all the men, from father to son. Your father ran away from it. Take care, you! Run away from it! Leave this house! Run away! Did he escape—your father—did he escape?"

"Yes; as you say, he escaped," said Lucian, impatiently.

"That dear old thing," he said, later in the evening, "your interesting pauper, Margaret, carries on the family superstition, I observe. Strange that my father himself—Well, never mind. Here is a letter signed Clarence Burghley—B-u-r-g-h-l-e-y, another variant of the name. Clarence John Calvert Burghley says that he is a grandson of the second son—the one who ran away and went on the stage. I dare say; I don't mind if he is twenty grandsons—and that he is about to forward to the Treasury papers, etc., etc., etc., and may he see the family portraits? Certainly, if you like to show them. Did the second son murder anybody, or forge anything? How did he distinguish himself?"

"He became, as the pauper cousin has just told us, a popular actor. That is all I know about him."

"Not much of the family curse upon him, anyhow. I don't think that was fair upon the others. Well, this Johnnie is going to be a claimant, and the Australian, I suppose, will have a look in, and the little American wants justice done, too. Justice shall be done."

"You like the little American girl, Lucian? Yes, I thought you did. She is proud and she is poor and she is independent, and if we don't help her she will starve—she and her tearful aunt."

"Well, my dear, why shouldn't she starve? That is the question."

"No, she must not. I want to help her, Lucian."

"Get her to go back to her own people. That is the best way to help her."

"Let me ask them to stay here for a little. It won't cost us much, Lucian—and to them it may mean everything—and you like her talk."

"Have your own way, my dear; you always do. Ask all the cousins—New Zealanders and all."

Then Lucian relapsed into his usual silent brooding.

"It is too ridiculous!" he said at last. "Here am I, a man of science, actually debarred from taking my own by superstitious folly worthy of the ignorant old pauper who believes in it!"

Margaret looked up, reproachfully.

"My father wanted me to make a promise. You wanted me to make a promise."

"You did make a promise, Lucian. Is it only the superstition? Is there not something to be said for the infamy attaching to the money?"

"The world cares very little how the money has been made. The world would not ask, my dear. There would be no infamy at all. Very great fortunes cast out reproach; just as successful revolutions are no longer rebellions. Everybody would know the past—old history! old history!—and no one would care twopence about it. Put the infamy theory out of your mind."

"I cannot. It would be always in my mind but for the thought that we have separated ourselves from them."

"Marjorie, be reasonable. Now listen, without thinking of infamy and misfortune and family curses. Do you suppose that I am thinking of this estate as a means of living with more magnificence? Do I want to eat and drink more? Do I want to buy you diamonds? You know that I cannot desire these things."

"No, Lucian, you cannot."

"Suppose that I saw a way to advance science—my science—the science of life—the most important of all the sciences, by using the vast funds which this estate would give me? Suppose that I had formulated a project—such a project as had never before been possible for the world—and that I could bring it into existence if I had this great fortune?"

"Your dream, Lucian, would turn to Dead Sea fruit."

"Again this bogie! Always this bogie! My dear, I am talking of things scientific, not of old wives' fables. I am dreaming of a world-wide service. Madge—wife!"—he laid his hands upon her shoulders and kissed her brow—"release me from that promise—set me free. Let me give this great thing to humanity."

"Release you?" She sprang to her feet and roughly pushed away his hands. "Release you, Lucian? Yes, if you first release me from my marriage vows; if you will promise that I shall never, never, never join that band of weeping mothers! If you will send me away, I will release you; and not till then!"

XXVI

A Shaky Partnership

The partnership began its autumn term badly. So badly that failure, bankruptcy, separation, looked imminent. The relations between poet and singer were more than strained; they were fast becoming impossible; accusations and recriminations were of daily occurrence. No more easy dropping into rhyme; no more brotherly discussions of tags and points of business. Anxiety gnawed the vitals of the poet, who, in return, gnawed his fingernails, unless he was gnawing the mouthpiece of his brier-root. Clarence sat in blackness and in gloom. Was this the light-hearted butterfly, the Cigale, the sweet singer and mirth-compeller?

For the visits to the September country-houses—usually so popular and so profitable—had proved a frost. There is nobody so easy to amuse as the man tired with the day's shooting. Yet Clarence failed to amuse him. He took down with him a portfolio full of new songs and little entertainments. Nobody laughed when he sang them. The shadow of a forced smile, a look of pity and contempt, or a sustained yawn was all the recognition he could get. And he seemed to overhear the people whispering: "Is this the most amusing man in London? Is this the fellow they made such a fuss about—this little cad?" You see that if a man invited to make us laugh fails to make us laugh, he becomes at once a little cad; that is understood. If he does amuse, he is a little god. "Why, he is as solemn as an undertaker." Just so; he *was* as solemn as an undertaker. He sat at dinner with the face of one sent down to conduct a funeral; he made no little jokes; lie told no little stories; and when he took his place at the piano and arranged the mesmeric smile, it was like the *croque-mort's* face suddenly lit up by a jet of gas. From every house the unfortunate mime came away with the conviction that he had failed, and that this would be his last visit.

"I knew how it would be," he said, naturally laying the blame on his partner. "I knew when I took the infernal things with me that the intolerable vulgarity would damn them."

"Vulgarity," the poet repeated. "Look here, Clary, I don't mind your calling the things vulgar. They were meant to be. For that class of people you can't be too vulgar. I'm not in the circles myself, but I know what everybody knows—that they like vulgarity. The vulgarity of the stage is meant for the stalls. If anything, they were not vulgar enough. But a poet who respects himself must draw the line somewhere."

"Why did they go as flat as ditch-water, then?"

"Because of the singer, Clarence, my boy. Because they were badly sung."

"They were *not* badly sung."

"They were. The songs are as good as anything I ever did. Went as flat as ditch-water, did they? Well, I should think they would, considering. Flat as ditch-water! Why? Because—" here he interposed some of those words which relieve the feelings and heighten the picturesque effect of the truth. "Because you're losing everything—everything—your art—your memory—your imagination—hang it, your very face is changed! I wish to Heaven you had never heard of this cursed estate, of which you'll never touch a single penny—you can't—with a case so incomplete. Your very nature is changed. You, with the happy-go-lucky laugh; you, with the light touch; you, with the twinkling eye; you, with the musical voice; you, Clary Burghley that was—good heavens! you look as if you couldn't laugh if you tried. You hang your head; you scowl; your eyes have gone in and your forehead has come out. It bulges. I say it bulges. To think that I should live to see your forehead bulge! You've gone back to your great-grandfather, the Westminster miser."

"I can't help it. It's the thought of the thing that's with me always—"

"Don't tell me. As if I didn't know! Now, look here, Clary. Let us understand each other. Ours has been a very successful business, so far, hasn't it? I invent the pieces and write the songs. All you've got to do is to sing them. You've sung them very well up till now, and I don't think I could find a better interpreter anywhere. All the same, clearly I can't afford to go on unless business is attended to."

"What do you want me to do, then?"

"Do? I want you to be yourself again. That isn't much to ask, is it? Look here, my boy. The thing presses. It'll get about like wildfire that you can't make 'em laugh any longer. Then you're a ruined Johnnie, because if you can't do that, you see, you can't do anything."

"What do you want, then?" Clarence repeated, sullenly.

"I shall find it difficult to replace you, Clary, but there are lots of other fellows who could do the thing. I've been talking it over with one—a man who's been on at the Oxford. He isn't a gentleman, and he'd have to go up the back stairs; so it wouldn't be quite the same thing. Still, one cannot sit down and starve. What you will do, my dear boy, with your face as glum as an undertaker's, I don't know."

"It's my claim that I think of all the time. If we could only connect my grandfather with the family. Because the missing son is dead long ago; he must be."

The poet groaned. "That's all you think about. I talk of the business, and you reply with this claim of yours."

Clarence looked all that his partner had described him—haggard, anxious, hollow-cheeked. The fever of the claimant was upon him. His face was full of anxiety. It was easy to see that, as his partner said, he had lost his art—at least, for a time. The ready laugh, the light of the eye, the quick smile, the easy carriage—all had vanished. You could not believe that this young man had ever been able to compel laughter.

"Must we dissolve partnership, Clary?"

"I can think of nothing but the claim. You must do what you like. Until this suspense is over, I can think of nothing else."

"Look here, Clary. At the best, the very best, it will prove a waiting business. They'll give the missing son or his heirs ten years' law before they consider the claimants—and when they do, I tell you plainly, your case is not established. Give over the dreams, therefore, and attend to business. Even if you succeed at last, you've got to keep yourself for ten years to come—perhaps for life. Attend to business, I say. Begin at once. Sit down at the piano and try to sing as you used to do."

"Stop a minute," Clarence replied, in the depths of gloom. "I've got something to show you first. It's about that connection. Suppose I had found another document"—he pulled out a pocket-book and opened it—"an important document—nothing less than a letter to my grandfather from his elder brother."

"Letter to your grandfather from his elder brother? Why, how came I to miss that among the papers? Why, such a letter might complete the chain."

"So I thought. And, in fact, here is the letter. It was not among the letters that I showed you. I only found it yesterday." He spoke with hesitation, and he drew from his pocket a piece of paper a little browned by age. It was the size of a royal octavo page. It was written in ink, now pale, but was still legible.

The poet opened it—looked up sharply and curiously—and then read the contents aloud:

DEAR HARRY,

Yours of the 15th to hand. I can do nothing for you with father. He is mad with you for running away and for going on the stage. Says that you've disgraced the family. He grows more miserly every day. I hope that your prospects will improve before long. They don't seem at present very rosy. I quite approve of your changing your name. The pronunciation, I take it, remains the same, in spite of the two letters stuck in the middle. My mother sends her love.

Your affectionate brother,
JOHN CLARENCE BURLEY
GREAT COLLEGE STREET, WESTMINSTER,
June 20th, 1818

When the partner had read this valuable letter he held the paper up to the light; he examined the writing; he looked at the edges.

"Most convincing," he said. "This letter establishes the connection beyond the shadow of a doubt. And this being so, Clary, you may rest at ease, and can give your mind to business."

He threw the letter on the floor carelessly and walked over to the piano, which he opened. Then he sat down, ran his fingers over the keys, and struck into an air—one of his own light, unsubstantial tunes. "Now, then, Clary," he said, "you are the heir all right. I congratulate you. Give up thinking about it for ten years. This is the song that ought to have fetched 'em and didn't. Come along and give it with your old spirit. Think of your granddad.

"Wanted, a Methusaleh! To tell us how they kept it up—
Our fathers in the by-gones, when they made the guineas run;
How they wasted time and drank it up,
and everything but slept it up—
And always had a new love on before the old was done.

"Wanted, a Methusaleh! Old man, let's have a crack again;
The port and punch, the song and laugh, the good old
nights revive again.
The gallop with the runaway to Gretna Green and back again,
The Mollys and the Dollys and the Kittys make alive again!

Come, Clary, your liveliest manner. It wants a laughing face all through."

Clary paid no attention. Then his partner shut the piano with a bang and a swear-word.

"You think, then," Clarence went on, as if there had been no break in the conversation, "that the letter establishes the connection?"

"Undoubtedly, my dear boy. I congratulate you. The connection is established, and, I repeat, now that your mind is at rest, you can go back to your work. In ten years' time, or thereabouts, we will consider the letter again."

"The letter is—is—all right, you think?"

"Oh! Quite—quite," James replied, airily. "We need not consider the thing seriously for ten years to come—otherwise—"

"Well? Otherwise?"

"Otherwise there would be one or two points requiring explanation. For instance, letters seventy years ago were written on letter-paper—square—size; a quarter-sheet of foolscap. Take a half-sheet of foolscap: there is your letter-paper of that period. This is written on a blank page cut or torn out of an old book. One edge, I remark, is freshly cut. Letters used always to be folded in one way—not this way. There was always a postmark of some kind on a letter which had travelled through the post."

Clarence groaned.

"Moreover, the Treasury must have heaps of documents in John Burley's handwriting. I wonder whether the handwriting corresponds."

Clarence made no reply.

"It looks to me like a modern hand; not unlike your own, Clary. Then I observe certain locutions which were not commonly used seventy years ago; they didn't, for instance, say 'mad' with a man, but angry with a man; and the modern poetical use of the adjective 'rosy' was then, I believe, unknown in common parlance. Further, in June, 1822, your great-grandmother, who sends her love, had been dead, according to the register of St. John the Evangelist, for nearly two years. These are points which in ten years' time may not appear of any importance."

He laid the letter on the table. "Shall we get to business, my partner?" he asked.

"I told you"—Clarence picked up the letter and looked at it gloomily—"that I should go mad or something. I haven't even wits enough left to forge a letter creditably."

"That seems rather a good thing, doesn't it?"

Clarence laughed. "What would my grandfather say? All he cared for was that the business—whatever it was—should be well done. Life was all stage business with him. Business of forging letters? Good business, sometimes. Pleases people. But must be well done. To think that I should expect a clumsy, self-evident, ignorant piece of work like this to deceive anybody!" He threw the thing into the fire. "Look here, I told you about the old man's comedy, didn't I? Everything was justified by the cause. So he opened letters, told barefaced lies, acknowledged them blandly when they were found out; borrowed money under false pretences, forged a deed, and all to save from dishonor the son of a dead friend. He would quite approve—I know he would—of my writing such a letter. I would write it, too, I would, if I knew the handwriting, in order to complete that claim. And I should never feel ashamed, or sorry, or repentant if I got the estates by it. I should not feel ashamed if I were found out."

"The moralist sighs," said the poet, "the friend sympathizes, the beak condemns."

"If I can't prove my case one way I will another. I am the rightful heir to millions! Millions! Millions!" He screamed the words and threw up his arms. It was like the screech of an hysterical girl. "Millions! And all that is wanted is a little letter connecting my grandfather with his own people. That is all. You may talk about honor as much as you like. I want my rights! I want my rights! I will have my rights!"

His voice broke, his hands shook, his face was drawn and convulsed. The other sprang to his feet, and caught him as he reeled.

"Sit down, old man," he said; "sit down and be quiet. Good heavens! This cursed claim will kill you, if you do not take care."

Clarence lay back—white—with closed eyes. Presently he opened them and sat up. "Don't mind me, Jemmy," he said. "I get carried away sometimes. Last night, in the middle of the night, I woke up and went mad over this business, and I think I had some kind of a fit. I found myself lying on the floor."

"This magnificent good-luck, Clary, this extraordinary windfall, seems likely to bring with it, in its train, a wonderful collection of blessings. Already it has robbed you of your powers; robbed you of your face; robbed you of your laugh, and robbed you of your voice. Good Lord! What a windfall! It has filled your mind with anxiety and gloom, made you commit a forgery, makes you regret only that it was a clumsy forgery, and tempts you to commit another and a more careful one! It throws you into fits at night and makes you hysterical by day! Clarence Burghley, there must be a devil in this fortune of yours. 'The Devil in a Fortune' might make a sort of recitative thing with a rattling air running through it. The Devil in a Fortune. Eh?" He took up the note-book.

> *"I tell of a mountain of gold—*
> *A monstrous, incredible hill;*
> *With a devil to guard it and hold,*
> *A devil of wonderful will.*

> *"And every sinner that dared*
> *To carry a nugget away*
> *With whackery, thwackery clawing of claws,*
> *Pawing of paws—*

I believe, Clary, we can make something of it when you get better."

"It is the wretched uncertainty," said Clarence, brooking the question of the devil.

"And all for nothing. Because you'll never get it—never, I am convinced. You will never get it—never—never. Now, Clary, I am going to see that other fellow, the man from the music-hall. But I would rather keep you, and I'll give you time. As for existing engagements, you won't keep them. You are indisposed—you have got influenza. I'll give you time—never fear—to pull yourself together."

"Why should I not succeed?"

"Lots of reasons. The malignity of fortune or fate—that's one thing. Fate dangles this wonderful prize before your eyes—puts it just, not quite, within your reach. History is full of malignity—witness Napoleon and Moscow."

"Talk sense, man."

"Very well. Other reasons. Because you can't prove that you belong to the people at all. To you and to me there is no doubt. But you can't prove it to the lawyers. Therefore you will never get it."

"Any more reasons?"

"Lots. The missing son or his heir will turn up and take everything."

"No. That is impossible, after all this time."

"They'll find a will."

"They have searched everywhere, and there is no will."

"There are more reasons—but I refrain. The long and the short of it is that they will give the son ten years at least before they consider the claims. And when they do, you will have no chance."

Clarence groaned.

"The question, therefore, between us is, shall the partnership be dissolved?"

Clarence groaned again.

"You can't get it out of your mind. Then put it in the background. Don't brood over it; something may turn up. The Treasury people, even, may find letters that will actually prove your claims. Take a cheerful view of the thing—and meantime go back to your work."

"I don't feel as if I could ever sing another song, Jemmy. Do without me. Get another partner."

The poet used a strong—a very strong expression—and slapped his partner cheerily on the shoulder.

"Not just yet, Clary. I can understand now how a man may be possessed by the devil. You are possessed by some devil or other. You are possessed by this Fortune devil, and it's only the devil that you'll ever get and not the fortune. "I'll wait a bit, dear demoniac."

XXVII

The Genealogist

Sir John went about for some days with an air of great reserve. Questioned about the clew, he smiled with importance and demanded patience. "But, of course," said the girls, separately and in a choir, "we understand. We are going to establish our connection with this mysterious, misrepresented, misfortunate, misled, misspelt family." Calamities many had fallen upon the family—yet it was an interesting family, and distinguished in a way. There are not many families which can boast of a fortune made, not lost, out of the South Sea Bubble; nor are there many who can show a real gentleman highwayman. And a real miser—one of the good old candle-end, cheese-paring sort—is an ornament to every family; he may, and has, occurred quite high up on the social ladder.

The girls looked on; they chattered among themselves and watched the paternal countenance. It was grave, it was pre-occupied, but it was cheerful. They comforted themselves, the clew was being followed; the clew would end in a key, the key would open a box, or a door, or a cupboard; and then the fair maid Truth would be found most beautifully dressed within. They called at the ancestral house; they filled the house with the laughter and the chatter of girlish voices.

In point of fact, Sir John Burleigh, genealogy in hand, and those ascertained facts connected with the Bristol sugar-baker, had called in the assistance of an experienced and obliging person who made it his business to ennoble the world, or at least to enlarge the too narrow limits of gentility—for a consideration. Provided with a clew, this benevolent person was getting on as rapidly as could be desired.

The artist in pedigrees, an old man now, presented the appearance and simulated the manners of a duke, or an earl at least. He was a handsome man still, who knew the value of good appearance and good dress; he was what is called a "clean" old man. Many old men who take a tub every day cannot achieve the appearance conveyed by this adjective. His face was shaven, except for a heavy white mustache; be was tall; his large hands, as white as his snowy linen, were covered with signet-rings. He sat in a room massively furnished; one wall was filled with a bookcase containing those county histories and genealogies which are so costly and such good reading, containing as they do the simple annals of the great. There are all the Visitations which have been published; with books of all sorts on descents, ascents, heraldry, the nobles, and the gentles. Over the mantel hung his own pedigree, a very beautiful thing, one branch connecting with royalty in the person of Edward I. For one should always practise what one preaches. Also, one should live up to one's profession. And to be always in the midst of noble ancestors and to find none for yourself would be a clear proof of professional incapacity.

The Professor of Family Ascents—who would not climb?—received Sir John with encouraging attention.

"You want to connect yourself, Sir John," he said, "with an English family? A natural ambition, especially when one has risen to the proud distinction of Knight Commander of the Order of St. Michael and St. George." He rolled out the title as if the mere sound of it was an enjoyment. "Now, Sir John, place me in full possession of all the facts—all the facts, if you please—and the papers—all the papers. Then I will do my best to assist you."

Sir John related the history as he wished the world to possess it. There was nothing false in his statement—only a *suppressio veri*. Well, you quite understand how he put it. We need not dwell upon the little suppression.

"I have noted your facts, sir. Father, named Charles Calvert Burleigh, born 1801, married somewhere about the year 1834 to a lady whose Christian name was Marian Welford. Emigrated to New Zealand in the year 1842, being one of the earliest settlers. Succeeded with his farm and acquired property. Died in 1873, and never told you—"

"I never questioned him."

"Never told you who he was, and your mother observed the same silence. Any more facts?"

"None."

"Perhaps he had quarrelled with his people. Well, Sir John, we need not speculate as to causes. We are here connected with the facts. Where are the papers?"

"There are none; not even my mother's marriage certificate. But we claim nothing, so it does not matter."

"Oh!" The genealogist placed his chin in his left hand and fell into meditation.

"There is, however, a presumption, based on what may be a coincidence."

"My dear sir," the professional discoverer lifted his head, "in our work we want all the presumption we can get"—he did not mean a double use of the word—"and all the coincidences we can find. Coincidence is the guiding-star of genealogy."

"This coincidence is nothing less than an extraordinary resemblance between ourselves—my son, my daughters, and myself—with a certain group of family pictures."

"Yes. Of course you are aware, Sir John, that such a resemblance may throw the door open to a fine field of scandal. The first Duke of—But you understand."

"I think that we need not fear that kind of scandal."

"Is it a noble family?"

"Very much the contrary."

"In that case, I should say, do not let us trouble ourselves about the resemblance, unless there are other reasons."

"This family is named Burley; their great wealth has brought them very much before the public of late."

"You mean the great Burley fortune? My dear sir, if you can connect yourself with that family—your name is spelled differently—but"—he shook his head—"it is one thing to connect a colonial or an American family with an English House—even a noble House—and quite another to prove things as lawyers require proof. Quite another thing, sir, I assure you. Quite another thing. And without papers, letters, or any kind of evidence, almost impossible."

"I think that you do not quite understand."

"What I mean, Sir John, is this. You come to me without any papers and two or three facts. If you say, connect me with this or that noble House, I am not hampered by any nasty facts. It is a mere question where to hitch you on—and matter of the expense you care to undertake. To make a man cousin to a coronet naturally costs more than to make him cousin to a baronet; and this again naturally costs more than a connection with mere tradespeople."

"Naturally. If it is only a question of inventing a genealogy—"

"My dear sir, we do not invent; we connect—we connect. It is always perfectly easy to connect any family with gentlefolk of sorts, and almost any real gentlefolk with nobility of some kind. If you like, I dare say I could connect you with royalty. Mere time, mere search, in order to find where to hitch on; that is all. But of course it is a great advantage to start practically unhampered, as you do. Now, you don't know your father's family. And you have no traditions about it. He never told you. What must we therefore conclude? That he was ashamed of his family or ashamed of himself."

Sir John changed color. "I do not agree," he said; "other reasons might be found."

"Illegitimacy, perhaps. Humble origin. Early escapades. One or other must be the cause."

Sir John said nothing.

"If we investigate with the sole desire to ascertain the truth we must expect humiliation. That is all. Let us go on. You wish to be connected with the Burley family—quite a middle-class bourgeois family—and you do not desire to claim their monstrous estate. As you have no papers, you would have no chance. If I were you I would soar higher, much higher; we might connect you with the Cecils or the Howards in some way—an illegitimate way would be the easiest; but as you will. Let us return to the Burley family. For my own purposes, I have been hunting for the sons of the famous Westminster miser—brothers of the money-lender. I cannot find any trace of them—"

"You must go further back to find my ancestor."

"Very well; you stick to your plebeian lot? Very well; I will investigate for you. Well, now, about the spindle line. On your father's side you will be plain Burley; but you had a mother. On her side, now, what can we do for you? On your grandmother's side—what? On your great-grandmother's? See what a vista opens before you! Why, only to go back so far as the accession of Queen Elizabeth, you had then 4096 living ancestors; to go back to Edward III, you had 131,072 ancestors. Do you think I cannot find you a noble family or two among so many? You want ancestors? Let me find you some that you can be proud of. Why, you are founding a family. You will become a baronet. If you like, you may become a peer. How will it be in years to come to read: 'This branch of a noble House, which traces its ancestry back to—shall we say Cardinal Pole? in the female line, was first distinguished by Sir John Burleigh, K.C.M.G., the well-known statesman of New Zealand'? What do you think of that, Sir John?"

Even a statesman is not above the softening influence of flattery. Sir John heard. Sir John smiled.

"You see; but if my hands are tied—"

"I do not wish to tie your hands. Connect me with any noble House you like. But you must first connect me with these Burley people. Mind,

I say again, I won't lay claim to the estate. I have the Burley genealogy with me. Here it is. I must belong to them. My girls, in fact, have seen the portraits, and there can be no doubt possible."

He took the pedigree and examined it. "And with which of these branches would you wish to be connected? Not too close to the money-lender, or you may have to be a claimant whether you like it or not; and then the absence of papers may clash with my work. An undistinguished lot—not one *armiger;* I should say, no coat of arms."

"I have mine. The College of Heralds found mine when I was knighted."

"You can give me that; it may be of use."

"I am morally certain"—Sir John winced a little at the utterance of this tremendous fib—"morally certain," he repeated, "that we come from this Joshua Calvert Burley, born in 1778."

"Morally! morally!—we don't recognize morals in genealogies, Sir John. But still, what is known about him?"

"He is said to have become a sugar-baker at Bristol."

"Sugar-baker? Oh! Sir John, why not a distinguished officer in the Austrian service?"

"Sugar-baker at Bristol," Sir John repeated, firmly. "He altered the spelling of his name to Burleigh—l-e-i-g-h."

"Oh! No documents, I suppose?"

"None. My father, Charles Calvert Burley, born in 1801, succeeded to his father's business, was unfortunate, lost his money; and in 1843, when I was six or seven years of age, went to New Zealand."

"Ah! Well, Sir John, you must leave it with me. Very unpromising materials—very unpromising indeed. Still, I will do my best. About the terms, now?"

The terms, when imparted and grasped, carried with them a wide extension of knowledge. If it takes time to build up a family, it costs money to buy one ready-built. To which nobody ought to object.

"Very well, Sir John," the genealogist concluded, "your instructions shall be followed out. Look in whenever you like, and find out how we are getting on. We shall certainly hitch you on to some good family somehow or other. It's unfortunate about these pictures and their likeness to you—because, you see, when a man has all the noble Houses in the country to choose from, there's no reason whatever—unless it's the money—why you should even begin with a middle-class lot like this. And your features, Sir John, if you will allow me to say so, possess a cut so aristocratic. A thousand pities! You remind me of the portraits of his royal highness the late Duke of Sussex. How should you like a royal grandfather?"

"I belong, you see, to the Calvert Burleys," Sir John replied.

"Good—good! After all, is there anything so admirable as family pride, even if it leads to a milk-walk? Leave it to me, and call again, say in a week."

And thus, you see, the clew, once found, was followed up.

Great, indeed, are the resources of science, especially the science of genealogy. After a surprisingly short interval, considering the extent of the necessary researches, Sir John was enabled to exhibit to his delighted family a genealogy complete in every branch. It appeared that his opinion was quite right, as the new genealogy conclusively proved. This branch of the family was descended from Joshua Calvert Burley, born 1778, who was Sir John's grandfather and the brother of the Westminster miser. The pedigree was most beautifully written on parchment, and illustrated with shields properly colored. Its appearance alone carried conviction to every candid mind. Leaving out the intermediate stages and the unnecessary names, the document ran as follows:

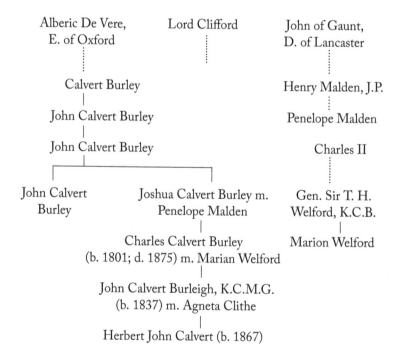

Alberic De Vere, E. of Oxford — Lord Clifford — John of Gaunt, D. of Lancaster

Calvert Burley — Henry Malden, J.P.

John Calvert Burley — Penelope Malden

John Calvert Burley — Charles II

John Calvert Burley — Joshua Calvert Burley m. Penelope Malden — Gen. Sir T. H. Welford, K.C.B.

Charles Calvert Burley (b. 1801; d. 1875) m. Marian Welford — Marion Welford

John Calvert Burleigh, K.C.M.G. (b. 1837) m. Agneta Clithe

Herbert John Calvert (b. 1867)

This, it must be acknowledged, was a genealogy worth paying for.

"It works out, Sir John," said the man of science, "better than we expected. Of course, when we do find a family connection of any pretensions, the rest is easy, because it has been done over and over again."

"This document, I suppose," said Sir John, thoughtfully, "will do very well for family purposes, but for a court of law—"

"As I warned you, a court of law requires papers. You would cling to the plebeian side, and there you are, you see. Don't blame me. Look at their vulgar names, spoiling the beautiful shields and titles above them! Sugar-baker! And he marries the descendant of kings!"

"Did you, in the course of your investigations, find out anything about my connections on this side?"

"I found out a good deal—oh, yes, yes, a good deal!" He looked hard at his client, who seemed entirely absorbed in his pedigree.

"About this Joshua, now?"

"Well, you told me about him, didn't you? Well, as you said—just as you said—he was born, as your genealogy states, in the year 1778, and he was baptized, as the books show, in the Church of St. John the Evangelist, Westminster. He was educated at Westminster School, and he became eventually, as you told me, a sugar-baker—a sugar-baker" (he yawned slightly, such was his contempt of trade), "in the city of Bristol. Here he married Penelope Malden, daughter of Henry Malden, J.P., a man also engaged in trade. Through the Maldens in the female line you descend from the Earls of Derby on one hand and the Barons Clifford on the other. His son, your father, married Marian—"

"Yes—" Sir John looked as if he wanted no discussion about his mother.

"Marian, daughter of General Sir Thomas Welford, K.C.B., through whom you are descended—not, of course, legitimately—from Charles II in one line, and from John of Gaunt, legitimately, in another. Really, sir, for the son of an early New Zealand settler, who knows nothing of his own people at all, I think you have come out of this arduous and dangerous—very dangerous—investigation admirably. Your connection with trade is—ahem!—unavoidable, but we have minimized it; whereas, two descents from royalty and three earls and barons in your genealogy make it, on one side, more than respectable."

"I think I ought to be much obliged to you"—Sir John rolled up the parchment and put it into its lovely morocco case—"very much obliged to you, sir. My children will be pleased; and my grandchildren, if I ever have any, will be placed on pedestals. I don't think I could have come to a cleverer man."

"You are quite right, Sir John," the other replied, with professional modesty; "it would be impossible."

"Or to a man who more readily understood exactly what I wanted."

"Exactly, Sir John."

So they parted. Sir John has never told anyone how much this important document cost him; but he has been heard to express his astonishment that the profession of genealogist remains in the hands of so few, seeing that its possibilities are so great. In these days of doubt as to a choice of profession, it seems odd, he sometimes says, that there is not a run upon it.

"Now, I wonder," said the man of science, when his client left him, "how much he really knows. He carries it off very well, if he does, for his father was a convict—it's all in the 'Annual Register'—a convict transported for life—most likely married another convict. Escaped. No one knew what became of him. Went to New Zealand. Well, I sha'n't tell. I wonder if he really believes all the truck?"

"I wonder," said Sir John, "whether the fellow really expects me to believe his lying rubbish? Sugar-baker—bankrupt—Baron Clifford—John of Gaunt. But, thank God! he does not know, and can never learn, the truth."

In the evening, after dinner, he announced that he had a discovery to reveal.

"Is it about the family?" they all asked.

"It is. In point of fact, children, you will be glad to hear that I have cleared up the difficulties, which, I confess, at first sight seemed insuperable. But they have vanished, and I am now going to lay before you"—he produced a leather case and pulled off the top—"the complete and veritable history of your family, so far as it has yet been traced."

"Oh! And that portrait—the later one—is that grandfather?"

"You shall hear. Meantime, I must tell you that, like yourselves, I was convinced that these resemblances meant a great deal more than coincidence. It seemed to me, as to you, impossible that we should all be so much like these people without some cousinship." Sir John spoke in his ministerial manner, which was, of course, that of one whose words carry weight.

"Certainly not," they chimed. "Oh, impossible!"

"So I considered. And it seemed to me that the best thing I could do was to put the matter into the hands of an expert—a professed genealogist, you know—one of those whose business it is to hunt up ancestors and to prove claims. This I did. I said: 'I am the son of So-and-so, who was born in 1801, and went to New Zealand in 1842, when I was about six years of age. I do not know where my father came from, or to what condition or rank his people belonged. I can only tell you that there is a group of family portraits in a certain house at Westminster which bear a most remarkable likeness, first to each other, so that they are all unmistakable, and secondly to me and my children—so remarkable as to make it absolutely certain that we must be related to them. Their name is the same as ours, spelled with a very slight difference.' Those were all the facts that I could give him, and after a little talk over them I left him to his work. He has now, after careful investigation, furnished me with exactly the information I desired. And here is the genealogy."

He spread it out and began to point out the wonderful acquisitions, and the great increase of family pride caused by this research.

"Your great-grandfather," he said, "is, you observe, not the owner of the first face so like Herbert's, but the son of the man who, some of us thought, was even more like Herbert; his name was Joshua Calvert Burley. He was educated at Westminster School; on leaving school he was placed in some mercantile office, perhaps as an apprentice. This matters nothing. You must be prepared for a somewhat humble connection on your grandfather's side. He became a partner or proprietor of a sugar-baking firm."

Their faces all lengthened.

"Sugar-baking! Oh! He was a baker."

"Sugar-baking is not exactly bread-baking. He was a sugar-baker. And why not? It is possible—or was possible—to become enormously rich by sugar-baking. Well, for some reason not apparent, probably because he thought it looked better, my grandfather changed the spelling of his name."

"It was done, then, at Bristol?" asked Lady Burleigh. "I have been thinking, since this business of the portraits, that your father, my dear, may have got into some scrape—debt—or something, and so thought it wiser to change his name."

"A scrape there was, but, according to my table, it was my grandfather who changed his name. Well, my father"—he hesitated a little, because it is really embarrassing at fifty-eight to start a new father—"was made a partner in the concern."

"The concern!" echoed the girls. "Have we discovered the long-lost great-grandfather only to learn that he was a sugar-baker and had a concern? What romance can we get out of a concern, however great?"

"And then something happened. The business fell into difficulties; your grandfather lost most of his fortune and emigrated. And that, my children, is all I have to say. The rest you can learn for yourselves from this document."

"Oh!"—the girls bent over the genealogy, their heads all together. "It might have been worse," said Lucy. "Herbert might have had the criminal ancestor that he wants so badly. Poor Herbert! He wants either a criminal or an aristocrat, and he will have to put up with a sugar-baker—a bankrupt sugar-baker."

"A sugar-baker!" Sir John repeated, with emphasis.

"I suppose, my dear," said his wife, "that all this is quite clearly proved."

"He has consulted the only authorities, where there are no better—the parish registers. I think we need never trouble to go over the ground again. Certainly I am convinced that it would be foolish and needless to do so."

"And as to the great estate?"

"There we must abandon all hopes. You will see that we are only the heirs failing the intermediate heirs—all the sons of the miser Burley first, and the money-lender Burley second. You will not be millionaires, my dears. You will go back to New Zealand, and you will live in comfort and plenty, thank God—and that is all."

But then the girls found out the magnificent connections on the spindle side, and pounced upon them. Heavens! A General and a K.C.B.! Splendid! And look—higher up—a long way higher up—Oh! Grandeurs! Heights! Soarings! Sky-scraping! Baron Clifford—Lord—Lord Clifford! That fine old title! And here the De Veres—De Veres—Earls of Oxford! Oh! actually the De Veres! That great and noble family! History is therefore full of the ancestors of these happy Burleys. And look! More grandeur! Royalty—Charles II! But he had no children. Go on. Things *tacenda*, yet not without more pride. And oh! oh! oh! Look! Look—everybody! John of Gaunt! Time-honored Lancaster! Old John of Gaunt! Good heavens! Here they stopped and gazed mutely at one another. "If John of Gaunt," they said, calmly reasoning out the thing, "then his father, and his great-grandfather, and so we get to William the Conqueror and King Alfred. Oh! King Alfred our ancestor! Father, is it possible? Is it really, really true?"

"There is the science of the genealogist, my girls. What else can I say?"

Nothing to be said—science is indisputable. So, when the girls had extolled their good-fortune and cried upon the heavens, in their amazement and their happiness they fell upon the paternal neck, and embraced with fervor the simple K.C.M.G. who united in his own person so many royal and princely and noble lines.

"But," they agreed, "these things must not be talked about. They are best kept to ourselves. At home people might be envious of John of Gaunt—time-honored Lancaster. Isn't he buried in the Abbey? Let us go and hang a humid wreath upon his marble brow. Oh! And Charles II. Well, but there is John of Gaunt—John of Gaunt—John of Gaunt!"

"And the sugar-baker," said Sir John.

XXVIII

A Physician's Advice

Another cousin, apparently." Lucian tossed a card into Margaret's lap. She read it. "Mr. Clarence Calvert Burghley."

"It looks as if he belongs to the family. Go and see him, Lucian. Perhaps, like the colonial, he will begin by having a pain somewhere."

Lucian was wrong. His visitor made no pretence of any pains, though he looked miserable enough for all the pains of purgatory. He went straight to the point. "I have seen in the papers," he said, "a statement that you have in your possession certain portraits belonging to the Burley family—my family—and I come here in the hope that you will allow me to see them."

Lucian looked at this new cousin curiously. He bore the stamp or mark theatrical. To begin with, he wore a fur-lined coat—Lucian held that fine raiment belongs to the other sex. His face was smooth-shaven, his speech was of a studied clearness, as if he was speaking words of a part—words written for him—not his own words. And his gestures were slightly exaggerated. He took off his hat as if the action itself formed part of his visit. These things slightly irritated Lucian. He thought the manner of the man was affected. It was not. The theatrical manner was natural to Clarence. Besides, at this moment he was horribly anxious and therefore perfectly natural. His anxiety was shown in the twitching of his nerves and the restlessness of his eyes.

"Your family?" Lucian repeated. "Why, your name, Mr. Burghley, is spelled differently."

"That is true. My grandfather, who was an actor, altered the spelling of his name when he went on the boards. Perhaps he thought the name looked better so."

Lucian looked at him again. The persistent Burley type was in his face, clearly marked and unmistakable, though the strength and the resolution had gone out of it.

"I don't know," he said, ungraciously, "that I am called upon to show these pictures to every stranger who wants to see them, on the ground that he belongs to the Burley family. There is a good deal of curiosity just now about this family. A great many people would like to be connected with them."

"There is no doubt about my connection, at all events. But if you cannot let me see them, I am sorry I disturbed you."

"Perhaps you would let me know the nature of your relationship."

"I am a grandnephew of the deceased John Calvert Burley. My grandfather was his brother, and the second son of the so-called Westminster miser."

"The second son. You are, then, the nearest in succession after the direct line."

"I am the nearest."

"You forget the missing son and his possible heir."

"They must be dead. Otherwise they would have turned up long ago. From your name, Dr. Calvert, may one gather that you are connected in some way with us? Are you, too, a claimant, perhaps?"

"Not a claimant—so far. Well, sir, if you can establish your connection to the satisfaction of the Treasury solicitors, and if the missing son does not turn up—nor any of his heirs—you will become, when they have made up their minds that the son is dead—say, in ten years or so—a very rich man indeed, perhaps the richest man in the country. I am told that the property, originally estimated at twelve millions or so, has been found to be actually worth a million or so more."

"Very possibly," Clarence replied, carelessly. "When one gets into figures such as these, what matters an additional million or so?"

"What, indeed? Well, Mr. Burghley, since you are so near the direct line, I shall not object to show you the portraits of some of your ancestors."

Clarence looked about the room. It now presented the appearance of a student's room; the table littered with books and papers; the bookcase filled with books.

"It was in this house," he said, "that the old man lived."

"He was born here, he lived here, and he died here. Your grandfather was born here, was brought up here, and ran away from here."

"Oh! Yes—and this would be his breakfast-room?"

"It was the old man's living-room; for forty years he never used any room in the house except this and his bedroom."

"And the portraits? May I ask how you obtained the portraits?"

"We took the house as it was, buying the furniture at a valuation, after the Treasury people had taken away the papers."

"Were there any—any—personal relics—or remains—of the old man?"

"I believe there was a pipe which he used to smoke. But that has disappeared."

"I meant, rather, things that would show us what the old man was like—note-books, account-books, letters, diaries in his handwriting—you know what I mean."

"You should ask the Treasury to show you these things. But I doubt if they will meet your views," Lucian replied, dryly. What did this man want with personal remains and relics in the handwriting of the deceased? "If you want to see the portraits, however, you can come with me."

Clarence followed him into the drawing-room. He saw all the portraits hanging on the wall, but he regarded them carelessly. He was thinking, in fact, of that scrap of writing.

"There are your ancestors," said Lucian.

"Humph! They are all exactly alike—till you come to look closer—wonderfully alike they all are!"

"Can you spot your grandfather?"

Clarence walked round the room slowly. Presently he stopped before the picture representing a dark Spanish-looking young man of eighteen or so.

"This is my grandfather," he said. "When I first remember him he was an old man with white hair. I should not have known him here, but we have a sketch of him in character as Mercutio, which is exactly like this picture. The eyes are the same, and the face. Oh, there cannot be the least doubt! I will swear to my grandfather."

"The fact should help your case, Mr. Burghley, because it is the portrait of the second son, Henry. You are welcome to have this portrait copied if you like, or used in any other way. That is to say, unless your case is already complete."

"Complete?" Clarence replied, with courage. "In every detail. In every link."

"Well. Then this resemblance illustrates your case. There is another point, Mr. Burghley. You are, yourself, unmistakably like your grandfather. You are thinner in the face, and you have not so much color. Otherwise you are exactly like him."

"I wonder if such a resemblance would be taken as evidence?"

"I don't think it would, except that it shows you to belong somehow to the family. But you are like other members of the family—especially you are like this ancestor." He pointed to the unfortunate prodigal.

"A good-looking fellow," said Clarence, examining the picture. "A dare-devil, rakish sort; would probably be called a Mohock in his day. Do you think I am like him? Who was he?"

"This man, unfortunately, came to the worst kind of grief; did a little highway robbery, and was hanged for it."

"Hanged? Really! My ancestor was hanged!" Clarence laughed. "This is an unexpected honor. Well, it was a long time ago; and people have forgotten it, I suppose. Oh! You think I am like him."

"Very much indeed. I mention it as another illustration of your case."

"The best thing I could do to prove my case might be to get hanged as well. Then there would be no doubt. I wonder if they would accept this likeness as well as the other as evidence?"

"Perhaps; but your claim, you say, is complete at every point already."

"Quite complete. The only thing is, how long shall I have to wait?"

"This man—the one who was hanged—was heir to a very large estate. His father was a very rich man—as wealth was then reckoned. But he could not wait, unfortunately for him."

"My case is so strong that I could, if I chose, raise any amount of money upon it," Clarence replied, with the appearance of confidence. "So you see, Dr. Calvert, there is no immediate necessity for me to be hanged."

Lucian laughed. The resemblance of this new cousin to the unlucky profligate was really wonderful. "I think I can tell you," he said, "most of your family history. Your grandfather, the second son, ran away, and, after adventures unknown, obtained a footing in some country company. His father never forgave any of his sons for running away, and in the end left the whole of his money to his eldest son. Your grandfather changed his name, and never held any communication whatever with his brother or with any other members of his family. Even when he came to London theatres he never made any attempt at reconciliation."

"I know all this. But how do you know it?"

"Circumstances have placed me in possession of a good deal of the family history."

"Dr. Calvert, I spoke just now of personal relics and remains. If you have any autograph letter of the late John Burley, I should greatly prize it, should you wish to part with it. Of course I don't know what you have. But there must have been something. The Treasury might not want papers of no interest—an autograph letter—anything—in the handwriting of a man so enormously wealthy, and my great-uncle. You can easily understand that I should greatly value anything of his—any little relic. It is a thing of sentiment, of course—but you will understand."

He spoke fast; his eyes became shifty; there was a false ring in his voice. He conveyed the impression—or the suspicion—that he did not really care twopence about his great-uncle; but that he wanted, for some purpose of his own, a specimen of his handwriting. Lucian—perhaps in consequence of these suspicions—thus knowledge confers power—power to lead on to disappointment—resolved to give him what he wanted.

"Perhaps," he said, "I understand you. Perhaps I do not. Well, I have certain papers and letters belonging to the late Mr. Burley—they were left in the house when the important papers were removed—because they were worthless. Among them is one at least which concerns your grandfather. You said that your case was complete. If it were not, this letter might assist you."

"My case is complete, of course; but yet—every case will bear strengthening. If you would let me see this letter."

"It is a letter which is written by the young man after he ran away—to his mother—speaking of the company which he had joined and of his change of name."

"Oh!" Clarence started into a natural eagerness. "It is the very thing I wanted. If you would let me see—copy—photograph—this letter."

"I will get it for you." He went in search of it. You have seen the letter already. It was one of those found by Margaret. "Here it is. You can make any use of it that you please. Your lawyers may copy it. I will lend it, or—it is useless to me—I will give it to you."

Clarence read it with a joy almost too great to bear. It was the one thing wanted to make his claim complete. He sat down, a little overcome. The Joyous Life was within his grasp at last—no doubt now. The connection was established. Then a most curious thing. For the physician, forgetting himself, began to warn this stranger seriously and solemnly against the very things he was himself daily, and all day long and all night long, practising, and this is what he said:

"Mr. Clarence Burghley"—Clarence heard Lucian's voice as in a dream—"I perceive by your manner and your behavior," the physician spoke with authority, "that you are greatly—dangerously excited by your anxiety about this claim of yours. This kind of anxiety is absorbing." Could he be speaking from personal experience? "It sometimes fills the mind to the exclusion of any form of work. I don't know what you do or how you live; but I can see in your eyes that you live in a perpetual fever of anxious thought; you build up schemes of what you will do when you come into your fortune; and your castles of Spain are always destroyed as fast as they are built by your terror that your case is not sufficiently strong. If I were to take your temperature at this moment, I should certainly find it much too high. I perceive, further, other symptoms— the trembling of your hands, the nervous twitching of your face, the black rings round your eyes; that you have no appetite, but that you can drink, and that you pass sleepless and restless nights. Is all this true?"

"You are a physician. I suppose you can read symptoms."

"Sometimes we can read symptoms—when they leap to the eyes. Now, sir, I have a little prophecy and a little advice. Will you allow me to offer both for your consideration?"

"Since you are so good as to give me this letter, I will listen gratefully to both."

"My advice is to send in your claim, and then to think no more about it—no more at all about it. To go on with your daily business as if there was no such thing as a claim or a fortune."

"Dr. Calvert," Clarence repeated, "I am indebted to you for the use of this letter and for a sight of the portraits, but I cannot promise to follow your advice in return."

"That is my advice. My prophecy is this: If you neglect it and any other warnings; if you go on letting your mind dwell on what may happen when you come into your inheritance, hope deferred will make your heart sick unto death or—worse—unto madness. The simple delays of the law may bring this trouble upon you. Unless the missing son turns up or is proved to be dead, they will wait for ten years at least. What will you do during the long years of expectancy and anxiety? Will you follow your ordinary work? With what heart, when this chance awaits you? You have seen a letter which, I am sure, greatly strengthens your case. Yet do not build too much upon it. And I tell you plainly, Mr. Burghley, that you will never succeed in your claim."

"Why not? Who is before me?"

"Accident—chance—the unexpected—are before you. There is, I believe, a superstition about this fortune. It is said that it brings disaster upon all who are concerned with it. We need not believe foolish superstitions, but it may very well be that the contemplation of or the longing after vast wealth may unhinge a man's mind. Be careful, Mr. Burghley. Too much thinking of millions cannot be wholesome."

Strange! This man, so wise for others, was at that very moment passing through the same experience himself. "Take care, I say, Mr. Burghley. Take care."

He opened the door. Clarence walked down the stairs and out of the house without replying. The warnings affected him but little. He had strengthened his case with the portrait and the letter. His claim was now completely made out. He went home with dancing steps; he threw himself into a chair and dreamed away the afternoon in visions of the Joyous Life when those millions should be his. And when his partner came home Clarence welcomed him with a shout and a laugh, brandishing the letter that established his parentage beyond the possibility of doubt.

XXIX

The Miracle

I came here yesterday, Margaret," said Ella, "and I am here today. I can't keep away from you, because you are the only person that I know in this country; we used to laugh and call it Little England. But it's Great England, Broad Britain, Big England, Thirsty, Sandy, Desert England, when you're all alone in it—with no—" She checked herself.

"Well, dear, you are always welcome."

"I can't sit still, or rest, or settle to work, or anything, I'm so miserable. I feel like jumping off Westminster Bridge."

"Sit still here, then, and rest."

"No; I must walk about or I shall go mad." The girl's cheeks were flushed, her eyes were too bright, her hands were hot. "Come out and walk with me. I want to feel the cool air."

Margaret led her into the large quiet square called Dean's Yard. "This is where I sometimes walk," she said, "when I wish to be quiet. But there are places here quieter than this. I will take you to the most hushed, still, and peaceful spot in the whole of London."

Under an archway, across an open court, through a broad arched corridor, she led the girl into a little square court, surrounded by a stone cloister; in the midst was a square of grass, with a fountain which ought to have been playing but was not; tablets on the walls commemorated dead men's names and lives. These tablets were all that remained of their memory. There were ancient doors and ancient windows of ancient, crumbling, worn stone, and above the corridor were houses which looked as if they were built at the time great Oliver ruled the realm.

"This is the old Infirmary Cloister," said Margaret. "It is the quietest place in the world. You hear nothing in these cloisters of the outside world—nothing but the striking of the great clock; you see nothing but the Victoria Tower. There is never any foot-fall here; the people who occupy the houses are in a conspiracy of silence. I come here often when I am troubled. Ella, dear, you are not the only woman in trouble; we are all troubled in these days. But the trouble will pass—oh! I think—I feel—that for all of us it will pass." Her eyes filled with tears. "Only to linger among the gray old stones soothes and comforts one."

The stones did not at first bring comfort to Ella—perhaps because she was too full of her trouble to notice them. She threw up her arms. She gasped. "Margaret!" she cried, "I am going mad. I am gone mad, I think, with the disappointment and the misery of it. Don't speak. Let me tell you first. I don't dare to tell Auntie. But she knows, poor thing. Ever since I began to think about the inheritance I have thought of nothing else—morning, noon, and night I have imagined and dreamed and built up castles about this dreadful money and myself. My very dreams are yellow with gold. I pictured myself the very greatest woman in all America—greater than the Vanderbilts, greater than the Astors—my name on everybody's lips, in every paper. Oh! the dreadful vainglory of it! And I was to be—oh! yes, nothing but that, if you please—yes, the best, the most generous, the most charitable of women! Oh! of course. The pride and vanity and self-seeking of it! That has been my dream, day and night—day and night. And now it is quite certain that it can never be anything but a dream."

"What has happened, dear?"

"Everything, I believe. You know that Auntie was always against it from the beginning. She's a prophetess, for sure and certain. She was for sending in her name and mine, and nothing more. But nothing would do for me but to come over here and claim the estate. I was so ignorant that I thought we only had to send in our names for the whole of the money to be handed over to us across a bank counter—sixty million dollars! I thought that we should be able to go home in a fortnight or so with a whole ship-load of dollars—millions and millions and millions of dollars—all in bags—and leave the Queen and the whole of the royal family in tears." She laughed through her own tears.

"Well?"

"They say that the Treasury must have proofs that the missing son is dead—or that he has left no heirs. Why, the world has been ringing with his name. If he was in the uttermost parts of the earth he must have heard that cry. Without proof, they say, they will probably wait for years. They tell me that when your General, Hicks Pasha, was killed in Egypt, they waited ten years for proof, because his body was never recovered, and not a soul returned from the battle to say that he had fallen. Ten years! When I heard that, my heart was as heavy as lead, for I saw that we might just as well go home again."

"Indeed, I think so."

"But that isn't all. Oh! I must go mad over it. I thought our claim was so clear and simple. Grandfather was Mr. Burley's brother. There's no doubt of that—and they say now that I must produce the proofs of his marriage. As if there could be any doubt of it! Why, I remember both of them. Proofs? It's an insult to speak of such a thing."

"But indeed, Ella, there are wicked people in the world. I fear they will insist upon the production of the proofs."

"I say it's an insult to suspect. Oh! it's impossible!"

"Yes, dear; but lawyers always want proofs of everything. It is not meant as an insult. And remember, we all—we all suffer from the—the follies of men—their follies and their wickedness. Lawyers will not take it for granted that there ever is a completely good man upon this earth."

"He wasn't married at Tewksbury. Grandmother—I recollect the dear old thing, lovely white hair she had—was an Englishwoman. She used to talk about her own people. They lived in a place called Bloomsbury, and they were lawyers. Her first husband was a lawyer, but a great deal older than herself, and he died, and then she came out to America with grandfather. I was only a little girl, and I never asked her name, else I might find out her people. And how in the name of wonder are we to find where a man was married sixty years ago and more?"

"It is not so difficult. There were only so many churches in London sixty years ago—perhaps not more than a hundred and fifty. The registers are preserved. An advertisement would procure you the proof—if it exists."

"An advertisement!" Ella laughed scornfully. "How are we to pay for the advertisement?"

Margaret took her hand.

"I have seen that coming, too, Ella. We are cousins, you know. Only I was afraid to speak. You are so independent and so proud."

"My pride is gone, then. Pride can't outlast want. And there's nothing left—nothing—nothing." She buried her head in her hands and burst into sobs that echoed strangely round the quiet cloister.

"My dear"—Margaret soothed her—"my dear, tell me all."

"We first spent the money we brought over with us, thinking it would be enough, and that we should only want it for a week or two. It is all gone—all but the rent, that must be paid tomorrow, and then there will be nothing left—nothing at all. Margaret, we are nearly starved. You would not believe on how little we have lived for the last three weeks."

"My dear, patience for a few moments; only while you tell me."

"We have spent everything. We have pawned our watches—our dresses—everything that we could part with. We have nothing but what we stand in. And more trouble. Auntie had a little money—not much. It brought her $200 a year. I had none, because father wasn't lucky. Auntie's money was put with a trustee, and he has just run away, bankrupt, and we hear that he has lost or stolen it all. Then we had our house—only a little yellow cottage with a slip of garden—but it was our own. We mortgaged it to get the money for coming over. And now we are told that the mortgage is the full value. Oh! it's roguery, it's treachery and roguery. So we're quite ruined, Margaret, and tomorrow we go out into the streets and w—w—walk about till we d—d—d—d—die."

"My dear child, this is most dreadful. Why did you not tell me of all this before? I only knew that you were pinched."

"Oh! you are a stranger; you are an Englishwoman. They used to teach us that Englishwomen were cold and proud. How could I?"

"Well, you have told me now, and so—we are your cousins, you know—something must be done at once, and—and—" She stopped short, for the trouble in the girl's face was terrible.

"I left Auntie praying." She burst into hysterical laughter. "She is always praying. She gets up in the night and prays. She asks a miracle. Poor thing! As if miracles come for the asking. There are none left. In these days, without money or work, we starve. If I talk about searching the registers, she shakes and trembles and begs me to give it up and go home again. Today finishes everything. This evening we shall eat up the last scrap of bread and drink the last cup of tea. Tomorrow we shall go out into the streets. And Auntie says we ought to go home! Is it better to starve in the streets of London among strangers or in the streets of Tewksbury among friends?"

"My dear, you shall not starve. It is all arranged. Only I did not know that the necessity was so close at hand."

She took Ella's hand. Without thinking whither they were going, Margaret led the way into the great cloister and through the little postern into the Abbey itself.

Afternoon service was just beginning. They took a seat in a retired corner, and then, while the silver voices rose and fell and rang and echoed from pillar to pillar and along the lofty roof, and the organ rolled, and the voice of the reader was like a single flute seeking to be heard through all this great building, the American girl wept and sobbed without restraint. It was a time for the opening of the floodgates.

When the service was over, Ella dried her tears. "Oh!" she said, "this place is full of consolation. I am better now. It's a lovely place. If I were to get that great fortune, I would buy it and take it over to Tewksbury, choristers and all. Thank you for bringing me. I almost believe that Aunt Lucinda will get her miracle, and I will not go mad."

"Well, then, dear, if you will promise not to go mad till I return, I'll take you home and leave you there while I go to fetch your aunt. And then we will have tea and talk—and you must be prepared for developments."

Aunt Lucinda was indeed in a pitiable condition. Half-starved, penniless, with the prospect before her of destitution, in dire terror lest a certain family secret should be discovered, she sat beside the black fireplace on that cold, autumnal afternoon with clasped hands and eyes that were blind with helpless tears.

"Aunt Lucinda," said Margaret, bursting in, "I have come to carry you away."

"Carry me away?"

"You are to come and stay with us, you and Ella. My husband is your cousin, you know. We invite you—Ella and you—to make our house your home for a while; till we have looked round and found some way out of the trouble. Oh! I know all about it; you need not tell me anything. Now let me pack up your things for you. Where are your boxes? I will do it all for you." She bustled about into the other room and back; she crammed the "things"—they were few indeed—into the two boxes; she talked cheerfully all the time; she gave the poor lady no time for thought or for protest. When all was done—it took ten minutes or so; no more—she brought out Aunt Lucinda's hat and jacket and rang the bell for a cab.

Then Aunt Lucinda's face began to twitch ominously.

"Come, the cab will be down below," said Margaret. "Let me help you with the things."

"Stay with you?" asked Aunt Lucinda. "We are strangers in a strange land, and you take us in! Oh! Ella said I prayed for a miracle; and there are no more miracles, she said—and lo! it is a miracle. Oh! The Lord fulfils the desire of them that fear Him. He hears their cry and saves them."

She stood for a moment with bowed head and clasped hands. Then she meekly followed this woman of Samaria.

XXX

"Confess Ye Your Sins"

When two troubles assail the soul it is not together—troubles very rarely fight in company—but separately. The stronger and the fiercer trouble overpowers the soul, enters, and takes possession. Then the lesser trouble goes away. He does not go far; he lurks in ambush till the present occupier withdraws. Then he sees his chance, and rushes once more to assault the citadel of man's soul. One might write a new allegory showing that fortress continually besieged by one trouble after the other—never at rest, never at peace. The biggest trouble of all, as the world has always been ready to confess, is the want of money. Not the want of plentiful money, but the want of needful money. As has happened to many, one sees the approach of the hour when there will be no more, not a penny more; no more food, no more lodging, no more resources, no friends, no work; then, indeed, this is a trouble so stupendous that the soul surrenders at once, and there is no room for any other trouble, hardly even for the pains of gout.

When this trouble was driven away for a time, Aunt Lucinda's soul was left open to the other and the lesser trouble—that, namely, connected with the claim, to which Ella now returned, but with somewhat mitigated persistency.

"As soon as we have found out how to make a little money, Auntie, we will advertise for your grandfather's certificate of marriage. I have thought it all out. Father was born in 1827—they arrived in Tewksbury in 1826—therefore they must have been married before they left London. Therefore the register will be easily found, and then our claim will rest on sure foundations!"

"Oh, my dear!" cried Aunt Lucinda, eagerly, "let us think no more about the claim. This fortune brings disaster upon everybody—even upon those who think about it and hope to get it, as well as those who have it. Margaret has shown and proved it to me. Think what misfortunes it has brought upon us! Do not let us think of it any more. There will be fresh sorrow if we do."

"I don't desire it any more, Auntie, for the vainglory of it. I don't want to be the richest woman in the world. But I should like—I should like—well—not to feel that we have come on a wild-goose chase. I should like our friends in Tewksbury to hear that we were really what we believed ourselves to be; and as soon as we have any money I will advertise."

This was the trouble that now vexed the poor lady's soul. To be sure, she knew that there could be no certificate in any church. But it is ill work to stir muddy waters. Things done may be remembered—may be handed down. The wife who left her husband in 1825, or thereabouts, and went off with young James Burley, had belongings, and the husband had belongings. The memory of the thing might survive. Therefore Aunt Lucinda trembled. She sat in terror all day long. She showed terror in her face—in her eyes—in her attitude.

"Ask her," said Lucian, "what is the matter with her. She is torn by some secret anxiety. She looks as if it might drive her mad. Ask her, Marjorie. I suppose you can't hint that an Egyptian mummy at the feast would be quite as cheerful as a face in affright. It will be a kindness to me if you bring her to a more resigned frame. There ought not to be spectres at the dinner-table."

Margaret obeyed.

"I can't tell you, my dear," the poor lady replied—"I can't tell anyone. It is a thing that I know and nobody else knows. And I live in terror day and night for fear of her finding it out."

"If nobody knows it but you—"

"Oh! But long ago, when it happened, many people knew. And some may remember, or they may have been told. Oh, if she were to find out!"

"I suppose it is a secret which affects—the—honor of someone whom you both know."

The poor lady nodded her head violently.

"My dear Aunt Lucinda, give your anxious mind a rest. A thing so old must surely be forgotten long since. All you have to do is to hold your tongue. Come, if we all think what might happen, where would be the cheerfulness of the world?"

"If she would only give up this dreadful claim I should be happy. But she won't. And she is walking right straight into the place where she will find the horrible, hateful, shameful secret."

"She can do no more than she can do. Everything is clearly proved except her grandfather's marriage." Aunt Lucinda clasped her hands and rocked to and fro, and her face turned red and white. Margaret pretended not to observe these signs. "The place and date of that marriage she has yet to ascertain. Perhaps she never will. Then she will never be able to establish her claim. I will tell you a secret which should console you. Ella will never, under any circumstances, get any portion of this estate."

"Oh, thank *God!*" She lifted her clasped hands. "There has been nothing but terror and misery since we thought of it."

"Ruin and Destruction!" said Margaret, the superstitious. "Ruin and destruction for all who make or meddle with this horrible estate."

"Will she give up looking for that certificate of marriage?"

"I think I can promise you that before many days she will definitely abandon all hope of the inheritance." This she said, thinking that Lucian would establish his own right, at least, whatever else he might do. "Tell me, Aunt Lucinda, do you want to be enormously rich?"

"No, I never did. I was quite happy at home when we were poor. We are nearly all of us women at Tewksbury, and we've got everything that the heart can desire—books, and a beautiful literary society, and courses of lectures, and churches, and meetings of every kind; nearly all of us are poor, and nobody minds. We aim at the Cultivated Life, my dear, and the Spiritual Life, and, oh! if you could hear Ella read her papers on Browning! I've got some here—would you like to read one?"

"Very much," Margaret replied, politely, but with little warmth, not feeling greatly tempted by the writing of an American girl who, she could not forget, was only—even English people say—only a clerk or cashier in a store. In this country we do not expect literature of the higher kind from such a girl. "Meantime, rest quite easy. What you fear cannot happen. It is impossible, since you alone know it. And as for this certificate of marriage, it might be found if one were to institute a search in all the parish registers—by offering a reward for its recovery. But you have no money, and, in a few days—how long, I do not know—the necessity of finding it will be past and gone."

"I am so thankful—oh! so thankful. I have prayed, night and morning, that this danger might be averted. Oh! Margaret, you don't know—you can't guess—what it is I fear—what would be the consequences—to Ella—the blight upon her life—the ruin of her pride—the shame and disgrace of it—"

"Hush, dear—don't tell me any more, unless it would relieve your soul."

"I will tell you, then, because I must. You are the first person to whom I have told it. I've known it for twelve long years—my brother never knew it, nor suspected it. And Ella doesn't know nor suspect. And when I learned it, for a time the sun went out of the sky—and I lost my faith in God—for I lost my faith in my mother—in my mother. Think of that! I have got back my faith, but my old happiness—that is gone—and oh! let me spare my child—my Ella—the shame that I have to suffer daily!" She clasped her hands and bowed her head and her lips moved.

"My mother was a pious woman," she continued; "one of those who go to chapel every Sabbath, and read the Bible at home. When father died, she read her Bible more and more. But she was not a cheerful Christian; her faith did not give her courage; her spirits were always sad and low. Sometimes she sat weeping for hours together. I thought it was because she'd lost father. But she never said anything to me until, twelve years ago, she fell ill. Oh! she spoke—and her words were like the scourge of an offended God."

Margaret took her hand. "Be comforted," she murmured. "If she told you of some great sin, it was a sign of repentance. Think of what a mother must suffer when she has to confess her sins to her own daughter. Think of her shame and of her repentance!"

"Yes—yes; I do—I do. It is my only comfort—to think of her repentance. She whispered—oh! I remember every word—she whispered: 'Lucinda, my dear, St. Paul says, "Confess your sins to one another." There is no one here to whom I can confess my sins, except to you—no one, because ray son must never know, nor his child. You must be scape-goat, to bear this secret. Women have to bear everything. You shall hear my secret!' And so she told me all."

"She told you all," Margaret repeated.

"The dreadful truth. Nobody would ever find it out; yet she could not die with that secret in her mind untold. I have thought of it, over and over again. Was it necessary to tell me? Why was I singled out for the secret? She told me, however—" She stopped again—she could not bring herself to repeat it. Yet, like her mother, she could not bear upon her soul any longer the weight of that secret. At last she strengthened herself. "She told me that she—she had never been my father's wife—she was the wife of another man—she had left him for my father—they came out together to America; and when they settled in a quiet, respectable town it would have been ruin to confess. So they lived and died in sin. That is what she had to tell me. That was the dreadful burden on her soul."

"A dreadful burden, surely. Yet, to tell her own daughter! Oh, think of the repentance and the pain!"

"She did not die. But she lost her speech, and lived so for three years more. And all the time her eyes followed me about, and they said 'Keep the secret—keep the secret. Don't let my son know, nor the child.' And every now and then I used to whisper that the secret was safe. But oh! the suffering!—to go among the people, to sit in church with them, to work with them, and feel that if they knew the truth they would shrink from me as from a leper!"

"But no one did know. And if you do not tell anyone, your secret is safe with me. How should Ella ever find it out?" Margaret did not tell her that close at Aunt Lucinda's elbow in the fire-proof safe was the whole of the family history, carefully drawn out by her husband's father, in which the circumstances of their flight were fully narrated.

"And then—Ella read in the papers about this inheritance—and she knew a good deal about the Burleys, for father liked talking over the old days, and it seemed to her, naturally, that she was one of the heirs, and so nothing would do but she must come over here to claim her 'rights,' as she called them; and then—think—then—oh! what was I to do? For she has no rights—I knew enough of law for that. I am illegitimate; so was Ella's father. Therefore Ella has no rights. Then, if she was to succeed I should be a wicked and deceiving woman, hiding the truth, and all the rest of my life, daily and hourly—all day and all night—so long as the consequences of the sin should endure, a breaker of the eighth commandment. I have turned that over in my mind. No one knows who hasn't thought it out—the consequences of sin. Think! Ella might, through me, get possession of all this money wrongfully; through me, generation after generation might be wronged; long after I was dead would arise the accusers against me."

"Do not fear, Ella will not inherit. If you had only told yourself that without that certificate of marriage the thing was impossible, you would have been quite tranquil."

"Oh, I might have told her so much and prevented this journey to England. But to tell her the whole dreadful truth! I could not! No; I could not!"

"No—you must never tell her."

"And then in the researches and the opening up of old stories, who knows what might be discovered? I have never been so wretched except in the first week after my mother's revelation." She sighed heavily. "It mattered nothing if we were put off and made to wait—I cared nothing at all about spending all our money. I wouldn't mind lying down to die and have done with it—only a Christian woman must wait to be called. If only Ella should never find it out—never find it out!"

This was the burden of her song—that Ella should never find it out. But she had relieved her soul. And straightway she began to mend; her pale checks put on a little color; her lips assumed the semblance of a smile; and her eyes lost the terror. "Thank Heaven!" said Lucian, "you have laid the ghost, Margaret—you are a witch."

XXXI

"Impossible to be Found Out!"

I mpossible to be found out!"

Is there anything impossible to be found out? Is there any man so old as to feel assured that the thing that he did sixty, seventy years ago will not be found out before he dies? Is there any man who can be certain that the history of his grandfather will never be revealed to the world? Why, an old letter, an old note-book, an old picture, a certificate of marriage—anything may be discovered. Or the thing is certainly known to some one else, and will by some one else be discovered and whispered abroad. Sometimes the thing is not found out till after death, which is merciful.

The other day they found a letter addressed by the captain-governor of a fortress to his Egyptian Majesty three thousand years ago! Shall they not, therefore, much more be likely to find letters written by you, most respectable Senex—love-letters—written to one Amaryllis, my Lady Light o' Love—only fifty years ago? "I have always taught my younger clients," said one of those practical moralists—the true father-confessors of the age, the family solicitor—"always to act in the full belief that the thing you are doing will certainly come to light." An excellent rule. Young readers will please to make a note of it.

"Impossible to be found out," said Sir John.

"Impossible to be found out," said Margaret, who knew it all the time.

You shall see.

After the romantic recovery of their long-lost ancestors, the Burleigh girls were naturally anxious to visit again and again the gallery of family portraits, and to keep Margaret informed concerning their great good-luck and the uplifting of the Burleighs.

"It is true," said the girls, "that John of Gaunt and Charles II and the noble lords our ancestors are all on the spindle side; but there they are. One day we may pride ourselves on the Red Rose of Lancaster, and another on the Stuart tartan, and another on the ancient barons. It's much prettier to say 'on the spindle side' than 'in the female line.' We are going to take the genealogy out to New Zealand, but it won't do to flourish it there. The New Zealanders would turn up their noses at such a magnificent display of ancestors. They would refuse to believe in them. For them we shall keep the other side—the spear side—fancy the pater with a spear!—the respectable family of the Burleys. It will be quite a distinction for us to be connected even indirectly with this mountain of gold—all the world has heard of the Burley millions—and nobody will be envious or jealous because granddad was only a bankrupt sugar-baker, and our cousin, the rich—very rich—incalculably rich—man, was only a money-lender. Perhaps you will let us copy one or two of the portraits just to show them in New Zealand."

Now, one day when they called Margaret was out; but she was expected home shortly, and they went in.

Sitting in the hall they found, also waiting for Margaret, the old woman, their cousin, Lucinda Avery, whom they had met on the occasion of their second visit. She was then in the workhouse dress, but this had now been changed for the ordinary civilian garb. Lucinda was no longer an "inmate" of the workhouse. Why do we reserve the word "inmate" for the workhouse and the lunatic asylum? She had been taken out by Margaret and intrusted to the care of certain respectable persons, who were instructed to keep her well fed, well warmed, and well dressed. To be warm within and without; to feel the physical case which belongs to abundant food; to have nothing to do—it was all this poor old soul asked of life—rest and warmth. It is, if you come to think of it, all that working people of every kind ask of life. When one is dead—"Requiescat in pace!" says the priest. "Let him rest from his labors." "He sleeps," say the people. "He is called to his eternal rest." As if to do no more work would be the greatest conceivable happiness. But the man of science says, "Let me work forever. To rest would weary me in a week. Let me be called to my eternal work."

The needle-woman sat humbly on the hardest chair, her hands folded in her lap, her spare form bent, quite patient, ready to wait as long as anyone pleased to make her wait.

"Why," cried the girls; "it's our cousin—Lucinda Avery!"

The old woman stood up meekly and courtesied. "Sir John's daughters," she said. "Sir John's beautiful young daughters. Yes, young ladies, Sir John is my cousin."

"And you are—you are—in the—"

"I was in the House. My fingers bent and got stiff, and I could work no longer. So I was glad to go in. But Mrs. Calvert took me out. She said that she'd found a cousin, and she wasn't going to leave her in the workhouse. I'm quite as comfortable where she has put me."

"Oh! But we are your cousins, too. Why should not we help? And where are you now?"

"I've got lodgings," she replied, "with respectable people. Mrs. Calvert pays for them."

"But you are our cousin, as well. Won't you come upstairs with us and talk about yourself? We are waiting for Mrs. Calvert."

The old woman followed submissively. She obeyed anyone who ordered her, as behooves one who knows nothing of the outer world but that it is strong and masterful, and must be obeyed. She followed, sheep-like.

In the drawing-room, at the writing-table, sat a girl who looked up from her work and rose.

"Our name is Burleigh," said the eldest. "We know Mrs. Calvert, and we have come to look at the family portraits again. They are the portraits of our ancestors."

"Why," said the girl, smiling, "I am named Burley, too. And they are my ancestors as well."

"Good gracious! and this old lady's mother was a Burley! Then we are all cousins together. But as for us, we cannot claim the big fortune, because we are descended from an elder branch. Perhaps you can put in a claim."

"I came over from the States with my Aunt Lucinda, to claim our share, if we could get it. But there are delays. They want more proofs than we can find. And they say they must wait for proof of the death of the man who should be the heir. So we must go back again—or find something to do here—and wait till it pleases them to be satisfied that he is dead. And that will be—I know not when."

She looked clever, this bright-eyed, sharp-faced American girl, and capable of self-assertion should the necessity arise.

"Let us shake hands and be friends," said the New Zealanders, through the eldest, "since we are not rivals. And let us all hope that you will get the fortune all to yourself."

Then they looked round the room and talked about the pictures, and found likenesses and common ancestors, and lamented such of the family disasters as they knew, and wondered about this person, and sighed over that, and agreed that the American cousin was partly like her great-grandmother—only prettier—but more like her great-great-grandfather. And it was all very pleasant. And they pressed the American cousin to bring the cousinship closer together, and to call upon her New Zealand kin at South Kensington. And it was all delightful, until the earthquake came.

It happened in this way. The old woman, whom they had placed in the most comfortable chair beside the fire—for it was a chill November day—sat placid and patient, her hands in her lap, her form bent, just as if she were still waiting in the hall. She did not know pictures; she did not like walking about when she could sit, and she did not understand the chatter of girls among themselves.

"And now," cried one of the New Zealanders, "let us hear, you poor old thing, all about yourself."

They sat and stood and grouped themselves about the old lady. Ella rang for tea, and they asked her questions, and made her talk.

She told what the old novels used to call her simple and affecting narrative; that is to say, she answered questions.

"Oh!" they cried. "What a life! What a dreadful story! What a cruel wretch the eldest brother must have been. How happy to have done with such a life! What do you do now? Do you read much?"

She shook her head. "No," she said. "I don't care about reading. "We never had any books, and I never did read, except on Sunday at church. I'd sooner stitch than read. But I like to have nothing to do. It's having Sunday evening all the week and all day long."

"What did you do on Sunday evenings?"

"We used to sit together, mother and me, in the dark, with the street-lamp outside, and she told me about her family. Every Sunday evening she talked about them. So, you see, it's this way. Because it's all Sunday evening with me now. I think about nothing but mother's family all the time."

They gazed upon this wonderful old lady with amazement. Was there anywhere else in the world an old woman who never read, except in her prayer-book; knew nothing—absolutely nothing; and had no food for her mind, except the recollections of her mother concerning her family. Ancestral worship can go no further. To spend the evening of one's days in remembering the history of an undistinguished—or perhaps an undesirably notorious—middle-class family.

"Tell us," said one of the girls, inspired of the devil—"tell us something about them."

It was half-past six; outside twilight had fallen; the firelight fell upon the faces of the girls gathered round the fire, and warmed up the thin cheek of the old woman with a rosy flush.

"Mostly I think about my mother's brother. But there was her father; she used to talk about him a good deal. He was a dreadful miser."

Here followed a chapter on the miser, containing many illustrations of the miser's miserly misery.

"The elder brother was John—my uncle John—who has left, they tell me, such a lot of money. He was dreadful fond of money, too, but he wasn't such a miser. He didn't stay at home and grub for money; he went out into the town and made more money."

Then followed the history of the money-lender so far as she knew. We have heard it already.

"And then came the next brother," suggested another of them, also inspired by the devil.

"The second son was Henry. He became an actor after he ran away. Mother lost sight of him, and never knew what he did nor how he got on. When he was a boy he used to make them all laugh by mimicking everything, especially his father. But he ran away, and his younger brother ran away; and when mother was left alone with her father and her eldest brother, she had to run away, too. And so she did, and married Captain Avery, my father."

Here followed the history of that unhappy marriage, with its sequel in the Fleet.

"Then there was the third son. He was named Charles."

"That's the one who is exactly like Herbert—our only brother," one of the sisters explained. "He is so like that we all thought he must be our grandfather. But he wasn't."

"Charles was a wild young man; I don't know what he did for his living. But he committed a forgery—"

"Oh!" They all drew breath together. "A forgery!"

"Yes. He wrote somebody else's name on a paper and got money for it. They caught him and tried him, and he was sentenced to death; but they let him off, and he was transported for life. They sent him to Australia."

"Where he died, I suppose? Well, it's a long time ago now. We need not feel very much shame over him."

"No; he didn't die in Australia. He escaped somehow, after a good many years, and came home. He would have been hanged if he had been caught. He found out mother—I remember him; it was when we were living in the Rules of the Fleet; and he came to see her, and brought his wife—her name was Marion, I remember—and their little boy—I remember the little boy—and he changed his name—spelled it different, but it sounded the same, and went away in a ship to New Zealand. And there, mother heard, he got on and got rich, and no one ever knew out there who he was nor what he'd done, nor where he came from. He told mother what he was going to do. His son was never to know, else he'd be ashamed. Got rich and prospered, mother heard. And it was never found out what he'd done," she concluded. She had forgotten that she was speaking to Charles's grandchildren. She was just repeating what her mother had told her.

There was dead silence. As five tall lilies for want of water hang their sweet heads and droop declining, so these five maidens drooped and bowed their heads in shameful silence. For the story could not be mistaken: the man who had forged that paper; the man who had been transported for life, and escaped; the man who had changed his name, "but it sounded the same;" the man who had a wife—"her name was Marion"—and a son; the man who prospered and grew rich—"and no one ever knew what he was nor what he'd done"—this man must be none other than their grandfather, and the beautiful genealogy was a long lie from beginning to end.

There was dead silence. Presently one of the girls sobbed and choked. The others choked as well—repressing sobs.

The old woman went on.

"Then there was the youngest brother, James."

The American girl, who was filled with pity for her cousins—because she, too, read the story and saw their shame unspeakable—shivered. Would there be anything terrible for herself?

"James was always thought a very steady young man—not like Charles or Henry—and not a money-grubber, like his eldest brother—mother said she was never so astonished in her life. He had an aunt who helped him—and he became a lawyer—and he was going to be a partner with his master, who was an old man, with a very young wife—and then—it's shameful to say it before young ladies—but the truth is—he ran away with his master's wife—and he took her out to America, and pretended she was his wife."

Then the sixth head bowed down.

And there was silence for a space.

Then the old woman got up. "I must be going," she said, cheerfully, after doing all this mischief. "Good-night, young ladies. I should like to tell you more some day. The family has had dreadful misfortunes. There was the one who was hanged, and the one who went mad. Oh! There's a deal to think about in the Burley family. I'll come and tell you all the troubles over again."

When she was gone they remained in silence. Presently the eldest of the New Zealand branch rose and touched her sister's shoulder, and they all rose and went out, leaving Ella alone in the room. And she sat there in the firelight. For the worst thing that could possibly happen, in her mind, was this thing: the worst crime that can be committed by any man, according to her Puritanic views, had been committed by her grandfather and her grandmother—she remembered them both—the grave and reverend grandfather, the wisest man in the town, the friend and adviser of all—and her grandmother, white-haired, reverend, dignified, pious, severe. Oh! was it true? Could it be true?

Margaret came home about seven. Ella had gone to her own room. She had a headache; she would be better alone.

The others went home by the underground railway. They had a carriage to themselves, and they all wept and cried without reserve. When they reached home they gathered together in Lucy's room.

"Mind!" said the eldest. "Not a word—not a look—not a syllable—above all things, the dear old pater must never know—never—never—never! Oh! it would ruin his life—" She broke down and sobbed. "And mother must never know—it would kill her. The shame of it—the disgrace of it—"

"Not a word! Not a look! Not a syllable!" they all echoed.

"Cathie"—Cathie was the youngest—"if you feel you can't sit down to dinner without crying, stay here and say you've got a sore throat or something. After dinner somebody must play—I'll get out the cribbage-board, and play with him. We'll go to bed early. We can't trust ourselves to talk. Mind! Again—no talking about it—even among ourselves. Never a word for the rest of our lives. If we marry, never a word to our husbands. And as for that wretched, lying, miserable genealogy, with its John of Gaunt and its Joshua Calvert Burley—and its sugar-baker and its Charles II—let the pater believe in it still. And we'll pretend—and let us forget. Oh! let us try to forget—if we never speak about it! If we go home soon—away from this unfortunate family—we shall be able to forget."

"We will forget," they cried. "We will try, at least, to forget. But—"

There was one thing more to be done.

Lucy, the eldest, did it. She went to the Church of St. John the Evangelist; she found the parish-clerk, and she examined the register. Joshua Calvert Burley. He was baptized on July 1st in the year 1778. So far the genealogy was right.

"There's a-many come here now," said the parish-clerk, "to search the Burley names. All trying to get a slice off the big cake, I reckon. As for the name Joshua, he occurs again."

So he did. Two years later, on October 3, 1780, little Joshua Calvert Burley breathed his last. It was hardly likely that in his short life of two years he could have found time to start a new branch of the Burley family tree—and therefore the portrait belonged to somebody else—and how about the sugar-baker? And how about John of Gaunt, and Charles II, and the Earl of Oxford, and the Baron Clifford?

XXXII

The Shame of it!

If you come to think of it, almost the most deadly blow you can strike at a girl is one which forbids the honor and respect due to those she loves—those nearest and dearest to her. Ella remembered the ancient lady, her grandmother, as austerely religious, constantly reading the Bible, always serious. Could the story be possible? Was it an invention of the old woman's?

That old lady, her grandmother, in the white widow's cap and black dress, who sat beside the stove, knitting in her hands for occupation, the Bible on her knees, her lips moving, but seldom speaking all day long—was she the wife of another man? To think of this terrible secret locked up in her heart all to herself! Oh! why was it suffered to be made known after all these years?

This dreadful story seemed for the moment to make self-respect henceforth impossible. We recover from some things. Not from such a thing as this, which can never be shaken off. It has to be accepted, like a humpback. To be sure, it can be hidden away, which the humpback cannot. Very many people, I believe, have got some such secret hump on their backs; the skeleton hangs in unsuspected cupboards; the young men and the maidens of a family grow up with the knowledge of what is behind the door. Learned in this way, and gradually, the story becomes a secret burden, borne without much pain. But to have a skeleton suddenly presented to you, cupboard and all; door wide open— door never seen before; cupboard invisible till then; skeleton never even heard of, a new and unexpected skeleton—this may be very terrible. One has to bear it as one can. No use whatever in crying over it. The thing must be endured, and one must go about as if there were nothing wrong at all—no pain anywhere.

No one would have suspected that this American girl had been robbed of so much. She became more silent, perhaps, and rather pale; but she made no other sign.

She kept it up for a week; then she broke down.

It was in the evening, after ten o'clock. Aunt Lucinda had gone to bed. The lamps were lowered; the firelight fell on the portraits.

Margaret sat improvising soft, sad music—letting her fingers ramble over the keys in harmony with the sadness of her thoughts. Ella sat in a low chair by the fireside. Lucian was downstairs in his study. Presently Margaret closed the piano with a deep sigh and came to the fireside, gazing silently and sadly into the red coal.

Ella took her hand and kissed it. "Margaret, you are unhappy; you sigh, and your face is always sad. Are we all to be unhappy?"

"You, at least, need not, Ella. Yet you are. Why? Not because of your horrid claim? If that is the cause, I can tell you something that will set your mind at rest. I have seen trouble in your face for a week and more."

Then it was that Ella broke down, and, in her weakness, confessed the whole.

"Margaret—that cousin—that old woman of the workhouse—Lucinda Avery—"

"Well?"

"Does she know all the family history? Is what she says about our people true?"

"I believe that her mother taught her nothing else."

"We were in the drawing-room, the New Zealand girls and I, and she was there; and we asked her about our people, and she told us. Margaret, for God's sake, do not let Auntie know! It would kill her—the shame of the thing would kill her."

"What did she say, dear? That is, if it would not pain you too much to tell me—"

"It pains me more to keep the thing a secret. She said—she told the New Zealand girls—who have got a genealogy a mile long—that their grandfather was a convict transported to Australia and escaped, and—is that true, Margaret? You who know everything, is that true?"

"Unhappily, Ella, it is true."

"And that my grandfather—my grandfather—ran away with his master's wife—who was my grandmother—my grandmother, Margaret. Since they never married in Tewksbury, they never married at all. Is that true, Margaret?"

"Give me both hands, Ella—both." Margaret took her hands, held them—kissed her forehead. "My poor child—it is true—"

"And you knew all along? Oh! how is it you know everything? And you never told me!"

"I knew that secret. Do you blame me for not telling you? I hoped that you would never find it out."

"And now I have found it out—as for my claim—that is gone—and a good thing too. Oh! Margaret—dear Margaret—don't tell Auntie—don't let her ever know."

"There is no necessity for telling her. You had better not talk with her about your grandparents at all. And now, Ella, my dear, don't think about this matter any more."

"Margaret"—Ella sat up in her chair—"what did you tell me—you, who know all about us? That disaster followed with that fortune—even on the mere endeavor after it. It has fallen upon me. I came over in search of it—I thought of nothing else. And now the punishment has fallen upon me. My father was the son of sin and shame."

"If you had stayed at home you would have escaped this evil. Yes, dear; it is true. Disaster falls surely and certainly upon all who touch that accursed pile of gold. God forbid that the smallest piece of it should come to you or yours—or to me and mine. It means shame and misery. To us women it means that we must bear the burden of the men's iniquities. To us it means the knowledge that our innocent children are only born that they may endure the inheritance of those sins." Margaret spoke with an earnestness that sank deep into her companion's heart.

"Ella, dear, I have seen them in a vision—in broad daylight—all the wives and daughters that you see upon these walls, and more. I have seen them, and I tremble lest their lot may be mine. Thank God, dear, daily, that you have escaped with nothing worse than the knowledge of a guilty pair."

"You, Margaret?—you, too, concerned about this inheritance? Then you must be—or your husband must be—one of us. Oh! when I first thought that we must give it up—because we could not find the marriage certificate—it seemed a most dreadful blow; now I don't mind it. I have come to see that both of us, Auntie and I, are most unfit for the burden of great wealth. If that was all—but I have got this awful secret to endure. I have lost my reverence for that dear old lady, so full of dignity—the memory of whom has always been a perpetual admonition of the Christian life. She is gone. What am I to put in her place—a shameful adulteress? I cannot, Margaret—I cannot."

"A repentant woman. The past forgotten and forgiven. The Christian woman that you remember. All that is left of her—pure and most womanly. It seems as if the most difficult lesson we can ever learn is that of the purifying fire of repentance. Let the old memory survive, Ella. So you will bear your burden better."

"I am glad that I told you. I feel happier again. Tomorrow I will tell Aunt Lucinda that we will give up the claim altogether. I feel lighter only to think of giving up the claim. That's enough about me. Now, Margaret—you who have done so much for me—can I not do something for you?"

"No; you can do nothing for me. There is but one person who can do anything for me. I am in a ship, and he is steering—and I see the rocks ahead, and he sees nothing but smooth water; and in a day or two, a week or two—I know not when—the ship will be on the rocks, and we shall be wrecked. That is the reason why I am unhappy, dear."

"It has something to do with this awful estate, Margaret. In America if we have religion we mean it. I shall pray for you. Aunt Lucinda says that we prayed for a miracle, and the Lord sent—you. If I pray, what will the Lord send? Something."

In the night, or in the small hours of the morning, Ella woke with a start, for she heard a voice. You know how a voice—which is no voice—does sometimes ring through the brain, crying, echoing, loud enough for all the world to hear. This was a voice that explained everything. Many things have been explained by such a voice; the school-boy in the night receives the solution of his problem from this voice; the hesitation as to this or that line of action is finally ended by this voice—it is not, you see, a voice that begins a new thing, or reveals a new truth. There are no revelations in dreams. But somehow in sleep, or at waking, the mind carries on the thoughts of the evening, and the voice brings a solution. This voice cried, "Lucian is none other than the grandson; it is he who may take the whole if he wishes. He has promised not to take it; but he is tempted more and more—and Margaret looks on, and waits, and dreads."

She received this message. Then she turned her head on the pillow and went to sleep again, for reflection would come better in the morning than in the dead of night. In the morning she perceived what a wonderful discovery she had made; and now she understood why Lucian was like his great-grandfather, Calvert Burley—the resolute, the masterful, and the unscrupulous. Resolution was his—and mastery; was the third gift also his already, or would he assume it with the inheritance of Ruin and Destruction?

XXXIII

THE STORY OF A DREAM

In this unexpected way the American girl discovered the secret of the House. Strange that no one else should have found it out. Why, his face, his eyes, his hair—all betrayed him. And what was he thinking about always, this strong man who sat so silent, his face exactly like that of the first Calvert, resolute and masterful? What but of the immense fortune that awaited him if he only chose to put out his hand and take it? A great and terrible temptation. For such a man as this would not desire wealth for its own sake—not for the life of pleasure, but for some worthier objects. She thought of her own castles when first she dreamed of getting it all for herself. As her dreams were, so would his be, but wiser—perhaps more generous. An American girl is not too ready to admit the superiority of a man. Ella watched him at breakfast and at dinner. She saw that the temptation was always in his mind. She saw his face growing more resolute, and she knew that the end was very near.

It is venturesome to interfere between husband and wife. Ella ventured.

"Lucian" (she attempted the thing in his study), "I've got something to say. Are you too busy? So—then—what is the matter with Margaret?"

"With Margaret?"

"Yes; she is nervous—she is anxious about something."

"I think that Margaret is quite well. But I will talk to her."

"Think she is well? Why, Lucian, what is the good of being a physician and a husband, and a lover, too, not to see that she is ill, without being told?"

"I will talk to her," he replied. How could he explain that between them stood a figure which to one showed like Dame Fortune in her best, her most smiling mood, and to the other looked like Siva the Destroyer? How should he guess that this girl saw the figure as plainly as either he or Margaret?

"You've got to talk to her, then, and to look after her, and let her have whatever she wants. You've got to think more about her, and less about your science and your profession, Lucian. If you were a lower kind of man, I should say you've got to think less about yourself."

"I will talk to Margaret as seriously as ever you can desire, Ella. She *has* looked nervous lately. I will see to it at once. I've had a good deal to think of."

"Lucian" (Ella took his arm-chair and sat down in it), "I often wonder why you are always thinking—thinking—thinking. Have you got some mighty discovery on your mind? Are you going to invent a bacillus that will inoculate the whole world into perfect health? That is the kind of bacillus we want—a ravenous bacillus that will eat up all the other bacilli, like Moses's serpent, and then spread itself out comfortably and expire. Is that what makes you so silent—I suppose I must not say moody?"

"Am I silent, Ella? There is something, perhaps, on my mind. You know one has to think of many things, and I—well—perhaps I have reason to think more than usual."

"I hope it will be successful thinking, and—oh! Doctor—Doctor Lucian—I hope it will be something that will make Margaret happy again. Cure her—cure her—cure her first, physician—before you cure the rest of the world."

Even the thought of Margaret was powerless against the temptation. His face hardened. He made no reply. Ella left him. She had fired her shot. Perhaps it would be useless. Perhaps it might recall him to a sense of what he was throwing away. For the shipwreck that Margaret foresaw would be the wreck of her married life—love, happiness, everything. She would never, Ella understood, join her husband in any part or share of this estate. "The ship," said Ella, "is very near the rocks."

At dinner the same day she made another attempt to combat the temptation. It was a silent dinner, but Ella forced the talk.

"Lucian," she said. He looked up abstractedly. "I want to tell you something. You have not spoken for at least ten minutes, which shows that you are now in a good mood for listening. Now, attention!" she rapped the table with the handle of a knife.

"Well, Ella?"

"I want to talk to you—and Margaret—about our claim, and all about it."

"Yes, we shall be very much interested."

"You know the Grand Triumphal March of the American Claimants, and the huge lump of solid happiness we've got out of our march, don't you?"

"I suppose we know something."

"Very well. We have withdrawn our claim. Auntie has tied up all the papers, and it has come to an end."

"Perhaps it was wise, considering the difficulties in your way."

"Perhaps; but consider—all the way from Tewksbury here, and all the time we have been here, I have had the most gorgeous dream that ever came to any girl—a dream of Boundless Wealth. I have been, like Tennyson, building for my soul a Palace of Art. I have been dispensing with both hands unheard-of blessings—and now it is all over."

"You feel, I dare say, a little lonely."

"Just a little," she interrupted. "Lucian, do you know what it is like?" She spoke simply, without the least suspicion of double meaning in her voice or in her eyes. "Did you ever have—you—a Dream of Untold Gold?"

Margaret started and bowed her head. Lucian started and dropped his fork. Why, at that very moment he was longing to wander away in such a dream—a vision in which he stood forth as the greatest benefactor that science ever knew. He dropped his fork—a thing no one ever does except at moments of sudden shock. In the last century, when a man was startled his mouth opened and his jaws stuck. That was the recognized and highly poetical manner of receiving the unexpected. In these days a man drops what at other times he never drops at all—his fork, his umbrella, his pen. The ancestral manner is the more striking. Lucian dropped his fork; he changed color; he looked up quickly and suspiciously. The girl's face expressed perfect, unsuspecting ignorance and innocence.

"I don't mean, you know, the ordinary wealth that makes a rich man such as we call rich—a man with a million or two—just independent of work—having to think before he spends ten thousand dollars—I mean Boundless Wealth—such wealth as I once hoped to inherit. The wealth that I came over in order to get—and haven't got."

Lucian picked up the fork and fenced, not with it, but with the question.

"I suppose," he said, "that we all have some such dream, at odd times. It does no harm to dream of things possible only for one man in a dozen centuries."

"Mine was a lovely dream. Would you like me to tell you about it? I know you won't laugh, Margaret, over the foolishness of my dream."

"Nobody will laugh, Ella."

"Then I'll tell you all about it. It began as soon as I was able to understand what it meant to be the heir of the Burley property. You can't rise to it all at once, especially if you are an American girl working in a store at five dollars a week. You understand ten dollars perhaps, or even twenty, but it wants great imagination for such a girl to get beyond that. I suppose it was a fortnight or three weeks before I even began to understand. I used to set down the figures, all in a row, and look at them till they got lengthened out—you know what eyes will do with things if you look long enough and let them have their own way. They stretched out—so"—she followed an imaginary line with her hand—"to miles and miles and miles of millions, till I used to think I was going off my head. The figures got the better of me for a time. If ever I shut my eyes, I saw along procession of them—round naughts without units—rolling wheels one after the other, never ending. Well, I got the better of them at last, and then the dream began. I had first to conquer the figures, you see, and make them feel that I was going to rule them. Did you ever feel that way, Lucian?"

"Not altogether."

"So the dream began; and I was the Queen of all the Treasure, and was doing with it—oh! the most inconceivable amount of good to the whole world. I just scattered blessings. I was the most benevolent fairy that you ever saw. That was how it began—just with blessings in the abstract—vague, you know—shadowy blessings. I think I enjoyed that phase of the dream best. Then it changed. Have you felt that way, Lucian?"

"Not altogether. But go on."

"Then I began to settle down—we were on board the steamer by this time, and the weather was awful, and as for poor Auntie—but I was too busy with my dream to notice things. I began to settle down, I say. I asked myself definitely what I was going to do. You see, I had made up my mind that I was going to get the whole estate—I had no manner of doubt about that. Well, where was I to live? Not in effete Europe, not in a corrupt European capital—that was the way I used to think six weeks ago. It must be in America—the Land of the Free. So I chose Boston, and I thought I would have one of the houses looking over the Common. And as for Tewksbury—which I then discovered, for the first time, to be quite a little place, I couldn't live there—that wasn't at all a fit place for the queen of all that treasure—but I would do something for it—What?"

She paused for anyone to make a suggestion. No answer.

"I thought I would build a great and splendid college."

Lucian started, and looked at the speaker with swift suspicion. No—innocence itself was in her eyes. Indeed, though I believe that her first question was artful and designing, and based upon her discovery, the rest was pure coincidence.

"A college—yes—a college for girls only, where they should learn everything that men learn—they do that already, almost. In my college they should do it quite. There are some things still left for men—mechanical engineering, ship-building, machines and engines, electricity—everything, everything, I would have taught in my college besides the usual history and languages and art and science."

Lucian nodded his head. "You would make them also navvies, ploughboys, hodmen, sawyers, carters, draymen?"

"Why not? There is no reason why they should not learn. Anyhow, I tell you I was just going to make the finest college in the world, and to plant it down at Tewksbury, and to leave them to work it out. Can anyone say that I was unmindful of my native town? Wasn't that a noble dream?"

"Very noble indeed," said Lucian, with a little restraint.

"I was afraid you wouldn't think so. Because, here in England you won't acknowledge—what an American understands quite well—that women are fast becoming the leaders of the world."

"No. I think we have hardly—"

"Not yet. But you will. The men will go on working; they will have to do the work that the women leave them. They will make things—all the men in Tewksbury make chair-legs, for instance—they will plough and reap; and they will do the buying and the selling—they will do the money-making. That is essentially a branch for the coarser wit of men. Of course it will not be considered in the future a noble branch of work."

"This is all part of your dream?"

"Of course. My college was intended to advance the supremacy of women. Oh! I know what you are thinking: no woman yet the equal of the greatest men. Why, you have never given us the opportunity, and you can't deny that even with our limited chances the average woman is far better than the average man. Woman is essentially the administrator. Why, it's the hardest thing in the world to get a man who can administrate; he must be a soldier or a teacher. But you may find a woman who is a good administrator in every other house."

"Your woman of the future—will she also fight?"

"Why not? The old fighting—the club and knife and fist—is gone. You fight from a distance. Your rifles are too heavy; but when you substitute electricity for powder, you will have a light weapon that we can carry as well as you. And as for endurance in a campaign, the average woman will endure far better than the average man."

"I understand," said Lucian, coldly.

"Yes, and the most beautiful point about it was that I did not want the fortune for my own use. I wanted it—all of it—for the advancement of the world. Oh, it was grand! There was I—just I by myself—on a pinnacle, a spectacle for all the world, five feet three in my boots—Ella Burley by name—native of Tewksbury, Massachusetts—a girl clerk in a store—who knew nothing outside my books—standing behind the great round world and rolling it uphill all by myself."

"Why not," asked Lucian, "if you have the money? That is the power."

"Ah! But, you see, that is a mistake. It is not the money that rolls the world—it is the man. I don't know whether my college would have taught the girls any better than any other college. But I do see now that it wouldn't have quickened or diverted the current one bit unless it was connected with a strong person—a man, if you like. Well, it's all over now," she laughed. "All over, and I am so glad—so glad; and so is Auntie."

"Since you are pleased, Ella—" said Lucian, feebly.

"Well, at first I was disappointed. It seemed a thousand pities to give up such a dream. Presently I remembered something in Browning. I can't quote the lines. He shows how everybody, who desires anything strongly, especially if he desires good things, feels like the Greek mathematician—that, if he only had a stand-point for his lever, he could move the world. But he can't—and he's got to be content to stand where he is placed, and to move if he can his own little bit of the world. So we must be content with our little bit. As for all that stuff about women leading—it was the kind of rubbish we talked—some of us; and my college, which was to teach them everything, what was it all but empty vanity and conceit?"

Margaret at this point looked at her husband. He lifted his eyes and met hers.

After a little pause he spoke. But he made no reply to the last little speech about the empty vanity.

"We are all of us moving the world," he said, "if we are working at science. I see no other way of moving or advancing the world. If your college had been founded, it might have been an excellent college, and a real centre for scientific discovery; on the other hand, it might have failed. There is no reason that I can see why women should not advance science. They have not done so as yet; but, then, very few have attempted in that direction. As for women leading the world, either in any high line or as administrators—there, fair dreamer of dreams, I venture to differ."

"Very well. But what would you do, Lucian," she asked, still with a look of open innocence, "if you—but of course you are too sensible—could entertain such a dream?"

"If I ever entertained such a dream as you say, it would be to advance science in some way."

"Just like me, then. But you would advance science only?"

"Yes; because I see no hope for the advancement of the world except by science."

"I have always been taught," she replied, softly, "that there was a larger hope. However, what do you mean to do for the world, especially by your science?"

"The possibilities of science are such that we can no more understand them than we can limit them. At the present we are still on the threshold. Future ages will ridicule us when they read that we thought only of prolonging life, destroying disease, alleviating pain, arresting decay. It will seem to them child's play when we proposed to lessen labor by the half—by three-quarters; to multiply food products indefinitely, to destroy poverty, to raise the standard, to lift up the poor to the level of the rich, and to make the world a garden for men and women as long as they like to live in it. Of life, in the long-run, there would be, I take it, satiety in the end."

"A world with nothing to do but to enjoy itself! Why, Lucian, your people would have to alter a good deal first. Only to think of pleasure! What a world it would be! Why, if you come to think of it, your science would produce a universal pigsty. Fancy taking all this trouble to produce a world with nothing to do but to enjoy itself! You are a very clever man, Lucian, but I do hope you will not get your college. If you do, I shall go and live on a desert island."

Ella laughed, but Margaret did not. She looked at her husband, who replied, gravely: "You do not understand, Ella. These things will not arrive all at once. The world will be prepared by gradual achievements. And in such a world the pigsty will not be permitted."

"People don't want much preparation for less work and more pay. But it's a curious thing, Lucian, isn't it, that your dream—a scientific man's dream—should be no better than mine? You are a biologist, a physician, and I know not what, and I am only a girl clerk from Tewksbury, Massachusetts, and we dream the same dream. And both the dreams are foolishness! Only think! Both foolishness."

XXXIV

ANOTHER DREAM OF DEAD MOTHERS

A fter this little discussion of the impossible dream there was silence for a space, three out of the four feeling guilty. Then Margaret rose. Lucian remained behind, shaken out of the even tenor of the dream, which now held him day and night. In the drawing-room the three ladies sat without the exchange of many words. As for the coincidence, what could be more natural than that Ella should speak of her dream? Everybody knew she had entertained such a dream, and had been living in it, and clinging to it, until it became impossible in the way that you have seen. But something was going to happen. Everybody knows the feeling that something is going to happen. The two women were expectant.

Something was going to happen. Anybody may say so much at any time. Something is always going to happen; something happens every day; but not something that may change the whole current of a life, may poison its stream, may turn sweet water into bitter; something that may choke the spring of happiness; that kind of something we do not expect, else were life intolerable.

Presently the clock struck ten. Margaret rose. "Good-night, dear," she said. "I must go down to Lucian, I think. We have to talk together tonight. Good-night, Ella; your eyes follow me about. You are like your grandfather's portrait. My dear, I know not what may happen. Perhaps tonight all my future—" She checked herself; she had said already more than she should have said.

She went down the stairs with trembling steps and beating heart. She stood before the study door for a moment hesitating. Then she opened it and stood in the doorway.

"Come in, Margaret," said her husband—"come in. You so seldom show up here since the American cousins came. Come in and shut the door. Let us be alone."

"What are you doing, Lucian?" He held before him a sheet of paper covered with figures and calculations. "Is it still the dream of unbounded wealth?"

"Always that dream, my dear," he replied, with forced cheerfulness.

"It never leaves me. I confess that for the time I can think of nothing else. That is not surprising when you consider the importance of it."

"And your dream, after all, is exactly the same as that of a girl, ignorant of the world, from an obscure village in the State of Massachusetts." Margaret had never before in all her life attempted to be sarcastic.

"Her dream!"—he laughed scornfully—"her dream compared with mine? My dear Margaret, you have not attempted even to grasp the greatness of my scheme. Every day it grows upon me—it throws out new branches in all directions, it brings forth unexpected fruit, it is going to be the most noble college of philosophy that the world has ever seen. Don't talk to me of that thing she called a college."

"Yet it is the same. And, like that girl, you want none of the fortune for yourself."

"None. I would not stir an inch, Margaret, believe me, to get this money for myself. So far, I respect my father's wish and my promise to you."

"But, Lucian, remember what that girl said. Though you say you want nothing for yourself, you see yourself everywhere—it is your own glory that you desire for yourself—glory as lasting as the monument you would raise."

He interrupted her impatiently. "You invent motives—what business has the world with motives? We want deeds; we need not ask the motives."

"In my husband I look for noble motives. Well, say that you desire to do some great thing for science. My dear, consider; you are young, you have begun well; go on in your line and do this great thing. It will be far greater for you if you do it—you yourself—than if you build a palace and hire laborers to do it for you."

"I have seen Nicholson," Lucian replied, evasively. "He tried to dissuade me from my purpose; but finding that to be impossible, he undertook the case, and has taken my papers to the Treasury today—all the papers in the case. He has, in fact, already put in my claim. And of course there can be no doubt and no delay. Well, Margaret, the thing is done."

Margaret dropped into a chair. "Oh," she moaned, "he has done it, after all!"

"It was necessary, if only that the unfortunate claimants who are hanging on and hoping on might be put out of their pain. I told you at the outset, Margaret, that if I could not have this fortune nobody else should."

"You have sent in the papers, you have put in your claim; and after your promise to me—a promise as binding as your marriage vows."

"Can you not see, Margaret, that a woman's superstitious whim cannot stand against interests so gigantic as these? I warned you. It has been evident to you what was coming. Besides, the claim is not for me—it is for the thing I am going to do."

She said nothing, but she clasped her hands and swung herself backward and forward as one who is in grievous pain.

Lucian went on justifying his own action to himself. "As for my father's wishes—I promised him that I would consider them, and I have considered them fully. Having regard to his natural dislike to the methods by which his father made the money, and his own school-boy humiliations in being reminded of the money-lending and the other notorious things, I can quite understand his wish to be separated from the past altogether; taking all these things into account, I can quite understand why he should attribute the various well-deserved shames and disasters of his family—which were clearly due to their own misdeeds—to the crooked ways of those who built up the fortune of the House, and to the third and fourth generation theory. But as a person not given over to superstition, and not in the least afraid of being taunted with things now pretty well forgotten, I am indisposed to accept his views, and I am disposed to take what is ready to be placed in my hands. You understand me, Margaret?"

"It is impossible to misunderstand you."

"Then—"

"You have not waited for my consent. You promised you would do nothing without my consent, and you have not even taken the trouble to ask a release of that promise!"

"The promise was nothing. It was made without understanding the facts of the case. But I do want your approval and your agreement with me. I do want your acknowledgment, my dear Margaret, that I am acting wisely and rightly."

"You have condemned your wife to life-long misery. Oh, Lucian, if any misery of my own—only my own—would make you happier—but—"

"Misery! Child! I don't want your misery. Margaret, Marjorie—mine." He caught her hand, but she drew it back. "I want your happiness. See—consider—we are poor. Between us we have no more than four hundred a year. There may be other claims on us as time goes on. I may never get any practice at all—most likely I never shall—I am not of the kind out of which successful physicians are made. And I don't want practice. I want to work all my life—research—work in a laboratory. That is my dream for myself. For you, ease and material well-being and no anxiety. That is all I want. But oh! the superstitious madness and folly of it! That you—you—should feel such mediæval, antiquated, ridiculous scruples."

"It is not superstition. What but misery has followed all the members of the family from generation to generation? Lucian, shake off the temptation. It is not yet too late. You to inherit this dreadful pile of gold, heaped up and gathered by pandering to the worst vices that can degrade and disgrace man! It was made by the ruin of gamblers; by the profits of infamous dens, where wretched men and lost women held their orgies! by lending money to profligate young men. Oh, Lucian, how can you, an honorable man in an honorable profession, the son of an honorable man—how can you, I ask, think for one moment of claiming this vast monument of shame?"

"I have considered all these things," he replied, coldly; "and I have told you that the use to which I design this wealth will be better, far better, than the abandonment of it."

"You will actually acknowledge yourself to be this man's grandson?"

Lucian laughed, but not with merriment. "I care nothing at all about the character or the history of my grandfather. He lived his life—a grovelling kind of life it was—and I live mine. As for the people he wronged—they are dead and their wrongs are buried with them. Good heavens! if we were to remember all the wrongs committed a hundred years ago! And as for the opinion of the world, I own to you, Margaret, first, that I care nothing at all about it; and, secondly, that the world cares nothing at all about me. The world is not greatly curious about any man's grandfather. Very often the world's grandfather, like mine, was of the reptile order. There must be crocodiles and alligators, I suppose. As soon as the facts are announced, and the world hears that the case is decided, and that the great Burley estates have been handed over to the legal heir, there will be a day or two of talk; the illustrated papers will have my portrait, with a brief account of my education and work; interviewers will flock here; there will be a speculative paper in the *Spectator* on the emotions natural to the sudden possession of great wealth; a good many stories will be raked up about Burley's Hell and Burley's Dancing-Cribs, and the old orgies, and the rest of it. What then? Silence will follow about the past; everybody will know the worst that there is to know; expectancy and conjecture will begin about the future. What is the rich man—the very rich man—the richest man in all the world—going to do with his wealth? And the first thing, of course, will be to make him a peer. This country could not go on unless the richest man in the country was made a peer. How should you like to be a countess?"

"Oh, Lucian! You can even jest about it!"

"Not at all. And then I shall found my college of science. That will be the serious work of my life. Come"—he changed his tone and spoke sharply, even roughly—"you have heard my dream. Let us fence with the thing no longer. It is not a dream—it is a settled purpose. I see before me a plain duty; an opportunity such as has never before been offered to any living man. If I threw away such a chance, it would be a blasphemy against science which could never be forgiven, neither in this world nor in the world to come. There are other rich men in the world, but their wealth lies in lands, houses, shares, and investments. If they attempted to realize their property they would lose two-thirds of it. I shall be the only rich man in the world who can lay his hand upon all these millions and millions of money and say, 'This is mine, to spend, to invest, to use as I please.' And you would prevent me from taking this magnificent, this unrivalled chance by a superstitious terror, or by some foolish objection as to the way in which the money was made."

Margaret sank into a chair and buried her face in her hands. It was no use to say anything.

"We cannot undo the past, my dear. Let us be reasonable. The money was not stolen; if it were it could be restored. The fortune was first begun, as my ancestor has artlessly informed us, by robbing the till; it was afterwards increased by the savings of a miser; and it was multiplied twenty-fold by trading on the vices of the town. What can be done with it better than to devote it all to science?"

"No," said Margaret, "we must not touch the accursed tiling. Why did your father leave it?"

"Again remember that I want nothing for myself except to be the founder of this great college. Margaret, have you no feeling for science? You are the wife of a man of science—do you not understand something of what might be done by such a college? Think. Science is the only thing in all the world that is real and tangible and certain. It is the only hope of the world."

"No. It is not the sole hope of the world."

"Yes; the only hope. You heard at dinner something of this. My college shall be the chief home of science, the chief servant of humanity, the teacher of that highest morality under which every man shall feel that he best protects himself by protecting all other men. That is my case, Margaret."

She sighed. She rose.

"Then you agree with me, Margaret? You are in consent with me? You release me from that promise?"

"No."

"Then, Margaret, once for all, I release myself."

She looked him full in the face. His eyes were hard, dogged, unrelenting—the determined eyes of his ancestor, Calvert Burley.

"The accursed thing is working in your soul already, Lucian. It has brought wretchedness, somehow or other, to all who hope to get possession of it—to Sir John; to his daughters; to Ella; to Lucinda; to that poor butterfly, the singer; to you. As for me, I am one of the wives; I can sit and wait and weep with them. Your mind is quite made up; I see it is; I read it in your eyes."

"It is quite made up, Margaret. There is no more to say, except—just at present, I fear, a useless thing to say—be reasonable, and trust in your husband's reason."

"I must go, then. I must think—I must find out, if I can, what is best to be done."

Margaret turned away sadly and climbed the stairs.

The house was silent; the lights were out. As Margaret went up to her room the air was filled with whispers—they were women's voices—for her alone to hear. They said, "You are one of us; soon you shall be one with us; one with us—one with us; you and—"

An hour later Lucian came up, stepping softly lest he should awaken his wife. He turned up the shaded gas-jet a little, and—where was Margaret? The tumbled pillow, the blanket thrown back, showed that she had been there. Where was she now? He looked round the room. He turned up the light higher. She was not there. Then he thought of the drawing-room. He opened the door. The curtains were drawn, the room was in black darkness; he lit a candle. The portraits all stared at him curiously, but no one was there. He returned to the bedroom; he thought she might be in Ella's room. He stepped softly upstairs; he would be able to see the light under the door, if there were any light burning in the room. He would hear their voices if they were talking. No, there was no gleam of light; there was no talking.

Then, while he stood on the stair in doubt, he heard Margaret's voice—she was talking quite softly, but as to her voice there could be no doubt, and the voice came to him from one of the garrets above.

Lucian was by no means a superstitious man, as we have seen. He regarded not omens, lucky or unlucky days, warnings or encouragements; he would have spent a night alone in a haunted house with unshaken nerves and the firmest resolution not to hear nor to see anything; he had an unbounded contempt for all the ghosts of Borderland. These ghosts know the scientific attitude; they recognize the folly of showing themselves to a man who refuses to see them; therefore, when the man of science steps in the ghost steps out. They only show themselves to the fearful. No argument, therefore, against the existence of ghosts can be founded on the fact that the scientific man never sees any. He *never will!* And now you know the reason.

Lucian was, then, the least credulous of men. But to hear your wife's voice in the dead of night, talking to non-existent persons in an empty garret, is a shock to the most profoundly scientific of men. Archimedes himself, Bacon, Darwin, Huxley, would be shaken by such a singular experience. Lucian felt his heart beat and his pulse quicken as he ran up the top-most stair. What did it mean?

The door of the front garret was wide open; a flood of moonlight fell through the windows, partly on the floor and partly on the dismantled bed and partly on Margaret herself, sitting on the mattress. A strange, weird picture she made, bathed in the moonlight, clad in a white dressing-gown, her bare feet on the floor, her long fair hair hanging over her shoulders, her eyes wide open, her hands moving in harmony with her words, her head carried as one who is eagerly listening and eagerly talking; her whole attitude that of one who takes part in a conversation on some subject of importance and interest. She was, in fact, in the midst of the wives and mothers; she was in her dream. Was this, then, a nightly practice with her, to steal away, and thus, sleep-walking, enact the dream? Lucian understood. He knew of this vision or this dream. To look on filled him with admiration of the case; it was a psychological study; the persistence of the dream was curious; in order to destroy it, his wife would probably require a change of thought and place and talk; this business of the succession once settled, he would take her away himself. As for any change in his own purpose, that was, of course, absurd.

He waited at the door—he knew she would not see him; he watched and listened.

"Yes—yes," she cried. "Oh! all you prophesied has come to pass. Even the desire for the inheritance—nothing but that—has brought shame and disappointment upon all, and now the time has come for me to feel what you have felt and to suffer what you have suffered—"

She paused and listened as if to one who stood at her right. Even Lucian could not avoid the wish that he also could see this company.

"The time has come at last. The temptation was too great. The desire has become a madness. He too will become openly your grandson and your great-grandson. He is exactly like your husband, madam, the Calvert Burley who brought upon us all this misery and the beginning of this wealth—perhaps he will end like him, in stony hardness of heart—and he is like your husband." She turned to another person. Lucian almost thought he saw that other person, with such reality did she turn from one to the other. But no—nothing was there but the moonlight, falling on his sleeping and dreaming wife. "He is like your husband, too, like the miser who drove all your children from the house, one after the other, so that some starved and some committed wicked things. Perhaps Lucian will in time become a miser. I think that already he begins to love money. He dreams all day about the money; he cannot think of his work—he will do no more scientific work. His gold will presently weigh him down and crush him."

She was silent for a few moments, but she turned her face from one to the other as if she listened to what each in turn was saying.

"You bring me no comfort. You give me no advice. It doesn't help me to hear from each of you, one after the other, the sadness of your lives. What am I to do? Oh! tell me, what am I to do?"

Again there was silence. Lucian shivered, for—against his reason—he imagined he heard voices in reply.

"No—no—no!" Margaret clasped her hands. "I will do anything for him—anything in the world except one thing. If it were for myself only, he should have my company in all the misery which he will bring upon himself. But mine alone. He shall not bring misery upon—" Here she was silent, while the others interrupted her, speaking apparently all together.

"It had been better," Margaret went on, "if you had left your husbands before your children were born. And that is the sum of what you say.

You all think so. Better—better for you—better for the world had you left your husbands before your babies were born."

She paused. Was it the murmur of assent that Lucian heard?

Then she rose and looked around. "It is very good of you," she said. "We will cry together often in the time to come. Only a day or two more and I shall be one with you—to share in all your sufferings, and to feel all that you have felt. Good-night—good-night. Oh, sad-faced mothers, good-night!"

The tears rolled from her cheeks, her voice broke, and then—a strange action when one of the two who embrace is impalpable and invisible—she raised her arms and made as if she threw them round the neck of one person after another and as if she kissed the cheek of one after the other. Then she looked round her—she was alone—her visitors were gone. She pulled open the chest of drawers and took out some of the things that lay there, things Lucian knew appertaining to infants. She unfolded them and held them up one by one in the moonlight. Then she carefully folded and laid them back again.

And then, still with eyes that looked straight before her and saw nothing, she walked past Lucian, and slowly, without touching the stair-rail, went downstairs, her husband following her. She did not hear his step; she walked on quite unconscious. She stopped at her bedroom door, hesitated a moment, and then went in and lay down upon the bed.

Lucian bent over her. She was fast asleep. Her eyes were closed. She was peacefully sleeping.

He lay awake watching her. She slept on, her breathing calm, undisturbed by any more dreams—exhausted. In the morning she would be recovered, she would be reasonable. Of course she would see the thing, as she always had before, with his eyes—from his point of view. She had always been that kind of wife who submits to everything which would make her husband happy. Presently he too fell asleep.

When he awoke in the morning she was gone. Not into the garret this time, but in a quite prosaic manner gone—down to breakfast.

WALTER BESANT

XXXV

Farewell!

L ucian's heart was softened. Remembering that acted dream—that strange drama of one visible performer with a whole company, invisible and inaudible—his heart became very soft. All the irritation caused by his wife's contumacy vanished in thinking of that sleep-walking. Clearly, he must take or send her away—to Freshwater, say, or Hastings, for a change. She had been dwelling too much on this foolish superstition; as soon as she understood the foolish unreason of the thing she would shake off her fears. Superstition, however, as this physician very well knew, is a hard thing to kill. Nothing but the most resolute defiance of the bogie is effective. There have been found men strong enough to beat down and destroy with hammers Odin, Dago, Kaloo, and the most venerable old idols; are there found men or women strong enough in these days to break looking-glasses, begin new work on a Friday, sit down thirteen to a table, or cease to believe that money gotten in certain ways must carry a curse with it?

Lucian considered these things with himself while he dressed.

He became charitable, even; there was, after all, something to be said for the superstition, especially by those who did not clearly perceive that all the disasters which fell upon the House were caused by wrong-doing. Certainly there were many horrid things in the family record; they had been presented to Margaret *en bloc* and suddenly; and, with them, his father's prejudices as regards the hereditary curse; and, really, if you come to think of it, the like of these disasters had seldom, if ever, been recorded in any middle-class family. In this middle way one is generally supposed to be tolerably safe. Down below, an appearance at the Criminal Court, with a pew in the very front—a stall in the front row—is common. Up above there are family histories, including losses at the gaming-tables, plunging on the turf, duels over ladies of the ballet, revelations in the Divorce Courts, and other scandals. Either up above or down below, such a family history as that of the Burleys, one supposes, might be equalled or surpassed. Not in the middle class, where there still lingers, we have been taught to believe, some regard for character.

Lucian's softening of heart did not include the least weakening of purpose; he was going to carry out that purpose—with or without his wife's consent. But of course she would consent. He never remembered any occasion, great or small, on which his wish was not her law. Naturally he supposed that his wish would under all circumstances always remain her law. Therefore he dressed and went downstairs in a perfectly cheerful frame of mind. He was late; he had overslept himself; the breakfast of the others was finished; Margaret was alone waiting for him.

Either by accident or design a chair stood before the fire, and between herself and her husband. Lucian did not observe that she was pale, except for a red spot on her cheek, and that she was trembling with some hidden excitement. He was only thinking of himself and his own magnanimity.

He stepped in, holding out both hands.

"My dear," he said, "I am shamefully late. You ought to have wakened me."

"Will you take your breakfast, or will you talk with me first? I have a little to say; it will not take long."

"Talk away, dear"—he lifted the lid of the hot-water dish and observed that there were kidneys—"go on talking, dear. I will take breakfast the while." He sat down, cut bread, poured out tea, and took a kidney. "How did you sleep, my dear?"

"As usual. I always sleep well."

"A dreamless, peaceful sleep?"

"I have one dream always. That is, hitherto I have had one dream. That will be changed now."

"What is the dream, dear?"

"It doesn't matter. Nothing matters any more."

Something—a little break—in her voice struck him. He looked up, sprang to his feet, and tried to take her hand. She drew it away. He stooped to kiss her—she repelled him roughly.

"*No*," she said, with decision, "that is ended."

"What is ended?"

She turned upon him a face so resolute, so stern and hard, so utterly changed from the fair face of smiles and love and submission to which he was accustomed, that he was amazed. He did not recognize his wife. For a while he could not speak. Then his masterfulness returned.

He laughed. "What has got into your head now, Margaret? I don't know you this morning."

"You forget what I told you last night. Yet I thought I made my meaning plain."

"You talked considerable nonsense last night, and I had to let you understand—more plainly than was pleasant—that a woman's superstition must not stand in the way of the world's interests."

"I told you that I would face any miseries that you might bring upon our heads if I were sharing them with you alone. But—"

"Well?" for here she stopped.

"I will not bring these miseries upon another. My child shall not inherit the curse of those millions."

"What?" he cried. "Your child? Your child, Margaret?"

"Did you not understand? Well, what your father did when he was grown up, I shall do before that child is born. I shall go away. The child shall never know its own people."

"Margaret, you do not mean this. Your child? your child?"

"I mean it most solemnly and seriously. You have chosen your part—you have sent in your claim. It must be granted. I go away before it is granted, because I will not, for one single hour, be a sharer in this wicked wealth."

"You will leave me, Margaret? But this—this—your child?"

"I am going away this morning, immediately. I have told your cousins, Lucinda and Ella. They will go with me."

"You will leave me?" He hardly understood the meaning of the words. And this was the girl who had seemed to have no life or joy except in doing things that would bring pleasure to him.

"It is too late, I suppose," Margaret went on, coldly, "to say anything more. You may, however, still keep me if you will agree to transfer your rights in this estate to the Treasury—or anybody—so that you can never—you or yours—have the least claim upon it, or upon any part of it."

"Never." His face became as the nether millstone. "What is mine I will take."

"Then, Lucian, I go."

"Stop—stop a moment. Your own people—your mother and sister—what will you tell them?"

"The truth. If they disapprove, which is very possible, I shall go my own way."

"But tell me again. Your child—your child—my child—"

"I will never consent to join that wretched company of wives and mothers who are waiting for me upstairs."

"Superstition! Come, Margaret, I will take you out of this house. It is too strange a place, too ghostly for a young wife with few friends. We did wrong in coming here. Come—you will forget, in new and brighter places, this company of wretched wives and mothers—the people who come to you in your dreams. And, my dear—you have told me—you will have new hopes."

"Therefore I must leave you, or my hopes will turn to terrors. Oh! Lucian, when you first heard of this shameful family you shrank with horror at the thought of claiming what you now call your own. Little by little you accustomed yourself to thinking of it till the thing became possible. Then it became attractive. Then it overpowered you. You have been tempted, and you have fallen. Yes—fallen. You are not the man I loved—your mind has gone down to a lower level—you no longer think of your profession and your own work; you think of the great power you are going to wield, and the great man you are going to be, by means of the vast fortune you have inherited—a fortune made out of men's vices by the coldest and most heartless villain that ever existed. This loathsome mass of ill-gotten gold will bring ruin and destruction upon your head, upon mine, and upon the child unborn unless I escape and flee—anywhere—anywhere away from this place. It is like being in a doomed city before the flames of Heaven descend upon it and destroy the city and the people in it. That is all I have to say, Lucian."

Without more words she left him alone.

He did not follow her. He stood still, thinking. Presently—the rebellion of a wife so submissive was inexplicable—his obstinacy returned.

"Wonderful is the power of superstition," he murmured. "She will come back. I will give her a day or two. Then she will come back, and I will make more concessions. Poor Margaret! As if I were going to give way to a woman's superstitious fad? Great heavens! To give up millions because the old man was a money-lender! Why shouldn't he be a money-lender? She will come back, and"—he laughed—"if she is right we must make suitable provision for the heir."

He sat down and took breakfast, his interest in the meal in no way diminished by the recent conversation.

After breakfast he should have gone to the hospital, but he did not. He went into his study, and sat down before some calculations as to the endowment of his students in the various branches of his college of science—a college which seemed about to cover half a county in extent. But what cannot be done with twelve millions of money? This morning, however, the figures seemed to run about of their own accord; they wouldn't stand still to be added up. And he kept listening. There were feet overhead, and the bumping of boxes. Margaret was packing up; she meant it, then.

Then the young husband, still the lover, experienced a pain such as he had never before thought possible. For he was drawn two ways, by two ropes—two forces—two invisible arms. One arm pulled him towards the door, while a voice inside his brain—it was the voice of his father—cried aloud: "Fool! Madman! Go to your wife and stop her. Give her what she asks. Stop her before a worse thing happens to you." And the other arm held him in his chair, while another voice inside him whispered: "Don't give up the money. Think of the power! Think of the position! Millions upon millions! The richest man—the greatest man—the most beneficent man in the whole country!"

The latter force prevailed. Lucian sat still.

Presently there was a knock at the door. It was Ella, dressed to go out. She had been crying, for her eyes were red.

"Cousin Lucian," she said, "I've come to say good-bye."

"If you must go, Ella. I suppose that Margaret has told you—"

"Yes—she has told us—I'm vurry sorry"—she was so moved that she forgot the London fashion which she had recently acquired, and called it "vurry"—"I'm vurry sorry indeed—I can't tell you how sorry I am."

"Indeed, Ella, you cannot be so sorry as I am—not only to lose you, but also—If you could bring Margaret to reason."

She shook her head. "Margaret is always reasonable—and you are wrong—oh, so wrong!" She sat down and began in her frank and direct way: "You are horribly wrong, Lucian. Don't tell me you want the money for your scientific college. So did I. But it was all rubbish. I wanted it for vainglory. The Lord wouldn't let me have it. He wouldn't let a simple girl like me, ignorant of the ways of the world, get the chance of doing mischief with that money. And what a relief it is to me, now, to think that I have done with this dreadful great fortune—and forever! Don't call me a hypocrite, Lucian. I do really feel that it would be too much for my strength—I should have been a lost soul. And it will be too much for you. Don't delude yourself; already I see a change in you. The weight of it will drag you down. Already you think all day long about your money instead of your work. But there! It's no use talking. If you won't listen to Margaret, you won't listen to me, and you wouldn't listen to the angel Gabriel."

He remained silent.

"Then good-bye. Aunt Lucinda is crying outside. When we get a lodging I will let you know, in case of repentance. It's always possible. The man must be far gone indeed when a door isn't left open for him to escape. Good-bye, then."

He took her hand coldly; the tears rose to her eyes; she ran out of the room, and he heard her sobbing as she banged the door—not with temper, but with grief.

When the wheels of the cab turned the corner of Great College Street, Lucian rose, put on his hat, and went forth to his morning's work at the hospital.

"What's the matter with Dr. Calvert?" asked Nurse Agatha of Sister Anne.

"What has been the matter with him for ever so long?" replied Sister Anne to Nurse Agatha.

"It's since his marriage," said Nurse Agatha, who was young and good-looking, and took an interest in holy wedlock. "Yet they say his wife is charming."

Sister Anne tossed her head. "They say! What do they know? He is always distrait, whatever the cause. As for the patients, he doesn't seem to care any more what becomes of them."

"Can anyone tell me what has happened to Calvert?" It was the editor of the *Scalpel* who spoke, and it was at the club that he said it. "I ran against him just now—he was passing without noticing me; I stopped him and asked about a paper he promised me. He seemed to have forgotten me and the paper and everything. Very odd. Must have had some kind of blow."

"Never the same man since his marriage," said another; "yet they say—"

"Hang what they say! We want our man back again."

This morning, especially, Lucian acknowledged to himself that he could bring his attention to bear upon nothing. To be on the point of stepping straight out of poverty, or, at least, slender means, into the possession of millions—many millions—that alone is enough to exclude from the strongest mind any other subject whatever. When one adds that the man had seen his wife—the wife of two months—deliberately leave him, it is clear that there was material for profound meditation.

He left the hospital as quickly as he could, conscious that the nurses were looking at him and wondering about him. He went into the street, where he met his editor, and entirely forgot who the man was and what had been promised to him.

Then he made his way to St. James's Park, and paced up and down that lonely southern walk. Here, at any rate, he could think.

For a scientific man his case was lamentable. To one who resolutely believed nothing except what he saw, felt, and could experiment upon, the case was almost insulting. For those two voices within him—actually two voices, two non-existent voices within the brain of a physician and a Fellow of the Royal Society—were continually crying out; the one that called him, over and over again, "Fool! madman! dolt!" the other that bade him rejoice over the great wealth that he had acquired, bidding him gloat over it, count it, plunge his hands into the mountain of gold, bathe in it, admire the yellow glow of it, consider the power of it, climb to the top of it, and stand there a monument for the world to envy—the great, the good, the illustrious, the fortunate, the dispenser of good, a modern savior of the world. "Now am I a god!" said the rich man of old—poor wretch! A king, he was too. "Now I am like Zeus the Cloud-Compeller." Zeus heard and did compel the clouds, and, lo! the lightning fell upon that man who was so like a god, and he lay prone, dead—all his divine likeness gone out of him, and his wealth piled up in mockery around his dead body. "Fool! madman! dolt!" cried continually the other voice. Both voices together, each trying to outbawl the other.

Then a doubt seized him, a doubt as to the papers. Were they, after all, complete? Was there no flaw in them?

He hurried as hard as he could walk to Lincoln's Inn Fields.

Thank Heaven! All was complete—Mr. Nicholson reassured him. The Treasury would certainly make as little delay as possible; he might reckon upon possession in a very short time. He would then be able to sit down, ascertain exactly what he possessed, and frame for himself his future course.

"Frame his future course." These were the lawyer's words. "Frame his future course." Why, he now remembered that he had not laid down any future course for himself—none at all. He was going to found his college. And then? Work in it all his life? Perhaps. But, then, there would be all this money. He would want a house to correspond with his income; there would be the management of the estates with so vast a property; and there would be the interests of the child—the child—the child—oh! there would be an immense amount of things to be looked after. Perhaps he would not be able to do any more research work.

He left Lincoln's Inn Fields and walked home.

Strange! The echoes had returned to the house—the echoes which he found when he visited it with Margaret; the echoes which rang from side to side up the staircase. They came back when Margaret left. Once more the house was empty. For a while there had been love in it—youth and love; youth and love and laughter and the music of woman's voice. Now it was empty again; it was as empty as when the old, old man sat alone all day long with never a whisper to break the silence, and the echoes ringing like funeral bells if one set foot within the hall or upon the stairs.

There was not a sound in the house; the two servants below went about their work as quiet as mice. The door at the top of the kitchen stairs was closed, and their voices could not be heard above.

Lucian shivered involuntarily. Margaret, he thought, would come back. She could not live without him. Meantime the house was horribly empty.

He hung up his hat and went into his study. He remembered his meeting with the editor; there was that paper he had promised. He found the pamphlet—a light and poetical *brochure* in German on the bacillus of some obscure disease—indolence, I think—and began to read where he had left off, pen in hand.

After half an hour he found that what he read with his eyes was producing no effect of any kind upon his brain—a disease requiring another bacillus. He pushed his paper from him as a rustic pushes his plate from him when he has finished dinner. Then his pen began of its own accord to draw figures—dazzling figures connected with the great inheritance. Thus: £12,000,000 for principal—what a glorious array of captive naughts! How many years of saving and success went for each oblong naught—each golden ellipse! At only 3 percent, £360,000 a year was the income from this capital sum.

Or, £30,000 a month—something like a monthly check!

Or, £1000 a day—counting Sundays.

Or, £40 an hour—sleeping or waking.

Or, 15s. a minute—every time the second-hand goes round.

Suppose he were just to leave it invested, as his grandfather had done, and to live on a small fraction of it—just to see what would happen. Well, to begin with, it would double in twenty-three years, and double again in twenty-three years more. He would then have £44,000,000 sterling; he would then be a little over seventy. Think of it! Forty-four millions!

He went on calculating, estimating, pleasing himself—it was a new sense—with the mere imagination (figures are the most imaginative things possible (of these great possessions. By the time he had learned to understand a little the peculiarities and the enjoyments of his grandfather, the money-lender, and his great-grandfather, the miser, he no longer regarded them with shame and disgust. As Margaret told him, he was changed indeed.

When he turned to the consideration of his college, he perceived for the first time that the sums he had originally proposed for it were much too big. It would only defeat his own purpose—he now understood—to make it so rich. Besides, there were other things which had to be done. He must not surrender all his power. Little by little; one endowment at a time. With an income of £360,000 a year one can do an enormous quantity of good. With such an income one is a demigod for power of benevolent endowments. Perhaps without touching the principal at all he might carry out all his designs. Two years' income—or three, at least—would be an ample endowment for a college. He might endow it with a million sterling, which means an income of £30,000; many colleges of Oxford and Cambridge are not endowed with so much.

And so on. For the first thought of the very rich man is how he can make himself still richer. With moderate wealth—say, the possession of £100,000—what our ancestors feelingly called a *plum*—with a plum in our pocket—a ripe, sweet, fragrant, delicately colored plum, an Orleans plum, or an egg plum, with its dewy bloom upon it—the average man is satisfied. He can sit down to enjoyment; he can give checks in charity, and so feel good all over; he can belong, in imagination, to Samaria and die comfortably, relying on certain texts. When the plum is a million, or two millions, or ten millions, one wants to make it more. It was quite natural that the last Burley but three should become a miser, and equally natural that the last but two should become a money-lender. They were so rich that they wanted more. And if you ask why this is so, you are referred to the German philosopher, who diagnoses the diseases peculiar to wealth.

Lucian had dinner served in his study. He reflected with the customary satisfaction of the rich man on this subject, that his household expenses would now become very modest; he thought that he might comfortably live on two hundred a year—so long as Margaret stayed away—but that would not be long; he would then have £360,000, less £200 a year, for his income. With this he could carry out the most precious designs— one year's income, perhaps, would do—and save the rest. Heaven! How the money would go rolling up!

He spent the evening in the same manner—over his figures. At midnight he went upstairs.

Even the room awakened no memory of Margaret. Only twelve hours or so since she went away, yet he had already forgotten her. A young wife on the one side, twelve millions on the other. Of course he had forgotten her. His brain was full of the millions. If he had remembered her, it was with a little feeling of disgust. She would cost so much.

One of the voices was silent. The other dropped with a murmur of encouragement and congratulation: "Oh, you are so rich! You are so powerful! You are so generous! And you will grow richer—richer— richer! More powerful—more generous!"

Dives sank into slumber, careless that the house was empty. So, you see, the work of the fortune was done. Love was driven out, and the loveless man felt not his loss. What more dreadful curse could have fallen upon him?

XXXVI

The Last Remonstrance

The next day Lucian sent out letters inviting all the cousins to meet at his house in Great College Street, on business connected with the estate. He proposed at this meeting, though he did not state his intention in the letters of invitation, to make an announcement of his own position, and to inform them of the fact that he had been recognized as the sole heir by the Treasury.

The first to arrive was Ella. She, however, instead of going upstairs to the drawing-room, ventured into the study, where she found Lucian at his table. Before him were papers covered with figures.

"You are going to proclaim yourself, I suppose," she said. "I thought to plead with you for the sake of your wife; but I won't. Your face is harder than ever. Well, we say in America, which is a very religious country, that the Lord sometimes breaks up hearts of stone. Perhaps He will break up yours."

Lucian laughed scornfully. The girl placed the tips of her fingers on the table and leaned over him. "You laugh," she said. "You will not always laugh. Oh, Lucian!"—she drew her slender figure to its full height, which was not much; but her dark eyes—the Burley eyes—flashed, and she looked tall, as every woman does who is deeply moved. "Cousin Lucian," she burst out, "I look at you and I wonder. I think of you and I wonder. You are a young man, your life before you." What graybeard counsellor could be wiser than this girl? "All before you," she repeated. "You've got a larger brain and a clearer eye than most; you might have become a man known even to us—even across the Atlantic—known to us; you have got enough money to live upon; you have got a truly lovely wife, whom you treat with your English arrogant condescension—American women won't be treated that way; and you throw it all away—everything—name and fame, gifts and talents—the calling to which the Lord called you—and your sweet and loving wife—you exchange these things—Oh, good gracious! What could the Lord give you more precious? What is there, out of heaven itself, more precious? Nothing—nothing—nothing! You have bartered everything away for a senseless, useless, mischievous pile of papers that they value at millions of dollars. Your life is done—finished; your course is run, because, masterful as you are, Cousin Lucian, without sympathy you can do nothing, and except from your wife you will get no sympathy. A common man, a small-brained man, might do such a thing; but you—you—you—a man of science—"

"It is because I am a man of science—" Lucian began.

"It isn't. Don't deceive yourself. It is because you have wickedly received into your mind and nursed and cherished a devil of greed and lust for gold. You pretend that you want the money for science—to make the world move faster. You can't; no man can make the world go faster. When the world is ready the man is sent—not before. You are sent into the world to be an officer in the army—a corporal or a lieutenant at most; and you want to make yourself commander-in-chief."

"I think I hear the people going upstairs," said Lucian, feebly.

"Let them go upstairs! I mean to say what I came to say. You will fail, Lucian. Your fine college may get built—I don't think it will, because you will grow more and more avaricious as the time goes on. But it may; and then—then the real work will go on, being done by the outsiders who've got no money. Get your men, and pay them for research; the more you pay them the less they will work. But I have thought this out. It is necessity which makes men work. Nothing great has ever come from a rich man—nothing, and nothing ever will. Your college is no better than mine, Lucian—no better than vanity and self-conceit."

"Thank you, Ella."

"Poor Lucian! We all thought so much of you; and now, unless that break-up comes quick, you are a ruined man. Dives *can't* work—he can't. You can't make a man more useless than by making him rich. Oh! when will the churches recognize this? Well"—she sighed, paused, and sat down, and then got up again—"I have nearly done—I have nearly said what was put into ray head to say. You have been tempted; you have fallen; you are blinded, so that you cannot see the sin and the shame of it. You are deaf, so that you cannot hear the warnings of it; and you are stupid, so that you cannot understand how much happier is the life you are throwing away than the life you desire. It is the way of all temptation," added this woman of vast experience. "Those who fall are blinded and deafened and stupefied, so that they only see one side of it—the side which attracts, and not all the other sides which threaten."

"Have you nearly finished?"

"How shall a rich man enter into the kingdom of heaven?" she asked. "Oh! I mean what ought to be your kingdom and my kingdom—not the kingdom with silver spoons and a carriage in it. He cannot, Lucian. You have thrown away the kingdom of heaven. Oh! what a thing—WHAT a thing to throw away! Margaret thrown away with it! Oh, WHAT a thing to throw away! Even the kingdom of heaven itself!"

XXXVII

A Conseil De Famille

The cousins were already assembled when Ella entered the drawing-room. The New Zealand branch, consisting of Sir John, the Rev. Herbert, and the five girls, were all gathered together at one of the windows. Lady Burleigh was not present. She was one of those philosophers who would rather begin a brand-new family than be connected with the finest old family possible, if the connection had to be established by wading back through generations of mud in the gutter. Therefore, she put the famous genealogy in a drawer, being persuaded, in her own mind, that poverty, and nothing else, had drawn her father-in-law, as it had drawn her own father, to New Zealand as an early settler. And she cared nothing about the Burleys, and felt no manner of interest in the illustrious progenitors, and took no pride even in John of Gaunt. Therefore, she refused to attend at this family gathering. Their branch was represented, in consequence, by seven instead of eight, and out of seven six came full of anxiety, and even terror. For the House of Burley was like an ancient museum, full of secrets, any of which might be revealed at any moment. However, they came prepared—the father for the sake of the daughters, and the daughters for the sake of the father—to rally round the genealogy, and to stand firm by the sugar-baker if anything should be said concerning Charles the convict.

Sitting by the fireside was the old woman, Lucinda Avery. But it was afternoon, and the chair was comfortable, and she had fallen fast asleep. "Hush—sh!" whispered the girls. "Do not wake her up. Let the poor thing rest."

They ran to shake hands with Ella. But their smiles were anxious. "She is asleep," they whispered.

"Goodness keep her asleep!" was the prayer that Ella breathed.

Clarence, with his friend and legal adviser, stood at another window. The completed claim had been sent in. There could be no dispute upon the facts. What did this gathering mean? The assembled company, he surmised, were cousins—claimants, like himself. But they were not descendants of the second son.

"It means compromise," his partner whispered. "I don't know why or how; but that's what I think it means. We'll wait a bit, Clary, and listen."

They all waited in silent expectancy for two or three minutes, when Lucian entered the room, accompanied by an elderly gentleman bearing papers.

"That's Mr. Nicholson," whispered the poet, surprised. "Firm of Nicholson, Revett & Finch, Lincoln's Inn Fields. Most respectable firm. I knew them when I was in my articles. They mean compromise; I'm certain of it. We will hear what they propose; don't let us accept too readily. I wonder who Dr. Calvert is—I wish I knew."

Mr. Nicholson drew a chair to the table. The audience all sat down. Lucian stood beside his lawyer.

"I have invited you here this afternoon," he began, "because you are all interested, as actual or possible claimants to the Burley estates, in the announcement I have to make. A step has been taken by the person most concerned in the matter which will, I fear, cause grievous disappointment to some present. But it is better that you should learn the truth in this way than from the papers, which will certainly publish the fact as soon as it gets abroad."

"I don't like the look of this," the partner whispered. "It's a bad beginning." He rose and addressed the House. "Before we go any further," he said, "I should like to ask, as Mr. Clarence Burghley's legal adviser—Mr. Nicholson may perhaps remember me when I was articled to his neighbors"—Mr. Nicholson bowed. "I should like to ask, if I may—it is a very simple question—by what authority Dr. Calvert calls together the representatives of the Burley family, what *locus standi* he has in the business, and what right he has to interfere at all."

"It is a perfectly legitimate question," Mr. Nicholson replied. "You all have a right to be satisfied on this point. Now, if you will let us go on our own way, I can promise that the question shall be answered in two or three minutes. Will you, please, meanwhile accept my assurance that Dr. Calvert has the best right possible to call you together?"

"I don't like it," the partner whispered—"I don't like it at all."

Sir John got up, looking responsible and dignified.

"On that assurance," he said, "I think we may safely proceed. But as far as I am concerned, we are here—although invited by Dr. Calvert— on what may be considered false pretenses, because we cannot claim the estates, or any portion of them, unless the whole of the branch represented by the man commonly called the Westminster miser, with his descendants, is extinct; and I believe that some present are his grandchildren. My connection with the family goes back to a brother of the Westminster miser."

The girls breathed hard and looked round at the old woman in the chair. Thank Heaven! she was still asleep, her head comfortably settled down upon her chest.

"I understood, Sir John, when you saw me—" Lucian began.

"Yes; that is true. It then seemed likely—even almost certain—from a remarkable coincidence of names and dates, and the resemblance of my children and myself to the portraits in that room, that my father was Charles Calvert Burley, third son of the Westminster miser. It has now been ascertained, however, without a doubt, that we are descended from his uncle, one Joshua Calvert Burley. His son, also called Charles, was born in the same year as the other Charles, who appears—ahem!— to have borne an indifferent character; most of you know, I dare say, the principal incident in his deplorable career. In losing him as a parent, however, we lose our claim to this estate. So that if the announcement we are about to hear refers to the succession, we are only interested as far-off cousins. That is to say, we are not claimants."

"I think," said Clarence, "that we ought to be told at once what my legal adviser asked—who and what is Dr. Calvert. If anybody has a right to take the lead in matters concerning the Burley family, it is myself, the grandson of the second son, Henry."

"You shall know, sir," said Mr. Nicholson. "Have patience for two minutes. The announcement that will be made will satisfy you in every particular."

Sir John sat wiping his forehead, unable to repress his anxiety. The girls observed with satisfaction that the old lady was still asleep. They whispered to each other and then to their father, who nodded his head and got up again.

"I think," he said, "that as this announcement clearly concerns the succession, we had better withdraw. To stay longer would be to invade the confidences of a—a—a closer family circle."

"No, Sir John," said Lucian, "please do not go. Nothing is going to be said that will affect you at all—nothing. Your name will not be mentioned, I assure you, or the names of anyone connected with you." Did he mean anything? Did he know—this terrible and mysterious physician, who seemed to know the whole history of the family? "Pray, Sir John, oblige me by waiting this out."

Sir John sat down. The girls looked round again to see if the old lady was still asleep.

Lucian continued.

"The heirs of the Burley estates would be, first, the descendants of John Burley's brothers and sisters. There were four brothers and one sister. I will show you who these descendants are, beginning with the youngest, James—"

"My grandfather," said Ella, as calmly as if she had the marriage certificate in her pocket, but with a red spot on either cheek. The Burleigh girls lowered their eyes, a sign of sympathy as well as of knowledge.

"Yes, your grandfather. James became an attorney. He emigrated to America, and settled in a town called Tewksbury."

"Mass.," said Ella.

"In Massachusetts. There he married—"

"No," Ella interrupted, "he did not marry in America."

"Then he married here. He had two children—namely, a son—whose only child, Miss Ella Burley, is here with us—and a daughter, Lucinda, unmarried, who is now in England. The ladies came over to claim the estates."

"We are no longer claimants," Ella explained. "We have not been able to find the register of my grandfather's marriage, and without that we have no case, it appears."

"You will find in a few moments that it would not help you."

"Clary, I don't like it," whispered the partner. "It looks worse and worse. He's too cool and methodical by half. There's something up his sleeve."

"The next son, Charles, came to grief. I believe you all know what became of him. He has left no descendants—at least, none are claimants. We then come to the daughter, Lucinda, who, like her brothers, ran away from home. She married a certain Frederick Avery, at one time captain in an infantry regiment. The man appears to have been a prodigal, or else he was unfortunate. He fell into debt, and ended his days in the Fleet prison, leaving his wife absolutely destitute. Her history is sad and extremely discreditable to the memory of the late John Burley. The man of millions refused to give his sister a farthing, or to render her any assistance. The unfortunate woman sank lower and lower until, with her daughter, she made a wretched livelihood by doing the roughest and most poorly paid kinds of needle-work. We found this lady's only daughter, now herself an old woman, in the Marylebone Workhouse. Her case is quite clearly established by the letters and papers which she has preserved. So far, therefore, this poor old pauper, ignorant and humble, is the only claimant to all these millions. Lucinda Avery, your cousin, is sitting with us. She seems to be asleep, and does not know even that we are talking of her."

A shiver and a rapid drawing of the breath from the five New Zealand girls followed this speech, because Lucinda at that moment lifted her head, straightened her back, opened her eyes, and looked round. Then she made as if she would rise and her lips parted, and the girls caught each other by the hand and blanched with terror.

But Lucian motioned her to sit down, and the old woman obeyed; and she closed her eyes again, and to all appearance went to sleep.

Lucian continued his story.

"The next branch," he continued, "is that of Henry, the second son. His grandson, Mr. Clarence Burghley, is here today. The connection, I understand, has been fully made out."

"Point by point—fully established," said the partner.

"I do not dispute the connection. I am perfectly willing to acknowledge that our cousin is the undoubted grandson of Henry Calvert Burghley."

"Our cousin?" asked Clarence. "Your cousin?"

Mr. Nicholson raised his hand as one who prays for patience.

"I don't like it—I don't like the look of things at all," murmured the poet.

Then Lucian went on.

"This connection established, there remains, therefore, only Mr. Clarence Burghley and that poor old lady asleep in the chair."

"Don't wake her," murmured all the girls.

"I will not. Let her sleep and rest. She has had very little rest in her hard-worked life. Out of all the claims which might have been made, there are only two which can be considered. But there is the eldest branch, the son of John Burley the money-lender; and since the announcement about to be made to you is the real purpose for which you have been called together, I will ask Mr. Nicholson, senior partner in the house of Nicholson, Revett & Finch, to make that announcement for me."

He sat down, and Mr. Nicholson rose. "Last May, five days before Mr. John Burley died, there died at the age of fifty-five my life-long friend, my old school-fellow, John Calvert, as he was known to the world, civil engineer. I had in my possession all his papers. I had been in his confidence ever since the day when—we were boys at the time—he refused to remain with his father any longer and ran away from home. He had nothing but a watch and chain that his mother had given him with a little hoard of a few pounds, which she placed in his hands on her death-bed. I had, I say, all the papers. Those which were necessary for our purposes I have placed in the hands of the Treasury. For John Calvert's real name was John Calvert Burley, and this gentleman"—he laid his hand upon Lucian's shoulder—"is the only son. Therefore, he is the sole heir to the whole of the Burley estates!"

Ella groaned aloud, thinking of Margaret. Up to the last moment she hoped that he would not do it. He had done it—he had sent away his wife.

Sir John laughed pleasantly. "I congratulate Dr. Calvert, or Dr. Burley—whichever you may prefer to be called."

"We must all rejoice," said Herbert, "that the right man has been found. Speaking for myself, I confess that I have had dreams—for the sake of the Church. But it is ordered otherwise."

"Take it quiet, Clary," whispered the partner—"take it quiet."

"Sir," cried Clarence, with flaming cheek, "this must be proved. I shall dispute every point of the assertion. It shall be proved in a court of law."

"The Treasury," Mr. Nicholson said, quietly, "have admitted the proofs. The rest is only a matter of necessary delay. Not only is Dr. Calvert the heir, but he is the acknowledged heir. Of course, it is open to anyone to bring an action, if he is so minded and so advised."

"How is it, I should like to know, that you have only just found out the fact?"

"Dr. Calvert has known the fact since the death of his father. The reasons why he did not immediately come forward are doubtless satisfactory to himself."

"That, my cousins," Lucian concluded, "is all that I have to say. I am myself the sole heir. Still, if any of you think that you are in any way entitled to any part of the estate, you will advance your claim in the proper way. Sir John, may I ask you if you think yourself—"

"No, no, certainly not. We descend from the higher branch."

Again the girls looked at the woman who slumbered. No sleep was ever more opportune or more gratefully received.

"Very well, then. Your daughters, Sir John?"

They all shook their heads.

"Cousin Ella, I look to you."

"Lucian, I would not touch a farthing, even if I had my grandfather's marriage certificate in my hand."

"Then, Mr. Clarence Burghley, what do you think?"

"Let me speak for him;" the partner rose, and spoke with some dignity. "My friend and client," he said, "is naturally much astonished—not only at this unexpected news, but at the treatment he has received. You remember, Dr. Calvert, that he called upon you; that he explained who he was and why he came. You received him, showed him these portraits, and gave him a letter which is very valuable in completing our chain of evidence. You did not tell him, as you should have done, that you were yourself the grandson and heir. You allowed him to go away, his brain fired with the thought that this vast inheritance would be his. Can anyone wonder that the anxiety has prevented him from doing anything at all? He has lost not only months of work, but has suffered detriment—great injury—to his professional reputation as an actor and entertainer. Cruel suspense, anxious nights, laborious research—for months—and all caused by your silence, Dr. Calvert. Under these circumstances, I submit, in the presence of Mr. Nicholson—a gentleman of the highest standing—that compensation, substantial compensation, is due to Mr. Clarence Burghley."

"Of course I ought to be compensated," Clarence broke in, savagely. "For four long months I have been unable to think of anything else. Who kept me in suspense? You. My mind has been unsettled—through you. I have been unable to do any work—through you. I say that compensation is due."

"You may leave your case in Mr. Nicholson's hands," said Lucian, coldly. He looked round the room. "My cousins," he said, "let us part, if we can, amicably. There are the portraits of your ancestors. If you wish, I will present to each the portrait of his grandfather. Sir John, behind you is a portrait of—of—it is said to be—your great-grandfather Joshua." But he knew very well that Joshua had died at the age of two, and that this was some other cousin. "Will you accept him and take him away?"

"Oh," cried the girls, "that will be delightful!" They clapped their hands with simulated joy—but gently, so as not to awaken the family historiographer. But their eyes rested on the portrait of Charles the convict, Charles of Australia, Charles the early settler, the handsome

Charles—so like their brother Herbert, and both so like the religious maniac, their great-great-grandfather.

Lucian took the picture from its nail and gave it to Sir John, who placed it beside his chair.

"I hear," Lucian addressed Herbert, "that you have professed a desire to be descended from a criminal." The girls dropped their heads and blushed. "It is a strange taste in ancestors—"

"I would be as one of the lowest and meanest of my people," said Herbert, hotly.

"Quite so. But your sisters, I believe, have no such ambition. However, I can gratify you even in this respect. Here," he pointed to the man who was transported beyond sea, "is your grandfather's first cousin, who was a forger and a convict. He is, therefore, your first cousin twice removed. You can boast about this noble connection among your people. The more they can drag you down to their own level the better they will be pleased, no doubt. If you are not satisfied, I can give you another criminal—the family is, happily, rich in malefactors. The man whose portrait is here was actually hanged at Tyburn Tree. You are connected with quite a group of criminals. It ought to make you proud and happy."

At the moment Herbert found nothing by way of repartee or proper rejoinder. An hour or two afterwards—a thing which often happens—he remembered what, as a faithful assistant priest, he ought to have said.

Then Lucian turned to Ella.

"Would you like the portrait of your grandfather, Ella?"

"No, Cousin Lucian. Aunt Lucinda has a miniature of him. I am quite satisfied with his American face. You may keep this."

He turned to Clarence. "And you," he asked; "would you like to take this portrait of your grandfather?"

"No," said Clarence, sullenly; "I only wanted to use the portrait for the sake of the connection. It's a vile daub, and I've got his picture in character. Keep it—if you like. It's no worse as a painting than all the rest. Keep it. The thing is only fit to decorate a room like this."

He left the room without dignity or any attempt to conceal the crushing nature of the disappointment. He was bent under it—his head hung down; he was pitiable to look upon.

His partner stayed behind to speak with Mr. Nicholson.

"When we have thought a little about this business," he said, "perhaps you will make an appointment. We ought to ask for a very substantial sum. I assure you that Clarence has been absolutely unable to do anything on account of his anxiety, and this blow is one from which he may never recover. Think of the awful blow of losing this vast fortune."

"Well," said Sir John, "since we expect nothing, we are not disappointed. Herbert, are you going my way?"

"We are going to stay a few minutes," said the girls. They stayed to talk with Ella.

Lucian went downstairs with Mr. Nicholson. The family council was concluded.

"Cousin," said Lucy, the eldest—"cousin in misfortune, are you going back to America?"

"No, we cannot, because we have no money for our passage, and nothing to live upon when we get there. Margaret is trying to get me something to do in England."

"Come out to New Zealand with us. We are going back very soon now—the sooner the better. We are the richer for our visit home by— that history which you have heard; you are the richer by your history. Come out with us. We will find you something—a lover, perhaps, if you want one—or a place, perhaps—you look clever—"

"I will go out to you, cousins, if I cannot find anything here. But I shall stay with Margaret if I can. Poor Margaret! Oh! There *is* a curse upon this horrible, hateful, dreadful inheritance. Ruin and destruction that old man brought with him to whomsoever he approached—"

At this moment the old woman in the easy-chair opened her eyes. She looked carefully round the room and then stood up, meekly folding her hands.

"The gentlemen are gone," she said—"Sir John and my uncle Henry's grandson and the others; only us left by ourselves. Mrs. Calvert says that those talk least who know most. Deary me! I knew everything all the time. But no—I wouldn't speak. I pretended to be asleep. Oh! I could have told everybody—"

"We are very much obliged to you for keeping asleep."

"Oh! I know my duty," she replied. "I'm a Burley, too, by mother's side. Do you think I would say a word to bring down the Burley pride or spoil a joyful day when all the Burleys meet together? With us women left behind, it doesn't matter what we say."

"Not—so much—not quite—so much," replied Lucy, the eldest.

"Daughters of Sir John Burleigh," she said. "Granddaughters of Charles—my mother's brother—who was unfortunate and was transported to Australia and escaped, and came back again and went out to New Zealand. And granddaughter of James, too—my mother's youngest brother—who ran away with his master's wife. Oh! yes. It's beautiful to see you, and to be asked to sit down with you, and to remember all about you. I wish my mother had lived to see you—such fine young ladies. And I hope, I do, that you will find good husbands—that you'll be more fortunate than your grandfathers. They were too high-spirited, mother always said. We have been an unfortunate family, she used to say, but never anything mean about us. Always high-minded. And always money in the family."

Ella heaved a profound sigh. "Now that one hears it for the second time," she said, addressing her cousins, "it doesn't hurt quite so much, does it? Perhaps it is not quite so dreadful as at first."

"It hurts enough to make us feel it all our lives," said Lucy, the eldest. "But, there—it matters nothing so long as the pater doesn't know it. Oh! my dears, so long as that dear old man never finds it out or suspects it, what does it matter if we suffer under this knowledge? We will go home and carry with us the humbugging genealogy, and talk about it as if we believed it, and even pride ourselves and stick out our chins on account of that grand old fraud, John of Gaunt—time-honored Lancaster."

XXXVIII

What the Press Said

It is announced in another column that the missing heir to the Burley estates has at last been found. In other words, he has thought proper, after a silence not yet explained, to come forward and to disclose himself. The facts of the case, if we may assume them to be established, possess a certain amount of romance not commonly met with. As regards the late Calvert Burley, the world already knows his history. The son of a man afflicted with the disease—if it is nothing less—of the miserly disposition, he saw his brothers and sisters fly one after the other from their wretched home and disappear. Search has been made after these brothers and sisters. There are descendants of some living in various parts of the world, but it would appear that, by some accident or other—a missing link in the evidence, a marriage not established, the absence of documentary proof connecting the possible claimant with the deceased—none of those descendants have yet been able to make good their claim. It is said that an old woman was found in a workhouse who was the daughter of John Burley's sister. And it appeared likely, in the continued absence of the son or grandchildren, that the estate would devolve upon a higher branch still, that represented by the generation of the Westminster miser. Had this happened, we believe that a well-known colonial statesman, a K. C. M. G., would have carried off the millions. As for the other claimants, who are numbered by the thousand, they have not, and never had, the least chance of inheriting anything. In any case, their dreams are now rudely dispelled, for the grandson has turned up and he will take all.

"This grandson appears to be a young man worthy of the great fortune which awaits him. He has hitherto been known as Lucian Calvert. He is a physician attached to the Children's Hospital, Buckingham Palace Road. He has also, by his biological researches, arrived already at the distinction of Fellow of the Royal Society. He has always been brought up under the name of Calvert and in ignorance of his real name and family. John Calvert, the son of the money-lender, being a sensitive youth, and unable to stand the reflections passed upon his father's various trades of gamester, proprietor of night-houses, and money-lender; and being also reminded continually of his relationship to the Westminster miser, whose memory still lingered in the locality, was disgusted with the pursuit of wealth in these directions, and resolved to leave his home, abandon his name, and to work his own way in the world without any assistance whatever. This project was actually carried into effect, one knows not how, by the son of the richest man in the country. He became an engineer: in the Forties and Fifties it was a profession which gave work to a great many and wealth to more than a few. John Calvert found work, but not fortune. It is said by those who remember him, but did not know his real name and history, that he always seemed to have a horror of saving or making money; a natural reaction, had his friends known it, from the money-making atmosphere in which he had been brought up. He died four months ago, a few days before his father. On his death-bed he first communicated to his only son the truth about his parentage. It is also said that he begged his son to take no steps whatever to make himself known to his aged grandfather, who knew nothing of his existence, nor to make any endeavor to secure any part of the estates for himself. The young man obeyed these wishes. But when the grandfather died, the day after it was found that he had actually died intestate. The Treasury, as we all know, stepped in; the whole of the papers were seized, and an advertisement called upon the heirs to come forward.

"The grandson, at this intelligence, was placed in a strange position. First of all, the thing which no one could have expected actually happened. The man who above all men, one would think, would have been careful of his succession, actually forgot, or purposely neglected, to make his will. Therefore, in the most unexpected manner, this young man found himself sole heir. On the other hand, there was no doubt that his father, who loathed the thought of money which had been a curse and a shame to his childhood, would have wished him not to claim his right, but to go on carving out his own way as brilliantly as he had begun, without the help of money. It is, indeed, the chief glory of our modern men of science that they do not use their knowledge, as they might, as a means of making money. But it is one thing to use science for the sake of making a fortune, and another thing to inherit a fortune already made. Dr. Lucian Calvert, F. R. S., may very well think that he can go on with the pursuit of knowledge whether he is rich or poor. Again, in the nostrils of John Calvert, civil engineer, this fortune stank. He remembered hearing of the miser creeping out after dark in his ragged old gabardine, picked up on the foreshore of the Thames, carrying a basket in which he put the odds and ends which he picked up—crusts, bones, bottles, bits of coal, nails, bits of wood—everything. That was how the family fortune was increased. He remembered hearing of the gambling-hell in St. James's Street, in which his father sat all night long, raking in the money, lending more money to the gamblers, and raking that in as well; the dancing-cribs which his father kept, making large moneys out of the vice and profligacy of the town; and the office in Cork Street where the money-lender sat, exacting his cent for cent with a relentless purpose to which Shylock never reached. To him the fortune stank. Time purifies even such a fortune as this. By the second generation the curses of the gamblers, the loud laughter of the miserable women in the dancing-places, the groans of the ruined borrowers, are silent and buried in the grave with the short-lived profligates on whom this human shark preyed. They are silent and forgotten. The years have flowed like a fresh stream over the pile of golden guineas; they are sweetened and cleaned. No one will scoff at the way in which that pile was accumulated; no one, indeed, ever inquires too closely into the history of inherited wealth: in general terms we know. Therefore we cannot wonder if Dr. Lucian Calvert, after due consideration to his father's views and the separation of prejudice from equity, has come to the conclusion that his duty, as well as his right, requires him to take his own."

That was the view taken, more or less, by all the papers. Of course, the amount involved being so enormous, there was an article on the subject by every paper in every city in the world. The London letter-writers had a topic such as seldom indeed occurs. The interviewers stood ten deep outside the door of No. 77, Great College Street. The evening papers produced long articles "From One Who Knows Him;" "From a Fellow-student," "From a School-fellow." No need to say who was meant; there was only one man for the moment in the whole world. Kings and presidents were neglected; revolutions were unheeded; the British empire was enlarged by a cantle of the earth as big as France; and no one cared. The only person thought of, spoken of, was Lucian Calvert, M.D., F.R.S., more rightly named Lucian Calvert Burley.

"We now understand," said Nurse Agatha to Sister Anne, "what has been the matter with the doctor. No wonder he was absent and absorbed. We thought him moody, and he was only wondering whether he should take his own or not."

"And now he has got it," Nurse Anne replied, "I shall ask him to endow the Nurses' Pension Fund."

"Everybody will ask him to give to everything. He will have to keep a staff of clerks with nothing to do except to say no."

Everybody did begin to ask. Wonderful it was to see the postman reeling and staggering to the door with letters. The secretaries of all the hospitals began; the clergymen of all the churches and chapels; the charities and charitable societies; the philanthropic associations; the societies for befriending people of all kinds; and, above all, the people in distress—widows, wives, and daughters; men out of work; men too old to work; men struck down by some disease or other; children bereft of parents—one would think that every other person in this island of Great Britain, to say nothing of the adjacent islands of Ireland, Man, Scilly, and Lindisfarne, was a destitute pauper reduced to beg for succor. Whether Lucian opened any of these letters I know not. Later on, Margaret found most of them in the dining-room. They lay piled on the table, and they ran over; they were thrown under the table, and they ran over and outside; they were turned out of the bag into the corners, and they ran over; they were piled in the drawers and the sideboard and the sofa, and they ran over. If it were not for the fear of exaggerating, one would say, calmly, that they lay heaped up as high as the pictures on the wall.

Some of these letters were threatening. Unless a certain sum was sent to a certain address a dreadful revenge would be taken. Dynamite would be employed; six-shooters would be exhibited; the immense fortune should not be enjoyed for long; the writer was a desperate man. Some were sarcastic. Would the owner of millions consider that a miserable hundred would put the writer beyond the reach of want? Would the very rich man condescend to listen to a tale of distress which could be relieved by a sum so small as to be absolutely unfelt? Some were religious. The owner of millions must consider himself a trustee. He held his property in trust; not to be lavished unworthily; not to be saved up. Now here was a case in which real good—good of such a kind as to soften things for his soul hereafter—was in his power. The enclosed papers would show. There were the letters of the professional beggar—the professional whine to be detected at once. There were the letters of inventors who only wanted a little capital to make a great success with their improved traction-engine; and the projectors who wanted nothing but a few hundreds to make their scheme the joy and wonder of the whole earth. And, lastly, there were the letters, familiar to every one, from all who were needy and oppressed; from the widow and the wife and the daughter; all madly passionate, praying, and imploring, so that a heart of stone would melt at reading their terrible tales. What becomes of all these cases of suffering and woe? If all the rich men in all the world answered these letters with five-pound notes, when these were spent the tale of distress would be renewed. "Let me tide over the misery of today," cries the widow; "my children want clothes and food." And what of tomorrow, madam? What, indeed? But of tomorrow we hear nothing.

As Lucian had as yet received no money, it was useless to open or to answer these letters. Therefore, as we have seen, he threw them all into the dining-room—which in those days of solitude he did not use—and left them there.

These days of solitude—he was quite alone—he felt a kind of fierce exultation in being alone. It was fitting, somehow, that the richest man in the world should be alone. Margaret would return presently, when the superstition left her, and she found that the lightning had not struck the inheritor of the Burley estates. Alone, he would meditate on his schemes. Alone, he would best bear the great shock of receiving all this wealth.

It was the *Spectator* which first asked in public, what everybody was asking in private, "What will he do with it?"

"Here is a young man," said this article, "who is suddenly lifted from the apparently modest income of a young physician and man of science, the scholar and student who has never had any thought or expectancy whatever of 'enjoying,' as it is called, a large fortune, or even an income large enough to admit of the generous life—the life which enables a man to have whatever he wants for his own pursuits: in the case of a scientific student, a laboratory and instruments, assistance and leisure for research. This young man, whose record is so considerable, suddenly finds himself in the possession of an income, the greater part of which, though there are whole streets of houses, is said to be safely invested in consols. It is also said, though these figures appear to be quite uncertain, that the income from all sources is nothing short of a quarter of a million. If, therefore, this modern Dives should resolve upon leaving his principal intact, he has every year, to play with, a quarter of a million. What will he do with it? He is said to be a young man of simple habits. He will certainly neither eat nor drink more than he has been accustomed to eat and drink. Perhaps in the course of time he may arrive at a more carefully critical taste; he may want his claret finer and his food more artistic. This, however, will not make a serious inroad upon his income. If he marries and has a family, they may, and probably will, demand a certain style in living; he may accept a title. He may purchase a country-seat. His expenses might rise gradually to £30,000 a year. That will still leave him £220,000 a year. What will he do with it?

"He might save it. This would be ignoble treatment. We will not consider the possibility of a man with a dozen millions desiring to add more. If, however, he were to save £200,000 a year, in five-and-twenty years he would be worth about £8,000,000 more, and then? No; we will not consider the possibility of saving. He must do something. What will he do? He might *give*, freely, all his life. There are many things which want donors and donations continually. In this way he would help to maintain a great many institutions of an admirable kind. There are hospitals, for instance; with so much money he might maintain, single-handed, half a dozen hospitals. But are there not too many already? Are not the hospitals used by persons who have no right to demand or to accept their charities? There are certain benevolent societies of which the Charity Organization Society has sometimes spoken harshly. It might widen the powers of these associations, and so enable them to pauperize the people much more effectually. In fact, the first danger that faces the rich man is that the more money he gives the more he weakens the self-reliance of the people. Therefore we believe that this young man will not give money for the relief of poverty. He will leave people, on the whole, to learn those wholesome lessons that suffering alone seems able to teach. Yet, since we are human and the sight of suffering that seems unmerited—as that of children—is always distressing, this rich man will, one thinks, give money to a judicious almoner. What else can he do? Formerly he might reclaim swamps and moors for agriculture. But who wants more land when so many thousands of acres are lying uncultivated? Or he might found scholarships and fellowships. There are enough of both; every young man who deserves assistance can get a scholarship. Or he might build almshouses; that is, it is true, the least mischievous form of preventing thrift. In these days he may create and endow technical schools and polytechnics. These are very excellent things, but our county councils will very shortly take over these colleges, or create others to be supported by the rates, or—better still—by all the people, for the people. Better to have national schools for arts and crafts than to depend on the possible foundations of rich men. Then, what will he do with it?

"He might present an iron-clad every two years; he might undertake the support of two regiments of the line; he might acquire an ugly street and make it a street beautiful—say Drury Lane; but a great nation does not want gifts from private persons. He might give his attention to the breed of horses or of cattle; to the improvement of machinery; to the advancement of inventions; but in all these things the ground is already occupied by those to whom these things are a profession or a trade. Again, therefore, what will he do with it?

"The more one thinks of it the more one finds that the difficulties increase. What shall the rich man do with his money? He might conduct a newspaper or a magazine or a review, as he thinks such things should be conducted, and without reference to popular opinion or to pecuniary success. But then one of two things would happen. Either his paper would be deadly dull, in which case it would neither have a circulation nor be looked on as an example, or it would become popular (and so make him richer), and beget a host of imitators. And suppose, after all, that his idea of a newspaper was wrong. Nothing more mischievous than a newspaper conducted on mistaken principles. To sum up, we fear that we can find no work for the rich man to do. When he has spent all he wants to spend, when he has given as much to distressful folk as he thinks safe and prudent, then will remain an immense sum every year, which this man will have to save if he does not wish to do mischief. There seems no help for him. His children will be cursed from the outset with immense fortunes and with no stimulus to work, and every temptation to luxury and vice. For them we entertain the pity and the curiosity that we reserve for those born with the silver spoon. Having expressed our opinion as to what cannot be done, we repeat the question, 'What will he do with it?'"

"Yes," said Lucian, "but they have not thought of my great college of science."

This amusement lasted for a fortnight. The popular imagination was touched. It is not every day that a man of no family, so far as he had ever discovered, finds himself the heir and the immediate possessor of millions. In the old lotteries a man fancied a number, saved, or sometimes stole, the money with which to buy a whole ticket—and—won the great prize; when the prize was declared the papers, then in an elementary stage of existence, always had a brief paragraph calling attention to the sudden accession of wealth, and there the matter ended; but deep in the popular breast lay the hope—the thought—the prayer, even—that a similar fortune might attend them—even now, when there are no lotteries to speak of, when the ordinary man has no rich cousins, when the old Nabob exists no longer. He used to come home with a liver like a bit of coral, with lacs upon lacs of rupees, just at the nick of time, in the hour when our need was the sorest. He exists no longer, and the sudden, the unexpected, the nick-of-time fortune comes no more. What we cannot get for ourselves, we cannot get at all. What we have not saved, we cannot use at a time of tightness. What we have not sown, we cannot reap. It is hard to lose the element of chance; there was always hope for the sanguine. Now hope, which chiefly means the looking out for luck, has fled to heaven, and the world is face to face with reality and fate and the consequences of extravagance. Better so, says the moralist. Perhaps, but still—Suppose, dear friend, some one were to present you, suddenly and unexpectedly, with a hundred thousand pounds. How would you feel about it? He would be robbing some one else, says the moralist again. Perhaps, but still—And this man, this Lucian Calvert, this thrice-lucky young man, who deserved no better than his neighbors, and expected no more, was standing up there, for all eyes to see, on his pyramid of twelve millions, or fifty millions, to demonstrate to the world that there may be still some kind of treasure-trove, some unexpected turn of Fortune's wheel.

For a whole fortnight, as everybody will remember, Lucian Calvert was the subject of talk, the subject of the journals over the whole habitable world. Nothing so romantic as the sudden elevation to riches and power of a young man known only to his little circle.

A fortnight; a short fortnight. Did the darling of fortune read what was said of him? He must have read something. But, for the most part, he stayed at home perfecting the plans for his college of science.

For a fortnight. And then—

XXXIX

Earthquakes and Showers of Fire

Then it was as if the broad earth trembled and all the foundations were swept; as if the stars fell from the heavens; as if the moon were darkened and the planets became invisible.

A certain newspaper got the intelligence before any of its rivals. How? No one ever knew; but as a writer at tenpence an hour happened to be in a certain room in a certain government office at the moment of a certain discovery, it was not difficult to conjecture. The secrets of the Treasury cannot be safely guarded at tenpence an hour. When a secret comes into the possession of tenpence an hour it finds its way to a newspaper office and becomes the property of the whole world. This newspaper, four-and-twenty hours in advance of all its rivals, naturally spread itself over the fact and made the most of it, with the news in leaded type, and the front page and longest leading article wholly devoted to the subject. The following is the paragraph:

"A dramatic discovery, reported in our columns, has just been made concerning the now famous Burley estates. It is a discovery which changes at a stroke the whole situation. A will has been found, dated thirty or forty years ago, by which the testator, John Calvert Burley, leaves his whole estate, real and personal, in trust, to the Council of the Royal Society for the foundation and endowment of a college of science. It is not to be a teaching college, but a college of research. The endowments of the professors, the nature and extent of the buildings, and all other details are left to the Royal Society. Such, briefly, is the will, which does not recognize the son at all, and was drawn up and signed before the grandson was born. If the will proves genuine, which there seems no reason to doubt, the grandson is absolutely disinherited."

And the following is a portion of the leading article, which, of course, was written on the same subject:

"The Burley estates have produced another surprise, and that of the most unexpected kind. The will of John Calvert Burley, deceased, has been discovered. The fortunate young gentleman, Mr. Lucian Calvert, M.D., F.R.S., whom all the world has been congratulating for the last fortnight, whose name has been on everybody's lips, has to lay down everything—to be sure he had actually received nothing—and to retire upon his old profession. As he had the strength of will to wait for four months before sending in his claim, it is hoped that he will have the philosophy to resign, with nothing more than a natural sigh, the power and authority which belong to such great riches. We commend him to the reflection that the abilities which have made him, at so early an age, an F.R.S., will continue to advance him in the honorable path he has laid down for himself. He wants no fortune to follow in the footsteps of the great men before him. As regards the will, it appears that when the Treasury seized upon the estate they found a vast quantity of papers, some in the house or office where Mr. Burley's managers, secretaries, solicitors, and clerks carried on his business of looking after the estate; some lying in Mr. Burley's private residence. These papers were, it was thought, all carefully examined and indexed. There was found, however, yesterday, a tin box which had been overlooked. Among the papers in this box was the will of John Calvert Burley. It was in duplicate with the original draft in the solicitor's own handwriting. The solicitor has been dead for twenty years. His son, however, who succeeded him, remembers that at his father's death Mr. Burley ordered such of his papers as had been in his hands to be sent to him. He remembers this box very well; and he is ready to swear to his father's writing and to the signature of the witnesses, who were two of his father's clerks. Under these circumstances, there can be little doubt that we have here the will of this rich man.

"It is a curious document, especially when we consider the manner of man who drew it up, and the kind of life he led. He leaves nothing whatever to his son; of his grandson, of course, he knows nothing. And he leaves the whole of his estate, now producing an income variously estimated between a quarter and a half of a million, for the foundation of a vast college of science, with endowments for research in every branch. Did miser ever before grub and heap up money, did moneylender ever before accumulate thousands, for the purpose of advancing a branch of knowledge of which he himself knew nothing and cared nothing? As a psychological problem, the question how this man, who raked in the mud all his life, ever came to think of science, will remain forever unanswered."

This intelligence was the first thing that met Lucian's eyes when he opened his paper at breakfast.

Soon after eleven his solicitor, Mr. Nicholson, arrived. He found Lucian still at his untouched breakfast; the newspaper lay on the hearth-rug. Lucian sat upright, his hands on the arms of his chair, looking straight before him.

"Lucian!" The old lawyer shook him roughly by the shoulder. "Wake up, man! What? You have read the news? So have I. More than that, I have been to the Treasury people—"

Lucian turned with haggard face. "Is it true?" he asked, hoarsely.

"Quite true," the lawyer replied, shortly, as if it mattered nothing. "True beyond any doubt, I should say. Well, then? We are once more just as we were. Eh? We have enjoyed an immense fortune, in imagination, eh? Something to remember. Once you had millions, eh? Rather stunned for the moment, eh? You'll soon get over that—put a bold face on it—make 'em laugh if you begin to cry, eh? Let 'em see that you don't care much—laugh at it—go to your club—make calls with your wife, eh?"

"Is it—all—quite true?"

"Oh yes. It is very simple. Your father left his home forty years ago. Your grandfather disinherited him. That is simple. When the lawyer died, he had his papers sent to his own office, where he employed salaried solicitors to carry on the work. The papers accumulated, and this box seems to have been overlooked in the search. Somebody ought to be sacked."

"In the search," Lucian repeated, not attaching the least meaning to the words.

"Very well, then. That explains how the papers got there. Of course, it does not explain how the Treasury people overlooked them. I think there is no manner of doubt possible. Perhaps the Treasury would get something done for you."

He stopped. His words made no impression. The look on Lucian's face alarmed him. "Is your wife at home?" he asked with changed voice. "I should like to see her."

"Margaret has left me. She left me because I claimed my own."

"Is it possible? Good heavens, Lucian! You have lost your wife and your vast inheritance as well. What was it your father said—that ruin and destruction would follow those who held any portion of that money? Lucian, don't sit staring. Pull yourself together, man!"

But he made no impression, and presently withdrew.

A black rage held Lucian's soul. It was chiefly directed against his grandfather. How unscientific a man can become on occasion is shown by this example. For he actually saw, as clearly as anyone can see anything, that old man tempting him, urging him to advance his claim; filling his mind with the splendors of possession, suggesting the great college—allowing him to be proclaimed the Prince of the Golden Ash-heaps—the Head—the young Lord; and then, with a malignant laugh, producing his old will, becoming himself the founder of the great college, and tumbling his grandson into dust-holes and ash-heaps which are not golden.

His face was dark; the room was dark, though outside it was high noon; his soul within him was like unto the soul of Job when, after seven days and seven nights, he lifted up his voice and cursed his day, even the day of his birth: "Let the day wherein I was born—let that day be darkness; let not the light shine upon it; let darkness and the shadow of death stain it. Let a cloud dwell upon it. Let the blackness of the day terrify it."

The ruin and destruction of which his father spoke had fallen upon him. Whether it was the curse of the House, in which his father believed, in terror of which his wife had left him—whether this superstition was real or not, ruin and destruction had fallen upon him by the hand of his grandfather. Misery and disaster were the work of that old man's hands, even out of the grave—misery and disaster on everybody. So much he now saw plainly.

On his innocent wife, driven from her home and from her husband. On those unfortunate New Zealanders, who came in search of an honorable ancestry and discovered an escaped convict. On that unfortunate American girl, who dreamed of boundless wealth and discovered the shameful secret of her father's birth. On the child of Piccadilly, who substantiated his case and already held out his hand to clutch the estate, when another stepped in to take it. And on himself, set up on high, to be dragged down again in the face of the assembled multitude. All the telescopes in the world were pointed at this unhappy young man as he sat bent down by this mighty blow—and behind the telescopes he could see the grin universal. Who would be laughed at by the whole world? He was Job, without even the pious admonitions of the three candid friends. He was Job in darkness, as Blake drew him. His spirit looked out upon the world, but could see nothing except universal contempt, shame, and derision. He got up at last, fired with a sudden thought. Murder, revenge, retribution were in his eyes. First, he took from his study-table a dagger-shaped knife—you will never find a man of science very far from a knife—and with this in his hand he swiftly mounted the stairs. He might have been going upstairs in order to put his dagger into that part of the frame where he could most comfortably and most painlessly stop the machinery. But Lucian was not so minded. A fuller, deeper, more satisfying revenge was in his mind.

He opened the drawing-room and looked round the walls—it was the look of one who counts his victims before the slaughter. He felt the edge of the knife with his finger. It was sharp enough. Then—how many times before this had he gone round the room and looked at the portraits of his ancestors?—he began again, as if he had never seen any of them before. "Calvert," he said, numbering them off on his fingers, "the rogue who robbed his master and laid the foundation—the master-builder; roguery and robbery make good foundations—honesty is but sand. Calvert's son—John the highway-robber and spendthrift and hangman's job. John Calvert the third—the religious maniac—poor wretch! John the miser—the creature who picked up bones and crusts, and drove out his children. John the money-lender—the owner of the dancing-cribs and gaming-hells; the man who disinherited his son and made me dream of the great college!

"Why," he murmured, "I am like them all. I have their face—there is but one face for all. It is my face. I have all their vices somewhere inside me. These I have inherited. I came back to them with these views—and yet they won't have me!"

The faces of the men scowled at him. Because this disaster had fallen upon him? But they had had plenty of disasters among themselves. The women looked at him coldly and carelessly, as if wondering for a brief moment who this poor wretch might be, and what he was doing among them all. Both men and women rejected him; if silent looks mean anything, then they would have none of him. Where, at this juncture, one asks with bewilderment, was divine philosophy? Where cold reason? For this man of science, this physician, learned and sapient, this student of the mysteries and phenomena of life, became for the moment like a superstitious girl. The curse of the House had descended upon him. He owned it in his soul; he felt it. His father had done rightly to escape by flight; he had returned, and this was his reward. Shame and disgrace of some kind or other must needs fall upon all who belonged to the House, and especially upon those who possessed, or desired to possess, the fortune acquired in dishonor, maintained in dishonor, and increased in dishonor.

As every one knows, in moments of great emotion the brain sometimes refuses the control of the master; it works independently; it goes off roaming in long-forgotten places. Thus, Lucian's brain, at this crisis, spontaneously presented him with a page of a printed book spread out before his eyes so that he could read it. Not a book in which he often cared to read, or a book which he regarded as necessary to be read; not a book of science; a book into which, as a rule, he never even looked. The page presented from this book, however, was one which he had himself found in Westminster Abbey for the speedier confusion of Margaret's superstitions. And now he saw it clearly spread out before him—on the wall—like the inscription which affrighted the king of Babylon. It was, in fact, none other than the page entitled "The Unjust Parable of the Sour Grapes."

He read the whole page through—that is to say, he remembered the whole page, which is the same thing; indeed, he thought he was reading it.

The last admonition, in the long chain of explanation and assurance, is not, it must be acknowledged, conveyed in words such as those now used by scientific men, nor does it take the form most likely to appeal to the scientific mind. Yet because he was able to detach the central thought of the passage from the words in which it was clothed, the admonitions fell upon his darkened spirit like a ray of sunlight.

"Cast away from you all your transgressions. Make you a new heart and a new spirit. For why will you die, oh House of Israel?"

Like a blaze of sunshine and light that printed page with its burning words fell upon his soul. Margaret once said that no one could help her. "Not even the Prophet Ezekiel." But the prophet did bring help. No curse at all, said the prophet. Every man stands or falls by himself. Why had this disaster fallen upon him? Because his grandfather was a money-lender? Not at all. The thing fell upon him quite naturally. The will was certain to be found, some time or other. Had he not deserted his own work, the work for which he was intended and equipped, on which he was already fully engaged, in order to change it for the administration of a vast and unwieldy mass of wealth for which he was in no way fitted, this thing would not have fallen upon him.

"Cast away from you—"

Was ever man of science so convinced before? He acknowledged no authority in the prophetic office; but he recognized the lucidity of the statement, the justice of the argument. "Transgressions"—why not use the word? A very good word it is. He had transgressed; he had stepped beyond his limits; he had bartered science for gold. Therefore—quite naturally—he had suffered. He had returned, in spirit, to the ancestors. Therefore—

"At least," he said, "there will be no more returning to my own people. They may be anybody's people henceforth. No Burley will I be. Calvert was I born—Calvert will I remain. My house shall no longer be decorated with the twopenny daubs of their portraits." He raised his knife. He cut the cord by which his original ancestor was hanging to the wainscot. He took down the picture, and then—it was like an act of cruel and deliberate revenge; it was an act which made every face on the wall turn pale and every lip tremble; speech they had none—he cut and hacked the canvas face out of the frame, and threw frame and picture on either side. "Down with you!" he cried, vindictively. "Down with you all! Out you go!"

He was something like that hero who, in the ecstasy of his rage, fell upon the cattle, thinking them to be princes. Lucian, in his great wrath, destroyed the portraits, intending to consign to oblivion the whole folk whose memory they preserved. "Not one shall remain," he said. Then he carried the frames and the canvases downstairs into the back garden and piled them up. But there was more that should be added to the pile. He climbed up to the garret—Margaret's room—the old nursery. He brought out the boxes of broken toys and trumpery; he kicked open the door of the highwayman's room, and seized his musical instruments and his easel and paints. He carried all these things into the back garden with his own hands.

Then he called his servants and informed them that they must clear out the whole of the two garrets; and that they might have the contents of the drawers, all the dresses and things left by the runaways, on condition that everything should be cleared out of the house in an hour. "Sell the things!" he cried. "Burn the things! Give away the things! Let me never find any of them here after an hour. Leave none of the old trumpery behind."

He was as eager to destroy everything old as if he had been a bishop over a city church.

Then he made in the garden a small but complete funeral pyre. The frames of the pictures formed the foundation; the wooden cradle and the toys lay on the frames; the pictures themselves were piled on the cradle, and above all lay certain bundles of papers. Among them were

Mr. Calvert Burley's Apology; the letters and household books found in the cupboard; the genealogy of the House, and the drawings, plans, and calculations concerning the great college of science, on which he himself had worked for the last month with so much zeal and patience and determination. Everything completed, he applied a light. After all, it was only a little bonfire; but you must never measure the importance of a bonfire by its dimensions. Otherwise the Fifth of November bonfire on Hampstead Heath, which is a magnificent blaze, might be considered more important than this little bonfire behind a house in Great College Street, Westminster. For Lucian's bonfire was the cremation of a whole family. Nobody will ever talk about them again; nobody will ever learn their history; the record of them is lost; only the great fortune will survive, for good or evil. No one will ever speak of him any more. Certainly not the New Zealander, who cannot think of the family without burning blushes; certainly not the American girl, for the like reason; nor the disappointed man about town; nor the poor old pauper, because her memory now fails her and she sits silent by the fireside; nor Margaret, to whom they have brought so much sorrow; nor Lucian himself, who owes them nothing but this humiliation and disappointment. They will all be forgotten; they are cremated; they and their acts and their power—if they had any.

A good deal more was burned in that bonfire. Our ancestors used to make bonfires at the corners of the streets in order to clear the air. This bonfire cleared the air. When Lucian fired it, he thought he was only destroying, once for all, everything that could in future remind him of his own people, from whom his father ran away—to whom he had returned, with consequences such as these. In that bonfire, though he knew it not, were destroyed the temptations that wellnigh wrecked his life, the unholy craving for the high place that seems to mean power and promises authority, and pretends to command respect. And in this bonfire were cremated the seven devils of the House of Burley—Devil Drive All, Devil Sweat All, Devil Scrape All, Devil Grasp All, Devil Hard Heart, Devil Loveless, Devil Ruthless. These devils had been with the family so long that they supposed they were going to stay; they looked already upon Lucian as their natural host and home. And, finding no admission at this supreme moment, they too fell shrieking into this astonishing bonfire.

The thirsty flames ran and rushed hissing and crackling—what in the world is so eager, so thirsty, as the flame?—in and out among the frames; they caught the wooden cradle, they licked up the toys in a moment; they made but one long spire pointing heavenward, quick to vanish, of the papers and documents. There was no wind in the little back garden, and the flames mounted straight and steady—a pretty sight. The bonfire lasted in all no more than ten minutes or a quarter of an hour.

It was interesting, though certainly not unexpected, to observe how, when the flames reached the canvases, when they were at their highest and brightest, there became apparent in the very heart of the fire, floating in the midst of the flames, the face and head of Calvert Burley himself, founder of this most distinguished House, separated from the picture, and hovering like a wingless cherub. Only for a moment. The eyes, which were turned upon Lucian, were full of reproach. His own descendant had done this. Other descendants had experienced the luck of the House in one or other misfortunes; none, until this man came, had visited the family disasters upon his ancestors. Now—now—now—he was losing forever the light of day; now—now—now—he was sinking forever into an eternity of oblivion. Only for a moment. The face sank back into the flames; there was a roaring and a hissing, and the portraits were all burned up. Farewell forever to the men of sin and the women of sorrow!

Afterwards, when Science resumed her sway, Lucian remembered that this reproachful face—this detaching of the head from the canvas—must have been a mere trick of the imagination. But he recognized the fact that on this eventful morning his brain had not been wholly under control, and that the things which he saw and remembered and did were not things in any sense scientific.

The cremation of the portraits, by itself, was by no means a scientific act. For how can a picture do any harm? And how can the destruction of a picture do any good?

The flames fell lower, their fiercer thirst assuaged. Lucian kicked into the embers outlying bits, and they rose again. Finally they died out, and there was left of this bonfire and all that it contained nothing but a heap of red ashes rapidly turning gray. Lucian stood watching it. Then he stamped his heel into the ashes, and sent them flying in all directions.

The day was over. In the twilight lay here and there about the narrow garden the red embers rapidly turning black. In a few moments nothing at all remained of that most lovely bonfire. Then Lucian left the garden.

XL

The Nobler Way

That is done with," said Lucian, looking down upon the white ashes. "I have now to go back to the old life."

He returned to his study. It had grown suddenly small—absurdly small. You see that when a man in imagination dispenses blessings from an inexhaustible pile, everything about him swells and expands; his house enlarges and becomes a palace. You cannot become Providence in person and live in a little back room of a house in Great College Street. When you cease to play that part, of course, your palace becomes once more a room fourteen feet by twelve.

Lucian looked around and shuddered—but not with superstitious fear. His wrath was over; the madness which ended in the massacre of the forefathers had quite left him. "The old life," he murmured. And that little shivering fit was caused by the sudden fear that perhaps he had spoiled himself for the old life by this long dream of boundless wealth. Instead of standing magnificently outside the world, driving, urging, persuading, pulling, pushing, shoving mankind to that higher level which mankind shows so little willingness to achieve, he was going to become once more a member of that company which works in the twilight, clearing away the tangled underwood and jungle, and draining the pestilential marshes which surround the circle of human knowledge.

He sat down in his wooden chair and took up his long-neglected papers. There were the books for review; there were the notes he had made; there were the pages of the unfinished paper written to explain and popularize the latest learned German's latest theory about the meaning of life. He turned over the leaves. Strange to say, he felt no disgust whatever. The old interest came back to him; he was eager to be at work upon it once more. There was a note lying unopened. It was from the hospital. He opened it, expecting a renewal of the disgust which had recently filled his mind concerning the daily drudgery of hospital work. Quite the contrary. The note interested him strangely. He must go over to the hospital as soon as possible. Splendid work, that of hospitals, for a physician.

He looked up from the table. Before him on the wall hung his father's portrait. Every day, every time he entered the study, he saw this portrait. For the first time he saw in it the Burley face—the strong type which came out in every one of the sons—the resolute face, the steady eyes, the firm-set lips: the face of Calvert the robber, of Calvert the murderer, of Calvert the maniac, of Calvert the miser, of Calvert the money-grubber; the face of every one, but transformed. There are two ways in which anyone of the gifts which the gods give to man may be used. These had chosen one way—the mean, the low, the sordid, the profligate, the selfish way. And it was stamped upon their faces. His father, the first of the race, had chosen the other—the nobler way— and it was so stamped upon his face. "Remember," that face spoke to him, "that I loved labor and hated money getting. Remember that I worked not for my own profit. Remember that I hated crooked ways. Remember that I warned you four months ago against touching this accursed pile."

Then this strong man—this masterful man—this obstinate man— bowed his head, and for very shame his heart became as the heart of a little child.

This shame will never leave him. For whatever a man does or says or thinks in the course of his earthly pilgrimage shall stick to him whether he is alive or dead, shall never leave him—never. It will be his companion forever; it will be like his shadow. Heavens! what companions do some of us hourly create!

The masterful man was ashamed. This was a sign, if you think of it, that the dream of boundless wealth was gone. Only the memory of it remained, and with the memory the shame.

They brought him a letter. It was from Sir John Burleigh.

"MY DEAR COUSIN," he said, kindly, "we are deeply grieved
to hear of this discovery, and of its consequences to yourself.
You will, I am sure, bear it with the fortitude that belongs to
your profession. Should you think of leaving England, let me
remind you that you have cousins in New Zealand, who will
always welcome you and your wife. My daughters desire to
convey to her their truest sympathy with her, and their most
sincere thanks for all the kindness she has shown them.

"I am sorry to say that my son Herbert, of whom we
hoped so much, has informed us that he is to be very shortly

received into the Roman Catholic Church, and that he intends to withdraw wholly from the world and to retire to a monastery—the strictest that he can find. It is curious that the member of our family whom he most resembles (his great-grandfather) was also a fanatic, or even a maniac, in religion.

"Public business calls me back to New Zealand. We return with an English connection and a family which, at all events, has given rise to a great deal of talk. I hope that further discussion into our family history will never again arise. As for us, we have got along, and we shall continue to get along, without any knowledge of that family or any help from them. It is agreed with my girls that we are to put the genealogy in a drawer. We shall be quite content with dating our history from the day when my father brought me with him to the shores of New Zealand.

"Again, I hope and trust that the loss of this great estate will be treated as a thing of no real importance, since the loss of it ought not in any way to injure your scientific career.

"I remain, my dear cousin,

Yours very faithfully,
JOHN BURLEIGH

"Strange!" said Lucian; "the man who wanted to be the grandson of a criminal—and who was, of all his family, the only one who did not know it—has fallen into religious mania, like his great-grandfather. He is to be a monk of the strictest rule. Heavens! what a race we are!"

While he was reading this note a second time, a card was brought in—"Mr. James Pinker."

The visitor followed the card. "Dr. Calvert," he said, "or Dr. Burley—whichever you wish to be called—"

"My name is Calvert."

"Very well. I saw the dreadful news in the evening paper. It came out—perhaps you saw it—"

"I saw it this morning."

"I tried to keep the paper from Clary—your cousin, Clarence Burghley—but he snatched it and read it, and then—then—"

"What happened then?"

"I've had the most awful night with him. I shall never forget it—never. 'Now,' he said, 'there's an end of everything. There will be no compensation for me. And I've lost my voice and my ear and my powers.' So he sat and gasped with a white face. And I certainly did feel low, too—because, you see, we'd been arguing it out—about the compensation; we were undecided whether to make it a million or a million and a half—and to tell the truth, Dr. Calvert, neither of us had tried to do anything for the last fortnight except to pile up the case for compensation."

"Well, Mr. Pinker?"

"Presently he got up, saying nothing, and went into his bedroom. I waited and listened, but I heard nothing. So I got frightened and went in after him. He was sitting with his collar off and his neck unbuttoned, with a razor in his hand. I made for him and got him to drop the beastly thing. 'I couldn't do it, Jemmy,' he said. 'It hurts too much.' Clary never did like things that hurt. 'And the horrid mess it would make.' Clary can't bear messes. 'But I must kill myself,' he said. 'I can't live any longer—I can't starve—I must die.' So I dragged him back and made him sit down. But he wouldn't listen. I fell asleep about two in the morning, and I was awakened by a noise. He had got a rope round his neck and was hauling at it. Lord! what a night it was! I got him down, and he owned that it hurt horribly, and I dragged him into the sitting-room again, and made him drink a glass of brandy. Then he began to cry."

"Well?"

"He dropped off asleep in his chair at last, and slept till nine o'clock this morning, and then he woke up, and then—it's the most wonderful thing possible—he actually got up and laughed. 'Jemmy,' he said, 'since there's no more chance of anything, let us go back to the old work.' So he sat down to the piano and rattled off one of the songs—a new song, 'Wanted, a Methusaleh! To tell us how they kept it up'—with all his spirit and fun come back to him. I declare I could have cried to see Clary himself again. I believe I did cry." Certainly tears stood in his honest eyes.

"He has come back to his right mind; I am glad. So have I, Mr. Pinker. We have all been off our heads over this damned money."

"I came round, Dr. Calvert, just to ask if you were going to set aside the will? I believe you could, if you chose. Then the compensation question will begin all over again."

"Good heavens, man! Do you want to drive us all mad once more? Set the will aside? I would not move a little finger to set the will aside."

"Thank goodness! Then I can go back to Clary. I shall make a song about it. You won't mind, I hope. It'll be sung in the highest circles only. It'll be rather vulgar, because we move in nothing outside the very smartest circles—that is, Clary does. My sphere is down below, in the grill-room."

So Jemmy Pinker went away.

Lucian set himself again to his work. But now his thoughts turned to Margaret, and he lay back in his chair thinking what he should do, and whether he should go to her, or first write to her, or wait for her. But another visitor came to him—this time Ella, who had spoken her mind with so much freedom; Ella, who had rebuked his counsels and derided his schemes and exposed his selfishness. Now she came laughing and running and holding out both her hands.

"Cousin Lucian," she cried, "I congratulate you! Let me look at you. Oh, what a change!" She became suddenly serious. "You have lost the gloom of your selfish dream—the gloom that you thought was firmness, and was only horrible persistence in evil-doing; it has gone. Tell me, Lucian—tell me that you are not regretting the loss of the dreadful thing."

"Just at the present moment I do not. But, Ella, I can't answer for what I shall think about it tomorrow. Just go on saying that it is a dreadful thing."

"Horrible, hateful, shameful, sinful, polluted—"

"Thank you, Ella. Adjectives, like alcohol, sometimes strengthen a patient."

"Isn't it romantic? There you were, only yesterday, on the top of a great—great—gallows—yes, gallows—and you thought it was a pinnacle—all of gold, with the sun shining on your face and making it as yellow as the gold, and your chin stuck out—so—and the devil beside you, and the people down below crying out, like boys, to begin the scramble. And now here you are, just on a level with the rest of us, and the gallows is surmounted by the crown of Great Britain and Ireland!"

"It's highly romantic," said the hero of this romance with a little grimace. "Please put in that all the world is laughing at me."

"No—they don't laugh; they only wonder how you feel."

"I have been in the clouds, Ella, and it is rather difficult, you see, to begin the simple life again."

"The simple life, he calls it." No one could be more contemptuous than this young person, so straight and direct of speech. "The simple life! What is the man talking about? Why, the simple life is the life with no work to do—simple and contemptible. That is what you were desiring—you—you—you *miserable* sinner! It is the complex life that you have returned to, filled with every good thing that can keep your brain at work. Simple life, he calls it! This it is to have been rich—only for a week or two."

"Yes," Lucian replied, meekly. "I shall get right again, presently, perhaps."

"Of course," Ella continued, critically. "I am different from the rest of the world. I've been through it all myself. We understand each other, don't we? First of all"—she took Lucian's seat and leaned back with her elbows on the arms, speaking as a professor—"first of all was the dream of unbounded possessions. It seemed splendid—it was like standing on a great plain—say in the midst of the prairie—and thinking that in whatever direction you walked all the land was your own. Next, that it would be so grand—so grand to turn the broad plain into a fair garden filled with happy people. You had that dream, didn't you?"

"Something like it."

"Of course you did. So did I. You were going to have a grand college. So was I—Oh! we've been through exactly the same experience. Then—oh! first of all it was to be everything for the world and nothing for ourselves—pure altruism—wasn't it? Then—by degrees—one began to feel—eh? I am sure you felt it, Lucian, because I saw it in your eyes. It seemed as if parting with everything would deprive one of power—one wanted to keep the power, all the power—so we began to think we would part with no more than the income and keep the principal. Did you feel like that, Lucian?"

"Child, you shall be taken away and burned for a witch. You are just too late," he said, glancing out of the window, "unfortunately, a quarter of an hour too late for my bonfire. Otherwise, you could have sat in the cradle."

"And then—then—oh, Lucian, let us lay our heads together and blush for shame—you began—I began—to think how the power would be increased tenfold if the money was increased tenfold. And you made calculations—I have seen you—showing how the millions could be doubled and quadrupled long before you would be an old man. And so there was creeping over you, faster and faster, the very spirit of your grandfather the money-lender, and that of his father the miser. Lucian, is this true?"

"It is true, Ella."

"Nobody knows except me, and I only know because I have gone through it myself. Lucian! What I am going to say is not the language you talk—but—you understand it—I said the Lord would break you up. Well, the Lord has broken you up. Your madness is driven out of you. You ought—but you won't—to go down on your knees and thank the Lord."

"Ella," he laughed, "I have taken a very serious step. I have burned the portraits, frames and all."

"Burned the portraits? Why?"

"I want every record, everything connected with the family history, to be destroyed. I have burned all the papers that were in my hands. Who knows now, besides ourselves, the history of these people?"

Ella shivered. "Oh! You have really burned the history—my history? And no one else will ever know."

"I have done more. I went upstairs and brought down all the toys and dolls and children's things that haunted Margaret. They are burned too. I would have burned the clothes in the bedrooms, but there wasn't time. So I gave everything to the servants on condition of the things leaving the house within an hour. I don't believe there is a scrap of anything except some of the furniture that can remind us of the people called Burley who once lived in this house. I believe their name was Burley. Some one told me so. There was some talk about money. My own name, you know, is Calvert."

"My name is Burley," said Ella, thoughtfully, "and I rather think that I am in some distant way connected with a family which once lived in this house. But I don't want to hear anything more about them. I have understood that they were a disreputable set. One of them actually ran away with his master's young wife! Oh! a dreadful family. But high-spirited, that poor old pauper said. Well, Lucian, I am glad that all the things are burned; and now, I hope, everything is to go on as usual."

"*Every*thing?"

"Everything. Without explanations, because we all understand each other. Margaret will have no more visions of mournful mothers and weeping wives and doleful daughters, and you will have no more dead ancestors calling and tempting and suggesting. Oh! it is so ridiculous that dead people should be allowed to go on as they have been going on in this house. Such things haven't happened with our people since they burned the witches."

"Everything as it was? Everything, Ella? You are charged to tell me that?"

"Everything. Aunt Lucinda and I are coming back to stay with you for a bit, if you will have us. I've found work. I'm going to lecture in a ladies' college on English and American literature, and afterwards in halls and places on American institutions. I believe that I am going to found another great Burley fortune, in which case—"

"Well, my cousin?"

"You will join the great fortune that you will have made with mine; and then—then—we will—what shall we do? For yours will be new stores of science; and mine—what will be mine? I know not; but this I know, that a true woman must needs become a rich woman, and the truer a woman is to herself and her womanhood the richer she becomes."

"Yes, Ella," he said, with meekness.

"Oh!"—she gave him her hand—"Brother Commander-in-Chief! The Only Substitute for Providence! Brother Dreamer! Brother Archangel! Brother Miser! we have sinned and suffered. Now you shall go to work again with a new heart."

She looked at the clock on the mantel-shelf. "Margaret," she said, changing her voice and dropping into actualities, "told me she would have tea ready by half-past five, and that she would ring the bell when it was ready. There is the bell. Let us go upstairs, Lucian."

THE END

A Note About the Author

Walter Besant (1836–1901) was born in Portsmouth, Hampshire and studied at King's College, London. He would later work in higher education at Royal College, Mauritius, where he taught mathematics. During this time, Besant also began his extensive writing career. In 1868 he published Studies in Early French Poetry followed by a fruitful collaboration with James Rice, which produced Ready-money *Mortiboy* (1872), and *The Golden Butterfly* (1876). Besant's career spanned genres and mediums including fiction, non-fiction, plays and various collections.

A Note from the Publisher

Spanning many genres, from non-fiction essays to literature classics to children's books and lyric poetry, Mint Edition books showcase the master works of our time in a modern new package. The text is freshly typeset, is clean and easy to read, and features a new note about the author in each volume. Many books also include exclusive new introductory material. Every book boasts a striking new cover, which makes it as appropriate for collecting as it is for gift giving. Mint Edition books are only printed when a reader orders them, so natural resources are not wasted. We're proud that our books are never manufactured in excess and exist only in the exact quantity they need to be read and enjoyed.

Discover more of your favorite classics with Bookfinity™.

- Track your reading with custom book lists.
- Get great book recommendations for your personalized Reader Type.
- Add reviews for your favorite books.
- AND MUCH MORE!

Visit **bookfinity.com** and take the fun Reader Type quiz to get started.

Enjoy our classic and modern companion pairings!